THE GREY HUSTLE

BY RICHARD LAWS

First published 2025 by Five Furlongs

© Richard Laws 2025
ISBN 978-1-7397026-6-3 (Paperback/E-Book)

This book is sold subject to the condition that it shall not, by way of trade or otherwise, be lent, re-sold, hired out, or otherwise circulated without the publisher's prior consent in any form of binding or cover other than that in which it is published.

This is a work of fiction. Names, characters, businesses, places, events, locales, and incidents are either the products of the author's imagination or used in a fictitious manner. Any resemblance to actual persons or organisations, living or dead, or actual events is purely coincidental.

*

For Ollie and Vicky Pears, Peter McCafferty, Rachel Laws, and the hundreds of wonderful racehorses and thousands of shareholders at Ownaracehorse, without whom my many years of involvement in this wonderful sport would not have been possible.

One

Staring blankly out of the rear window of the taxi, Laura Fenwick caught her glum reflection in the glass and winced. Her afternoon at the races had meant to be exciting, innocent fun – and so it had been, up to a point. Indeed, by the time the third race of the afternoon had run, in differing ways, she'd already won twice.

Laura's first win had come at 2.30pm when the young colt she owned, Kaleidoscope, had recorded a resounding success on debut. According to her trainer, this performance was an important stepping stone to a far more important race at Royal Ascot in a few weeks' time. Her mood darkened again as she recalled her second 'win' of the afternoon, a success with unexpected consequences. Laura had been won over by a devastatingly handsome man she'd met in the Beverley racecourse Owners and Trainers bar.

With her husband, Andrew, away in Dubai on business once again and being thoroughly bored with the lengthy, inane chatter she'd had to endure from her terribly dry trainer, a casual chat with the rather dashing man who introduced himself as 'Sebastian Savage, Racehorse Trainer' at the bar, had been a welcome distraction. A distraction that had turned into a discussion, a flight of fancy, and finally, a proposal.

She wasn't a flirt. At least, Laura didn't think so… and yet, as she thought back to five hours ago, perhaps she had been a little *too* welcoming to Sebastian's advances, possibly even a shade tipsy, thanks to the celebratory champagne after Kaleidoscope had won his race. But Sebastian had made her feel so alive! So attractive, and even… *desirable*! Thanks to his good looks and attentiveness, Laura had found herself acting like a vivacious eighteen-year-old again. She'd almost forgotten how thrilling it felt… experiencing that fluttering of attraction in the pit of her stomach once again. Andrew hadn't made her flutter like that for ages. Her husband managed to serve up the odd tingle of attraction brought about through familiarity, but Sebastian had pressed buttons Laura had long since forgotten.

It had been a wonderful, crazy, and memorable afternoon. They'd left the racecourse within an hour of meeting. Taking up his offer of a tour of his stables in Malton, sure, she'd been slightly nervous, but also terribly excited. Sebastian had whisked her off in his open top Jaguar, down country lanes shaded by softly whispering trees to his training stables, arriving at his mansion in a matter of minutes. At first, she thought he owned the entire Marsh Mansion. It turned out Sebastian only occupied a set of rooms in one wing… but what a wing! After filling her glass with champagne he'd taken her on the tour of his rooms and Laura had been entranced. It was like walking through an issue of Ideal Home magazine.

However, there came the moment when Laura's reverie had flattened. They'd reached Sebastian's bedroom and she'd hesitated at the door, a sudden wave of guilt crashing over her. Sebastian had entered his bedroom and gestured for her to join him on his bed. His demeanour had been suggestive. In return, she'd baulked and provided him with an embarrassed but heartfelt refusal.

Sebastian Savage had fallen silent, receiving her rebuff with no more than an understanding smile. He'd rolled off the bed, smoothed out the bedclothes until they were wrinkle free, and suggested she finish her glass of champagne. They'd gone back to the lounge and after admiring the view for a short time - down on his training yard, nestling below the start of the Yorkshire Wolds – she'd leaned back on the incredibly comfortable sofa and feeling sleepy, had closed her eyes, just for a moment.

Laura had woken, immediately feeling uncomfortable. Her dress was askew and she'd somehow felt *wrong*. Still on the sofa in the lounge, she'd sensed something warm and heavy across her stomach. Sebastian's arm was wrapped around her. He had appeared to be asleep. On the wall, a huge flat screen television was quietly showing racing replays from that afternoon. According to the screen, it was early evening. She'd been asleep for almost two hours. Sebastian stirred and Laura took the opportunity to lift his arm off her. Getting to her feet, she'd been forced to pause, hold out her arms, and steady herself. An intense pain had shot across her forehead and she was gripped by a disarming dizziness.

An unwanted hand had rested on the small of her back.

'Hey, sleepyhead,' Savage had said as Laura had spun away from his touch, 'Take it easy.'

'I should be going,' she'd blurted automatically, 'Call me a taxi. Just... call me a taxi will you?'

'Of course,' he'd replied lazily, stretching to reach for his phone, 'I apologise. We must have fallen asleep.'

She'd noticed a glass beside his phone on the occasional table. It held the dregs of a spirit, probably whisky, and three lumps of ice. The ice had still been in cube form, hardly melted. He'd been awake, waiting for her to stir.

The scales had fallen from Laura's eyes. But before she could question him, Sebastian had spoken again. It was such a simple, sensible suggestion. And yet it had been laced with such threat.

'If that colt of yours, Kaleidoscope, was trained here at Marsh Landing Stables,' Sebastian had suggested with a rakish flick of an eyebrow, 'We could enjoy all of this on a regular basis... It could be... fun. So how about it?'

'I couldn't do that,' Laura had replied with a shake of her head, suddenly realising she was barefoot. As she looked down, she'd noticed several buttons on her dress had popped open. She began scanning the room for her shoes.

Savage's eyes had became hard, 'Why not?'

'It wouldn't be fair to my current trainer... besides, Kaleidoscope was given to me as a gift from my husband. The trainer was his choice.'

'Oh, I don't know,' Sebastian had said as he'd swirled

the last drop of Glenfiddich, clinking ice around his glass, 'I'm sure we could find a suitable excuse, and it would mean we could share some regular, quality time together…After all, you'd want to keep a close eye on Kaleidoscope's progress through the summer season, wouldn't you?'

She'd met his eyes in that moment and it was as if she could read his thoughts. How could she have been so stupid? This suave, devious, and … well, good-looking little weasel hadn't wanted *her* at all. Well, perhaps a little, but he wanted her blasted racehorse more!

The whole afternoon had been a lie. They'd argued. She'd become angry and he'd reacted with… a grin! A victorious smirk had landed on his perfectly shaped, glistening lips. He'd laid languorously on his designer sofa and in a firm, uncompromising tone told her to, 'Chill the hell out!'

Sebastian Savage had ordered her to sit back down and listen carefully to what he had to say. And then, he'd succinctly laid out his proposal and the consequences of Laura's refusal to co-operate.

As Laura reflected further on her time with Savage, her taxi swung out of Malton and headed for her home in one of the more desirable villages on the outskirts of York. Her feelings of regret soon turned into anger. He had been so calm, so assured. It was as if Sebastian Savage had done this a hundred times before…

Two

Saturday nights are sacrosanct if you're in your late teens, but especially if you work in a racing stable. It's usually the only chance each week to really let loose.

Sundays are still regarded by most horsemen as a day of rest, or at least, a day where stables tend to be run on minimal staffing, offering both horses and humans one day a week to take it a little easier. Despite the programme book stubbornly fielding one or two race meetings most Sundays, racing stable staff will tend to only work one in every three sabbaths. And that's why Saturday night offers these minimum-wage-earning youngsters in the racing industry the opportunity to seize the evening for themselves. And for some, blowing off steam comes with little regard for the consequences.

It was with this exact aim in mind that Jack and Cam boarded the busy Scarborough train, only slightly tipsy after downing a duo of pre-night-out drinks at their Malton digs. It was like student accommodation, a house they shared with four other young people, all employed in horseracing, and appropriately named by the charity that ran it, The Racing House.

Being a popular rail route to the east coast town and only a two carriage train, the teenagers' preliminary search for a couple of seats together was unsuccessful. Moving into the second carriage, they discovered their only option was to fill up a four-seater table presently occupied by a couple of well-dressed, and coiffured older ladies who had berthed themselves opposite each other in the window seats.

Even before Cam's backside had contemplated dropping into the seat beside her, he was being hailed by the tall, upright lady in a chic blue tartan jacket and matching calf-length skirt. The jacket was fastened up to just below her chin, and the colour matched her eyes, a sharp, penetrating blue. Her hat was of broadly similar tartan material, but it was the two six-inch pheasant feathers placed at a jaunty angle that drew the boy's eye as he sat down beside her.

'Good evening, gentlemen!' the lady exclaimed effusively, in turn aiming a smile up at Jack and then Cam.

'Please join us! Scarborough for the evening is it? I'm Lucille, and this is Emily,' she said, gesturing to the woman sitting opposite.

'I see you're eying my hat, darling boy,' Lucille

continued at a pitch louder than was necessary, 'Don't worry, I didn't shoot the unfortunate creature myself. I had a man to do that for me!'

Lucille possessed the type of plummy, confident voice rarely heard, except perhaps in BBC between-the-wars period dramas. It instantly carried down the carriage, and possibly into the second compartment. With such clear diction, and volume set just below a shout, her words were wholly unavoidable to anyone within a radius of twenty yards.

Jack smiled politely as he clambered into his seat beside the rather mouselike woman called Emily, whilst Cam grinning at Lucille, landed in the seat beside her with more of a thump than he'd intended. This potential impropriety forced him to pause a moment. A privileged upbringing had been thrust upon Cam and it was this imbued sense of duty that now forced him to reflect on the loss of his inhibitions, thanks to his alcohol intake. There were many aspects of his childhood he'd rather forget, or chose to ignore, but good manners was not one of them. The last thing Cam wanted was to be perceived as impolite.

To his relief, Lucille's immaculately made-up face crinkled into a broad smile as she recognised his slightly inebriated state, but more importantly, the glint of devilment in Cam's eye. Her new travelling companion was going to be interesting, and possibly fun… at least for the next twenty-five-minute train ride!

'Good to meet you, Lucille and Emily,' Cam returned, holding out a hand to Lucille whilst holding her gaze and subsequently acknowledging Emily with a nod, 'I'm Cameron Camberley, otherwise known as Cam, and my friend over there is Jack Goodman.'

Lucille took a long moment to look Cam up and down over the rim of her glasses, 'Scottish?'

Despite living in Malton for the last year and a half, try as he might, Cam hadn't shaken off the Scottish accent that pervaded his speech. Having grown tired of the weighing room banter created by his Scots accent, he'd made an effort to dampen it down with something akin to a Yorkshire twang, but as Jack had pointed out, he'd ended up sounding like a Scottish version of Del Boy Trotter. As a result, he'd given up, and embraced his Scottishness, although the odd Yorkshire vowel managed to break through every now and again without him noticing.

'Och, Aye!' Cam confirmed with eyes twinkling, before adding, 'And I have to say, Lucille, that is a truly terrific bonnet. It looks even better close up. You can really appreciate the full effect!'

Cam spent a moment in admiring mode before meeting Lucille's eyes again, 'So, where will you ladies be gracing with your presence tonight?'

Lucille beamed appreciatively and cleared her throat. On the other side of the carriage a bald chap sitting in an aisle seat ruffled his copy of The Daily Mail testily and sighed, giving the distinct impression he'd already been regaled with this information and had no wish to hear it again.

Jack shot him a friendly, inquiring look that wasn't reciprocated.

'Oh, ignore him,' insisted Lucille in a stage whisper that definitely reached the Daily Mail reader, 'We're on our way to Scarborough. Emily here is appearing at the theatre! But tell us about yourselves? A night out on the town for you two young bucks, is it?'

She placed emphasis on 'young bucks', which Cam took as an invitation to be ever so slightly flirtatious.

'Our one night off,' Cam explained with a smile, 'So we're hitting Scarbados.'

'Scarbados?' Lucille queried.

'Scarbados,' announced Jack, prompting Lucille to transfer her gaze to him, 'Cam calls Scarborough, The Barbados of the North,' he added with a roll of his eyes.

Lucille nodded her understanding, 'Ah, irony! I see. Scarbados... yes, I like it.'

She paused a moment, as if in thought.

'Although… as seaside towns go, Scarborough certainly has plenty to offer. However, I admit the sea is unlikely to match the temperature of Barbados waters. But they do have a rather exciting looking water park in the North Bay…'

'Swimming isn't on the agenda tonight, Lucille,' Cam reported with a wink, 'We're in party mode.'

'Oh yes? Any particular reason?'

Cam's eyes darted around the carriage ahead of leaning forward in conspiratorial fashion. Lucille leaned in too, eyes wide in anticipation, clearly enjoying the amateur dramatics.

Holding a hand to the side of his mouth and speaking in a whisper that was sure to carry the length of the carriage, he told her, 'Jack rode a winner, and I was placed second at the races today.'

'Oh! You're jockeys!' exclaimed Lucille, immediately slamming her ring-laden hand to her mouth in mock consternation, 'But aren't you far too tall and handsome to be jockeys?'

'Sorry!' she quickly added, waving away her question, 'I didn't mean to embarrass you,' she said coyly, noting with pleasure the radiant smiles from both young men.

'So whereabouts did your riding prowess result in success?'

Emily, who up until now had been passively following the conversation, straightened in her seat, her curiosity apparently pricked. She turned her head to Cam, awaiting his answer.

'Beverley. We're apprentices, and we were riding in a division of the apprentice handicap at the start of the card, earlier this afternoon.'

Lucille screwed her mouth to one side, 'Division?'

'One race split into two because of the high number of entries,' Jack explained.

'So between you, the spoils were landed. Well done boys! We should celebrate your success!' said Lucille, diving into her handbag and busying herself with its contents.

Cam gave Emily a questioning look as Lucille continued to scrabble around. Emily returned him a wan smile and shifted her gaze to peer through the grimy window to where the platform was slowly moving away as the train picked up speed.

'I tell you darlings, I could kill for a G and T!' Lucille stated, producing a sizeable flask and four plastic glasses from her voluminous bag, carefully laying them out on the small table.

Across the carriage the Daily Mail man emitted another sigh, ruffled his newspaper and added a shake of his head for good measure.

Jack and Cam shared a grin across the table. It looked like the twenty-five minute journey to Scarborough was going to be far more fun than they'd anticipated.

The train jerked forward as the fourth glass was filled with a pre-mix of gin and tonic and the two apprentice jockey's achievements earlier in the day were toasted by all four occupants of the table.

Three

Perching on her stool behind the counter, the cashier's gaze never left the female customer as she stumped frustratedly back to the betting shop front door, yanked it open, and swept outside without looking back.

'Women!' Bert grumbled from his seat at the small table closest to the betting counter, a position the inveterate punter inhabited week days from opening time to the end of racing.

Using his elbows as rests, Bert leaned over his newspaper. His copy of The Sun was open at the double page spread detailing todays racing. It was heavily marked with blue biro. Pen in hand, head down, he somehow managed to sigh, draw a line on his newspaper, and speak at the same time.

'Right funny onion, that one, Sue.'

'Now now, Bert,' Sue gently chided from behind the counter, 'She was new to betting, that's all.'

Bert rolled his shoulders and puckered his lips, his eyes never leaving the list of runners in the first race at Wolverhampton.

But he had a point, thought Sue. The woman had asked some strange questions, given she'd admitted to being a first-time punter. And she had become so easily frustrated once she realised there was no way her bet could be accepted. Sue had dealt with a long line of difficult customers in her thirty year career in betting shops. And in comparison, this had been an instantly forgettable encounter… so why was she left with this sense of unease gnawing at her?

It wasn't busy in the betting shop, just a smattering of the usual faces. The morning rush had eased off to a dribble and Sue soon found herself replaying the conversation with the mystery women in her head, trying to tease out a reason for this particular encounter leaving her with such an uncomfortable feeling.

On the other side of the counter, Bert ruffled the pages of his newspaper and offered his own verdict on the woman in his familiar gruff tone, 'Up to no good if you ask me. Don't let it bother you.'

Sue stared down at him through the glass partition. Say what you wanted about a seventy-five-year-old who spent all his waking hours in a betting shop betting minimum stakes… Bert could be surprisingly adept at reading her mood.

'She got her wires crossed,' Bert continued as his biro ringed a horse's name on his newspaper, 'Dangerous… having information about a racehorse, when you don't know how to make the most of it.'

Sue squinted over Bert's shoulder and down at his newspaper. She couldn't quite make out horse the old man's heavy blue oval was highlighting. Then she remembered the name of the horse the woman had mentioned at the counter before she'd got angry and stomped out.

'She knows it's going to lose,' Sue said sharply.

She blinked, surprised at the sound of her own voice. She hadn't meant to blurt out her revelation.

'Aye, lass,' Bert replied, 'That's why she asked all those dumb questions. She thought she could lay the horse to lose in a high street bookies. A woman new to gambling, asking how she can profit from a horse losing… getting angry when she couldn't put her bet on. What's that tell you?'

For the first time that day, Bert lifted his head and met Sue's eyes, patiently waiting for understanding to arrive.

Sue found herself nodding back at Bert as the jigsaw pieces fell into place. The stilted conversation now made perfect sense! The woman believed the horse won't win.

'I didn't realise,' Sue said thoughtfully, 'I could have told her to go to one of the online betting exchanges…'

She trailed off into silence. The fact the woman *knew* a horse wouldn't win… that wasn't right.

Slipping off her stool, Sue went to the corner of the counter closest to Bert and leaned over. His biro was still outlining the same horse, running in the first race at Wolverhampton and due off in a matter of minutes. She checked the screens that covered the far wall and found the betting on the race and the horse. It was the favourite.

'Sunset Blaze,' rumbled Bert, 'Ridden by Jack Goodman.'

A punter Sue knew by name approached the counter. She went back to her stool, acknowledging him with a smile. He returned a grimace and pushed a betting slip under the glass partition along with a banknote. She examined the ten pounds bet on Sunset Blaze, then glanced up at the man, considering whether to say anything.

'What the matter with you? Can't you read it?' he inquired with an angry glare.

Sue shook her head, rang the bet through the till, and

smiled sweetly as she returned him his receipt.

Four

'So, you're on the favourite! What's your take on its chances, Jack. Are you on the winner?' asked Cam. He was hardly able to keep the crackle of laughter from his voice.

Jack's answer was returned swiftly and directly.

'Shut it, Cam.'

Even so, Jack couldn't help but smile to himself whilst leaning forward to run a calming hand down the neck of the three-year-old he was aboard. The winners and weekend fun in Scarborough were now nothing more than a hazy memory – he and Cam were back to business. It was Monday afternoon, and this was the first race of the day, a race limited to apprentice riders only. His gelding, named Sunset Blaze, was impatiently twitching his front legs and snorting, waiting for the gates to release him from his prolonged incarceration within the starting stall.

Jack knew his best friend's comment wasn't intended to offend. There was no malice attached, it was simply a jibe at the fact Sunset Blaze was a short price, whereas Cam was aboard a rank outsider, a filly called Restless Kiss, a course specialist, but shouldering top weight, she was a less-fancied runner in this seven furlong apprentice-only handicap.

Jack slid a long, wide-eyed stare Cam's way two stalls to his left, as if softly admonishing a mischievous puppy, but remained silent.

'Oh, go on! Say it, Jack,' Cam pleaded as another runner and rider slid into the stall between them.

Jack sighed inwardly. Cam's request was now picked up by some of the other apprentices in the adjoining stalls and soon enough, four or five more jockeys had joined the chorus demanding an answer to the query, 'Are you on the winner, Jack?'

A stalls handler passed in front of Jack's stall and despite his hurry to complete his task, glanced up at him. In on the joke, an amused grin was bending the young handler's mouth to the edges of his protective helmet.

Checking there were still three horses to load, Jack gave in to the cacophony of requests and clearing his throat, replied in a clear, authoritative voice.

'I was *born* to win, and *expect* to win.'

There was a good-natured cheer and a couple of laughs around him, soon curtailed when the starter announced there were only, 'Two to go.'

Cam pulled his goggles down, still grinning, pleased with the pre-race banter. Jack's rendition of that phrase always took him straight back to their first day at the Doncaster Racing College, and the day they'd met, almost two years earlier. It was the day Jack had uttered those exact words in reply to a tutor going around the class one by one, asking each of the budding young riders how they would approach a horse race.

Whilst most of the class had fumbled around with bland, often lengthy generic explanations, Jack's concise reply, delivered with such earnest intent had prompted Cam and a few others to initially burst out laughing, amused with his deep South Yorkshire accent and deadpan delivery.

He'd subsequently thought hard about Jack's words, impressed with his directness, and after the tutorial, Cam had introduced himself. The mix of Cam's exuberance and sense of fun, combined with Jack's determination, self confidence, and a dry sense of humour had seen the two young men become firm friends. Their friendship was further cemented once the two of them realised they were both imbued with enough raw riding talent to see them push each other to new heights and battle to become the top apprentice rider of that year's intake. It was a battle Jack had won.

Since that first meeting, Cam had repeated Jack's snappy, yet dourly delivered one-liner mantra a hundred times or more. So much so, it had become a good-natured running joke among the apprentices they'd trained alongside. Somehow, it never became tired, and what's more, Jack was true to his words. He had a natural talent, being strong in the saddle, intelligent in the run, and if Cam was honest, Jack was the better rider. And his mental attitude meant he did expect to win.

Yet at the end of their time in Doncaster, it was Cam who had been offered a quality apprenticeship at a large, busy Malton based yard, run by a trainer called Sebastian Savage. And at least initially, he had tended to get better rides compared to Jack. Why? Perhaps it was the way he spoke, thanks to his private education, his genuine smile, thick blonde hair, and dazzling blue eyes. Or perhaps it was the ease with which he was able to mingle with owners and trainers. Cam had a way about him that transcended class, status, and colour. In short, he was instantly likeable.

With good reason, Jack didn't invest trust in people easily, preferring to remain quiet and restrained. Nevertheless, he eventually managed to secure an apprenticeship with a smaller, rather old-fashioned trainer called Paddy Doherty, also based in Malton.

Gripping his filly's reins, the banter forgotten, Cam focussed on how he was going to give his mount every chance to win. Sensing the last horse was entering the stalls to his left, he hunkered down in his saddle, ready to push Restless Kiss from their stall three draw. It was imperative he got a good start, especially around this circuit.

'Jockeys!' hollered the starter.

The stalls doors made a metallic thud as they sprang open and twelve three-year-old racehorses, each carrying their inexperienced apprentice, kicked forward. Breaking well, Cam got his filly up to speed and was able to hold a prominent position as the field left the seven furlong spur behind and rushed to the first bend.

Only too aware this All-Weather racecourse was full of

potential pitfalls for apprentice and pro-jockeys alike, Cam didn't push too hard. He reminded himself that Wolverhampton's tight oval dictates that a decent track position is always paramount. Go into any of the bends four or five wide and you'd gift a huge advantage to those riders on your inside. But whilst a decent start was important over any distance on this artificial surface, it was an imperative over seven furlongs, as the first bend was reached after a mere fifty yards. But it wasn't all about speed. Being slow to start might consign you to a poor outlying position, but being too quick in the early stages could see you burn your mount's energy reserves and be running on empty in the final furlong. As if that wasn't enough to contend with, as you turned into the back straight it was essential not to find yourself boxed in on the rail and behind a horse unable to go the pace, otherwise you could be shuffled down the pack on the inside rail, with nowhere to go but backwards.

Cam sat tight in fourth position as he and his three-year-old entered the back straight, hugging the inside rail. Dropping his hands just enough, he allowed the filly to bowl along without extending herself too much, whilst maintaining his position. She had a welter burden in this handicap, having been penalised six pounds for a win two weeks previously. It would be weight that beat her today, and saving ground by racing on the inside might just be enough for her to follow-up that win with another competitive performance.

Cam angled his filly into the rails once more as they reached the top turn and asked her to kick off the final bend, managing to pass a flailing opponent on its inside and take a share of third. Asking the filly for her final effort he made further ground into second over one and a half furlongs out.

Some way behind, Jack had been playing his cards in a completely different way. Slowly away, and quietly stalking the field in a share of last, one off the rails, he now pushed Sunset Blaze energetically as they entered the home straight, crossing to the inside rails when the chance came, slicing through a number of rivals already flat to the boards.

Meanwhile, Cam was asking Reckless Kiss for maximum effort. He edged out to give himself a clear run to the finishing line, still holding second place as the furlong pole whipped past. The filly was trying hard to counter her top weight, responding to his urging, holding her position, but achieving little else. The leader was two lengths in advance of her; too great a divide for Cam to make an impression.

A thump of hooves announced the sudden arrival of a gelding on Cam's outside, and he recognised Jack, riding low in his saddle, whip still resting up his horse's neck, his gelding enjoying a hands and heels introduction to the business end of the race.

Cam gave his filly another flick of his whip, but recognising his chance of maintaining second was already gone, switched into maintenance mode. It was at this moment that another memory from his time at the Racing College filtered through Cam's mind, this time their tutor's terse reply to Jack.

'Your arrogance aside, young man, you may be *born to win* and *expect to win*, but it should not be at any cost. Competent race riding isn't just about winning. There comes a time in most races where you'll realise you're *not* on the winner. Whatever your skills as a rider may be, you can't force a beaten horse to run quicker. You must judge when your mount has given everything. Knowing when you're beaten, and looking after your horse whilst attaining the best finishing position possible, is a skill in itself. A skill you ignore at your peril.'

The tutor's retort had dispelled the atmosphere of frivolity in the classroom and Cam had watched Jack take on board this advice, nodding reverentially back at their tutor, a serious expression on his face.

Cam could sense Restless Kiss had given him everything. He would see his way home in third without punishing a horse whose stamina was rapidly ebbing away.

Cam watched on as Jack, now two lengths in advance of himself, produced Sunset Blaze in the last half a furlong to lay down a challenge to the long-time leader. Jack's signature low riding style had now become a power-packed thrust in time to his gelding's stride. It was surely a one-sided contest, Jack, under his willing partner, bearing down on the weakening leader, his whip still stowed, only a stride away from hitting the front and tasting victory.

Cam kept pushing, sure of holding third, but transfixed by the sheer artistry of his friend's last-gasp, perfectly timed win. First and third from their only rides of the day… it would be an upbeat drive back up the motorway to Malton.

He only caught a glimpse. A momentary snapshot that told Cam something wasn't right with Jack. Still, his friend had the race won, Cam was sure of that.

Concentrating on riding out to the line, the cheers from the crowd combining with the frenetic commentary, Cam went past the finishing post to a barrage of noise and after negotiating his filly around the bottom bend, began to pull Restless Kiss up. She'd done well, considering her concession of weight to the field.

With the hub-bub from the small, but feisty crowd dying down, it was with some astonishment that Cam heard the public address system announce that Jack's gelding had finished second.

Cam pulled up alongside Jack down the back straight and instead of immediately returning to the winners enclosure in front of the grandstand, he engaged with his best friend.

'What happened there?'

Jack looked over, a single frown line showing below his helmet and his eyes crinkled into a query, 'What do you mean?'

'I was convinced you had that race won. You were travelling so well, and had the speed… until the last few strides where you…'

Cam searched for the right words. He wasn't the sort to fire his mouth off after a race, let alone question another jockey's riding. But he knew Jack so well. They were alone down the back straight. No one would hear what he said…

'…you looked out of sync? And… you were whipping air.'

Jack considered this for a moment, his eyes becoming slits as he concentrated. He shook his head having reached a conclusion.

'I was never going to get there,' he replied positively, 'He was going weak under me, and you're mistaken about the air-shots, I could feel them making contact.'

Despite his robust response, Jack's brow furrowed within his helmet as he stared down at Sunset Blaze's fine head and pricked ears. For a long moment he reconsidered his previous statement. Presently, he closed his eyes and shook his head, as if casting all negative thoughts aside.

'Naa. This lad didn't have it in him,' Jack added in his broad Yorkshire twang, giving the gelding's neck a consoling pat, 'We weakened in the last three strides, I was lucky to get as close as I did.'

Cam didn't reply, preferring to provide a nod of acknowledgement rather than persevering and potentially starting an argument. It was an unsatisfactory answer. Jack had to know he'd screwed up. Why wasn't he just admitting to his mistake?'

But they were friends. Best friends. If he couldn't say it to Jack, after what they went through at Racing College, what was the point?

Cam ventured, 'I guess you were trying too hard and might have got unbalanced?'

Jack didn't answer, and Cam wondered if he'd taken his comment as a statement, rather than a question. Jack was now urging his mount into a steady canter back to the winner's enclosure, in front of the grandstand. Slightly irked at not receiving a reply, Cam followed and waited trackside, watching as his friend was reunited with a stable lass and Sunset Blaze was led into the winners enclosure. Jack slid off the gelding's back underneath the second position marker. Once he'd retrieved his tack, the gelding's trainer immediately button-holed his jockey and they bent their heads together in a hushed, private conversation within the tight confines of the winners enclosure. The trainer was relatively young, in his late twenties, but was managing to generate a name for himself in his second season by improving horses with moderate pedigrees to win valuable handicaps.

The trainer's name came to Cam as his own filly was being led into the winners enclosure – Freddie Jones. He and Jack had discussed the trainer during their car journey to the racecourse that morning. Jack had been quite excited to get his first ride for the young, emerging handler.

Jack's conversation with the young trainer seemed to go well, with trainer and jockey breaking apart sharing a smile and a handshake. Jack immediately headed off to weigh in. I must have been mistaken, thought Cam. Perhaps Jack had been a shade untidy in the saddle, his air-shots just an oversight. Still, he'd like to see a replay, he couldn't believe Jack could muck up a straight-forward challenge like that in the last few strides.

'Hoy! You getting off her, then?'

It was the filly's stable lass, intent on disturbing his train of thought. Hair scraped back into a bun and pale to the point of sallowness, her upturned face was staring expectantly at him. The title of 'Stable Lass' did Jackie no justice - she had to be in her mid-forties and was a capable horsewoman, more so than either of the younger barn managers back at the Savage yard.

'Sorry, Jackie! My mind was elsewhere,' Cam replied, flashing her a hopeful smile to strengthen his apology.

'Yeah, well,' the woman sniffed as he dismounted, 'I need to get this lass a drink.'

As Cam unbuckled the tack from his sweating, but

perfectly static filly, the owners approached. He prepared himself, smiling as an excited trio of men and two women surrounded him. He gave his report on Restless Kiss's run, making the point that her admirable consistency, and the handicappers reluctance to drop her rating, was responsible for her many placed efforts and the lack of a follow-up win. Owners satisfied, Cam turned to address Jackie.

'Thanks. She's really genuine. With a bit of luck, the handicapper will drop her a few pounds and give her a proper chance next time.'

'I doubt it.'

Cam pursed his lips and gave a small nod of acknowledgement. Jackie was a 'glass half empty' type and doubting any further conversation would be forthcoming, he pressed his tack to his chest and made a move towards the weighing room. He was halted by the sound of Jackie clearing her throat.

'Keep your mouth shut,' she said, a warning in her eyes.

'Err.. what?'

'Your mate, Jack Goodman. Don't mention that ride to him. I know you want to. I can read your thoughts. It was an iffy ride, a *very* iffy ride. My advice is to keep shtum. You're green, but have good hands. You've also got a decent head on your shoulders and if you put the work in, could make it to pro, even though you're too honest and far too good looking for your own good. Don't muddy your reputation by getting involved in… whatever shady stuff that scally's into.'

Before Cam could form a reply, the grandstand reverberated to the sound of the public address system announcing, 'Horses away, horses away, please.'

His mind racing, and stunned by Jackie's unexpected advice, Cam remained stationary, his mouth lolling open.

Jackie turned Restless Kiss, and forced to wait a few seconds to allow another placed horse to depart the winners enclosure, she took the opportunity to sidle up close to Cam.

'Listen, Cam. The key to survival in this game is to

surround yourself with good people,' she said in a low voice, 'Mark my words. Based on that ride, your mate Jack is turning into one of the bad people.'

Five

With an index finger hovering above his mouse, Cam watched the replay of the 2.05pm at Wolverhampton on his laptop for the umpteenth time that evening. His finger taps were becoming increasingly agitated in order to pause the letterbox shaped oblong of video every few strides up the home straight. Sitting upright on his single bed, laptop across his knees, he noticed the time. It was a few minutes after midnight. He'd been replaying the race for over an hour.

Aware he needed to be up and out riding work in a mere five and a half hours, he closed the laptop lid, swung his legs over the side of the bed and allowed his head to droop until it met both his hands. Closing his tired eyes, he massaged his face, trying, and failing, to empty his mind.

No matter how many times Cam watched the Wolverhampton race, he wasn't able to shake the clear and obvious conclusion. Jack had thrown the race. He'd been producing air shots up the home straight, failed to push his gelding out, and at one stage it looked like he actually angled his mount into the quarters of the winner in order to slow his forward momentum. And what was worse, Cam couldn't shake his view that all these actions had been skilfully disguised. He was convinced Jack's mount should have won, and as much as that thought pierced his heart, he knew. It was his friend's fault.

Cam got to his feet and without being aware of it, started to pace his room, the Victorian floorboards squeaking beneath his socked feet. Jackie Bell's words came back to him – 'Don't muddy your reputation… shady stuff…' Jack had never been involved in shady stuff before… or had he?

Jack wasn't the sort to volunteer personal information about his past, but reading between the lines Cam reckoned he'd been involved in some pretty ropey stuff as a youngster. Surely nothing like that had gone on since Jack had started riding? But the evidence was there for all to see... he'd thrown the race. Cam reflexively shook his head and scrunched his face up in disgust. How could he even think of such a thing about his best friend? And yet... the evidence was damning on the reverse head-on replay. Thank goodness, it was a camera angle rarely shared with the public.

Cam drew to a halt on his fourth circuit of his bedroom, his eye catching the headline emblazoned across the front page of an old copy of the Racing Post lying on his desk. The full colour picture showed a close up profile shot of leading pro jockey Mickey Manton superimposed on a background of Newmarket's final furlong. Having won the first two classic races of the season, both the 1,000 and 2,000 guineas, the headline screamed, 'Manton The Magician'.

Cam snorted derisively. Two years previously the same Mickey Manton had been making headline news for his abuse of cocaine and being found guilty by the rulers of the sport of betting on himself to lose races. There were also rumours that he'd been systematically passing information to a brace of the most powerful international bookmakers and throwing races on demand, although no hard evidence or charges had been brought against any of them. And yet twenty-four months later, he was at the pinnacle of the sport, being lauded by the same newspaper that had previously castigated him.

Everyone loves a story of redemption, thought Cam wearily, picking up the paper and tossing it into his waste paper bin. So why was he still wrestling with the aftermath of this one ride from his best friend?

The answer came to him quickly. He could have accepted it as an exceptionally bad ride. Every jockey has bad rides from time to time, but this was more than a bad ride. This was a *purposefully* poor ride. And the reason he was so wound up about the race was... Jack wouldn't admit he'd thrown it. In fact, he wouldn't countenance the possibility he'd made any sort of mistake!

During the drive from Wolverhampton back to Malton that evening, Jack had maintained that he'd been beaten fair and square. They'd argued, Cam pleading with him to watch the replay and explain his actions. In the end, they'd dropped into a sullen silence for the last hour of their journey and upon their arrival back at Malton, Jack had stumped off up the two flights of stairs to his room at the top of the Racing House charity-run accommodation.

The converted Victorian house over three floors was home to a total of six stable lads, lasses, and jockeys under the age of twenty-five, so when a knock came on his bedroom door it wasn't a big surprise, despite the late hour.

Cam opened the door and his heart pumped a little faster when he discovered a tired looking Charlotte dressed ready for bed. He noted the fluffy red felt dressing gown with a white sash and the pair of pink crocs on her feet, greeting her with, 'I'm loving the Santa look, Charlie.'

Charlotte, or 'Charlie' as she preferred to be called, didn't say anything, she just stood in the hallway, arms crossed, staring expectantly at Cam. Lodging directly below him on the ground floor, she was a stable lass at the same place as him, the Sebastian Savage yard. Short, but in Cam's opinion, perfectly formed, right down to the diamond stud in her snub nose, Charlie was never without a boyfriend, or girlfriend for that matter, on her arm, and being something of a social butterfly, she'd been difficult to pin down and get to know at first. It took a night of Christmas karaoke in the house to put that right, as she sang like a lark and Cam bellowed like a warthog. Their rendition of Fairytale in New York had been memorable. Since then, they'd slowly become good, if grudgingly from his point of view, platonic friends. Presently, the nineteen-year-old girl raised one perfectly sculpted eyebrow in a silent query of, 'Really?'

'What is it, Charlie?' Cam shrugged.

'You're walking circuits of your room again,' she said, pushing her way into his bedroom, 'I can hear you from downstairs, pacing here, there, and everywhere.'

She plonked herself on the edge of the bed, crossed her bare legs from the knee down, and after rearranging her dressing gown, patted the space beside her, 'Come on then, give!'

'Sorry, Charlie,' Cam said with a heavy sigh, 'Am I really that easy to read?'

'Absolutely. You're completely transparent. Real heart on the sleeve stuff. And your footsteps are loud enough to keep me awake! But, you're also fair, honest...'

Boring? Cam thought to himself miserably, wishing she'd add good-looking and fun to be with, to her list.

'...and I can't sleep when I know something's bugging you, it's all the squeaking from the floorboards. What's with all the walking in circles, anyway? Why can't you just burst into tears like everyone else?'

'I'll bear that in mind for next time,' he intoned darkly.

Charlie gave one of her barking laughs and Cam felt a little brighter. Picking up his laptop he joined her on the bed, making sure not to get close enough to touch, and for the umpteenth time that night, set the race video playing.

'Watch Jack, he's on the runner-up. Sunset Blaze.'

Six

It was fast approaching half-past midnight when Cam and Charlie climbed the stairs and knocked on Jack's bedroom door at the top of the house.

'He's bound to be asleep!'

'Then why is there light coming from under his door?' Charlie said in a tired, and slightly frustrated whisper.

'Maybe he's afraid of the dark?' muttered Cam.

They waited, Charlie adjusting the belt on her dressing gown and Cam examining the ceiling, as a means of not staring at her bare legs.

'I told you, he's asleep,' said Cam, walking away a few paces.

Charlie bent her head to the door and listened.

'Someone's coming!' she mouthed silently, waving at Cam to rejoin her. She jumped back from the door as it opened a crack.

'Oh, hi!' said Jack warmly upon seeing Charlie. As he swung his door open and noticed Cam, he added, 'Oh… hi,' in a deeper, significantly laboured tone.

'Another jockey who can't sleep?' Charlie ventured as she impatiently pushed her way into the room. Jack was still fully clothed and she noted the iPad lying on his bedside table was displaying the Racing Post website.

'Come in, why don't you,' Jack grumbled as he shut his door behind his two late night guests. He cleared his throat and to Cam, said, 'Actually, I thought about coming down to see you tonight.'

He stole a glance at Charlie before returning his gaze to Cam, 'I wondered if you and me…'

'She knows about the Wolverhampton race,' Cam cut in, 'She got it out of me.'

Jack rolled his eyes, 'Any port in a storm, eh?'

'Hey!' Charlie barked, 'I'm not *any* port, and you're the one in the storm.'

Jack visibly deflated, 'Yeah, I know.'

Cam frowned, 'You know?'

'I've watched the race video…'

Jack studied the concerned faces of his two friends and dropping his eyes to the floor, rubbed thoughtfully at his bony chin.

'You were right, it does *look* like I threw the race. It would take a proper horseman to see it, but there are moves I made… actions I took… Thing is…'

Jack had been inspecting his feet. Lifting his head, he blinked rapidly, his eyes glistening with moisture. Resisting the urge to wipe the frustrated tears away, he stared resolutely at Cam, and then Charlie.

'The thing is, I don't remember the race that way.'

Charlie tipped her head to one side, 'What are you saying?'

'I mean… I didn't ride the race that… way. Look, I know it sounds like I'm crackers, but… in my head, I did everything to win that race,' Jack insisted, his reply punctuated with sighs of frustration.

Cam was relieved, pleased Jack had seen sense, 'Well at least we're on the same page now.'

'But I'm not!'

'You threw the race, and you're admitting it. That's all I…'

'No, no. You don't understand,' moaned Jack.

Becoming animated, his hands waving, he fixed Cam with a serious stare, 'I don't remember that race. I don't remember riding like that. I've gone over it all night, again and again. In my head, I rode the perfect race!'

Suddenly shooting to his feet, Jack ran a nervous hand through his hair before making a fist and gently biting on it, worry lines appearing across his forehead. Charlie jumped up from the bed and placed a comforting arm around him.

'I'm amazed the stewards didn't call an inquiry,' said Jack, his voice catching slightly, 'After all, I was on the favourite.'

Cam said, 'Maybe because it was an all-apprentice race they let a few mistakes go. But the ride didn't go unnoticed.'

Charlie sent a warning frown back at Cam, still sitting on the bed. He responded with a defensive shrug.

'I've shown you the comments on social media!' he complained.

An exasperated and wide-eyed Charlie replied, 'Yes, but just at this precise moment they would be unhelpful, *wouldn't they?'*

Cam made a mouth-zipping motion, but as the contemplative silence built he couldn't help himself. The question bursting within him had to be asked.

'Why, Jack? Why ride like that? Is someone paying you? Do you owe someone money? Are they threatening you? I mean, it's just not like you… not at all!'

'No! None of those,' Jack insisted.

'So what made you ride like that?' Cam pressed.

Charlie thought about giving Cam another warning glare, as tears were starting to brim in the bottom of Jack's eyes, but her curiosity got the better of her. Jack was mild-mannered, sensible, and despite his background, or maybe because of it, incredibly centred. Presently he was also indisputably the best apprentice jockey in Malton, having quickly amassed the twenty-five winners required to cut his seven pounds claim down to five, and well on the way to fifty winners, having ridden with plenty of success through the winter on the all-weather circuits. She waited for him to answer, but was ready to forgive him if he couldn't, or wouldn't.

Jack took a deep breath and turned to Cam, looking him straight in the eye.

'I can't explain it,' he growled in a low voice, 'Like I've said, I came away from that race believing I'd ridden a text-book race and given Sunset Blaze every chance to win. I don't recognise myself on that replay… it's like…'

Jack trailed off, his face a mask of concentration.

Cam waited, allowing Jack time to grapple with his explanation and locate a string of suitable words.

'… like I wasn't in that saddle.'

Silence returned to Jack's room. With the only chair tucked under the small desk, all three of them were lounging on his bed, trying to make sense of what Jack was saying, compared with what they knew to be true. Similar to the other five bedrooms in the house, Jack's room was sparsely furnished. Along with the single bed, each room came with a free-standing wardrobe, desk, chair and waste-paper basket. The decorating was equally minimal, featuring white painted walls, although the tall ceiling conferring a sense of air and space. Faded yellow curtains only just met in the middle to shield Jack's one window. None of this, nor staring at Jack's few personal effects, or the various paper posters tacked around the walls, helped Charlie or Cam come any closer to solving Jack's predicament.

'It's late,' Charlie announced eventually, 'And I've got to be at Savage's yard by six-thirty. I'm off to bed. Both of you should get some sleep too, you both look shattered.'

She rolled off the bed, 'I bet you're both still feeling the effects of that bender you went on in Scarborough on Saturday night.'

'How do you know about that?' Cam asked, clearly perplexed.

Charlie gave him a prim smile, 'Don't you remember? You both came into the house singing a Marc Almond song so loud I couldn't hear my television. I had to shush the two of you and send you both up to bed. So I guess this is the second time I've had to do that in only a couple of days! Now come on, get to bed.'

Cam frowned. Only the vaguest recollection of Saturday night in Scarborough came to him, although the haunting lyrics, 'Say Hello, Wave Goodbye' were suddenly travelling through his mind. Something clicked and he remembered: the Soft Cell tribute band they'd seen at… now where was it they'd seen them?

Addressing Jack as she headed to the bedroom door, Charlie said, 'It's just one race. It will be yesterday's fish and chip paper by tomorrow, as my Auntie used to say. All forgotten about.'

Jack nodded and provided her with a faint smile.

'Thanks, Charlie. I hope you're right. I'm riding out that decent horse for Freddie Jones tomorrow. I just hope he didn't watch the replay of that Wolverhampton race.'

'Ach, all the trainers around Malton think you're bloody wonderful,' Cam assured him as he joined Charlie at the door, 'Including Freddie Jones.'

He allowed a yawn to stretch his mouth open before adding in a tired voice, 'Tomorrow's another day. Like Charlie said, people forget.'

'Hand!' barked Charlie, elbowing Cam in the ribs, 'I don't want to see your tonsils!'

As if to demonstrate, she immediately yawned, the back of her hand covering her mouth. Cam noticed how petite and delicate her fingers appeared against the lightly tanned skin of her face.

Jack was weary, but still managed a grin. Well aware of his friend's attraction to Charlie, it amused him that Cam hadn't yet plucked up enough courage to ask her out.

'Go on you two. Get out,' he said amiably, 'It's almost one o'clock in the morning.'

With assurances to his friends that he, 'Would be fine. And also, I have three rides at Ripon tomorrow afternoon,' Jack ushered them out into the hallway, promising to see both of them in the morning. Once the door was closed, Jack surveyed his room. It seemed tremendously empty without them, and his single bed felt seriously uninviting.

As he got under the duvet and tried to make himself comfortable, Cam's words came back to him.

'It was an apprentice race, mistakes are expected because we're still learning. And like Charlie says, it will soon be old news.'

Jack turned over, pulling his duvet tight. Cam was right, he was making a bigger deal out of this than was necessary – he should accept his friend's explanation, that for whatever reason, he'd not been himself at Wolverhampton. He had to forget it and move on. Besides, what were the chances of such a strange experience in the saddle happening a second time?

Seven

Since moving to Malton almost a year ago, Cam had discovered that being apprenticed to the Sebastian Savage yard did have its benefits, but just lately, he'd found himself dwelling increasingly on a number of major drawbacks.

Unlike Jack, he didn't own a car. Jack had bought a really old Renault with his first prizemoney cheque from Weatherby's. Cam simply didn't earn enough to afford to buy or run a car of his own, based on his low salary and number of race rides. Both he and Jack had an agent, but his best friend was averaging a dozen rides a week, whereas he was lucky if he got a leg up once a week on an outsider for the Savage yard.

When he couldn't beg a lift, Cam used pedal power to get around Malton and its sister town of Norton. His daily cycle from his digs each morning, through the centre of Malton's old town, and then out into Norton and finally, half a mile into the countryside where the Marsh Landing yard was located, was only a fifteen minute journey. He used this time to fill his mind with which horses he would be variously, riding out, breaking, moving around the yard, or which boxes he would be cleaning out. However, over the last few weeks, he'd found himself dedicating this fifteen precious minutes to grousing about his employer. It seemed he became more disgruntled with every revolution of his pedals.

Turning off Beverley Road he slowed in order to navigate his way around the potholes in the track leading into the yard. As he carefully avoided another five inch rim-killing gouge in the track, he considered whether his current disgruntlement with the trainer to whom he was apprenticed could be blamed on anything other than the man himself, Sebastian Savage. He ruled it out. Savage was definitely at the root of all his disappointment with his career.

Cam supposed lack of sleep might be to blame for his depressive state of mind, but he quickly ruled that out too.

He'd always been able to cope with very little sleep. No, there was another reason, and the hollow feeling in his stomach was testament to his own guilt. It was the upward trajectory of Jack's race riding exploits, compared to his own excuse for a riding career, that was the reason for his melancholia.

Stowing his bike in one of the old, wood-built, and rarely used stables around the back of the yard, Cam headed for the tack room to consult the work rota and pick up his riding kit.

Marsh Landing Stables had been a historically significant yard in the Malton area, with a glittering history of racing success spanning more than a century. Initially famed for producing a gaggle of Guineas, Derby, and Ledger winners between the wars, the stables had once housed more than two hundred equine athletes. Arguably, its heyday had been in the fifties and early sixties, when Brigadier James Oswald White had been at the helm. Having fostered close relations with a number of the better studs in the area, his glory years had included several classics, and numerous wins in the big northern handicaps, most notably the Northumberland Plate and the Ebor, the 'Brigadier' having had a penchant for training stayers.

A variety of barns, paddocks, and other training facilities, old and new, huddled around a suitably grand mansion, and the current setup based around this venerable country pile of the Whites still traded on that heritage, although the site had since been broken up into five, and then seven smaller yards during the eighties and nineties.

Sebastian Savage trained from the Marsh Landing Stables, having taken over the lease when his father, Terry, died of a heart attack on the gallops. Despite the yard managing to produce twenty to thirty winners each year, the days of potential Classic and Group horses being sent up the Norton gallops from the Marsh Landing Stables were long gone. With an average of forty horses through each flat season, Savage set out his stall to a basic, and rigid methodology. His system of training saw him buy in a large number of unraced, sprint-bred juveniles, keeping the best of them to farm the northern racetracks with sprint handicappers that ran frequently, and won in their turn. A decent ninety-plus rated sprinter would pop up every few years, allowing him to race at York or Ascot, and just about keep the stable in the public eye. With an average win rate of a mere six percent most seasons, Savage settled for quantity over quality. This thought brought a smirk to Cam's face, as the same could also be said for Savage's private life.

In his mid-forties, Savage was single, preferring to remain available, seemingly for whoever happened by and took his fancy. At six-foot-two, the trainer's lean, muscular frame exuded a natural agility. And retaining most his own hair, Savage combined a wardrobe of fashionable country clothes with what Cam imagined to be a punishing grooming regime. To women of a certain age and social tier Savage was able to appear as a dashing, handsome sort who maintained his fitness and jaunty good looks by frequently riding out. Whilst female company was easy to come by, he boasted few male friends.

Cam had noticed his Guv'nor had a particular attraction to petite, busty blondes. There was a running joke in the yard that should Dolly Parton ever stroll into the yard, the Guv'nor would be courting her with his disarming charm before she could say, 'Nine to five'.

It seemed Savage was able to attract a never-ending array of both single and married ladies, often a shade older than himself, into the East Wing rooms of the Marsh Mansion where Savage lived alone. Many of them ended up owning a horse, or part of one, until they discovered their syndicate was made up of similarly busty types and put two and two together.

None of Savage's private shenanigans were of concern to Cam. Until now, he'd kept his head down and concentrated on his work, riding every morning, mucking out, feeding and inevitably, sweeping. In return, he was given the odd ride in public, almost exclusively in apprentice races. However, he was becoming disenchanted with the lack of riding opportunities. There had been promises from Savage of allowing him outside rides from other trainers and using him and his 7lb claim for standard non-apprentice races, but those opportunities had yet to materialise. Cam had one win and a couple of places under his belt from a paltry fifteen rides. Meanwhile, his best friend was apprenticed to a much smaller yard, but able to visit other yards and ride two or three lots a day for a large variety of trainers. Jack had already reached twenty-five winners from just over a hundred and fifty runs, had his 7lb allowance reduced to 5lbs, and was making giant strides towards becoming a professional jockey.

Cam was satisfied petty jealously of his best friend wasn't causing his disenchantment with his boss. He applauded and celebrated all of Jack's wins as if they were his own, and Jack reciprocated. No, this was about a lack of opportunity. Cam was sure he deserved to be getting outside rides, but Savage refused to release him, instead using him as a skivvy around the yard.

'Penny for 'em!' someone called out from between the hanging rows of tack. Cam immediately recognised the voice of Miguel Gomes, one of Savage's two barn managers. Along with the other barn manager, Dean Rice, and Jackie Bell, the travelling head lass, Miguel did most of the heavy lifting around the yard. Whilst Savage flitted here and there supposedly overseeing things, Dean, Jackie, and Miguel did the heavy grunt work with the help of a mixture of seven full and part-time stable lads and lasses.

'You've been gazing longingly at that saddle for a full minute,' Miguel pointed out in his thick Portuguese drawl, 'Any chance you're going to pull it down and get some work done? I've got you working four this morning and cantering another two.'

Cam forced a smile onto his face, 'Yeah, had a bit of

trouble sleeping last night. I guess I'm just a bit…'

'Hung over? Too much booze?' Miguel suggested, flashing an amused eyebrow.

Cam shook his head. He was about to reply, but a third voice spoke first.

'We can't have you on a horse's back if that's the case, Cameron,' said a familiar voice from the tack room door.

Cam cringed. There was only one person in the yard who insisted in calling everyone by their full Christian names. It was one of many ways he asserted his dominance. Turning slowly, Cam found Sebastian Savage leaning against the tack room's doorframe, his arms crossed and wearing an expectant look.

'I swear I haven't been drinking, Guv'nor,' Cam said in a flat, determined tone, 'I'd never get on a horse unless I was a hundred percent sober.'

Savage regarded the boy for a long moment, eventually allowing the twitch of a smile to break out. He didn't really care if the boy had been on the lash the night before. In fact, he half expected it, either that, or spending his night with a good woman. Both were decent ways to lose a night's sleep in his opinion. Nevertheless, you never passed up an opportunity to remind staff of who was boss.

'Good to hear it, Cameron' sighed Savage, his interest in the boy suddenly exhausted, 'Miguel? I'm going to watch the first three lots from the marker. I want to get a grip on the juveniles, so send the fillies first lot, then the colts and geldings. Make sure the two running on Saturday get an individual three-quarter pace gallop.'

Miguel's shoulders drooped slightly. Not only did it ruin his planned morning's work, it meant that his boss would be standing on his own private viewing platform all morning, right beside the top end of the All-Weather gallop. That meant his work riders would be on edge, and he'd have to turn the lots around extra quick. The Guv'nor wasn't the most patient of men and the nip in the air was sure to test that patience.

'Yes, Guv'nor,' Miguel replied dutifully, noting that Savage had already turned his back. His boss was striding away and probably hadn't waited to hear his response.

Hesitating for only a moment, Cam decided to seize the opportunity to speak with Savage and hurried after the trainer. He caught up with him half-way across the quad that acted as the centre of the yard. The first splashes of rain were hitting the concrete as Savage ground to a halt and spun around in response to Cam's call of, 'Mr Savage? Guv'nor!'

'What is it, Cameron?' Savage asked, lifting his eyes to the sky to squint at the massing dark blue clouds rolling over the Wolds towards them, 'Make it quick. This tweed jacket stinks if I get it wet.'

'I just wondered when I was going to get the opportunity to ride out for other yards...' said Cam, 'I've been with you for almost a year now, and I thought...'

Savage had raised a flat palm and closed his eyes. Cam took the hint and his query trailed off.

'Cameron Camberley,' said Savage, managing to pour enough condescension into his name it made Cam's heart shrivel and his blood pressure rocket.

'You're my apprentice. That means you're *mine*,' harped Savage, 'You're mine, to do as I wish. That's what you signed up for. In return I give you rides. Do I not give you rides?'

'Yes, But...'

Again, the flat palm appeared. Cam's heartrate continued to build. The rain was coming down in earnest now and Savage had hunched his shoulders to stop drips finding their way down his neck.

'But nothing, boy,' Savage said, his eyes narrow slits, 'You need experience, and I give it to you. That's the deal. You ride work, muck out, lead up, feed, sweep, and basically do anything that I instruct you to do and I give you a couple of spare rides at the racecourse. *That's* how you learn.'

Cam took a breath.

'I appreciate that, sir, but I'm an apprentice *jockey*. That means I learn to ride at the races. If you use me more often for your horses, or allow me to ride out for other yards in Malton, I can get more experience and become a better…'

Savage's hand raised once more, cutting Cam off. Cam could feel the faint buzz of anger rising in his chest. It was building within him. He so badly wanted to slap that patronising palm away and shout in this idiot's face. All he wanted was *a chance*. A chance to ride horses with real ability, not the no-hopers and those running just to get a few pounds back from the handicapper.

'I'll release you to ride for other trainers when your race riding skills are of a high enough quality not to embarrass me in public,' Savage said curtly, 'Now get out of my sight, I'm getting wet!'

'And how, exactly, do I prove myself when I'm only getting one or two rides a month?' Cam said to Savage's retreating shoulders.

Savage came to a rigid halt. He turned and walked the five paces back to Cam, a snide grin bending his mouth sideways. Without warning Savage's hand shot out and roughly grabbed Cam's polo shirt by its collar. Dragging the thin teenager toward him, Savage grimaced, lifting his quarry to his toes, until their noses were only an inch apart. Cam had his hand on the trainer's arm, but didn't struggle, shocked by the sudden physical contact and the iron grip on his shirt.

'You put your head down, work hard, and do as I say,' Savage snarled into Cam's face.

Savage released him by thrusting Cam backwards with both hands, 'And speak like that to me again and I'll make sure you don't ride a rocking horse, never mind a racehorse.'

Still in shock, his chest heaving with pent up anger, Cam watched as the Guv'nor stump off in the direction of his private rooms in Marsh Mansion. Cam had to tell himself not to race after him and give Savage a piece of his mind. Instead, he lifted his head and closed his eyes, allowing the rain to strike his face, run down his cheeks and pool around his collar.

He stayed like that for some time, counting and breathing, allowing his anger to slowly ebb, desperately attempting to clear his mind of the violent retribution he'd like to rain down upon the pompous oaf. Within seconds of him reaching an inner calm, a whispered conversation started up close by. Cam opened his eyes and found a group of four fellow stable hands and work-riders discussing him from under a stable awning where they were sheltering from the shower. Crestfallen, Cam shot them a defiant look, dropped his chin, and walked self-consciously back into the tack room.

***

'Head down, work hard, and do as I say.'

Savage's words of wisdom bounced around Cam's head throughout the morning. He rode two lots in a funk, ideas of walking out, or having it out with the boss again bending his mind one way, then the other.

He'd reached the bottom of the gallop on his third ride of the morning and took his mount, a headstrong three-year-old colt, to one side, allowing the rest of the group from the yard, three unraced youngsters, to follow a seasoned handicapper up the gallop. Miguel had asked him to ride the three-year-old alone, giving the horse a three-quarter pace workout, ensuring his best work was in the last two hundred yards up to the summit of the hill, passing Savage just as the colt was stretching out.

Cam was starting to come around to brazening out the rest of the day and sloping off home to discuss his woes with Jack when his phone rang. He took a quick call, getting rid of the cold caller a few seconds later. Another two riders had appeared behind him so Cam gave his colt a nudge with his heels, an encouraging click of his tongue, and they set off up the hill.

The gallop was built on a gradual rise, only wide

enough for two horses to work side by side. It was uphill all the way, the final furlong of the seven being up the steepest of the inclines. Going along at a full gallop, it took a fully fit, decent sort to reach the top of the hill without weakening, or taking a big blow. With the first two furlongs being flat and relatively straight, Cam allowed the three-year-old to trot, then canter for a few strides before getting him into the rhythm of a good, swinging gallop. Negotiating a small dip, horse and rider entered the one sweeping left-hand turn and Cam rebalanced the colt for the remaining five furlongs arrow straight up the gently rising hill.

With three furlongs to run, Cam loosened his grip on the reins and allowed the colt to quicken. There was still more under the bonnet, but Miguel had told him in no uncertain terms that a three-quarter pace workout was all that was needed today.

Two out, Cam squeezed the colt just a tad and he responded with a longer stride. Between the colt's ears, Cam spotted Savage, standing in his usual position on his personally created plinth, only a yard or two away from the All-Weather track. Too close to the gallop, in his opinion. He'd always reckoned Savage brought owners to his private vantage point in order to impress them with the speed and majesty of their horses as they shot past only yards away. Standing so close to the All-Weather gallop always brought gasps of astonishment. But today, a potential new reason for Savage to camp out so close to the gallop sprang into Cam's mind. Perhaps his boss simply liked to intimidate his work riders…

As he drew closer to the trainer, that suppressed tingle of dissatisfaction with Savage renewed itself and soon became something more, not quite anger, but Cam sensed his hackles were raised. The sun was out now, the rain having been blown out onto the Vale of York. The Guv'nor had removed his coat and hung it on a post placed at the back of the plinth expressly for that purpose. His phone was held to his ear and

Savage was looking down, idly brushing the sand on the nearside edge of his plinth with his toe. Cam grimaced. Savage couldn't even be bothered to look up and watch him.

Cam started to push the colt, keeping him up to his work, but still not allowing him to extend to a full gallop. It's probably his latest girlfriend, Cam decided. That's who'll be on the end of the line. Yet another blonde with Rubenesque proportions... He wondered what would happen if he allowed the colt to open up?

'I can't wait, cooed Savage into his mobile phone, 'I've been looking forward to meeting you again ever since we bumped into each other at the races.'

'Oh, *have* you?'

'Oh, yes. It's been *six long days*,' Savage replied, placing emphasis on his last few words.

He was treated to a sycophantic giggle from his eager female listener.

'I'd better get going, my dear.'

'Awww!' she bleated back.

'Until Saturday, then,' Savage replied smoothly, before finishing with a small, impassioned growl. Experience had taught him that this strange little noise tended to produce a response that helpfully indicated where they lay in the seduction process.

'Mmmm!' his date replied enthusiastically.

Savage could imagine her big blue eyes rolling enticingly at him. It was certainly promising.

She added, 'You know something Sebastian, I can't w...'

Savage's eyes had been cast to the ground in concentration during this attempt to woo the divorcee. His morning's work on the gallop had gone well - he now had this pretty little blonde from Wetherby booked in for a meal out in York on Saturday, and Sunday lunch in his apartment with a rather comely woman from Hull. He'd been working on that latter liaison for several weeks now, so a half decent lunch could turn into an interesting afternoon... Allowing himself a satisfied smirk, he finished the call. The sound of imminently approaching hooves caused Savage to frown. They'd sounded unlike the normal slap of a horses foot on the sand, wax, and fibre that made up the All-Weather surface. This had the distinct thump of hoof on turf and all of a sudden it was uncommonly loud.

As he lifted his head, his mobile phone slipped through his fingers and he lunged forward to retrieve it from the harrowed fibresand at the edge of the All-Weather gallop.

Savage never had time to wipe the surprise from his face, let alone avoid his fate, as over half a ton of horse plus eight stones, eleven pounds of Cameron Camberley encased in a body protector, cannoned into him.

Eight

'Jack? Is that you?'

'Cam! What's wrong?'

Jack transferred his phone to his right ear and slapped a hand over his left as the racecourse public address system belted out an update on the non-runners later on the card at Ripon.

'Sorry, Cam. I'm at Ripon. I couldn't take your calls earlier because I was riding, and you know I can't make calls from inside the weighing room... No, I'm outside now. Five missed calls... I'm guessing this is important?'

'Thank god,' Cam breathed, his relief flooding down the phoneline to Jack in a single, emotive wave, 'I've been trying to get hold of you for the last hour. Can you come to York? I could really do with your help.'

'York? Cam... What's going on? You sound like you're in a railway station. I can hardly hear you for all the background noise.'

There was a couple of seconds pause where all Jack

could hear was people chattering, and incessant clicking and a strange clanking and squeaking.

'I'm at York Hospital. Actually, I'm right between two blasted vending machines and a mass of people in the Accident and Emergency department. Oh, and I've got a policewoman with me. I think she's making sure I don't run away.'

Jack closed his eyes and tried to imagine the scene at the other end of the line.

'Are you hurt?'

'Yes, erm… Not badly. Well, not as bad as him. Just bruising and a twisted ankle.'

'Him? Who's 'him'?'

'Erm… the Guv'nor. They've rushed him off somewhere to X-ray his arm. They reckon it could be broken. And one of the nurses said something about bruised ribs. But since I've got here they won't tell me how he is.'

'And the policewoman?'

A couple of seconds of silence ticked by.

'She's… er, fine?'

'No, you dummy! I mean why have you got a policewoman with you?'

'Oh, right. I think I've been arrested. Oh, no. Hold on…'

Another short pause filled with the sounds of coffee being dispensed and a distant conversation concluded with Cam returning to speak once more.

'Meera. Erm… the policewoman, is saying I'm not arrested, but I've got to be questioned and make a statement,' he confirmed, 'Can you come? She's taking me for questioning at…'

Once more a short silence developed.

'…Fulford Police Station. I could *really* do with knowing you're there.'

Jack looked down at himself. He was in the Ripon Racecourse car park, the easiest place for a rider to make a call from without breaking the BHA's jockey communications rules – it was only a step out of the back of the weighing room. He still had his silks and riding attire on from the previous race, and was due to ride in the last on the card in over two hours' time. Letting the trainer and connections of the handicapper down by leaving now would be unprofessional. But it was Cam, and by the sound of it, he was in trouble. Jack knew all about trouble, as he'd rarely been out of it throughout his childhood. Cam was only the second person he'd ever considered a true friend and Jack knew the value of having someone like that in his life. Priceless. Far more valuable than the few minutes of frustration it might cause the owners and trainer to find a replacement jockey for the 46 rated filly he'd been booked to ride in a Class 6 five furlong handicap in the last at Ripon on a Monday afternoon.

'I'm setting off now,' Jack told his friend, 'But first, tell me exactly what's happened.'

Jack listened. By the time Cam had finished his story, he'd removed his silks and body protector and was standing just outside the weighing room back door in a thin vest.

'I'll be with you in an hour,' Jack promised as he cut the call. He immediately placed a call to the trainer of his mount in the last race on the card, before rushing back into the weighing room building to finish getting changed.

Nine

Fifty-five minutes later, Jack walked into the reception of the modern office block that was home to Fulford Road Police Station. He crossed over to the reception desk, noting that the building was only a stone's throw from York Racecourse's back straight.

Once he'd asked the heavily moustachioed, bull of a male policeman on reception whether Cameron Camberley was still in the building, it was explained to him that yes, he was. Jack waited for more, but the policeman's dull gaze indicated that if he wasn't careful, their conversation had every chance of developing into a game of twenty questions.

Jack dropped his shoulders and sighed. It was always the same when he encountered the police, traffic wardens, security guards, well-heeled owners and trainers, and even bouncers on the door of night clubs. Even though he was gainfully employed and had remained on the right side of the law for over two years now, a certain set of people had an innate ability to identify him as having once been a wrong 'un. Jack had long imagined his past misdemeanours must somehow be written into his face, part of his hairstyle, or sewn into his clothes.

'Can I see him?'

A shake of the head, 'No, Sir.'

The policeman managed to fill the word 'Sir' with so much contempt, Jack couldn't help being impressed.

Jack looked around the reception area. To the right of the reception desk were a number of single and double doors interspersed with pot plants. He smiled inwardly. Everything in York came with a touch of quality. In Sheffield the local nick was a barren place where anything not nailed down, such as pot plants, would have soon been lifted by the clientele. Beyond the reception he could see offices and a stairwell. He couldn't see anywhere to sit and wait.

'Any idea how long he'll be?'

Another shake of the moustache.

'A guess?'

This seemed to amuse the policeman. A swift pout rolled his upper lip and made his moustache ripple.

'I'm afraid not, Sir.'

'Can you tell me what's happening to him?'

The policeman cocked his head to one side and the moustache consulted a computer monitor.

'He's being interviewed.'

'Great, so once he's been questioned he can leave?'

The policeman smiled for the first time.

'That rather depends on his answers, Sir.'

He's been waiting to deliver that line, thought Jack as he forced a smile. He was finding it difficult not to stare at the officer's moustache sitting under a pair of large nostrils from which protruded a thicket of hair growth.

Whilst contemplating his next question a set of double doors opened with a swish and a squeak behind him and a voice he recognised called out his name, initiating a half-smile.

He turned, and Charlie rushed up to him. She was wearing her tight-fitting, weather resistant work clothes, her very short blonde hair almost completely covered by a bright red woollen hat that had a home-knitted look about it. With only the lightest touch of make-up, and her athletic physique, she could pass as male or female. That's Charlie, he reasoned, she's happy with who she is. Such a shame that her sexuality confused many of the people around her, and no matter how hard he tried, that included him.

The policeman watched the two teenagers embrace awkwardly before loudly clearing his throat.

'Sir is welcome to join Mr Camberley's entourage in our waiting room,' said the policeman.

Jack noted the contemptuous look Charlie gave the receptionist and guessed she'd received a similar treatment to him. Taking hold of his arm, Charlie guided him away from the reception desk, back through the double doors, and into a waiting room. Among the further array of tastefully placed potted plants, plastic chairs were lined up back-to-back. There had to be twenty chairs, but only one was occupied. Charlie pulled him down into a seat in a corner well away from the sole occupant of the seat, ten yards distant.

'Have you spoken with Cam? What did he say?' she demanded, her eyes filled with concern. If he wasn't mistaken, she'd also shed a tear or two on her way to York as her usually blemish-free cheeks were uncommonly rosy. Her right knee jiggled as she bounced her leg on the toe of her trainer.

'Yes, he called me at Ripon. I came straight here. How

about you?'

'Never mind me,' she scolded, 'What did he say? Did he sound... okay?'

'Yeah... he was a bit weirded out by being brought in for questioning. I don't think he's ever had a run-in with the police before.'

'Yes, but was he hurt? What did he say about the accident?' she pressed.

'He's shaken up, but otherwise fine,' Jack assured her, 'All he said was that he'd had an accident on the gallops and he and his Guv'nor had been hurt. But don't worry, he only had bruises and a couple of cuts.'

'It's not his idiot body I'm worried about,' she said with a wince, 'I'm worried with what they're going to charge him with! I've heard Savage is in a bad way. I'd already left for the day, but I spoke to Joanne, one of the stable lasses at the Savage yard, and she said they had to call an ambulance and it took twenty minutes for the medics to scrape the Guv'nor up off the gallops!'

'I have a feeling she may have been exaggerating slightly,' said Jack sagely, 'Cam said he thought Savage had a broken arm and had a cracked rib or two. But that's what you get for standing in the way of a galloping horse!'

Her foot stopped jiggling for a moment and Charlie seemed to relax a little.

'Joanne's not the sharpest. Hopefully you're right. Apparently Savage was screaming all sorts,' Charlie added, hugging herself, her jiggling leg starting up again. That limb has a life of its own, Jack thought. He considered placing a calming hand onto her skin-tight riding breeches in order to arrest her nervous tick, but decided to let it be.

Charlie continued, 'Joanne said Savage was blaming it all on Cam. He said Cam rode straight at him, bashed into him, and whilst he was on the ground stole stuff from him.'

'What? Why would... what sort of stuff?'

'I don't know exactly, from his jacket I think. A watch,

his wallet... oh, and his diary?' Charlie shrugged, her voice beginning to rise in pitch to match her concern, 'They'd had some sort of argument earlier that morning in the yard and Savage told the police Cam was attempting to kill him for not giving him rides!'

A boy in tracksuit bottoms and a hoodie that shrouded his face in shadow was sitting facing them, his back against the far wall. He now adjusted himself in his seat, making his chair leg squeak on the shiny laminate floor. Charlie shot him a quick look, having forgotten they weren't alone. Jack followed her gaze, trying to catch a glimpse of the stranger's face within the hood. Raising his head a fraction, the boy stared sullenly over at them from under the edge of his hood. Jack reckoned he was probably a teenager, seventeen, maybe slightly older.

Charlie quickly broke eye contact, hugging herself tighter. Jack matched the teenager's stare. Eventually the boy scowled, slumped back in his seat and pulling his hood down, became insulated from inspection once more.

A silent minute went by before Jack, speaking quietly and trying to be as circumspect as possible, posed Charlie the question he'd been wanting to ask since she'd appeared through the waiting room's double doors.

'I was just wondering... You and Cam. Is there anything, you know, between the two of you? It's just, in the circumstances... you being here...'

Charlie's leg stopped jiggling. She snorted softly, her mouth opening to reply, but she thought better of what she'd been about to say. Jack was usually quiet, almost introverted, for him to ask such a forthright question was out of character. With his black hair, brown eyes and bent nose, this burst of intensity was almost scary, especially when his dark eyes seemed to be joining with hers, linked in some sort of dance, as they tried to read each other's thoughts.

'Why are you interested?'

Jack bit the inside of his mouth. As he'd expected, this

conversation was going to be tougher than he wanted, or it needed to be.

'I'm his friend. His best friend, and I... suppose I care about him. Things haven't been easy for Cam lately...'

'Eh? How do you mean?'

'The race at Wolverhampton on Monday. It shook us both up. Cam more than me.'

'Tell me about it,' Charlie insisted, 'After we met up last night he was still pacing around his room like a caged tiger.'

Jack considered this for a moment before adding, 'And we both got a letter from the authorities this morning, saying we've got to see a BHA representative at Haydock on Saturday. We've no idea what that's about. It's put Cam on edge, not to mention the fact that Savage has been treating him like cheap labour around the yard for the last year. Limiting his rides for the yard, and not allowing him to take outside rides is burning Cam up inside.'

'You're not helping either,' she pointed out, 'What, with you banging winners in left, right, and centre.'

This gave Jack cause to fall silent for a moment. He hadn't considered the impact his own success on the track might be having on Cam. Charlie might have a point. Whilst admitting to himself that Cam might be a little jealous of his winning streak, Jack knew for certain it was Charlie who should also tread carefully. After all, she was the apple of Cam's eye.

'Look, when Cam comes out after being interviewed under caution, he'll need our support. He's bound to be tired and emotional. You know how he gets! What happened today will affect him. I don't want him getting hurt... emotionally'

'Hurt by me, you mean?' she demanded, failing to look away under Jack's determined gaze.

'Listen to me Jack,' Charlie growled quietly, anger spicing her words, 'Cam and I are good friends. That's all. I'm here because I like him. He's a sweet boy who is fun, full of life, sensitive, and more than anything else, doesn't judge me.

The last thing I want to do is add to his problems!'

On the other side of the room, the hooded boy emitted what sounded like a chuckle.

'And you can belt up too!' Charlie called out angrily across the waiting room.

An uneasy silence shrouded the room for the next two minutes. If the roles were reversed, we'd be in better shape, Jack thought. If he'd been the one to skittle Savage over on the gallops he'd cope with the police's questioning and wouldn't be worrying. If Cam was out here, he'd be saying the right things to Charlie, and perhaps even the hooded boy. They'd be eating out of the palm of his hand. He had a way about him… Cam could talk people around, make them see other points of view, make them trust him. It was a skill Jack admired hugely, and a regular reminder of how poorly he managed his own relationships. Luckily, most trainers judged him on his ability in the saddle, not his conversational skills.

He made a meal of turning his head to look at Charlie beside him, hoping she'd notice and provide a smile. She didn't make eye contact with him, opting instead to glare broodingly at the far wall. Jack settled in for an extended wait.

Presently, Charlie gave a small sigh and leaned into Jack until their shoulders touched.

'Tell you what, you give me the reason the two of you are so close, and I'll tell you about myself and Cam.'

'How long you got?' Jack asked, relieved she'd initiated the conversation. He'd begun to worry they'd be sat together in silence until Cam finally showed up.

'At this rate, all night I imagine.'

'Okay. Here it is. What Cam probably hasn't told you is that he saved my life.'

Jack paused for effect.

He'd never told this story to anyone before, and yet he'd run the entire tale through in his mind countless times, choosing his language carefully, and even his mannerisms, so that when the right opportunity arose, the story would land with impact. It deserved that much.

Charlie waited, encouraging him to continue with eyes wide and insistent.

'And Cam didn't save me in the way you'd imagine. He didn't stop me being trampled by a horse, or disarm someone attacking me with a knife. He just said the right thing… at the right time.'

Ten

'And so from being enemies, we ended up being closer to each other than I could ever imagine,' Jack said, finishing the story with a ragged, emotional breath.

He looked over at Charlie beside him and was disappointed. She was trying hard to suppress a giggle.

'Sooo… ' Charlie said eventually, sucking air over her teeth, 'That was a *really* interesting story… But it's complete bollocks isn't it?'

Jack frowned, but couldn't maintain the seriousness in his eyes.

'Dammit, yes. It's a story Cam tells to impress women. He tells it so well. In his hands that story always has them laughing, then crying.'

'Well you managed to get a giggle from me. But I can't believe I allowed you to get to the end,' she said, shaking her head, 'For future reference, including the spoon and the miniature pony was just stupid.'

Jack smiled and shrugged his shoulders, holding them hunched against his neck, his arms out wide. Charlie finally broke into a broad white-toothed smile that bunched her cheeks.

'What can I say, when Cam tells it, it's perfectly believable.'

Charlie laughed, giving one of her funny snorts that told Jack it wasn't false.

'What's the real story about you two?' she asked.

He shrugged, 'You know, boy meets boy…'

'Oh, come on!'

'Nothing really, we just clicked. Can't say why. You must know that Cam's from a really wealthy family, had a private education, and owned ponies and horses from the age of four, and I…'

'…have been in prison twice, no family to speak of, and got recommended for the Racing College because you happened to get work at a racing stable as part of your outbound community service whilst at a Youth Detention Facility. Yeah, I know, Cam told me,' Charlie finished for him.

'He told you all that?'

She nodded.

'So what about you?'

'What about me?' she said, clearly revelling in being obtuse.

Jack leaned back in his seat and pouted, 'All I know is that you're about twenty, you've been in the Racing House for sixteen months, five more than me, and I've only shared about two conversations with you. You date both men and women, and you're attracted to Cam. So…'

'Cam's only a friend,' she cut in.

'So… out of the twenty years, I'm missing nineteen.'

Charlie slowly uncrossed, then re-crossed her legs, fixing Jack with a steady gaze. He got the impression she was trying to work out if he was genuinely interested.'

'Seriously, you know all about me,' he argued, knowing full well this wasn't true, 'I'd like to know a bit more about you. This seems like the perfect opportunity, given we're stuck here waiting until Cam pops up, or we find out they're charging him with something.'

'They wouldn't do that would they?'

Jack grinned ruefully, 'I doubt it, not from what he told me. And no changing the subject. Come on, spill.'

She gave him a reproachful stare, but soon relented,

'Okay. Potted version. Brought up in a small town on the North East coast. Father walked out when I was two, Mother kicked me out of the house at sixteen. I love horses, so found a stable lass job. Been doing it ever since. Fell lucky when I got the chance to get a room in the Racing House. I've actually been in the house for over two years.'

'So, you and Cam…?'

'We're good friends and that's all,' Charlie replied, landing a soft, playful punch on his shoulder.

'So what about…'

'No! You've got too much out of me already. Let's talk about something else!' she insisted, 'How about telling me what the two of you got up to on Saturday night in Scarborough?'

Jack was a little taken aback by the question.

'You know, Saturday night? The night the two of you could hardly make it up the stairs?' she prompted.

'Oh, yeah, a great night out…'

Jack peered blankly into the middle-distance. He'd expected to recall the entire evening immediately, but bringing it to mind, it all seemed a little muddy and confused.

'So what happened on Saturday night?' Charlie persevered, 'You were both back by eleven o'clock, and usually you'd both be rolling drunk. Instead, you were… well, you weren't drunk, but you weren't all there, so I assumed…'

Jack's forehead rolled up into a frown.

'No. no way! We didn't touch any drugs. Absolutely not!'

'Well… your eyes were glazed and neither of you could walk straight.'

Jack shook his head and repeated his denial.

'And you're wrong about the time,' he claimed, 'We didn't get back until well after midnight and I know for sure Cam was worse for wear. He drank a load and could hardly walk, I had to help him up the stairs.'

'Oh, I'm not saying that you weren't *tired*. Both of you

looked exhausted. But you hadn't been drinking – at least not to excess by the smell of you both. And you're wrong, you did get back early. I missed the last five minutes of an episode of Vera on my TV to watch you two making a hash of getting up the stairs, and that finished at eleven o'clock,' Charlie insisted.

She paused to examine Jack's face for evidence of another attempt at bare-faced tall-story telling. Instead she saw confusion. There was none of the fake earnestness he'd employed during the telling of his make-believe tale. Charlie made a mental note to play Jack at poker if the opportunity ever arose, she reckoned she'd be able to read his bluffs all night long.

'Answer me this…' Charlie said, 'Did you or Cam have a hangover on Sunday morning?'

Jack wasn't listening. He was trying to remember his Saturday night, but drawing a complete blank. How could he forget what happened only two days ago? His recollection was hazy at best. He could always recall the highlights of a night out, even when he'd been *really* drunk. And why hadn't he thought about this on Sunday? Had their drinks been spiked? Would that make him forget the entire evening?

He became aware of Charlie's voice, repeating her question about a hangover.

'I think so… I can't exactly put Saturday night and Sunday morning into any order,' he admitted in a faraway voice.

'Seriously, don't ever play poker,' retorted Charlie.

One of the double doors to the room squeaked open and a familiar face poked through gap. The face split into a smile and the figure of Cam Camberley stepped into the waiting room.

Upon laying eyes on Jack, Cam's relief was palpable, his shoulders dropping as tension was released, although a tired grimace didn't budge from his face. However, as he met Charlie's gaze, Cam eyes widened and he treated her to a surprised smile.

'Hey, Charlie, thanks… for coming,' he exclaimed as she met him half-way and gave his shoulder a playful punch.

'Couldn't leave you all alone to rot in a cell,' she joked, grabbing the cuff of his jacket and giving his arm a quick, self-conscious hug.

Cam shot Jack a questioning look over Charlie's shoulder, receiving a shrug in return and a whispered, 'She's nowt to do with me!'

'I went to the train station as soon as I'd heard,' Charlie explained, pulling away from Cam and rolling her eyes at Jack, 'I didn't reckon on *him* coming. I saw Jack was riding at Ripon, and assumed he'd be there until after racing. I thought you'd be alone.'

She paused, then added, 'I thought you could do with a friend being here.'

The dark patches under Cam's eyes wrinkled, and he produced a weary, appreciative smile for Charlie.

'You look done in,' Jack commented.

Cam blew out his cheeks, 'Been a long day.'

'You're okay to leave?'

Cam's grimace returned, 'Yeah, let's get out of here.'

As Jack headed to the exit, he gave the policeman behind the reception desk a sarcasm ladened vote of thanks.

'What use will that do?' Charlie huffed as the automatic doors slid shut behind them.

'Can't help it. Force of habit,' Jack replied, 'When you've had as much experience with the fil… erm… *police* as I have, it becomes second nature to wind them up at every opportunity.'

Charlie frowned at him, 'That's only the second time I've ever been in a police station. The first was a visit with my local brownie pack. Surely treating policemen with respect is a better way of dealing with them?'

'You'd think so, wouldn't you,' said Jack with a pitying look her way.

The three of them stepped out into twilight that was

rapidly becoming night. A set of globes on poles lit up the pathway to the car park and a quick look at her phone told Charlie it was half past seven.

'I've been in there three hours, but it felt like more,' she said, blinking up at a sky full of clouds dappled with greys and dark blues. A sharp, icy breeze whipped around them and a shiver ran through her.

Jack saw her bunch her shoulders. Despite it being mid-May, there was still a chill to the air.

'I have to agree with Jack,' Cam said, 'Meera Akbar, the DC who took my statement spent the whole time sighing and asking me if I was sure I hadn't got it wrong. She was convinced I was lying. And when she left me in reception I had to give that guy on the desk answers to a bunch of questions, including my inside-leg measurement, before he'd tell me where you were!'

Cam was still grumbling as they got into Jack's car, taking the passenger seat. Charlie clambered in the back and they sat there, waiting. Jack didn't start the car. Instead, he turned to Cam, crossed his arms and waited. Malton was a small place, and news travelled fast in the racing community - the internet had been set ablaze by Cam's accident.

'Forty-five texts and... I can't count the WhatsApp messages!' Cam complained, 'There's one from the BHA too, reminding me again I'm being interviewed by some chap at Haydock on Saturday.'

'I got that one too,' said Jack, 'It looks like he's desperate to speak with both of us.'

Cam continued to inspect his phone, its bright screen lighting up his face, unaware Jack was studying him intently. He tapped on a message from Miguel at the Savage yard and swore under his breath a few seconds later.

'What?' asked Charlie.

'It's a text from Miguel.'

'Who?' asked Jack.

'He's one of the barn managers at the Savage yard. It

says I'm not to go back into the yard until 'today's incident' is cleared up.'

Cam stared at the message again. Deeper within the text it talked about his immediate suspension from duties. The word suspension made him curl up inside. Without a job in racing, his room in the Racing House was at risk. He looked up from his screen and found Jack eyeing him expectantly.

'Can you take me back to the hospital?'

First Jack, and then Charlie, sticking her head in the gap between the front seats, explained why this was a bad idea.

'Savage is blaming you,' she told him, 'It's all over my social media. He's accusing you of attacking him, and stealing his diary… Well, he calls it his notebook. Here, take a look.'

Passing him her phone, she watched Cam's face as he frowned and groaned his way through a number of feeds. Tapping and swiping the screen, his expression deepened into disbelief, and finally, disgust.

Charlie watched him as he read, 'You didn't pick anything up at the scene, not even accidentally?'

Cam tapped his pockets, 'No, nothing here. Besides, the police went through all of that. When I came round, I was more interested in making sure Savage was breathing.'

Cam's attention returned to his device.

'Hold on!' he suddenly protested, 'They're saying here I tried to kill the Guv because he wouldn't let me take outside rides!'

The cabin inside the car went silent for a moment.

'There's also this,' said Jack, passing his own phone over. Cam squinted at a headline in the Racing Post that said, 'Are We Treating Our Apprentices Fairly?'

'Well, it's about time,' Cam said, after reading the synopsis, 'It's dealing with the exact problems I've had with Savage.'

'Go to the bottom of the piece, the last three paragraphs,' prompted Jack.

Cam's eyes sped down the article until he saw a

reference to Malton. He read the last few paragraphs, handed the phone back to Jack, then sat very still, his eyes closed.

'…and now we have a young, impressionable jockey taking his frustration with the apprentice system out on a trainer, with potentially devastating consequences…' he said quietly, echoing the last paragraph of the report.

Jack caught sight of Charlie's concerned face in the rear view mirror. She was watching Cam carefully and Jack could tell she didn't know what to do for the best. The two of them had spent time during their wait for Cam trawling through social media sites and discussed whether they should let Jack see all the online chatter about the incident, eventually deciding it was best he knew the worst.

'My career is ruined,' Cam said, his head in his hands, 'What trainer will employ me? I'll be lucky to get a ride on a merry-go-round after this!'

As if to confirm this assertion, Cam's phone began to ring. The first few bars of Paul McCartney's 'Frog Chorus' rang out, it's comedic quality starkly out of tune with the atmosphere in the car.

'It's my mother,' he gulped, staring wildly at the screen and then over at Jack.

'Take it. Get it over with,' Jack advised. Turning the key in the ignition, he added, 'In the meantime, I'll get us home.'

To the sound of Cam desperately trying to placate his mother, Jack found his way onto the A64 and pointed Corbyn, the name he'd given to his first ever properly bought, paid for, taxed and insured car, towards Malton.

Behind him, a small silver city car followed at a distance, careful to have at least one other car between them at all times. Thirty minutes later, Jack pulled into the Racing House, located on a Victorian terrace in Malton's sister town of Norton. He guided Corbyn through a pair of tall stone gateposts and parked under a mature tree. Passing the entrance to the house, the silver car eventually pulled over and halted beside the kerb a hundred yards further down

Langton Road.

The driver used the car's mirrors to watch the entrance to the Racing House for a few minutes, keys in the ignition, ready to flee - should the need arise. Tugging a hood up over their head, the driver exited the car. With hands stuck into grey legging pockets, the bent over figure sauntered past the entrance to the house at a slouch. A long glance down the driveway provided confirmation of several kinds. Crossing over the road thirty yards later, the figure took time to examine the upper floors of the Racing House during their dawdle back to the car. After a final few minutes casing the Racing House, the silver car pulled away from the kerb and slipped quietly away into the night, the driver satisfied with their evening's work.

Eleven

Detective Constable Meera Akbar should have been off duty over an hour ago. She sucked in another deep breath of faintly antiseptic hospital air through her nose and, for the third time, tried to finish her sentence.

'… and at present, Sir, we have no evidence to suggest…'

'No evidence! You're looking at your bloody evidence. It's lying here in this hospital bed. I've got three cracked ribs and a broken arm!' Sebastian Savage screamed indignantly.

Akbar regarded the invalid with a glazed expression. It was seven o'clock in the evening. She was supposed to be at the pub quiz in an hour. There was no way that was happening, thanks to this posh, whining little…

'…We have no evidence to suggest that Mr Camberley's actions were an attempt on your life,' Akbar squeezed in before Savage could draw another breath.

Savage screwed his face up, then exploded.

'He purposefully aimed, then ran me over with a

racehorse!'

Akbar maintained an unreadable expression.

'Mr Camberley maintains you were standing too close to the edge of the gallop. Like you, he suffered a concussion as a result of his fall from the horse, added to which, there were no other witnesses. As a result of your accusations, Mr Camberley was interviewed under caution and believes the colt…'

Akbar lowered her eyes and scanned the half-dozen lines in her notebook before continuing, 'Jinked to his left and either he, and/or the horse collided with you due to your proximity to the All-Weather track.'

Attempting to gesticulate at the constable, Savage's growl of anger became a groan of pain as he jolted the sling holding his right arm.

'What about my belongings? Did you find them on him?'

'Ah, yes, Sir,' Akbar responded, 'You said in your statement that when you woke up Mr Camberley was…'

Reading from her notebook once more, Akbar stated, '…was going through my pockets, trying to find my notebook, wallet and phone.'

'And you've found all of them?'

'No, Sir. A colleague searched Mr Camberley at the scene and he had nothing on his person. However, a search of the nearby area did recover a phone and a wallet.'

Akbar unclipped a secure pocket and handed over a thin wallet and a phone with a distinctive orange cover. Savage gave a grunted harrumph as the items were handed over and noted the phone was working, despite a new crack in its screen.

'Can you confirm these are your…'

'Yes, yes,' Savage said irritably, almost immediately discarding both.

'Then I will leave you to recover,' Akbar said, making to leave the small, private room.

'What about my notebook? Camberley must have taken it. It wasn't in my jacket when I checked in the ambulance. It was definitely in my inside pocket, I'd been… um, using it before the bloody idiot slammed into me!'

Akbar liked her job. It was a daily challenge being a woman of mixed race and only standing five feet six inches tall. She had to deal with a host of issues her six foot plus, white, male colleagues hadn't even dreamt of. But that was okay. The job was reward enough. She got on with most people, and most people got on with her. Except… time wasters. It rankled her, that such a small group of selfish, opinionated, and often petty people could take up so much of her day. Mr Sebastian Savage was definitely in this category, but there was something new in the creases around his eyes, a concerned lilt to his voice… he wasn't bothered about his phone or his wallet. But the notebook. His notebook on the other hand...

'Valuable is it, this notebook of yours?' she inquired.

Her interest managed to subdue Savage for the first time, his reply sombre and serious.

'Er, no. Not to anyone else but myself… it has sentimental value. It was originally my fathers.'

'If you could describe what your notebook looks like, and its contents, I can add the details to our incident report.'

'Can you search Camberley's house?' Savage asked with renewed hope, 'He must have handed it on to an accomplice before he was searched.'

'That's not an option, Sir,' Akbar said quietly, her own notebook open, pen ready.

'Tell me, where was your notebook?'

'In my jacket.'

'And the jacket?'

'Hanging on a post at the back of my viewing plinth.'

Akbar diligently wrote something in her notebook.

'The next people on the scene of your accident were the riders in the next lot coming up the gallop, they saw Mr

Camberley get to his feet and stagger over to you. He was then seen to immediately make a call, which was to the emergency services to bring an ambulance to you. Mr Camberley was never seen going anywhere near your jacket. We're assuming your notebook, like your phone and wallet, has been lost, not stolen.'

Savage scowled at Akbar, and muttered something she chose to ignore.

'Your notebook description?' Akbar queried, pen at the ready once more.

Savage gave the dimensions of his red, leatherbound pocket notebook with its paisley patterned indentations and tin reinforced corners, but refused to say what it contained, beyond, 'personal information relating to my business.'

Akbar left Savage and walked the hospital corridor in a thoughtful mood. She'd spoken with several people about Savage earlier in the day, those present at the incident, and at his yard. The reviews had been mixed. He was either a fine employer and boss, or they loathed him, whereas Camberley was universally liked. After his interview in Fulford she'd been sure Camberley was being truthful, and this was nothing more than a freak accident. But the notebook… and Savage now had use of his phone…

She doubled back, and sure enough, Savage was already engaged in a phone call. Paper-thin walls to his private room helped, but Savage was speaking in a low voice. Standing with her back to the room door, Akbar strained her hearing and managed to catch the bare bones of the conversation. It was clear that Savage was desperate to recover his notebook.

It soon transpired that whomever he was speaking with didn't have the answers Savage was seeking. Akbar sensed the trainer didn't hold power over the person he'd called, being assertive at first, but his manner becoming far more defensive, possibly desperate, the longer the conversation lasted.

A senior nurse appeared in front of her, giving Akbar a questioning stare, silently pointing to the exit. Suitably embarrassed, she left.

Apart from the paperwork, she was finished on this case. Akbar told herself that Savage's strange call was probably nothing more than him running his day past a friend. It had been a long day, and Savage *had* been bowled over by a horse, even though his injuries had turned out to be relatively minor. And didn't the trainer have every right to feel aggrieved that his property had gone missing? So why did she have a bad feeling about the man?

Akbar followed an elderly man in a dressing gown as he shambled out of the main exit to the hospital. Outside, she breathed in the evening air. To her disgust, it smelled of cigarettes. Still blocked by the painfully slow patient, Akbar left the path and dodged around him, moving onto the road for a few steps. She glanced back as the patient joined a clutch of dedicated smokers loosely huddled together outside the entrance to the hospital. The pensioner was already trying to dislodge a cigarette from its packet. Two things struck her. Firstly, despite his slow walk and haggard face, he can't have been more than forty-five. Secondly, to her amazement she realised that two or three of the smokers were holding onto saline drips.

That look of desperation in the shambling smoker's eyes dragged Akbar's thoughts back to Savage. He'd had the same look of utter desperation when it came to his notebook. It was a craving. Perhaps that was why she'd gone back to his hospital room? Maybe it was why she had such a bad feeling about Sebastian Savage.

Akbar's walk slowed as a new thought struck her. What would be the result of a craving like that not being satisfied?

Twelve

'Tell us what happened on the gallops,' Jack queried.

Cam groaned, 'I did all that for hours in the police station!'

'Tell us what happened, again!' Jack insisted.

'Uhh!' Cam complained, flopping down onto Jack's bed and rolling to lie flat on his back and stare at the ceiling. Jack's room was at the top of the house, with Cam's directly below, Charlie below him. They'd climbed the two flights of stairs to Jack's room expressly to distance themselves from everyone else in the house.

Cam, Jack, and Charlie had already faced a battery of queries from the other three boarders at the Racing House the moment they'd walked in the door. Grace and Olivia had been okay to deal with, both stable lasses who rode in the odd Amateur riders race under rules. But it was the final boarder, Ben, who turned out difficult to deal with. A jobbing stable lad who worked at several yards, including Savage's, he had been quizzing the other work riders in the lot prior to Cam going up the gallop and crashing into the trainer. Ben had wanted to know about Cam's argument with Savage and nothing else, having already made his mind up that Cam's actions on the gallops were, in Ben's indelicate words, '...a classic case of workplace rage and revenge'.

'How can people condemn me like that?' Cam asked as he lay on the bed, contemplating Jack's bedroom ceiling.

'Oh, forget what other people think! Tell us what happened on the gallops today,' Charlie demanded, far more forcefully than Jack thought was necessary. She'd crossed her arms and was now glared at Cam. He glanced at her, but didn't react, returning to staring up at the single light in the centre of Jack's ceiling, covered by a hideous orange paper shade.

'Oh, come on!' he said closing his eyes, 'I told you in the car, I don't... exactly... remember. Leave me alone you two.

I'm too tired. I just want to go to bed.'

'I want never gets!' warned Charlie petulantly.

'Oh, *please* let me go to bed,' Cam pleaded.

'We need to hear everything from your argument with Savage this morning, right up to when you met us at the police station,' said Charlie, ignoring his plea.

Why is everyone so wound up? Cam wondered. Surely a good sleep would see everything making more sense…

'Come on, start talking!' she shouted angrily when Cam allowed his eyes to close again, 'You might forget important details by tomorrow!'

On sufferance, Cam blinked his eyes open, his brow bending into a hurt frown.

Much to Jack's surprise, Charlie doubled down.

'Don't look at me like that, Cameron Camberley! Your poor little rich kid routine is of no use to you now. Stop feeling sorry for yourself for five minutes and concentrate on what's important!'

Cam sat bolt upright, finally realising Charlie had lost patience with him.

'Everything, mind you, Cam! Leave nothing out,' instructed Jack, flashing Charlie a fleeting look of thanks to which she mouthed a surreptitious, 'You're welcome'.

Sitting on the edge of the bed, Cam forced himself to swallow his self-pity, put his tiredness on hold, and started to recall his version of events for his two best friends, in as much detail as he could. It was the first for them, but the umpteenth rendition of the truth for Cam.

When he'd finished, Cam lay back on Jack's bed, held his hands to his throbbing forehead and announced he was, '…going to bed, I'm exhausted,' and promptly fell asleep on Jack's bed. They decided to leave him there. Jack folded his duvet over him, and he watched with a pang of jealousy as Charlie placed a cooling hand on Cam's forehead and held it there, a doting half-smile on her face.

'I love watching people sleep,' she said quietly.

She removed her hand, but folding her arms and tilting her head, she continued to study Cam's supine body for a long moment.

'You *watch* people sleeping?'

She turned to him, a broad grin on her face, 'Don't worry, I don't creep around at night visiting everyone's bedrooms and sit there watching them sleep!'

'Well, thank goodness for that,' replied Jack a shade uncomfortably, not one-hundred percent sure he believed her. She must have read his thoughts, as when she spoke again, she was on the defensive.

'There's literally hundreds of thousands of videos online of people sleeping, so it can't only be me that finds it fascinating - especially when they're dreaming.'

She crossed the room and opened the door, 'You shouldn't be so closed minded, there's still a ton of things we don't know or understand about the human brain.'

Charlie looked back at Cam curled up on Jack's bed, his chest gently rising and falling, his face slack.

In a whisper she asked, 'Who knows what's going on in his head at the moment?'

'Based on what he told us about bashing into Savage at a three-quarter pace gallop and the fact he then fell off and seems to have lost consciousness for an unknown amount of time, I reckon he'll be trying to make sense of it all,' replied Jack, clicking his bedroom door closed.

He followed Charlie down to Cam's room on the first floor and she loitered outside.

'You don't believe Cam meant to collide with Savage, do you?' she asked. It was a presumptive question, but Jack sensed a hint of seriousness about her tone. He replied positively and immediately.

'There's no way Cam meant to hurt anyone.'

'Are you sure? You've only known him, what, a year and...'

'Over two years,' Jack confirmed, 'And I can assure you,

he hasn't got a revengeful bone in his body. Yes, he was frustrated with his treatment as an apprentice jockey, but Cam believes that fundamentally, everyone is good. It's what drew us together. The times he calmed me down and kept me from losing my head at the Racing College... He...'

Jack felt his throat catch. No one else could understand what Cam had done for him. His friend's selflessness was the only reason he was here, race riding, and with a future. If he hadn't met Cam...'

Shaking the memory from his mind, he sniffed and tried to lighten the mood.

'Now if it had been *me* on that colt...'

'Don't tell me *you* could have run Savage down?' Charlie scoffed.

Jack drew in a breath and held it as he looked fixedly over her shoulder, deciding whether he should be truthful or not.

He exhaled with a small groan and dropped his gaze to fix her with an earnest stare.

'There was a time when I wouldn't have thought twice.'

Her eyes flickered around his face as she tried to work out whether or not he was joking. After a few seconds of awkwardness, she stepped back and looked at her feet.

'I'll sleep in Cam's room tonight,' said Jack, gesturing at the door to his friends room.

'Yep. It's been a long day,' Charlie said, turning to leave. She stopped at the top of the stairs and looked back, 'Let's get together with Cam tomorrow and try to work out what we can do to help him.'

He nodded his agreement and Charlie departed. Jack watched as her shoulders, then her short blonde hair disappeared down the stairs, cursing himself for being too honest about his past. How he wished he could rewrite the first sixteen years of his life.

***

At 2.00am Jack was cursing the ease with which Cam had fallen asleep. Try as he might, he couldn't discourage the day's events from churning around in his head, particularly the time he'd spent with Charlie with whom, he now realised, he'd developed an attraction of sorts. His thoughts would settle and make sense as he followed a linear line of inquiry, the next moment his concentration would spin out of control, galloping off in a new direction without answering the questions he'd left behind. It was infuriating, his mind felt like a washing machine that kept erratically jumping from the wash to the spin cycle.

Cam's mishap on the gallops was worrying, but Charlie's completely different recollection of what happened on Saturday night was equally troubling. Add to that his failure to experience what was happening in the race on Monday… and then there was his ride today.

Had the same thing happened today? His mount, a low level handicapper had been sent off as an uneasy favourite in a sprint, but the gelding had never settled after getting excited in the stalls, rearing, and bunny-hopping out and gifting the rest of the field a two length advantage. Jack had been forced to use unnecessary speed and stamina to get him into a prominent, challenging position by the time the two furlong pole flashed by. Unsurprisingly, the gelding had faded in the closing stages to finish third.

A horrible thought wormed its way into his head, causing an uncomfortable sweat to bubble up on his forehead and under his arms. Throwing off his duvet, he perched on the edge of Cam's bed and reached for where his phone should be, only to find that his bedside table, lamp, and charging cord weren't there. He was in Cam's room, damn it! Hunting around, he found his phone on the floor. A few moments of bleary-eyed tapping brought up the Ripon race replay. Was he losing his grip on reality, or had that ride felt… fuzzy? Just like the Wolverhampton race the day before.

In less than a minute, the race was replayed. But Jack hadn't been too bothered about the last fifty-seven seconds, he'd known something wasn't right even before the stalls had opened. He'd rocked back in the saddle. Why? There was no good reason for it, and he'd given the gelding, full of nervous energy, a golden opportunity to rear up at a critical moment... ending any chance he had of winning the race.

But that wasn't how he remembered today's ride. How could he believe he was riding one race, and yet the video replay clearly showed he'd acted out almost the reverse? Bringing up Google, he frantically searched for 'conditions that bring about memory loss'.

Five minutes later Jack was in a hazy, information fuelled stupor, having read enough about memory loss to scare himself into something akin to a panic attack. The phone fell through his fingers. Realising his heart was racing and he was becoming short of breath, he steadied himself with both hands gripping the edge of his mattress and said, 'Four, seven, eight,' to himself, then whispered it aloud.

It was Cam who had taught him the 4-7-8 technique, back at the Racing College. It had helped cement their friendship. It was Cam who had placed himself between Jack and a fellow pupil he was about to pulverise. Cam - who had read the situation and stepped in to bring him back under his own conscious control and avoid the dire consequences a fist fight would bring. It was Cam who subsequently made sure he didn't allow the rage that dwelt deep within him to bubble up, and explode. But the 4-7-8 technique also worked in other situations. Situations like this.

Inhaling for four seconds, Jack held his breath for a further seven seconds, and then exhaled slowly for eight seconds. Concentrating on his counting and nothing else, he was back in that stable in Doncaster, Cam counting out the breaths with him, the young apprentice who had been the subject of his rage looking over Cam's shoulder with a puzzled look on his face.

Jack shivered after the third rendition of Cam's calming mantra. The exercise had worked, his heart had stopped it's manic beating, his breaths were now coming easily and he was in control once more. However, he sensed his sleep deprived mind was only a single step away from racing away once more, filling with the potential maladies he could be suffering from, everything from a stroke to early onset dementia.

Wide awake now, Jack's bleary eyes tracked around Cam's room, full of photos, racing books, magazines, and posters. His own bedroom was positively stark in comparison. It was the plethora of family photos that felt alien to Jack. So many smiling faces, all of them judging him. A sudden need to be out of the room saw him throw on Cam's dressing gown and head down to the ground floor and into the communal kitchen and lounge.

Surprised to find the kitchen light on, he entered briskly and almost fell over Grace, who was bent over, examining the contents of the open fridge.

'What the hell!' she exclaimed, holding a hand to her heart as Jack pitched backward, issuing an apology as he did so.

'You scared the bejesus out of me! What you doing in here at half-two in the morning?' the twenty-year-old added.

'Probably the same as you,' Jack replied hoarsely, 'I couldn't sleep and thought I'd get a drink of milk, or even a cup of tea…'

His voice trailed off as he realised Grace was blushing furiously. Even her ears had gone red, allowing him to notice her small silver earrings, each with a tiny silver moon hanging from them.

'You need to cover up, Jack. Your… um, robe is a bit…'

Embarrassment hit immediately. Cam's dressing gown was woefully inadequate for Jack's much smaller, but wider physique. Thank goodness he was still wearing underwear! He'd known the gown was inadequate, but hadn't expected to run into anyone. As he collected the errant elements of his robe together Jack felt his cheeks burning.

'I'm so sorry, Grace…'

'No worries,' she replied, cutting him short and batting his apology away with a wave of her wrist. She dived back into the fridge and emerged holding a bottle of ready-made chocolate milk, 'I've seen worse.'

Unlike himself, Grace was dressed appropriately, wearing a set of pyjamas and a dressing gown that reached her ankles. A pair of substantial slippers with rabbit features completed her ensemble. Her accent didn't advertise the fact she was a west-coast girl. If he remembered correctly, she came from Liverpool, but she spoke without a Scouse twang. Jack didn't socialise with her outside the Racing House, but he was aware she was never without friends. Grace was talkative, liked to laugh, and could be self-deprecating, something of a rarity among the stable lasses he'd come into contact with so far. However, he was always a little careful around her, as she was known to have a fiery temper. Just recently he and Cam had received several angry bangs on his floor and ear-bashings at breakfast just for playing his music or his TV too loud, as she lived in a ground-floor room partly beneath Cam's.

Grace slapped her plastic choco-milk bottle down on the kitchen island and pulled up a tall stool, 'Want some?'

He thanked her, but shook his head, 'I think a glass of water will do me.'

'You sure?' she asked as he found a glass and filled it from the tap, 'After what happened today to Cam, the taste of something sweet might be reviving. Is that what's keeping you up?'

Jack clambered onto a stool opposite her and took a sip of his cold water, 'So many questions, Grace!'

She grinned, 'It's not every day someone I know rides a three-year-old colt over their Guv'nor! I've had people messaging me all day. They reckon I must know something because Cam and I live in the same house and I was on the gallops when it happened.'

Jack shot her a questioning look. A jolt of anticipation putting him literally on the edge of his seat.

'You were on the gallops?'

'Sure, I was with a group from my yard. We watched Cam kick off from the bottom of the gallop.'

'Really?'

'Yes. Really!' she said, her eyes wide, gently mocking his response.

'Sorry, It's just the police told Cam there was no one else there.'

'Well, we never saw any of the actual accident. We reached Cam and Savage about a minute or two after it happened. But we got Cam sorted and helped deal with Savage. Boy, that man can scream for England! You should have heard him, he made a right kerfuffle.'

Learning she hadn't actually witnessed the impact, Jack's excitement drained away, 'It's a shame you didn't see Cam run the colt into Savage. He can't remember too much about it.'

'Yeah, he looked pretty dazed when we got there,' she agreed, 'He was babbling something about a Magpie at first, but came to his senses soon enough.'

'A Magpie? Like the bird?'

'Yes, the bird. Perhaps it was the name of the horse he was riding?' Grace suggested, 'Cam need not have worried, the colt was fine. He was caught at the top of the gallop. Not even a scratch on him, so we reckoned Cam couldn't have bashed into Savage at full pelt. If it helps at all, we reckon Savage was making a right meal of it. Even if he did break an arm and crack a rib or two, he was hollering like it was much worse.'

'Did you tell the police that?'

Grace shrugged, 'Mmm... I think so. To be honest, if Savage hadn't been kicking up such a fuss, I reckon it would have been reported as just a simple accident on the gallops and the police would have left us to it as soon as the ambulance turned up. Cam has his Guv'nor to thank for winding up the police and getting them so deeply involved.'

The two of them sipped thoughtfully at their drinks in silence for a short while. Jack was considering going back upstairs to bed when Grace spoke again.

'There was one more thing...' she said slowly, as if still mulling something over, 'The only reason we saw Cam kick off at the bottom of the gallop was because he took a phone call. I remember because it took ages and eventually we had to shout at him to get going up the gallop.'

'Yeah, he said he got a cold call.'

Even as the words came out of his mouth, Jack was wondering who would be making a cold call to a jockey at eight-thirty in the morning. And why would he answer it?

Grace continued, 'But something struck me afterwards. By this stage we were only ten or fifteen yards away from him. Cam was sitting on that colt, ignoring us, phone to his ear for... what, two minutes? And yet, I never heard or saw him speak. Not at all. He just listened. He didn't acknowledge us or even say goodbye at the end of the call, he just put the phone in his pocket and set off up the gallop.'

Jack gawped slack-jawed at Grace.

'What?' she said self-consciously, 'I don't think he did it on purpose. You know Cam's not like that. It was just... well, you do wonder who he was talking to before he set off up the gallop to run his trainer over.'

'Erm... yes, I guess so.' Jack replied, his stomach churning as he recalled what Cam had said about that phone call... over in a few seconds, and it being a cold call. Other anomalous facts also began to take hold of his thoughts, all of which were calling him back upstairs to Cam.

'I'd better get back to bed and try to get some sleep,' he murmured, sliding off his stool.

'You're riding Rosy Glow in that nice race at Haydock

at the weekend aren't you,' stated Grace.

Jack nodded, 'Yeah, and I've a ride up at Carlisle tomorrow.'

She cast her gaze over to the digital clock on the cooker. It was past midnight.

'Actually, that ride is *today*.'

Jack blinked hard before focusing on her again, 'Dammit! Yes, I see what you mean! I should be in bed...'

In three, no, *two* days' time he was due to get the leg up on his highest profile ride of his season so far. No! His career! And he'd completely forgotten about it with everything that had gone on with Cam. In the meantime, he was riding at Carlisle in less than ten hours' time!

'Actually, there is one other thing,' said Grace.

Jack gave Grace a weary, but expectant look.

Dropping her voice to a whisper, she said, 'I would be careful with what information you and Cam share with Charlie.'

Jack frowned. This wasn't like Grace. She wasn't the sort to tittle-tattle about her housemates.

'It's just... I accidentally overheard a phone conversation after I came in from morning stables. I was sitting on the sofa over there... and Charlie mustn't have seen me. She got this phone call and I'm sure it was from Savage. I recognised his voice, he was shouting. Charlie got pretty upset, kept saying she wouldn't do it, but Savage talked some more and soon enough she said she'd go. I don't know where. Then she left the house. The next time I saw her she came in with you two a few hours ago... I'm sorry, it sounds like...'

Jack pursed his lips for a few seconds, biting back his disappointment.

'Yes, it does sound like... that,' Jack said slowly trying to keep the bitterness from his voice, 'You did the right thing in telling me. Thanks, Grace.'

'It doesn't feel like the right thing,' she muttered.

Jack started to make for the hallway but slowed up and

turned around when he reached the kitchen door, 'By the way, Grace, why are *you* up at this time of night?'

She screwed he face up, 'Insomnia. Had it since I was a kid. But being a stable lass helps. It means I can catch up a bit later in the day. I often grab some extra sleep after morning stables. Don't know why, but I can sleep better in the late afternoon.'

'The late afternoons,' he echoed thoughtfully, 'In future I'll… um, try and keep the noise down for you when Cam and I are in his room during the day.'

She took a swig of her chocolate milk, 'That would be much appreciated.'

'Good night, Grace. And thanks for the chat.'

She took another gulp of her chocolate milk and raised the plastic bottle in salute, 'No problem.'

***

'Cam?'

He was still in the same position he and Charlie had left him in two hours ago. Jack gave him another nudge.

'Cam?'

There was a groan and a sleepy complaint, muttered from under the duvet.

'Cam!' Jack insisted, rocking his friends shoulder, 'You have to wake up!'

Cam lifted his head and moaned, 'What is it?'

'This is important. Saturday night. Do you remember last Saturday night?'

Cam buried his fair hair into his pillow and let out an agitated groan, 'What does it matter? Let me sleep will you!'

Losing patience, Jack grasped the edge of the duvet and whipped it off the bed. Cam wriggled, complained, and finally rolled over and sat up. Realising he was still almost fully clothed he teetered on the edge of the bed, gave a grizzled sigh and hung his head low.

'Don't you dare fall asleep again!' Jack ordered, placing his palm under Cam's chin and lifting his head.

'Come on, tell me what we did on Saturday night.'

Cam sighed, rubbed the back of his neck, and sighed even deeper.

'We went to Scarborough on the train.'

'Okay, and when we got there, what did we do, where did we go?'

'We had one too many drinks and came home.'

'No! Think! *Where* did we go?'

'Oh for the love of…' Cam started to complain.

'It's an easy enough question. Where did…'

Cam screwed his face up, 'Doh! Just tell me!'

Jack got hold of both of Cam's cheeks, turning his head until they were eye to eye.

Speaking ever so slowly Jack said, 'If I could remember everything, I would tell you what we did.'

Cam studied his friend's face. It held a serious expression that told him he wasn't getting back to sleep until Jack was satisfied with his answer. Closing his eyes, he cast his mind back.

'We had a couple of drinks here, then went into Scarborough on the train. We met that hilarious lady on the train and then we started drinking at the Dog and Duck, then… then we went to… Did we go and see…'

Jack waited until Cam's eyes were back open. He was in the midst of a deep frown when he finally finished his sentence.

'…a band? A seventies cover band… or was it a cabaret?'

'A cabaret?' frowned Jack.

'A mix of acts,' Cam explained, 'You know, singers, dancers, maybe a comedian… I remember singing something…'

'Where did we see a band?'

Cam scratched his head, 'At… I can't remember. Then

I'd guess we got the last train back to Malton as usual.'

Cam looked up quizzically at Jack, 'Actually, how *did* we get home, Jack? I've no recollection of the journey home.'

'I think you're right. We went to see a show, I have a hazy recollection of a stage, maybe in a theatre?'

'Cripes, we must have been as drunk as lords,' Cam grinned.

Jack reciprocated with a grin of his own, amused at Cam's turn of phrase rather than marvelling at how much alcohol they'd managed to sink.

'And how did you feel on Sunday?'

'Hung ov… '

Cam didn't finish, 'Actually, I was fine. And so were you! We got up early and went for a run up the Wold gallop didn't we?

Jack nodded, the start of a smile appearing around his eyes.

'Charlie says we came home *early* on Saturday night. About eleven o'clock. And she reckons we weren't drunk. She said we were both humming a tune, claimed to be tired, and went straight up to bed.'

'Did we sober up on the way home?'

'When have we ever done that?'

'Mmm… never.'

The room fell silent, both teenagers searching their minds for the lost pieces of Saturday evening. Presently, Jack spoke.

'It's no use, I don't know if either of us will be able to remember. But after you fell asleep, Charlie said something that stuck in my mind. She said we were being weird when we came home on Saturday night, or at least, weirder than normal, and she reckons everything that's gone wrong in the last few days started on Saturday night.'

Before Cam could reply, Jack fired a question at him.

'How long were you at the bottom of the gallop before you set off on that colt this morning?'

Cam scratched the side of his head.

'Miguel told me to set off half a minute after the others. I got a call, but put it down within a few seconds because it was someone selling something, broadband I think. So I set off pretty much when I was supposed to.'

'Not according to Grace. She said you waited at the bottom of the gallop for two to three minutes – the length of your phone call. In the end she shouted at you to get moving. So you have no recollection of that?'

Cam shrugged, 'Nothing until the police arrived.'

'Then there's the race at Wolverhampton on Monday. I have no recollection of the poor ride I gave that filly. It's like we're both losing chunks of our memory, and it all started…

'…on Saturday night,' Cam finished in a hushed voice.

'The only thing I can recall in any detail is talking, or rather, being talked at, by that posh woman on the train.'

Cam grinned, 'Oh yes! She was a hoot!'

Jack gave his friend a sideways look.

Cam sighed, 'I know, I know. My turn of phrase is advertising my privileged upbringing again, isn't it?'

Jack looked thoughtful.

'There was another women at our table on the train. Didn't she tell us something about a show? At some theatre… why am I thinking it was beside the sea? You know… the smaller lady who was sitting beside me?'

Cam rolled his eyes, 'You mean the quiet one who spoke really softly and slowly.'

'Yeah, what was her name?'

Cam concentrated hard for a few seconds, closing his eyes and scrunching up his face. He opened his eyes and sighed.

'No… can't remember.'

Jack tried again, 'What about the other lady? The loud one in the tweed jacket and… the hat with feathers?'

Cam closed his eyes again, trying to dredge up a name.

'Beaumont,' he said, clicking his fingers together.

'No, no... that doesn't sound right,' Jack complained.

Cam sucked his cheek in, concentrating hard. Jack was correct, it wasn't quite right.

'Beau, Beau... Beau...fort!' Cam exclaimed.

The surname brought the lady's first name to Jack.

'Yes... *Lucille* Beaufort,' grinned Jack, pleased with his contribution and he grabbed for his phone, 'And didn't she say she was from Harrogate?'

Typing a quick query into Google he scrolled through a few of the results.

'Gotcha! Lucille Beaufort is on Facebook.'

Cam commented, 'There couldn't be more than one Lucille Beaufort in Harrogate could there?'

Jack scrolled further down the page, 'No, this is definitely her – look at the photo. She's married, fifty-eight and works for... ah, here we go, a company called Moncille. And they have her address here in Harrogate!'

Cam nodded and smiled, 'Weird that she should stick in our memories, but nothing much else does about the rest of the night!'

'Then that's where we should start – from where we can remember,' said Jack, demanding a high five from Cam, 'With Mrs Lucille Beaufort from Harrogate. Hopefully she can tell us what the hell we did on Saturday night.'

'We need to talk to her soon. Ideally, tomorrow,' he added after a moments thought.

'Why tomorrow?' Cam said between yawns, tiredness beginning to crowd in on him once more.

'Because it's only two days until Saturday, and I'm riding Rosy Glow in a Group Two at Haydock. I want to know I'm not going to put in another clunker of a performance on him like I did on Sunset Blaze.'

'Ah... yes,' Cam conceded, 'Saturday at Haydock... aren't we being interviewed by that chap from the BHA's integrity team?'

Jack grimaced, he'd forgotten about that.

'Get back to your own bed, Cam,' Jack said, pulling his friend to his feet and guiding him to the door, 'I need to catch up on my sleep and I'm missing my duvet.'

Cam was closing the bedroom door when Jack remembered something he'd meant to ask him.

'Magpie!' Jack called out, just as Cam began drawing the door closed behind him, 'What do you know about a Magpie?'

The door stopped moving, leaving a crack of two inches. The gap remained, hovering between two and three inches. Cam had to have his hand on the door handle, Jack decided.

'Cam?'

Cam didn't reply.

Jack went to the door and with a little effort pulled it out of Cam's hand and opened it wide, called out to Cam once more.

Cam was standing, or rather, leaning stiffly against the door jam, eyes closed, apparently asleep. Jack prodded him gently in his chest and Cam's eyes fluttered and came to rest half open.

'You're knackered,' Jack observed, realising it wasn't the time to be grilling Cam about magpies. He carefully turned Cam around and placing his friend's hand on the banister, guided him down the stairs.

'Go straight to bed!' he called down the stairs once Cam had reached the landing and was standing still, swaying a little.

Cam obeyed. Jack watched him trundle the few feet to his room and disappear inside, satisfied when he heard the door click shut and the squeak of mattress springs as Cam fell into his bed.

Jack yawned, and was in bed within a few minutes. Before he switched off his room light he made a mental note to ask Cam about that 'Magpie' comment of his in the morning.

Thirteen

Checking the address with Cam for the third time in less than a minute, Jack leaned forward and cocked his head over his car's steering wheel. He peered up through the bug splattered windscreen at the impressive mock Tudor residence purporting to be the home of Lucille Beaufort. Corbyn, his Renault Laguna, had just crunched up thirty yards of gravel drive and come to rest in front of a porch framing a large oak door sporting metal braces and studded with black bolts.

With it being late evening, it had already fallen dark and a set of movement sensitive lights had flicked on as they'd rolled up, illuminating the porch and surrounding driveway. Jack winced a little, as the stark light highlighted the fact that his much loved, but ancient Renault was currently filthy following the long journey up to Carlisle racecourse and then over to Harrogate.

'Not bad, as homes go,' Jack noted as he inspected the building, 'This has to be three times the size of the Racing House.'

Cam curled his upper lip, 'Take it from me, size isn't everything. My mother's Camberley Hall has sixteen bedrooms, three reception rooms, two sitting rooms, a library, a ballroom... well, you get the picture. And yet my mother and sister only live in about three rooms and spend most of their time complaining about the heating bills.'

'At least it looks like someone's in,' said Jack, nodding toward a light coming from the nearest window. The bay window numbered six long panes of glass set into a stone surround. A set of drawn curtains were being peppered by several tiny, but bright light sources from within the room.

Once they were standing in front of the door, and unable to locate a bell of any sort, Jack stepped forward and gave the door a hard knock, taking time to scan the porch whilst waited for an answer.

'I presume you want me to do the talking?' asked Cam.

'Yeah, I think that's best. I suppose this is the sort of luxury you're used to.'

'Only until I met you,' Cam shot back with a grin, 'That's when luxury went out of the window.'

He paused for a second before adding, 'Actually, this porch reminds me of the entrance to my rooms at boarding school. I first walked through an entrance like this when I was seven.'

Jack gave his friend a wicked smile, 'It reminds me of a house I burgled when I was fourteen.'

Cam was about to investigate this claim when a click of heels on floor tiles and a female voice became audible from behind the door. A lock clunked home, the door swung inwards, and a female face both boys recognised, smiled expectantly down at them despite being in mid-sentence.

'...and he didn't flinch. Oh, I know! I almost died, darling.'

It was Lucille Beaufort, perfectly made up, hair sculpted, pearl earrings and heavy silver necklace disappearing into the neckline of a boldly printed, multi-coloured dress that clung to her wispy frame. Despite a phone being clamped to her ear she maintained her smile but shushed the boys by placing an index finger to her lips.

'Yes darling, that's right,' she barked loudly into the phone after a four second silence, 'I know! In the restaurant of all places, I tell you, it was tres embarrassante!'

Jack shot a glance Cam's way. His friend's eyes were fixed on Lucille, his face a mask of simpering delight. Jack tried to crack a smile as Lucille stood, her gaze fixed on some point over their heads, as once again, she listened to her caller's response.

'I know. It's simply not on. Please tell Trevor he needs to apply them with more Fixadent next time, we can't have his false teeth falling out every time he eats!' she instructed, 'Well, I must go, darling. I've two fantastically good-looking young male guests at the door and that doesn't happen every day!'

As Cam's mouth opened, Lucille's halting hand was produced again. A shorter silence descended this time, after which she sniggered at a presumably suggestive comment and glanced at the two boys before adding, 'Small, but perfectly formed, darling.'

As Lucille nodded energetically at what was being said, Jack listened hard, but couldn't hear any of the caller's words.

'Adore you! Adore you, darling!'

Lucille tapped at the phone and dropped her gaze to the boys, giving them a longer once over this time, coupled with another endearing smile.

'I'm so, so sorry! So sorry!' she blustered, 'I don't know why it gets manic at this time of the day, but it always does… Oh my! It's… oh, now don't tell me… darling Cameron and hunky Jack isn't it?'

The 'hunky Jack' description brought a quickly masked frown to Jack's face, as a small flood of memories from Saturday's train journey were re-awakened.

'Good evening! We met you on the train to Scarborough, Mrs Beaufort,' said Cam, softly brushing a little of his fringe away with a slow hand, his glacier blue eyes steadily meeting her gaze.

Jack smiled inwardly. The lazy hair swipe and soft stare were mannerisms he'd seen Cam employ on many occasions. His Scandinavian good looks, offset by this slightly self-conscious movement wasn't a silver bullet, but to date it had always produced a positive effect, somehow warming the atmosphere around him. Jack had seen that simple movement work wonders on both men and women. You could watch as the tension dropped from them. And without knowing it, Cam's audience would start to reciprocate with similar mannerisms. And Cam had no idea he was even doing it. On the one occasion Jack had covertly mentioned it on a night out in Doncaster, Cam had shrugged it off with a deprecating smile that had made him even more endearing.

'Of course! I remember you Cameron... and you Jack! And what a night we made of it...' Lucille said with a theatrical wink, 'Oh, where are my manners? Please, come on in my darling boys.'

Whisking her guests into a wide hallway, Lucille made a meal of closing and bolting the door, affording Jack and Cam a little time to inspect the inside of the house. Jack was a little disappointed, it was a dark and chilly hall. At some point in the past, perhaps ten years or more, the house had been decorated to a high, and no doubt, expensive standard. However, the years had taken their toll and despite being meticulously clean, there were signs of neglect. A flaking in the paintwork here, a crack in the mortar there. It gave the entrance to the house a tired, worn-out air.

Lucille had struck Jack as the sort to fill her house with colour, rather than the dark, burnt orange paint on the hallway walls, lit by a few very subdued candle lights. However, an impressive set of stairs with an intricately carved banister brought the hallway up somewhat. There were paintings dotted around, and a long line of framed photos travelling up the stairs. Jack squinted, they looked like shots of Lucille and a man together in various locations around the world. However, the major adornment to the hall was a large oval mirror whose silver was parting company with its glass at the edges. It was set into an ornate red ceramic frame that dwarfed the semi-circular telephone table over which it hung.

'Follow me, darlings,' Lucille sang out, swishing past them and to the first door on their left. Entering a large lounge Jack's faith in his ability to read people was restored; this was a major contrast to the hallway. Not only was it colourful, it was warm.

Neither Jack nor Cam said anything for a few seconds, needing time to take in the sumptuousness of their surroundings. Even Cam, whose family residence had conditioned him somewhat to privilege and the effect of affluence, was blown away by the conspicuous grandeur on show.

They stepped onto a huge silk rug which in itself was worthy of closer inspection. It employed a pink, white and blue spiral pattern that covered most of the floorspace. Two carved lions bookended the ornate wooden surround to an open fire, with a plethora of memorabilia weighing down the mantlepiece. A huge, clover leaf mirror with bevelled edges topped the fireplace, that was belting out heat. Elsewhere, the combination of regency furniture and array of somewhat eclectic original artwork filling the walls combined to take the breath away. Looking up, Jack stared in awe at a sparkling glass chandelier. A strong lamp at the centre of the cut glass chandelier was bouncing spears of light onto the walls and the drawn curtains. The strange dots on the windows now made perfect sense.

One household item didn't quite fit the room's aesthetic. It was a large, thin television incongruously placed beside one of the lions, bigger than Jack had ever seen before. The sound was muted, but Jack easily recognised an old episode of a BBC sitcom, also noticing the TV was positioned to be watched from the sofa rather than one of the trio of armchairs.

'Shall I call for some tea?'

'Call for some…?' Jack heard himself say softly.

'That would be wonderful, Ms Beaufort,' Cam interjected, 'And I have to say, I absolutely love this room… It's simply stunning.'

'Oh, please, boys! I thought we'd got this sorted on Saturday,' she chided with a wave of her hand, 'Call me Lucille.'

Before Cam had the opportunity to use her first name, Lucille was on her feet and at the lounge door, shouting through the house for a pot of tea.

'What a poppet you are, Monty!' Lucille trilled, presumably to an unseen servant or possibly a husband at the back of the house, 'A pot of tea for three would be lovely, and perhaps a few biscuits? My callers look positively anorexic!'

Jack shared a sobering look with Cam. She had a point, there wasn't an ounce of fat on either of them. With a natural weight of eight stone four pounds, he didn't need to manage his diet too closely. Cam, mostly due to his height, was forced to adopt a stricter regime of weight-watching in order to remain in the region of nine stones. Weight wasn't something he and Cam discussed, but the subject fascinated others, particularly people from outside the horseracing fraternity.

Once Lucille had clicked the door to the lounge closed she rejoined them around the fire. She took a seat on a dark red velvet sofa closest to the fire, and directed them to a pair of armchairs. Before she sat down on her sofa, Lucille cleared away a copy of The Times. Jack noticed it was today's edition and both the newspaper's quick and cryptic crosswords had been completed.

Cam waited until Lucille had settled back before getting down to business.

'We're sorry to drop in on you unannounced, Lucille, but we were wondering whether you could help us with something?'

'Fire away!' she barked with a smile, 'It's the very least I can do. I had a wonderful night with the two of you in Scarborough, the best for a long time, I can tell you!'

'That's great,' said Jack, 'Because… well, we can't quite remember our movements on Saturday night, beyond getting on the train and meeting you and your… um, friend.'

'My… friend?'

'On the train,' Cam said with a smile, 'She was sitting on the same table with us? Emma, wasn't it?'

'Emily,' interjected Jack, the name having popped into his head unbidden.

'Ah, yes! Emily. I forget her surname,' Lucille said with a frown, 'I probably *called* her a friend, I'm terrible like that, I'm something of a hoarder when it comes to friends. But we actually only met for the first time on that train journey. Emily joined me at Leeds. We got chatting before you two joined us at Malton.'

Cam smiled back at her. She was clearly a force of nature, and he could easily believe Lucille collected friends everywhere she went on a night out. It sounded like she'd *collected* himself and Cam along the way on Saturday.

'Did we go our own way at Scarborough station? We both have this faint recollection of you being with us in a crowd.'

'Oh, my boy! I managed to talk the two of you into joining me at the theatre. You must remember, darlings? The lady… Emily was it? Anyway, she offered me a free ticket to her show, and you two got one each too. Surely you remember?' she chided.

Lucille continued, 'You were so gallant the two of you! You accompanied me to the cabaret show at the Spa Theatre… Ah, Monty and I loved it over there…'

For a few seconds Lucille became distant, caught in her own private bout of reminiscing.

'So, what happened when we reached Scarborough station?' prompted Jack, keen for Lucille not to roam onto another subject.

'Of course, darling!' she said, snapping back with alacrity, 'Where was I… ah, well, we got a taxi down to the promenade, went for a few drinks in the theatre bar and then I sat with you in the auditorium, well, for most for the time, until you both left me and went up onto the stage.'

Jack scratched his head, bewildered by this latest snippet of information. He'd never describe himself as an introvert, but he couldn't imagine himself happily get up in front of a packed theatre! Cam, on the other hand, could be a bit of an exhibitionist…

'We went onto the stage?' Cam asked with a fascinated grin.

'Oh yes,' Lucille replied brightly, 'When Stefan asked for volunteers from the audience.'

'Stefan?' Jack queried.

'Yes, don't you remember, darling?' Lucille smiled back, 'Stefan Kreihn. The hypnotist.'

Fourteen

Hypnotist? Jack couldn't remember any hypnotist! That said, he was still struggling to believe he'd been to the theatre at all last Saturday night. Though when he really concentrated, there was a vague, fragmented memory of him standing on a stage. The scene was emerging from the depths of his mind, slowly, almost painfully, more of a shadow of a memory, or a dream…

While Lucille went in search of their pot of tea, Jack concentrated on this new information. He'd been laughing in a bar, leant against a round glass table, then he was sitting in some red, high-backed seats and looking to his right, Cam was happily singing along to something, and on his left was Lucille, dressed in her tweed outfit and that hat with the feathers… she was clapping along. The stage was only a few yards away, and two blurred figures were moving around. The lyrics 'Say Hello, Wave Goodbye,' washed over him…

Lucille came back into the lounge carrying a tray, apologising for their wait, a lack of custard creams, and a surfeit of bourbons. Jack relaxed and came back into the moment, the interrogation of the deep recesses of his mind having given him the early signs of a headache. Tuning back into Lucille's voice, she was repeating a name he now half recognised.

'Yes, Stefan Kreihn,' said Lucille, 'I've seen stage hypnotists before, of course, but it never gets old because the audience are the stars of the show. Not that either of you featured for very long.'

'You're saying Jack and I went up on stage?' Cam asked.

'Yes, Stefan had the entire audience pushing the palms of their hands together to create pressure, and then everyone had to concentrate on his voice,' said Lucille, frowning a little, 'Then he invited those who wanted to be placed fully under, to join him on stage. You two jumped up like jack rabbits! It was a shame, really.'

'Sorry, Lucille. What was a shame?' Jack queried.

'Neither of you made it. You know…' she looked at both of them expectantly, 'You weren't sent fully under… they couldn't hypnotise either of you for some reason.'

Her comment was received with two blank looks. Realising further explanation was required, she continued.

'Stefan had about thirty or forty people volunteer. He soon weeded out the ones pretending, and I assume a few had been drinking heavily. They were returned to their seats straight away. At first, he seemed to have a problem with you, Jack, and eventually both of you were walked into the wings by his assistants. Before you ask, I'm not sure why. Stefan got on with his show and neither of you came back to your seats until after he had taken his final bow and the theatre lights came back on.'

Cam was leaning forward, hanging on every word, 'So we *didn't* get hypnotised?'

Lucille bunched her perfectly painted blush red lips together, 'Oh, I wouldn't say that, you both looked pretty vacant afterwards so I bundled you into a taxi outside the Spa and took you straight home, rather than waiting for the train.'

She broke into a smile, 'You both kept singing that song, the one about waving goodbye, like you were drunk or something.'

'Say Hello, Wave Goodbye,' Jack murmured.

'That's the one!' Lucille chortled, 'The taxi driver was ever-so pleased to see the back of you two when we dropped you off!'

'Thank you for seeing us safely back home,' said Cam.

Lucille flapped a hand at him, 'No need for thanks, I

had a whale of a time! You're extremely entertaining company, and it was rather nice to have a couple of young bucks on my arm for the night!'

Twenty minutes later, Lucille was watching from her front door as Jack and Cam's car disappeared down the drive. She gave them both a final little wave. Cam wound the window down and stuck his hand out to reciprocate.

'Stefan Kreihn,' Jack said once they were heading out of Harrogate on the York road, 'Do an internet search on him will you? Find out where and when he's next appearing.'

Cam responded by fiddling with his phone.

'Whitley Bay Playhouse... this Saturday,' Cam reported, 'It looks like he and that Soft Cell tribute act are touring.'

'Is there a photo of him?'

Cam tapped his phone a few times more and turned the screen towards Jack. The overall impression was of a lean, slick, confident man in his late thirties who could have just walked off the film set of a James Bond movie. But his role was of villain, not hero. His oval-shaped face was topped with short black hair, parted with precision and neatly drawn across his forehead. In the background a dark stage was lined with bright white spotlights that sliced through the murk and the photographer had managed to catch Kreihn with an eyebrow raised and his thin lipped mouth turned up at one side in order to flash a quizzical smile.

'I don't recognise him,' Cam sighed, 'How about you?'

'No, but I think we should see him perform... again.'

'This Saturday?'

'I don't know about you, but I've started to remember more about the theatre, and I've got this memory of being stood in the wings of the stage.'

Cam nodded his agreement, 'Yeah, when Lucille said about us going up on stage I could see myself with you, standing deep in the wings, looking onto the stage. It felt like a dream... I couldn't understand why people were eating onions as if they were apples, and there was a chap playing a cucumber like it was an electric guitar...'

Staring at the road ahead, Jack frowned, 'Don't s'pose you remember a teenage girl playing, or rather, slapping the heads of two bald men like bongo drums?'

Cam nipped the bridge of his nose between finger and thumb, 'Now you come to mention it...'

Jack gave a small snort of discontent, 'We'll head up to Whitley Bay and catch the hypnotist show after I've ridden Rosy Glow at Haydock on Saturday afternoon. I reckon Mr Kreihn owes us some answers.'

Fifteen

During his enforced incarceration at York hospital Savage had spent a good proportion of the day pondering the best approach to ensure Cameron Camberley was punished for the bruising, headaches, and dizziness he'd endured for the first few hours of his stay. The doctor confirmed he had a couple of bruised ribs and his right arm had sustained a hairline fracture. Both ailments would heal quickly, so he'd been told, but just for good measure Savage had been exaggerating his pain and milking the good nature of two nurses he'd identified as soft touches. He was eventually discharged in the late afternoon.

One objective filled his thoughts as he was driven back to Malton by taxi. He needed to retrieve his notebook and had become convinced that its disappearance had been the sole reason for the entire enterprise. Quite how his apprentice had discovered the value of the notebook was unclear, but he would get to the bottom of that too.

That Akbar policewomen attached to his case had given the impression she wasn't interested in pursuing the matter, despite his protests. Savage presumed Cameron had managed to convince the female detective that their coming together was accidental. Savage thought otherwise, instead pursuing other avenues of potential recompense... firstly by recruiting a couple of people who owed him a favour, and secondly, by lodging a formal complaint with the BHA. Any pressure he could bring to bear on the boy would help him force the notebook's return, which is why within twenty minutes of returning to the stables he'd left his rooms at Marsh Mansion. He was currently climbing the Racing House stairs, on his way up to Cameron Camberley's room.

He'd made a point of speaking individually to each member of his staff on the gallop that morning, but garnered nothing in terms of the notebook's current whereabouts. Only he and Camberley had witnessed the incident, and the boy had been beside his unconscious body when two of his work riders had doubled back and found them. It had to be the boy who had taken his notebook.

Savage reached the first floor landing and listened at the door to room three, having been reliably informed this was Camberley's room. He knew it was risky doing his own dirty work, but he had several good reasons for being fanatical about his notebook. It annoyed him that his precautions had been so easily circumvented by a moody teenager. He rarely produced it in public, only updating its contents in private. It always resided in a zipped or buttoned inside pocket of whatever jacket he was wearing, only ever buying jackets or coats that offered his own particular brand of quirky security. Ideally, he liked to feel the notebook's sharp, tin-reinforced corners against his chest as he walked. Without it, he felt strangely incomplete. With his arm currently hanging from a sling, wearing a jacket on his right arm was impossible – he had it draped over his shoulder instead.

Savage shivered as he listened to a television blaring inside Camberley's room. It took a long moment, but he smiled when he heard two male voices discussing whatever they were watching. Good, Savage thought, Camberley had his apprentice pal with him.

Propelled by the gnawing thought of his notebook being in someone else's hands, Savage readied himself. He allowed a little more anger to bubble up. Taking a step back from the door, Savage adjusted his sling, balled his free fist, sucked in a breath, and held it.

Sebastian Savage didn't give Cam the chance to invite him in, because rather than knocking, he announced himself by kicking the door in. With his first, well-aimed kick, the locking mechanism was wrenched from its housing, capitulating with a satisfying splitting of wood. His second kick slammed the door wide open.

'Guv'nor!' Cam exclaimed, more in puzzlement than shock, as Savage entered his room. Initially, his attention was drawn to his flimsy bedroom door swinging on a single hinge, rather than his extraordinarily angry ex-employer burdened by an arm in a sling and his left hand clenched in a fist.

Given the young lad's age and size, Savage had plumped for intimidation, hence his robust entry to the room. Depending on the lad's reaction, he would alter his plan accordingly.

'Good evening, Cameron!' said Savage, his words benign compared to the undercurrent of vicious intent in his eyes, 'I'm here to…'

Jack was already on his feet. Living many of his formative years in care and borstal meant he had an in-built speedy reaction to any threat, especially when it involved a booted-in door. A sudden, uninvited entrant into your private space meant only one thing – an imminent beating – and had to be dealt with appropriately. Lightening reflexes put him on the front foot.

Savage had moved too slowly. By the time he'd made it into the room and said his opening line, Jack had already sprung to his feet, grabbed the nearest heavy object off a shelf, and smashed the knuckles of his left hand into the trainer's windpipe. Savage's eyes popped in surprise and he tried to scream, but only managed a wheeze.

'I'm here to…' he gurgled, whilst pounding a fist into the side of Jack's head. Jack proceeded to stamp on Savage's foot. Unbalanced, it was easy for him to pin the trainer to the far wall, pressing in on the man's ribs, which he correctly reasoned still had to be bruised and therefore, susceptible to pain when squeezed. It brought another yelp from Savage, tears to both his eyes, and the trainer wobbled, falling to his knees. Jack then warned Savage in no uncertain terms what he would do with the glass snow globe depicting a scene from Whitby, currently held above his head, if the trainer didn't calm down.

Sometime later, Cam reflected that this all happened in a blur, during which time he hadn't moved from his bed, watching wide-eyed and with his mouth open as his former boss was brought to his knees by his best friend. It only took another few seconds for Jack to back off and Savage to regroup, get to his feet, and deliver what felt like a pre-prepared speech.

Cam and Jack had been interrupted whilst watching a live football match on television, so the trainer, already hoarse from Jack's attack on his larynx, had to bellow over the sounds of Newcastle United scoring an away goal in the League Cup and ten thousand Geordies screaming their appreciation.

His face like thunder, Savage grimly addressed Cam.

'You two have got my notebook, haven't you?' he blustered, whilst keeping a wary eye on Jack.

'What notebook?' asked Cam.

'Don't bother lying to me, I know you've got it. Why else would you attack me as soon as I knocked on your door? I saw you, Cameron, kneeling over me after you'd tried to kill me on the gallops!'

Throughout his discourse, Jack noticed Savage had been casing the room, looking, no, *searching* for something. Presumably, his notebook.

Jack took a threatening step forward. Savage took a step back and scowled at him, 'You've ridden your last race for me, son. You're an animal, you deserve to lose your licence.'

Without hesitation, Jack responded, 'Not riding for you suits me down to the ground.'

'I don't know what you're talking about,' Cam insisted from behind Jack, 'You've got this all wrong Guv'nor, I kept the horse straight. You were far too close to the gallop and when the colt jinked…'

'You were angry with me before went out onto the gallop, so you rode the colt into me on the gallop and tried to kill me,' Savage declared, waving his forefinger accusing, 'And all because you fail to understand that I'm giving you a fair and proper grounding in race riding!'

'A proper grounding?' Jack replied contemptuously, 'You've been using Cam as cheap labour for the past eighteen months and only allowing him the minimum number of rides on horses with little or no chance.'

Savage couldn't deny himself a smirk.

Something about the trainer's expression made Jack feel uneasy, a feeling he'd just walked into a trap.

'Exactly! I've fulfilled my obligations as his employer,' said Savage in a stronger voice, 'I came here tonight to offer an olive branch, in return for my property being returned. I've always been fair, but in return I've been attacked. And when I'd been left for dead you stole my private notebook. And now, the two of you have attacked me again because I've come to ask for it back!'

Cam frowned, 'What? No! I've never even seen this notebook of yours. I've heard about it from other lads in the yard, but…'

Cam faltered, frustration getting the better of him. He glanced over at Jack and shrugged, unable to find the words to reason with a man who was being so unreasonable.

Savage licked his lips, pleased to have broken the boy. However, he wasn't any closer to retrieving his notebook. It was time to show them who they were dealing with.

Jack tensed as Savage straightened, then stepped towards the broken door. He turned and dropped his voice so it could only just be heard above the sound of the television.

'Listen, boys. I'm not the type to hold a grudge. If my notebook comes into your possession in the next few hours, and it's handed back to me in one piece, I'll drop the charges I've lodged with the BHA against Camberley for injuring me on the gallops, and I won't go through with the charges I'm about to file against you, Goodman.'

Savage waited for his words to hit home. Jack's snarl of pure disgust told him he understood. It was Cam who needed further explanation.

'What charges?' asked Cam.

Savage grinned, dipping his free hand into the depths of his sling and removed a mobile phone. He flashed the screen at the boys to show it was currently making an audio recording.

'No, Camberley, Goodman... please! Don't...' shrieked Savage, then threw himself against the last hinge on the door to Cam's room. The bracket came away easily and the door fell to the hallway floor with Savage on top, groaning loudly in pain.

Cam stared down at his employer, his mouth hanging open in bewilderment, not comprehending what had just happened. Meanwhile, Jack darted forward, his intention to retrieve Savage's phone and delete the recording. He knew exactly what Savage was up to. They'd been manipulated. The trainer had manufactured an incriminating recording. Jack had no doubt the taping had started *after* Savage had broken Cam's door down. It would account for the pause before he strode into the room. The recording would start with his warnings to Savage, and the sounds of him rendering Savage immobile.

'Leave me alone!' screamed Savage, adding a few more groans as he rolled needlessly around on the remains of the splintered door on the hallway floor.

'What's he doing?' asked a bemused Cam.

'He's trying to frame us. Everything he's said and done since he kicked the door in was just an act.'

As Jack bent down to roll the hollering trainer over Charlie appeared on the hall landing, closely followed by two more housemates, Grace and Ben. Jack sighed and backed off. There was no way he could rip Savage's phone from him now, it would only incriminate them further.

Helped to his feet by Charlie and Ben, Savage made a show of shying away from Cam, hiding behind Ben whilst continuing to feign painful noises.

'They... they attacked me!' Savage said with a wince, 'And Goodman threw me against the door.'

Jack noticed Savage's hand slip into his sling. The slimy toad was switching his recording off. He had witnesses now. Savage had won... for now.

'He's lying,' countered Cam indignantly, 'He broke the door down himself! He smashed his way into my room and threatened us...'

Charlie frowned, 'So why is the door lying in the hallway, Cam? It has to have been broken from the inside.'

The arguments and recriminations continued for another minute between the housemates, Savage remaining silent, simply nodding in agreement as required. Jack too was quiet, although his gaze never left the trainer.

Tiring of the bickering, Savage groaned loudly and told Grace he was going to Malton hospital to be checked over, and could she drive him there? She agreed, and after rinsing Cam and Jack with a number of choice words regarding the depravity of those who resorted to senseless violence, she and Ben guided Savage down the stairs. Cam stared after them. Grace was still shaking her head with disappointment as she and Savage reached the ground floor.

Charlie remained on the landing, listening to Cam plead their innocence. When the front door to the house slammed shut, she caught Jack's arm.

'You're very quiet?'

'It's all lies,' he replied, walking back into Cam's room and muting the television, 'This missing notebook has got Savage rattled. He seems to think Cam stole it and now he's going to ridiculous lengths to force him to give it back.'

'So the question you need to ask, is why,' Charlie said levelly, 'Why is his notebook so important to him?'

Outside the room, the sound of Cam manhandling his door could be heard. There was a soft thump as he leaned it up against the hall wall.

'I've no idea. Not yet anyway,' Jack said in reply, closing his eyes and sighing, 'He's a slippery sort for sure. Savage could be up to anything. Perhaps his notebook contains all his internet passwords... who knows?'

'Whatever's in that notebook is worth him going to extraordinary lengths to retrieve it,' Charlie said, bending over to pick up the locking mechanism from the corner of the room.

'So you believe us?' asked Jack, genuinely surprised.

Charlie winked at him then crossed back to the damaged door frame, 'I never did too well in physics lessons at school, but even I know that there's no way this lock could end up over there unless it was kicked from the outside.'

She held the mangled lock up to its original housing and added, 'You can see where the wood has splintered inwards from the force of his kick. I bet the outside of the door is dented inwards, where Savage's kick landed.'

'Impressive!' Jack admitted.

Cam nodded his agreement, simultaneously delving into his jeans pocket for his vibrating phone. Having read the text message, he showed the screen to Jack and said, 'It's from Savage.'

'Didn't take him long to back-up his demand,' Jack noted bitterly.

'What's it say?' asked Charlie.

'He wants his notebook back, or he'll see to it that

neither Cam nor I work in racing again.'

Sixteen

For the first time that year Jack sensed there was a proper feeling of summer in the air as he waited with the rest of the jockeys just inside the weighing room. It was a warm Saturday, probably the first decent weekend of the year, and it had brought out a bumper racing crowd. The towering trees in the Haydock paddock had started to unfurl their young, bright green leaves and for the first time in a week, a clear blue sky held no threat of rain.

Although the flat season was into its eighth week, it being the last week of May, Jack felt *his* flat season started today. He was about to ride the most exciting racehorse he'd ever had the privilege to get legged up onto, in a Group race worth more than seventy-thousand-pounds to the winning owners.

Haydock racecourse was buzzing, racegoers having just witnessed an epic finish concerning five horses closing to within half a length of each other in the Group Two Temple Stakes, the winner surviving an incredibly close photograph finish and a Stewards Enquiry to land the spoils by a nose. However, it wasn't that five furlong sprint that concerned Jack, it was the following Group Two race, the six furlong Sandy Lane Stakes for three-year-old colts and geldings that would determine his level of success today. In fact, his week, entire month, and possibly the rest of his season's success was hinging upon whether he could get Rosy Glow to deliver a performance that made the colt a legitimate Royal Ascot prospect.

Despite the pressure, and the lack of a good night's sleep, Jack was calm and collected, as the group of jockeys grew around him and their entrance into the paddock became imminent. He was surprising himself. This felt *right*. It was where he was supposed to be. He was about to walk out onto the biggest stage he'd ever encountered in the sport, yet he would do so with confidence, and without fear. Three years ago he'd have never dreamt such a thing was possible.

The first of his weighing room colleagues stepped out into the sunshine and he followed, careful to skip down the steps without tripping. Once his booted feet touched the closely clipped grass of the parade ring he felt the sun's heat on his shoulders suddenly cut out. He'd entered the shadow cast by one of the mature trees within the misshapen oval parade ring, its borders encased with bright white railings.

Still buzzing after the Temple Stakes, the crowd pushed in, six deep in places as the final few colts and geldings entered the ring to complete the contingent of fifteen runners for the second feature race of the day. Jack looked around a busy ring for Freddie Jones, Rosy Glow's trainer, but instead spotted David Hayton, who looked after the syndicate of six people, the owners of the colt.

Nothing more than sheer dumb luck had connected him to the colt on a drab, wet evening at Newcastle six weeks earlier. His agent had called him after he'd ridden an outsider into second place in the apprentice handicap, the first race on a twilight card at the All-Weather track, asking whether he was willing to stick around at the cold, windswept racecourse for another two hours? With the opportunity to bag another ride to help pay for his petrol, Jack had said yes to the ride without asking the horse or trainer's name. That horse had been Rosy Glow, a lightly raced three-year-old racing in a Class 4 Novice over a mile. It turned out to be the most fortuitous spare ride he'd ever ridden.

Freddie Jones had met him before the Newcastle race and explained this outing would be an educational run. Despite having an option in the 2,000 Guineas, the colt had raced extremely green first time out under the yard's usual professional without showing anything special. He had been instructed to jump as cleanly as possible from the stalls, tuck him in at the back, and pass a few in the closing stages without knocking the colt about. In the event, Jack had known after only a few seconds on the colt's back that Rosy Glow was unlike any racehorse he'd ever sat on. The colt oozed class. He could feel it coming off Rosy Glow as he moved.

Following orders, Jack had allowed the colt plenty of time from the stalls and managed to switch him off at the rear of the field, sharing last place in the ten runner field. As if bored, the horse had dropped his head and despite keeping up the gallop, showed little interest for the first half of the race over the straight mile. Over two out Jack had watched the race fall apart in front of him, and giving Rosy Glow the faintest of flicks, he'd asked for his finishing effort.

Nothing. Absolute zero. Despite continuing to travel well, the colt had been content to cruise along out the back of the field. Loathed to strike him again, given his instructions from Freddie, Jack had started pushing him along, and as the colt's head came back to him, he'd shouted, 'Go get 'em!' into the horse's ears.

Rosy Glow had picked up as if scalded. He passed all nine horses in the final furlong. Through his reins, Jack had felt the colt gaining confidence with every single competitor he left in his wake. Under a hands and heels ride, Rosy Glow had won by half a length, going away from the field at the finish, and in a fairly decent time. Afterwards, he'd told Freddie Jones he thought a drop in distance would be in order for the colt to be shown at his best, pointing out that the colt had been dossing out the back for the best part of three furlongs, and was in his opinion, capable of going a much quicker pace throughout, without blunting his finish.

The trainer's surprise, combined with the unbridled joy from Rosy Glow's connections at getting a 50/1 winner, Jack had hoped he might be considered for the colt's next outing. When he learned that it was to be a crack at the 2,000 Guineas he'd lived in hope for the next fortnight, praying he would get the call to ride at Newmarket.

However, Freddie Jones sent the colt straight to the 2,000 Guineas four weeks later at Newmarket and the phone call Jack had hoped for, never came. Rosy Glow was ridden by a professional jockey favoured by the yard, and Jack had watched with mixed feeling as the three-year-old was ridden from a position in midfield and ended up well beaten, finishing fourteenth of the nineteen runners, losing by over thirteen lengths.

Believing his association with the colt was over, Jack had been shocked to receive a phone call from Freddie Jones a week after the Guineas. Would he come over to his yard and ride Rosy Glow out, with a view to racing him over a shorter trip next time?

Twenty-one days after the Guineas, Jack was here at Haydock, a five-pound claiming apprentice riding an outsider in a Group Two. Not unheard of, but definitely a feather in his cap – there were no other apprentices riding in the race. As he strolled across the parade ring he had all on to control a smile of excitement from working too far across his face.

Jack saw a familiar arm in the air and headed over to where Freddie Jones was currently entertaining his owners. David Hayton, a large, thick-set man with a pinball smile and a billiard ball head welcomed him into the group with a warm shake of his hand. The unofficial leader of the small syndicate, David never had a bad word for anyone, and certainly not for his horse, whom he doted upon, living vicariously through Rosy Glow's exploits. A shade gauche, and with a tendency to be ostentatious - he always wore a cream suit and a cravat, rather than a tie - David introduced the remaining five owners, three men and two wives, all of whom had remained relatively placid before the Newcastle run, but who were, without doubt, as high as kites today, given the prestige attached to the race.

'So, a change of tactics today,' Freddie told the group, once Jack had been reintroduced, 'We're drawn in stall seven, right in the middle of the field, and we're racing over six furlongs today, rather than a mile. We want to make the most of his ability to travel at speed, so young Jack has been schooling him to race at pace right from the kick, and race prominently.'

Freddie had taken to calling Jack 'Young Jack' from the first time he'd arrived at his yard to ride work. The nickname grated a little, as Jack felt it highlighted his inexperience, but not wishing to rock the boat, he'd not made any mention of it. To be fair to Freddie, Jack had worked out that he did have another employee with the same name, although he doubted the trainer referred to the forty-year-old stable lad as 'Old Jack'.

'We won't get the 50/1 today, more like 14/1, but that will do us!' David Hayton chipped in, 'And Jack's 5lb allowance will be really helpful.'

'Although you've been losing on a few favourites this week, haven't you, young man?' said a quiet voice.

Freddie frowned but didn't reply for his jockey. Instead, he gave Jack an expectant look and simply introduced the speaker as, 'Leslie'.

Jack had to peer around David's bulk to discover where the comment had originated. He found a bespectacled chap in his sixties, no taller than himself, who was studying his reaction keenly. Neatly dressed in a well-tailored three-piece suit, Leslie had a receding hairline with one or two errant strands flying in the breeze, but was otherwise impeccably turned out. Leaning ever-so slightly to the right up against his walking stick, Leslie waited patiently for his reply.

'It's the way it goes sometimes,' Jack replied levelly.

Leslie smiled, his eyes remaining stony, 'No mistakes to be made from racing from the front though, are there?'

A shiver ran through Jack. Was this man referring to his inexplicable Wolverhampton ride on Monday? Or had he noticed the other favourite he'd failed to ride out properly the following day? Did he want him to explain what had happened in those runs?

He blinked, mouth open but nothing to say, aware a sudden flow of sweat was making his forehead stick to his riding helmet. Fiddling nervously with his whip, it fell from his gloved grasp. As he stooped down to retrieve it, someone spoke.

'Thank goodness we're not favourite today then,' Freddie offered Leslie with a grin, 'Young Jack here may not be as loquacious as you'd like, but he can judge pace. That's all Rosy Glow will need from him today.'

Jack hadn't quite understood what loquacious meant, but from Leslie's reaction, and the fact that Freddie now put an arm around him and marched him off in the direction of the colt, he wasn't going to have to explain himself. Relieved, he and the trainer reached Rosy Glow who was being led around the edge of the parade ring by, of all people, the other Jack.

'Sorry, Freddie. I didn't know what to say to that chap.'

'Don't fret kid. Leslie is a professor at Liverpool University. As far as I can work out, he spends his time slicing brains up and trying to make sense of them. I reckon he speaks to everyone in that condescending manner.'

The call on the public address system was for jockeys to mount, and thirty seconds later Freddie launched Jack into the saddle with a flurry of last-minute instructions he'd already given him twice before.

'I bloody hope you're right about the trip, kid,' he said with a grin, 'It'll be the biggest win of my career. But hey, just enjoy yourself.'

Jack didn't know whether to grin or be serious. In the end he did neither, leaving his legs out of the stirrups he concentrated instead on keeping the colt calm until he was released onto the racecourse. Once he'd kicked off and began jogging Rosy Glow to the start, all swirling thoughts of his poor rides this week, Cam's problems, the impending meeting with Stefan Kreihn, and his growing feelings for Charlie were placed on hold.

The racecourse commentator was calling the runners as they went to the post. As the details for horse number nine, 'Rosy Glow, ridden by apprentice Jack Goodman, claiming 5lbs, in green with the white star, and the white cap,' rang out over the public address system, a young-looking face in the grandstand with a small, sharp nose concentrated on Jack. Those soft eyes never left the horse and jockey until they were well past the three furlong marker.

Nine minutes later the stalls clanged open and Jack squeezed the colt with his ankles and held him together tightly. Rosy Glow leaped forward and immediately stole half a length from the field, catching his stride perfectly. Knowing pace was critical, Jack allowed the colt to accelerate, but unlike the Newcastle race, he didn't have to worry about him switching off. He had the lead. Rosy Glow galloped just as he had at home when he was without a wall of horses in front of him, free moving and with an energetic ease. From between the horse's ears Jack looked up Haydock's straight six furlongs to the finish he would be crossing in less than seventy seconds time.

The four furlong marker swept into view with remarkable swiftness, but Jack was sure he had Rosy Glow on the right stride pattern. Although there hadn't been rain today, the ground was soft, he could hear hooves slapping the turf, their metal plates digging grooves in the surface around and behind him.

Three furlongs left, then two. If anything, the going was helping his mount, as Rosy Glow continued to skip effortlessly over the top of the grass, maintaining his half a length lead without Jack having to resort to anything more than a gentle push of the horse's head as his front feet hit another stride.

It happened at one and half furlongs out. Rosy Glow faltered. It was only a minor slip, a back leg not meeting the turf at the right angle, but Jack felt it go. He let the colt take two strides without pushing, fearful he'd gone wrong behind.

The loss of momentum allowed another horse to move upsides, and Rosy Glow was headed for the first time.

The third stride felt good, and Jack pushed tentatively on the fourth. As if to tell him he was good to go, Rosy Glow changed his lead foot and pointed his toe. That same surge of power he'd experienced at Newcastle came from beneath him and Jack, still only working hands and heels, overhauled two challengers to his left, and surged past the new leader. A gasp of admiration was drawn from the crowds in the grandstand as Rosy Glow powered away in the closing stages to cross the line three lengths clear of his nearest rival.

Deep in concentration, Jack hadn't heard the crowd, nor the commentary, despite its loud, brash noise filling the racecourse. It wasn't until he'd successfully taken Rosy Glow around the bottom bend and into the false straight that the rest of the world started to penetrate his mind once more. Bringing the colt to a canter, then a trot, and finally a walk, the calls of congratulation from his fellow jockeys began to register.

The next twenty minutes were a blur of smiles, handshakes, interviews, weigh-in, presentations, and so many congratulations, his head was spinning. All around him he heard the words, 'Commonwealth Cup' and 'Royal Ascot' being thrown around. He didn't make the connection until later, instead, he found himself being swept along, relieved he only had one more ride on the card. It was in the last race, an apprentice-only handicap.

Dazed, and not a little embarrassed by the attention, Jack was initially uncertain how to take the words of adulation from his trainer, owners, and myriad of other people who kept popping up in front of him. He settled into a concentrated, serious smile, whilst trying to remain centred, using short, pointed answers when he was required to speak. To his surprise, his stoicism was well received, and even praised the next day in the press.

The one comment that meant the most had come from

Freddie Jones. He'd caught up with him as he was re-entering the weighing room following the trophy presentation and provided him with one simple sentence.

'You should be proud of yourself, young Jack.'

It wasn't a line, or a sentiment he'd ever had said to him before. Not from his mother, and certainly not from his absent father, nor any teachers or friends. He'd let the heartfelt comment rest on him for a few seconds before thanking the trainer. As Freddie had turned away to rejoin his jubilant owners, Jack entered the weighing room with a warm buzzing in his chest.

Outside the weighing room, beyond the jockey's walkway and behind the white rails, a pale face with a sharp nose watched Jack Goodman disappear into the bowels of the restricted access building. The watcher pulled a dog-eared racing guide from their jacket pocket and re-checked the last race on the card.

Seventeen

The changing room at Haydock was generally a hive of activity, but for a brief few minutes, Jack found himself in an island of tranquillity. Standing by his changing bay, silently reflecting on his ride earlier in the afternoon, he wasn't aware Cam had entered the changing room and jolted upright when his friend burst forth with an excited congratulatory scream.

'Just incredible!' Cam kept repeating as he embraced Jack from behind, not letting go, jiggling him up and down like a rag doll thanks to his extra height.

'Seriously, Jack,' Cam added, spinning him around and hugging him, 'That was just… I'm lost for words. You're on your way. A star was born today. You're… you're…'

'…just lucky,' Jack finished, 'I'm just incredibly lucky.'

Jack sat down on the bench and Cam joined him.

'Tish Tosh! This is no time to be humble! That's some

colt, and you were brilliant! We have to celebrate. It's Saturday! We should go out tonight to...'

'Scarborough?' Jack suggested with a wry smile.

'I was going to say...' Cam replied, visibly wilting, 'Yeah, okay I was going to suggest Scarborough, but I suppose we could go to Brid if we had to...'

'We're going to Whitley Bay,' said Jack levelly.

Cam contemplated this option, screwing his lips sideways, and finally gave up on the boys night out with a defeated shrug.

'Yep, I suppose you're right.'

'And I've still got my ride in the last. I need to get my head right for that. My lad looks like he has a great chance.'

'Yeah, the bookies have made him a strong favourite,' agreed Cam ruefully.

Jack caught Cam's eye and was swamped with guilt.

'You'll find another apprenticeship,' Jack assured him, clapping Cam on his knee.

Cam squirmed uncomfortably on the wooden slatted bench for a few seconds before letting out a long breath. As well as banning him from the yard, his ex-employer had jocked him off the two rides he'd already been declared to partner this weekend. It transpired Savage was determined to remove all trace of Cameron Camberley from his business. There was also a rumour going around Malton that Savage was going to bring a civil case against him if the police didn't go ahead and press charges for nothing less than grievous bodily harm. Cam had always known his boss was arrogant and self-obsessed, but he could now add liar to that list.

With a shake of his head, Cam finally replied, 'It's not your fault you're tasting success.'

Jockeys, both male and female, began to filter into the room, some receiving the attention of valets dealing with their clothes, boots, and changing requirements. The two teenagers remained sitting in silence as the sounds of their sport filled the room.

'Before long I won't be able to sit in here. Once Savage cancels my apprenticeship the BHA will rescind my race riding licence,' Cam said mournfully.

'Unless you can find another yard to take you on.'

'Who will do that once they hear I'm the Malton Mower?'

Jack gave him a querying look.

'It's what the online stable gossips are calling me after I mowed Savage down,' he explained miserably.

'Ah! It could be worse though.'

'You reckon?'

'Give me five minutes. I'll come up with one.'

'I can't wait.'

Jack bit the inside of his mouth for a moment before venturing, 'I could ask Paddy…'

Paddy Doherty ran a small thirty strong yard on the outskirts of Malton. It was a yard overlooked by most young riders as a source of apprenticeship, but Jack had clicked with the distinctly working class trainer, and struck lucky. The yard was producing a decent number of winners, and Paddy was more than happy for Jack to take outside rides, the two of them striking up a good working relationship based on mutual respect for their shared hard work ethic.

'You can ask. But I doubt Paddy will be able to take on two apprentices with the limited amount of firepower he has.'

'I'll ask him on Monday,' Jack stated positively.

Sensing he could chance a question he'd been wanting to ask Cam for some time, he lowered his voice, 'You said anything to your parents yet?'

Jack watched him shake his head. If anything, the mention of his family seemed to transport Cam deeper into depression.

Their childhoods had been strikingly different, and yet both boys had recognised a strange similarity in each other, a common bond that united them – a broken relationship with their family. Cam's family seat stretched across the Scottish borders, based around a small town to which the family gave its surname: Camberley. A private schooling and high parental expectations had led to their disappointment and ultimately, frustration that turned into anger when Cam announced he was leaving, having secretly gained a place at the Doncaster Racing School. His issues were predominantly with his mother, who didn't share Cam's love of horses, nor understand his talkative nature and lust for life.

'A dyed in the wool Scottish skinflint,' was how Cam described his mother to those who inquired. And to the handful of people whom he trusted, he would add, 'She also possesses a liking for psychological blackmail.'

Jack wasn't so savvy about sophisticated mind games, but knew plenty about domestic violence, having witnessed more than enough from the string of lowlife, drug addled boyfriends who used his mother as a punchbag. When he was five she'd become attracted to a particularly nasty sort called Keith who had inveigled his way into their council flat and proceeded to victimise both of them for the next four years. Jack had experienced violence on a predictable, daily basis until the Sunday of his ninth birthday when his mother's drug fuelled argument with Keith saw Jack attempt to protect his mother. Rather than the odd drunken punch or cigarette burn that was the norm, on this occasion Jack was badly beaten. Trying to flee, he only made it as far as the street outside his home, and was rushed to hospital by a concerned neighbour. During his absence his mother and Keith disappeared from the flat, and from his life.

The authorities duly stepped in and took control. Moulded, and to a certain extent, trained by his experiences with his mother, Jack went on to fight another battle with those charged with looking after him from nine to sixteen. Small for his age, and a quiet boy, Jack had been a natural target for bullies. A fierce, streetwise intellect and a tidy pair of fists had kept him in and out of trouble on a daily basis.

By the time he was due to leave, Jack had nothing but

contempt for his local authority, their care system, and the low expectations it harboured for its young, trapped inmates. Jack left believing his care home was acting as a finishing school for a life of crime, addiction to drugs or alcohol, and usually, both. However, there was one comment on his release papers that had surprised him. The head of the care home had said, 'Jack has an unhealthy disregard for his own safety. Nevertheless, having been in his company for over seven years I have concluded it is this complete lack of fear, regardless of the situation, that has enabled Jack to not only survive, but thrive. It is his willingness to ignore any sense of danger and thrust forward that makes those around him want to follow, and yet he rarely places his trust in any of them.'

Another apprentice, Ricky Lowe wandered into the changing room and without looking around called out Jack's name.

Still in deep thought, Jack was oblivious, however Cam called back on his behalf.

'That BHA bloke wants to see you now,' Ricky announced and reversed out of the door, his task completed.

When Jack didn't respond, Cam slapped his friends knee again, 'Hoy, Jack! That BHA fellow is asking to see you.'

Jack stared, not comprehending for a few seconds.

'Get going, Jack,' Cam ordered, 'Remember what they said at college? You never leave anyone from the BHA Integrity Department waiting!'

Jack blinked. Reminded of the strict and unforgiving lecturers at the horseracing college in Doncaster, he almost glazed over once more. Cam pushed at his friend's shoulder, 'Get going will you? I'll wait for you.'

'You've no choice, I'm driving,' Jack reminded him, jumping to his feet and searching around for the pair of shoes he'd arrived in.

'Forget them,' Cam insisted when the search proved fruitless, 'He was in a right mood when I saw him earlier. He's called Chief Integrity Officer Cupcake. Don't make him wait!'

Jack left the weighing room in his stocking feet, still wearing the body protector and sky blue silks he'd ridden to success thirty-five minutes previously. Cam watched Jack depart, a grin working its way onto his face.

Crossing to the other side of the weighing room building, Jack passed the clerk of the scales, busy weighing the riders back in from the latest race. No one noticed Jack or even looked up – it was quite normal for half-dressed jockeys to be wandering around the weighing room building. He kept on going, down a corridor sprinkled with doors, each one sporting a single window containing horizontal yellowing blinds that were drawn closed. Turning a corner, he immediately came across the door he was looking for. It was emblazoned with three letters picked out in tarnished gold leaf - BHA.

Jack knocked on the door and waited. A muffled response to enter came from within and he twisted the doorknob and stepped inside. It was a small, largely empty room apart from a cheap, thin table behind which a large man was hunched, typing on a laptop.

Taking his first breath inside the windowless room, the taste of nicotine hit the back of Jack's throat. He clicked the door closed and waited, swallowing down the urge to cough. The British Horseracing Authority integrity department investigator neglected to look up from the laptop he was busy tapping, instead, lifting his right hand from the keyboard he pointed a hooked finger in the direction of a plain dining room chair in front of his table.

Jack could feel the cotton in his socks sticking to the cheap carpet as he made his way to the chair and wondered whether he should make a crack about his lack of footwear in order to lighten the mood. He decided against it, Cam had read the situation perfectly, this chap had a harassed air about him. Besides, he'd been warned about the sense of humour bypass that each officer was required to undergo in order to work for the integrity department.

Jack studied the back of the man's laptop screen, his chair being so low he was robbed of a view of his face. Straightening, then sliding slightly to one side he managed to glimpse a little more, but nothing of note. Around late forties, perhaps early fifties Jack guessed, but he hadn't got a good look at him yet as the laptop screen was still between them. However, he appeared to be sporting a double chin as he crowded in on his computer.

Jack settled in for a wait. He'd been briefed about the integrity department by some of the pro jocks, as well as one or two trainers he rode out for. They were the horseracing police, and you gave them a wide berth. The general advice was to say as little as possible. If you were called in for 'a chat' then you dealt with them carefully, and only spoke when answering their questions. Keeping your answers succinct was preferable, and according to the advice he and Cam had received from a pro jockey with a colourful history of involvement with the Integrity Department, he'd advised limiting any replies to, 'Yes', 'No', 'Maybe', and in some cases, 'If you say so.'

Jack intended to follow this advice.

The investigator continued to tap away and looking around, Jack noticed there was a lit cigarette lying in a saucer acting as his ashtray. A teacup was a few inches away, busy embedding a warm ring into the table's varnish. Meanwhile, the abandoned fag was sending a narrow shaft of smoke up to the ceiling where it was collecting into a blue fog.

'I'm John Cupkiss,' said the man without warning. He spoke in a much deeper voice than expected, making Jack jump a little in his seat, and also stifle a grin as he realised Cam had either misheard the man's name, or more likely, he'd been trying to fool him into calling this rather stern investigator, 'Mr Cupcake.'

'Good to meet you, Mr Cupkiss. I'm…'

'I know who you are,' said the investigator, cutting Jack short, 'I know *all* about you.'

A pair of sausage fingers with unnecessarily long nails reached over the top of the laptop screen, slapping it shut. His sunken eyes, altogether too close for the size of his face, squinted down a flat nose at which Jack found it hard not to stare. An accident or a fight, he presumed.

'I like to introduce myself to every apprentice jockey,' continued Cupkiss, the nail of his finger tapping an uneven beat on the hard plastic of his laptop, 'It allows me to get a measure of the man. It also gives you young lads...'

He paused, as if remembering something that irked him. The nail tapping continued, starting to annoy Jack.

'...and lasses, of course... the chance to cast away all thoughts of playing fast and loose with the rules of racing. Given you've attended the Doncaster Racing School, I assume you're fully briefed on what is expected from you?'

'Yes.'

'Good, then you're already a full ten percent of the way there.'

'Only ten percent?' Jack queried, shooting a look at the man's finger, religiously maintaining the insane, irregular tapping. He returned his stare to the man's face.

There was the slightest twitch of Cupkiss's lips that Jack took as a sign that the investigator was pleased with his reaction.

'Are you familiar with the question of nature versus nurture?'

Jack winced as the tapping got louder, filling the long moment he took to consider his answer. Unable to concentrate properly on the investigator's question, he shook his head.

'Of course not,' Cupkiss said in a condescending tone, finishing his comment with a disappointed sigh, 'I've read your profile. It's not your fault.'

Jack felt the hair on the back of his neck prickle.

'What's not my fault?' he asked brightly.

The tapping stopped abruptly and Cupkiss opened his laptop. After a short delay to blow his nose on a once white, but now tawdry grey handkerchief, he began to read.

'You're a Sheffield lad. Only child, brought up by your mother until the age of nine, after which you fell under the care of the local council.'

He paused, squinting a little at his screen before saying at a slower pace, 'No sign of a father.'

His tempo picked up again, 'History of truancy, several fights at school leading to expulsion… twice, and a bunch of shoplifting offences as a minor. Left school at sixteen with no qualifications and after being caught breaking and entering, a short spell in a prison for young offenders. Worked out a six month spell of community service in a livery yard south of Chesterfield where you learned to ride, before applying to the Racing School…'

'College,' Jack interrupted, 'It's a College.'

Cupkiss eyed him keenly, which Jack took as a warning not to interrupt his flow again. As if to reinforce his warning, the investigator restarted the tapping. Jack noticed he was now using the little finger on his left hand to make the noise.

'You're currently…' Cupkiss paused again as he inspected his screen in greater detail. It looked to Jack like he man was doing some mental arithmetic, 'Eighteen years old and apprenticed to Paddy Doherty's yard based in Malton, after you graduated with top marks in your class. You've been in a scuffle at a local pub since joining Mr Doherty fourteen months ago, for which you were given a caution by the local police force and a warning from the BHA.'

Jack grumpily crossed his arms and looked away, focussing on a scuff half-way up the grubby partition wall. Cupkiss was spot on. It was all true. He didn't like to be reminded of some, if any elements of his past. The caution and subsequent ticking off by the BHA had been particularly galling, but he'd never had, and never would, back down to a bully.

The investigator leaned forward, the tapping on his laptop forgotten for a few precious moments.

'I believe thieves, tricksters, and those people who resort to violence are born, not made,' said Cupkiss, slowly closing his laptop and placing his elbows on the desk, 'It's in your nature, lad. However, you've been given a chance. And with the right nurture, you can change...'

Jack stared back at the much older man, not really registering what was being said. He'd heard versions of this speech dozens of times. He resorted to nodding and maintaining a calm, sullen, poker face.

Eventually the investigator closed his laptop and asked, 'Can you do that for me?'

He nodded in reply. It was a standard closing statement Jack had heard all too often and a positive nod usually did the trick. But Cupkiss didn't dismiss him.

'Now then, lad. I don't just want you to keep your nose clean, I actively need your help. It's in both our interests to keep racing clean, so if you see or hear anything you think could be bringing the sport into disrepute, you must report it.'

Mmm... switching to 'good cop', thought Jack.

Cupkiss took a deep breath and launched into another speech, 'Wherever there is gambling, there are crooks wishing to bend the odds in their favour...'

Jack went back to his default nodding as Cupkiss did his best to warn him against consorting with gamblers, bookmakers, and accepting any sort of payment for racing information that could, however vaguely, potentially point to the outcome of a race.

Cupkiss eventually talked himself out five minutes later.

'I agree, Mr Cupkiss,' said Jack, 'And I will do as you say.'

This was received with a blank stare and a gruff, 'Good.'

To Jack's disgust, Cupkiss re-opened his laptop, clicked his mouse once or twice and stared at the screen. The incessant tapping started up again. A full thirty seconds went by, Jack feeling the beginnings of a headache thumping in his temple as the BHA Officer's index and middle fingers drummed away on his keyboard.

Mid-drum the tapping ceased.

'So what happened at 2.05pm on May 28th at Wolverhampton in the Class Five handicap over seven furlongs?' demanded Cupkiss, slowly closing the laptop once more whilst aiming an anticipatory glare at Jack.

Eyes wide and mouth open, Jack blinked several times at Cupkiss before full control of his facial features returned.

He inspected the wall of the office, searching for an answer, but as his silence extended, he decided a shrug would have to suffice.

'Let me remind you then,' Cupkiss said with a forced smile that his eyes knew nothing about, 'In my opinion you threw that race. It was clever, mind you. Only the rear view camera actually revealed the true nature of your endeavours to ensure you never hit the front.'

'I don't remember,' Jack said with another shrug, 'Was there a Stewards Enquiry?'

'No,' Cupkiss replied after a moment of rumination, 'Your inaction was missed by the stewards.'

He leaned forward across the table again, his gaze never leaving the young man now sitting uncomfortably in the seat before him. In a slow, voice he said, 'But not by me.'

'If the Stewards had referred your ride to us in London, I'd have been all over you like a rash,' he continued, pushing back in his chair, 'As it is, you got away with that one. It seems to me, your past nature got the better of you on that occasion. Nature versus nurture… it's a tough one to break.'

Cupkiss got to his feet, and for one magical second Jack believed his grilling was over. He really hadn't wanted to try to explain the unexplainable – that he'd been sure he'd ridden a perfect race on that gelding, even though the video told a completely different story.

Cupkiss placed his hands on his hips and Jack noticed

the man had a sizeable paunch with which his shirt was struggling to cope.

'Whilst the Wolverhampton race was bad... I've not seen anything like that from you since. However, I've recently learned that your nature had drawn you to that friend of yours, Cameron Camberley.'

'Not really. He's nothing like me,' frowned Jack, confused as to why the conversation had veered in this direction.

'Indeed. One could say Mr Camberley has led a charmed life! The son of a wealthy family, grown up with horses at the bottom of his garden in his own private stables by all accounts... and yet, and yet...'

'What?' Jack spat, his initial dislike of Cupkiss quickly descending into loathing.

'I would have imagined it would be *you* who would lose his temper and do something stupid, given your upbringing, but no...'

'Cam did nothing wrong. The police aren't pressing charges. It was an accident. That colt should have been gelded a year ago, it was known to be headstrong, and it was its first run up the gallop after weeks on the walker. He was bound to be a handful. Besides, Savage was standing far too close to the gallop.'

Jack took a breath. Cupkiss had got to him. He'd said too much.

Cupkiss bunched his lips together in contemplation, neglecting to reply. He adjusted a couple of sheets of paper on his desk with a poke of his index finger.

'Your mate may still pay the price for his lack of control over his mount. Sebastian Savage may not be the most pleasant or popular employer in racing, but when a trainer makes an official complaint, we have to take it seriously. The man certainly believes in retribution.'

Again, Cupkiss paused, as if anticipating a reaction. This time, Jack remained stoney-faced and silent. The Integrity

Officer responded with more lip-bunching before continuing.

'I've informed Mr Camberley that Mr Savage will not be cancelling his apprenticeship.'

Jack frowned, not understanding.

'That's good isn't it?'

Cupkiss grimaced, 'If Mr Savage holds onto your friend's licence it means he controls where Mr Camberley can work, and what rides he can take, right up to the end of the season.'

It took Jack a moment for this to sink in.

'Savage can stop him from getting any rides for the next six months?'

'Seven,' Cupkiss confirmed.

Jack shivered as he realised what Cam had done, speaking with him in the changing room, all congratulations and smiles. Cam had made sure he didn't come into this meeting with Cupkiss and immediately shout his mouth off, defending him. His friend knew him well.

'That's... not fair,' Jack breathed, trying to remain calm.

'Maybe. Maybe not. But Mr Camberley will need support from his friends over the next few weeks, okay?'

Jack nodded.

Cupkiss sighed, 'I don't suppose you know anything about a lost notebook?'

Jack shook his head.

'Well, if it does magically appear, get it back to Savage. He's making my life a misery at the moment,' said Cupkiss aiming his eyes at the office door, dismissing Jack.

He made to get up, but this last comment from the Integrity Officer had made him seem far more human. Perhaps this Cupkiss wasn't so bad, he thought.

'Erm.. Has Savage made any other accusations against Cam and myself?' Jack asked casually, wondering whether Savage's doctored recording of his visit to Cam's bedroom had landed with the BHA.

'Not that I'm aware of?' Cupkiss responded, sounding a

little too suspicious for Jack's liking, 'Why? Should I be expecting another damning report about Mr Camberley to come across my desk?'

'No. Absolutely not, Mr Cupkiss.'

Relieved, Jack rose and made his way to the door.

'Send in Kieran Bassett, will you?'

Jack said he would. As he pulled the door shut, Cupkiss called out his name one more time. He paused, regarding the investigator through the gap in the half-closed door.

'I saw your ride. Earlier, in the Novice race. You've got ability in the saddle and a decent racing clock in your head. Don't waste it, Jack. Regardless of what you think you know, you're young and inexperienced. With your background, you're bound to be approached. Do yourself a favour, don't get involved. If you do, I *will* catch you, and I *will* crush your chances of becoming a pro rider.'

They locked eyes for a second. Jack got that uneasy prickle down the back of his neck again. He nodded back at Cupkiss, dropped his eyes to the floor, and quietly clicked the door closed.

Eighteen

The changing room had emptied once again with the general exodus of jockeys for the fifth race on Haydock's afternoon card. With the reduction in noise, Cam was left without a distracting conversation in which to participate or overhear. As he waited for Jack to return from his interview with Cupkiss, the now almost silent changing room had taken on an oppressive feel as his thoughts turned to Savage, his useless apprenticeship, and the subsequent ramifications if he couldn't move stables.

It wasn't just the loss of his job, there was his room at the Racing House. It was written into his tenancy agreement. If he wasn't employed in the racing industry, he would be required to give it up within a month and find alternative accommodation. It would be virtually impossible in Malton, there simply weren't any cheap rooms to rent, and having burnt his bridges with his mother, he couldn't rely on a handout from her.

To stay in Malton, he had to find a job. Any job in racing would do, even if he had to become a yard boy. He could put up with not riding for a short period, he told himself. Anything would be better than having to go back home to Camberley with his tail between his legs.

He knew it so well. That look of self-satisfied victory on his mother's face. It flashed into his mind's eye and Cam winced, an unwanted heat building around his collar. He took a calming breath and determined there was no way he would be forced to return home to Scotland. He may have wrecked his apprenticeship with Savage in that one moment of lost concentration, but he would rather earn minimum wage, sleep in a tent, and work his way back up to apprentice again, than go cap in hand to his mother.

When Jack appeared in the doorway, Cam could hardly contain himself. He jumped to his feet.

'I need to find another job,' he said with sorrowful overtones, 'And quick. Can you help?'

Jack nodded, 'Cupcake told me about Savage's complaint. I guess you'll get kicked out of the house if you can't find a job, and I won't allow you to go begging to your family.'

That was the thing about Jack. When it came to big decisions, he had a quick mind. Cam immediately brightened at this thought. Jack might be the quiet one, but he was always a step or two ahead of the people around him.

Cam cocked his head to one side, 'That's why you're a decent jockey.'

He punctuated this statement with a smile.

Jack frowned, unable to make a connection.

'Always a move ahead,' said Cam, 'In any horserace,

you and I know there are two or three moments where a split-second decision has to be made. Getting those decisions right often makes the difference between winning and losing.'

Placing a hand gently on Cam's shoulder, Jack asked, 'Are you feeling alright?'

Cam cracked a soft laugh, 'I'm fine. How was Cupcake?'

'Cupkiss? Oh, he was as expected, until he told me about the complaint he's had lodged against you.'

'Aye, I've thought about that. I'll start looking for a new job on Monday.'

Jack met his gaze and Cam could feel his friend's eyes boring into him.

'What is it now?' Cam queried.

'I don't think you've grasped what's going on. If his complaint is upheld you may not ever find another apprenticeship, and you'll find it difficult to get any job in racing. Savage is going for your jugular and won't let go until…'

'Okay, I get it,' said Cam, holding up a flat hand.

'Somehow, we've got to convince him to drop the complaint.'

A roar from the crowd in the Haydock grandstands filtered through the weighing room and placed a perfect exclamation mark behind Jack's words.

'I've got to get ready for my last ride,' said Jack, 'We'll discuss your options on the drive over to Whitley Bay.'

Cam confirmed with a silent nod, thankful for Jack's concern and commitment to his cause. They really did share some sort of affinity, despite their radically different backgrounds. At Racing College they'd been like two magnets, inexorably drawn to each other.

Twenty minutes later Cam was sitting outside on one of the wooden benches set against the weighing room wall, watching the crowd massing as the horses for the final race of the day toured around the parade ring. Seeking a clearer view, he got to his feet and sidled over to stand against the paddock rails, turning his head to the weighing room entrance as the first gaggle of colourfully clothed jockeys made their way out across the veranda, down the steps and into the parade ring. Jack was one of the last out, whip in hand, already scanning for his trainer and connections as soon as he stepped outside.

A voice, young and clear, called Jack's name and a racecard and pen was thrust towards him. It was a lad in his teens, no older than Jack himself, but slightly taller. He wore a baseball cap with a brim so large, it shaded most of his face. An involuntary smile came to Cam's lips as he realised Jack was about to sign what was probably the first of many autographs. The win on Rosy Glow in a Group Two had raised his profile as a jockey and would undoubtedly boost his career. Whilst his own race riding career was stalled, or possibly over, Jack's was just getting going. And good luck to him, thought Cam. It was only what his friend deserved.

The autograph hunter looked pleased, almost excited as Jack approached, transferring both his racecard and pen to his left hand, and reaching out his right to offer a handshake.

It was a rather robust, jerk of a shake, sending Jack slightly off balance and towards the taller boy, who leaned in to speak with him privately, head bowed. Cam caught a snatch of the boys thin, sharp nose before the back of Jack's head blocked his view. Losing interest in the autograph hunter, Cam looked to the parade ring and watched Jack's mount, a gelding called Captain Trouble, being led around the ring. He knew the horse well as it was trained in Malton and being a seasoned handicapper, was a regular runner around the northern racing circuit.

A hold-up sort, Captain Trouble could be a difficult ride if he wasn't in the mood, and it was well known by the yard and punters alike that he needed to be produced late. Ideally his jockey had to hit the front later than late, as in the very last stride of the race. If not, Captain Trouble had a habit of immediately pulling himself up – quite embarrassing if you were still a hundred yards away from the winning post. Nevertheless, he was favourite for this Class 5 handicap, looking to have an obvious chance at the weights.

Unbidden, an image of a young face drifted into Cam's mind, and a memory stirred. Whipping his eyes back to where Jack and the autograph hunter were still locked in a private, whispered conversation, Cam plotted a direct route to Jack. He'd seen that face before. The day of the accident on the gallops. The teenager had been in the waiting room at York Police Station.

Jumping to his feet and dodging between racegoers, Cam made his way along the weighing room veranda and rushed down the steps, calling out Jack's name and receiving no response. As he approached, the young autograph hunter raised his head just enough from under his cap to reveal cool blue eyes above the sharp nose. They widened, startled to see Cam bearing down on him.

A renewed shot of worry ran through Cam. Jack looked half asleep, his head lolled to one side… surely he couldn't be dozing, could he?

'Hey, what's your game?' Cam demanded, ready to grab the young lad.

As Cam made his final stride to meet the two of them the lad bobbed his head back down and swiftly whispered something into Jack's ear. Cam noticed the lad still, inexplicably, had hold of Jack's right hand, the one he'd shaken.

Cam made a grab for the autograph hunter, intending to seize a handful of his jacket, but instead found himself grappling with Jack who had somehow toppled backwards into him.

Giving Jack a small push, the autograph hunter simultaneously pulled his hoodie over his cap, leaving just the brim showing, then cinching it tight, he turned and ran. Without looking back, he dived in and out of the racegoers, most of whom were static, watching the horses, trainers, connections, and jockeys in the parade ring. He didn't slow his pace until he'd reached the base of the grandstand, then hurried behind the huge building. The crowds immediately thinned out and as the racecourse gates drew close, he eased into a hurried trot. As he'd calculated, to allow for the mass exodus after the last race of the day, the exit gates were already wide open.

Back on the weighing room steps, Cam righted himself, and grabbing Jack's shoulders with both hands, looked into his friend's eyes. They were heavily dilated. He appeared dazed and distant.

'What did he do to you? What did he say?'

The quickfire questions had a transformative effect on Jack. His eyes immediately lit up, becoming sharp, and recognising Cam, Jack grinned.

'Who?'

'The lad talking to you! The autograph hunter!' implored Cam, straightening to stand on his toes, desperate to spot the hooded perpetrator.

Jack frowned, 'What auto…'

'Are you feeling okay?'

'I feel amazing,' he admitted with a broad smile, waggling his whip, 'I'm right up for this ride!'

'Seriously?' Cam checked, holding onto Jack's shoulders, staring into his eyes, assessing.

'Sure!' Jack insisted, but sensing Cam's urgency he added, 'Why? What's up with y…'

'Go win your race,' Cam cut in, and set off after the autograph hunter.

Passing through the racecourse gates a waft of cool air played onto the autograph hunter's face as he turned into a light breeze. He dropped to a walk to get his bearings, not immediately sure which area of the vast car park he should be headed. Pleased to see there were only a smattering of people around, and little in the way of traffic, he located the general area of his vehicle and set off at a jog again. A moment later he was stalking between cars, a set of keys in his hand.

The car's engine started with the minimum of fuss and despite the odd bead of sweat dripping from his forehead, around his eyes and down his cheek, he was feeling pretty good about himself. His heart was still racing, but slowing with every second and every yard he put between himself and the racecourse exit. As he pulled out of his tight-fitting parking bay, he allowed the smallest of grins to bend his lips upwards. Reminding himself that he'd only discover if he'd been successful when the result of the race was known, he wiped the grin from his face and concentrated on driving the car to the end of the row of parked cars and executing a left turn onto the main road out of the racecourse.

A ripple of pride crept over him though as he straightened the steering wheel. He'd been careful to plan his escape route, just in case he was followed. By driving up through the main car park and over to the narrow road on the side of the straight, he would exit at the top of the course, instead of the main entrance. Less well-known and an underused way out, it would ensure a quick getaway and give him access straight onto a major road.

A glance into his wing mirror had his heart racing again. An instantly recognisable blonde-haired man had just careered out of the racecourse gates, onto the road, and was now running at full pelt towards him. He pushed his foot down hard on the accelerator and praying no one would walk out into his path, the autograph hunter shot through the canyon of parked cars, furiously scanning the road ahead as he left Cam Camberley behind.

Cam slowed to a jog and swore at himself for not committing the car's registration to memory, watching as the small car reached the top of the five furlong straight. Despite being as fit as he'd ever been, he was used to a steady run, rather than an all-out sprint. Coming to a shambling halt, Cam soon found himself bent over, both hands on his knees as he tried to get breath back into his lungs. Straining his neck upwards, he kept an eye on his lost quarry. Where was the autograph hunter going? Surely there was no way out at the top end of the racecourse...

Nineteen

'I don't understand. I just... don't understand!' whined Cam from the passenger seat of Jack's twelve-year-old Renault.

'What don't you understand? Jack said lightly, 'How I managed to pull off a double on the card?'

Cam shot him a look that landed somewhere between disgusted and amused.

'I've watched that horse throw away races a ton of times, as soon as he hits the front,' he complained, 'But the Group Two Guru gets on him and the little sod saunters into the lead two out and wins head in chest!'

Jack forced a high-pitched laugh out but kept his eyes fixed on the road as Corbyn's need to pull to the left required small and constant corrections.

'It's like Captain Trouble loves to be in the lead all of a sudden!' grumbled Cam, 'But that's not what I meant when I said I didn't understand... I want to know what that lad in the hoodie was saying, or doing to you, and why he ran.'

'I told you, I can't remember... or at least, it's all a bit hazy. All I do know is that after he spoke with me, I signed his racecard, and I felt on top of the world, like nothing could stop me from winning.'

'You must have transmitted that feeling into the horse,' Cam sighed, 'What was the winning distance again?'

'Nine lengths.'

'Nine... sodding... lengths,' Cam breathed, 'And to add insult to injury, the lad in the hoodie managed to escape at the top end of the racecourse. I didn't even know about that exit!'

Jack shook his head, 'Don't worry about the autograph

hunter. If he did do something, it only helped me win!'

Cam unhappily grunted his agreement.

Jack continued, 'I know you're convinced that the autograph hunter was the same boy in the police station waiting room, the day you mowed down Savage, but even if it was, I don't care. I didn't ride poorly, or throw the race, did I?'

'No, you managed the exact opposite,' said Cam, 'And Captain Trouble was returned the favourite. His odds shortened. There must have been plenty of money for him in the last few minutes before the off.'

Jack went quiet for a moment, 'I... didn't know that. Anyway, I think you might have just spooked a genuine racing fan. He should be the least of our worries.'

'Why? What've you heard?' asked Cam absently, his mind still concerned with the shaded face and the young figure's retreating back as he'd run from the racecourse.

'From what Cupkiss said to me, if Savage doesn't get his notebook back into his grubby little hands, you won't be race riding for the foreseeable.'

'But what can I do? I haven't got it! And I checked yesterday – I walked up the gallop and looked around for his blasted notebook. I searched around that plinth Savage stands on, there was nothing there.'

'You don't suppose one of the work riders who found you and Savage might have taken it?'

Cam shook his head, 'I was seeing straight by then, and by the time the first riders arrived I'd made it over to Savage to check he was okay. I would have seen if anyone had started rifling through his jacket. Besides, Savage woke up and was looking for his jacket way before anyone even got close to us. It was only when he had his jacket in his hand that he started complaining about his arm and ribs.'

'Yeah, Grace told me as much the other night.'

Cam looked over at his friend, his eyes wide, 'The other night?'

'Nothing like that! She has trouble sleeping, and I

bumped into her in the kitchen. Actually, she was… interesting.'

A silence developed and another mile slipped by under Corbyn's tyres, both jockeys in deep thought. Presently, Jack spoke, continuing as if there hadn't been any gap at all in their conversation.

'She thinks Charlie came to the police station because Savage told her to. If that's true, I'm guessing Charlie wanted to find out whether you had his notebook.'

'I get the feeling Grace has been avoiding me for the last couple of days,' Cam announced as Jack aimed his car down the slip road, off the motorway and onto the A66 towards the north east and Whitley Bay.

'Me, too,' agreed Jack, 'Although I've caught her watching me reverse Corbyn out down the drive a couple of times. She seems to think I can't see her twitching her curtains.'

'Grace won't even listen. It's like she doesn't want to know me anymore,' Cam grumbled, 'I went down to her room last night to try and explain about Savage's lies. It was useless. She wouldn't even let me in. I started telling her how he'd tricked us and she told me to leave her alone until I'd given Savage his notebook back, then slammed her door in my face.'

Jack didn't react. There was nothing to say. He too had tried to make things right with Grace following the incident with Savage and Cam's door. He'd caught her making breakfast in the shared kitchen and starting to explain. She'd refused to listen, telling him to give back Savage's notebook.

'Grace will come round, eventually,' Jack advised without much conviction, 'In the meantime, we need to concentrate on getting to Whitley Bay Playhouse for seven thirty. Something happened to us on that night out in Scarborough and we'll find out tonight by offering to get hypnotised again by Stefan Kreihn.'

Twenty

For their first thirty minutes inside the Whitley Bay Playhouse auditorium Cam and Jack surveyed a virtually empty theatre, having arrived an hour before the performance was advertised to begin. According to their tickets, the Soft Cell tribute band was to be a brief support act for the main event of the evening, which was billed as, 'The Stefan Kreihn Experience'.

Their box office tickets didn't indicate specific seats, so Jack chose a pair in the centre of the stalls, ten rows from the front, to ensure a clear view of the stage, a partial view of each of the wings, and also to hopefully remain fairly inconspicuous. At a quarter to eight the safety curtain rose and three musicians emerged onto the stage to play to a meagre, but enthusiastic audience of about a hundred people. However, during their half-hour set the theatre steadily filled with a mixture of students, middle-aged couples, and noticeably towards the back of the venue, a number of rows occupied by silver-topped pensioners. By the time the lead singer of 'Softer Cell', who to be fair, did sound incredibly like Marc Almond, had crooned his final number, the place was almost at its six hundred person capacity and an atmosphere of excited anticipation was hanging in the air.

In contrast to the promotional photos on his website, Stefan Kreihn was far less intimidating in person. In fact, both Cam and Jack were surprised to discover he wasn't just smaller and older than expected, Kreihn was far more charismatic than his cheesy promotional shots and amateurish website had led them to believe.

Entering the relatively bare stage, consisting of a series of graduated charcoal coloured curtains, the spotlighted Kreihn appeared in a thin, black, polo-necked top, sleeves pushed up to just below his elbows, black jeans, and shiny, black boots. He received a rapturous reception and accepted the adulation with several flowery bows, thanked his audience for returning once again, and grinning expansively, announced they must be 'gluttons for punishment!' This received a hearty roar of approval from all areas of the auditorium. It seemed Kreihn enjoyed a somewhat fervent and regular following.

'Do you think he's the autograph hunter?' asked Cam.

Jack studied Kreihn for a long moment, eventually resignedly shaking of his head.

'Yeah, me too,' Cam agreed with a disappointed grimace.

After a short list of rules – no videoing, no drunks on stage, and a reminder that everyone was here at their own risk - the show quickly gathered speed. Ominous music struck up from the on-stage speakers and Kreihn asked for any of those who wished to be a part of the fun to hold their flat hands together and push palm-to-palm, exerting just the right amount of pressure to make their arms tremble.

Jack elbowed Cam, 'Okay, time for me to get onto that stage and see if I can find our autograph hunter,' he whispered, placing his palms together, 'Keep your eyes peeled. If you see anything strange, wave at me.'

Cam put a hand on his friends arm, 'Just remember, don't allow Kreihn to hypnotise you!'

Jack returned him a look of determined optimism, although now he was here, with the audience buzzing round him, he wasn't so sure. He could now understand why a livewire like Lucille loved to watch the show and not be hypnotised. The anticipatory suspense was flowing around the room as if it was electrically charged.

Kreihn asked everyone participating to chant, 'Deep Sleep!' for about half a minute. The chant grew bigger and as it began to reach its zenith, Kreihn invited everyone with their palms still together to stand. About ten percent of the audience did so.

'Deep sleep. Deep sleep. Now... come up and join me on the stage!' cried Kreihn into his small headset microphone.

Jack got to his feet, muttering the mantra under his breath and shot his friend a parting wink, only to find Cam's hand shooting out to grab hold of his arm.

'Shouldn't I come with you? 'You know, to find out what happens on stage... just in case?'

Jack looked into Cam's blue eyes and detected concern wrapped in a blanket of uncertainty.

'If I get hypnotised... come and get me. But don't worry, I won't!'

Cam released his grip and followed his friends progress along the row of seats, into the aisle, and down to the front of the stage, where he and about fifty other audience members were organised into a queue beside a set of wooden stage steps. One by one, the willing stooges stepped up and into the bright white lights illuminating the stage.

Kreihn continued to speak to the audience while three assistants dressed in a tight-fitting black polo-neck sweaters sorted the hopefuls. One of the assistants, a thin-limbed woman, now milled between the potential stars of the show, helping Kreihn sift through them. Some of the audience were immediately asked to return to their seats. Cam presumed they were the ones with too much alcohol on their breath. Others were quietly spoken with and subsequently released back to their seats, and the remaining chosen few were lined up, facing the audience, at the back of the stage.

Cam watched Jack hawklike as his friend waited in line, still chanting the 'deep sleep' mantra and pushing his palms together. Kriehn went through the same process with each successful candidate; with his microphone switched off he would say something to them, then place a hand between their neck and shoulder bone and jerk them forward slightly whilst still speaking. A teenager three places in front of Jack was immediately returned to her seat, but the chap in front of him one was rocked a little by the hypnotist, spoken to, and sent to join the growing line of participants at the back of the stage.

Cam was impressed, Jack was blending in well, although anyone concentrating just on him would have noticed he kept taking surreptitious glances around him and into both the wings of the stage. Whilst a little suspicious, several of the wannabe stars of the show were doing the same. One or two were smiling, or even waving at their friends in the audience, although once this was noticed, they were promptly dispatched back to their seats by Kreihn or his assistants.

As Kreihn reached Jack, a series of loud thumps inside Cam's chest made him gasp and he realised he was holding his breath. Nervous tension, he decided, as he re-inflated his lungs.

Kreihn went through the same process with Jack and was about to place a hand on him when his female assistant popped up at the hypnotist's side, delaying the anticipated jerk to Jack's shoulder. A short whispered conversation led to a nod of understanding from Kreihn and passing Jack over, he moved on down the line, allowing his assistant to clap her hand on Jack's shoulder, and rock him forward so their heads almost touched.

Until now, Cam hadn't paid that much attention to the female assistant buzzing about the stage, sorting the volunteers like wheat from chaff, as more often than not, she had her back to the audience. But now she turned, her arm around Jack's waist, to guide him into the wings of the stage. As she did, she offered the audience a reassuring smile.

A shudder of ice-cold horror ran through Cam.

The assistant's smile now fell benignly onto her new charge, as with an arm still around him, the woman gently gripped Jack's elbow and they disappeared into the wings and out of sight.

On the edge of his seat, seeing where Jack was headed, Cam had already sprung to his feet. That face. That assistant. He'd seen that woman's face before. But where?

Kreihn had almost finished the sorting of his cast of

characters, only a trio remained, still chanting 'Deep sleep' and holding their palms together. Determined to rescue Jack, Cam set off to the stage.

Pushing his way through legs, shoes, boots, bags, and issuing apologies to a string of complaints from the people on his row, Cam reached the aisle and hurrying to the front edge of the stalls, stared in puzzlement up onto the stage as he caught a glimpse of Jack with the assistant.

Jack was barely recognisable, standing zombie-like just inside the far wing, closely attended by the hypnotist's assistant. Meanwhile Stefan Kreihn, having released the last two hopefuls, was now going through his line of nine potential stars of the show.

The assistant turned, took a step forward and looked over at Kreihn. As she did, she crossed the ghostly beam of a spotlight. Giving the hypnotist a satisfied nod and a thumbs up, she moved back again and the shaft of silver light caught the side of her face providing a moment where her profile was perfectly lit. That snapshot made Cam's brain sizzle with reflective connections. Like the correct piece falling into place in a jigsaw, Cam linked her face to a location. The train to Scarborough. The assistant was… damn it! He couldn't remember! Something to do with that train…

An urge to scream, 'Stop right there!' at the woman leading his friend even deeper into the shadows of the wings bubbled up in Cam. He fought it down, the last thing he wanted was for her to run, and there were questions that needed answers. And then there was Jack. He was clearly hypnotised – could he be somehow hurt whilst he was 'under'? Cam didn't know, but he wasn't going to chance it.

On stage, as the suspenseful music started to edge towards a conclusion, Kreihn was talking with his back to the audience as one by one he sent each of the remaining members of the public into a standing sleep. Every other potential candidate had rejoined the audience, so Cam stood alone, his presence at the foot of the stage going unnoticed by

Kreihn, but he was starting to get a few catcalls from the people behind him whose view of the action on stage he was obstructing.

Cam knew his way around a stage. His private schooling, and his confident, flamboyant nature had afforded him the opportunity to appear in several theatrical productions. It wasn't something the racing world would appreciate, but his performance as Puck in A Midsummers Night's Dream had been well received at his school, although only his father had ever bothered to make the seventy-five mile journey to watch him perform.

Cam took his chance. As Kreihn's back was still turned, he shot up the steps to the stage, immediately cutting into the wings opposite Jack. Worryingly, wing stage right was a hive of activity. Trying to appear relaxed and confident, Cam strolled up to a couple of whispering men, presumably stage hands. To their left, a woman with a headset was sitting behind a small bank of buttons, knobs, and a tiny monitor. Cam assumed they were either lighting or sound controls. One of the men glanced at him and frowned, but didn't challenge him. Backing further into the darkness, and ignoring what was happening on stage, he stared over into the opposite wing, but couldn't see anything clearly. There was movement, but exactly what and whom, was uncertain.

Standing stock still, Cam watched Kreihn walk with a confident swagger to the centre of the stage and address the audience via a microphone taped to his cheek. Beyond the hypnotist, in the wings on the other side of the stage Cam now caught sight of the assistant. She had her back to him. Meanwhile, the show had started in earnest, the audience braying with laughter as two of Kreihn's stooges bit into large, unpeeled onions with unbridled abandon and agreed with Stefan that they were the tastiest, sweetest, juiciest apples they had ever eaten.

Cam ignored the on-stage antics, more interested in what was happening in the opposite wing. The female assistant was remonstrating strongly but silently with a new, younger male in similar black clothes. Another two or three people were also moving around in the shadows.

Cam's heart jumped. He tried to get a better view – the young male... Was he the autograph hunter from Haydock?

The woman gesticulated wildly with her hands, rolling her eyes, and ramming her pointed index finger into the young man's chest. Meanwhile, the much younger man stood with hunched shoulders, head bowed, eyes fixed on the boarded stage floor, taking her abuse without protest. Finally, the older woman threw her arms up in the air in silent admonishment and holding her left arm out straight, pointed deeper into the shadows where to Cam's relief he could just make out Jack, his head tilted into his shoulder, apparently in a standing sleep.

Almost every theatre stage provides a crossover, an alleyway or hallway that enables actors to exit into one wing and appear from the other. Knowing this, Cam turned around and careful not to trip over taped wires, discarded props, and other accumulated junk, found his way deeper backstage. Sure enough, down a few steps, and behind a thick drawn curtain he discovered a thin passageway that ran for twenty yards behind the stage. Another burst of laughter came from the audience as Cam made his way along the poorly lit alley, and reaching the end he cast another curtain aside. His bold approach had worked so far, so he leapt up the half-dozen steps like he owned them.

A young stagehand, about the same age as Cam, dressed in the ubiquitous black sweater, dark trousers and trainers blinked in surprise at Cam's sudden arrival. He had been slouched in his chair, but swiftly scrambled to become erect. Beside him a table was filled with a plethora of eclectic props including a range of vegetables, numerous balloons, hula hoops, and several beakers filled with a green liquid. Cam's attention was drawn to a set of pink skullcaps, whereupon he shuddered, with no understanding of why.

With the confidence often found within oneself when you have no other option but to wing it, Cam placed his finger to his lips and shushing the teenager, closed the distance between them.

'I'm a friend of Stefan's,' Cam whispered, a hand cupped to his mouth, 'Sorry, didn't mean to come out of nowhere like that! Stefan said I could watch the performance from the wings.'

The repeating of the hypnotist's first name had the desired effect and with a furious nodding of his head the young stagehand pointed Cam upstage. Following his extended finger, Cam lifted his gaze to where Kreihn's assistant was busy, hunched over, speaking with Jack, a faraway look on his face, her hand on his shoulder. Beside her, the teenage boy Cam had spotted from the other side of the stage looked on.

The young man was the first to recognise Cam coming towards them, saying something so short and immediate into the woman's ear it made her jerk her head around to meet the fierce, determined expression of the handsome apprentice jockey. Noticing he also had his fists balled, she went ramrod straight, although Cam noted her right hand remained stubbornly gripped onto Jack's shoulder.

Able to study the woman's facial features up close for the first time, Cam came to an abrupt halt. He definitely knew that face… the hair was different, and she was wearing a thick layer of stage make-up… Desperately trying to make a connection, it wasn't until she cocked her head a little to whisper something to her fellow assistant that at last, a name came to him… Emily.

'Emily…' Cam said slowly, his eyes crinkled up in concentration, 'Emily… '

'Harris, the woman finished for him, 'Emily Harris'.

The woman didn't appear overly surprised. With an accepting nod and purse of her lips, she dropped her hand from Jack's shoulder, 'And this is Robert, he isn't audience facing, and neither is Saul, back there on the props table.'

The newly introduced boy failed to say anything or meet Cam's accusatory stare. Head bowed, he preferred to stare nervously at the floor. Cam interrogated the boy's face, but disappointingly, this wasn't Jack's autograph hunter. His face was too pudgy, his frame wide, and too well built.

'What have you done to Jack?' Cam demanded, going over to his friend and placing both his hands softly on his shoulders. He looked sleepy, but was awake.

'Hey, mate,' he said, peering into his glazed expression.

Jack's face was pallid, his skin slack, as if every facial muscle no longer functioned. Most alarming were his dreamy, unseeing eyes, half hidden by drooping eyelids.

'Bring him out of… whatever you've done to him… now!' he said, barking his demand at Emily over his shoulder.

Emily and Robert shared a quick glance.

'I'm afraid your friend has … umm… had a bad experience,' Emily reported.

'Of course he has!' exclaimed Cam, 'You've hypnotised the poor sod!'

'No, no,' replied Emily, elbowing her way back in front of Jack and inspecting his eyes, 'This boy should never have been allowed onto the stage. It's the same issue we had with him last week in Scarborough.'

'Last week?' Cam queried.

'Your friend is highly susceptible to hypnosis and coupled with his incredibly strong sense of self, and some sort of trauma in his past, he's reacted badly to being put under. If we're not careful, he could end up suffering from a bout of psychosis. I'm slowly bringing him back to full cognitive function to ensure there's no lasting effect.'

'What do you mean, no lasting effect?' Cam questioned, scrutinising Emily's face.

She gave nothing away, except a flash of impatience.

Cam continued at an increased volume, 'Would that effect make Jack lose his race whenever he's riding a favourite?'

Emily stared uncomprehendingly back at him.

'I don't know what you mean,' she said with a shake of her head.

'Even though he believes he's ridden the perfect race?'

This time Cam fired his accusation at Emily in a shout.

Both Emily and Robert cringed, shooting nervous glances onto the stage where Keihn was busy setting up an elaborate set of linked events with his hypnotised stooges. The stage hypnotist shot a wide-eyed query into the wings and after receiving a pacifying wave from Emily, went smoothly on with his show.

'I'm waiting!' exclaimed Cam, demanding their attention.

'Alright, alright!' Emily capitulated, 'All I ask is that you remain calm and speak quietly. As much for your friend's benefit as ours. I'm a trained hypnotist with many years' experience and your friend will be perfectly fine in about thirty minutes if you just calm down and allow me to do my job!'

Emily took a sharp intake of breath and continued, 'Yes, you were both hypnotised last week. It was a mistake. An awful, awful, mistake. When we shared that table on the train, I gave everyone free tickets for the performance. You came along, and both of you came up on stage to be hypnotised. You were fine, but he… It's Jack, isn't it?'

Cam nodded.

'He reacted badly and went into a low level psychosis. We have protocols for that, so we brought him into the wings and looked after him. But you… you caused us a few issues.'

'What do you mean?'

Distracted for a moment by what was happening on stage, she held up a hand, 'Just a minute.'

Waving at the boy on the props table, Emily called out something and he picked up a tin horn with a large black squeeze bulb at the end and moved over to stand in the wings.

Stefan Kreihn came over a moment later and still talking to his audience, took the horn out of the boy's outstretched hand and continued with his act.

Cam noticed Robert was studiously keeping an eye on Jack, who to his relief was now blinking and holding a hand to his head.

'Hey, Jack. You okay?'

Swaying a little, Jack gave his friend a hazy smile.

'Cam?'

'Yep, I'm here.'

'I feel like by brain's been squeezed out through my ears.'

'Excellent! Jack's coming around,' Emily said brightly, 'He'll be feeling much better in a few minutes. Stay and watch the rest of the show from here. There's a nice little restaurant café over on the seafront, we can go there after the show. I can explain everything without all of the backstage chaos going on around us.'

She drew closer to Cam and in a conspiratorial whisper she added, 'And they make their own, incredible chocolate cake!'

Twenty-One

It was more of a fish and chip café and takeaway, rather than a restaurant, although at ten o'clock on a Saturday night, The Silver Grid on the Whitley Bay seafront was surprisingly busy serving teas, coffees and, to Cam's delight, chocolate cake. Ten of its fifteen plastic-topped, easy-wipe tables were occupied and the reassuring smell of chip fat hung in the air.

'You're looking better, Jack,' Cam declared, forcing a smile, 'Not so green around the gills now!'

Bringing a smile to his friend's face was proving a challenge. Having failed miserably to stop Jack from being hypnotised, and managing to bungle his rescue, Cam had watched the remainder of the show with Emily Harris and Robert from the wings of the stage. Riddled with guilt, he was hoping against hope that the woman would be true to her promise - to return Jack to his normal, fun-loving self and explain what on earth had gone on last week in Scarborough. Whilst he'd woken up bright and refreshed, Jack had since looked like he had the mother of all hangovers.

Hugging a mug of strong black coffee, Jack took a sip and smarted at the bitterness of his drink.

'What does green around the gills even mean?' he griped, 'I've never heard of it… has anyone got any painkillers? I've a crashing headache.'

'I can only apologise… again,' said Emily Harris sitting opposite the two of them. She scrambled for her handbag and digging deep, handed over a couple of aspirin.

Cam lifted a wedge of homemade chocolate cake from his plate and, pushing his guilt aside, took a large bite. No wonder this place was busy, this cake was to die for. He allowed the combination of the moist, coco infused cake, melted real chocolate topping, and thick, sweet ganache sandwiched between three layers of cake to linger in his mouth, his tastebuds tingling wantonly before he swallowed. He licked, then smacked his lips in satisfaction.

'Seriously? Do you have to do that *every* time you eat cake?' groaned Jack.

'I only get to eat it once in a blue moon!' Cam complained through a second mouthful of chocolate heaven,' I have to make the most of it.'

'It's alright for you, Goodman,' Cam added with a devilish grin, 'You could eat cake until it comes out of your ears and not put on a single ounce. I can put on a pound by simply walking past Greggs and sniffing the air!'

Cam swallowed, licked his lips and then smacked them with obvious relish. Readying himself for his next chunk of loveliness, he bobbed his head towards the woman sitting opposite, adding, 'And Emily offered to pay!'

Jack rolled his eyes and winced at the pain it caused in the muscles around their sockets.

'Come on Emily, what happened at Scarborough?' Cam asked through another mouthful of chocolate cake, 'Hurry up, spill the beans.'

Emily girded herself, 'I'll do my best. I'm so sorry, it all got rather out of hand…'

In the corner of the room, his back to the boys and the café's entrance, Cupkiss watched with interest as the unknown woman began speaking with the two apprentices. He was certain neither of them were aware he had been following them. First from Haydock after their strange altercation with a young racegoer, then into the theatre, and trailing them from the stage door, into this steamy little café. He had a bad feeling about these two, despite their assurances in their interviews earlier in the day. Keeping his head down, his hat brim just above his eyeline, he toyed with his teaspoon, wishing he could hear what was being said. By the look on the boy's faces the woman was telling quite an engaging story.

His gaze centred on a large framed advert featuring a toucan claiming it was a lovely day for a Guiness. But it was the reflection in the glass, not the pithy marketing message that interested him. He congratulated himself on his slyly covert method of observation before dropping his eyes to the menu card on his table for a moment. He grimaced. Only in the North East of England, he thought, could you find traditional afternoon tea and a deep fried Mars Bars on the same menu.

His attention flicked to another of the framed photos on the back wall. In this picture the glass provided a decent reflection of the café entrance. The shop door had opened and a new customer of average build, average height, and average looks came in. He was wearing a raincoat similar to his own. Before approaching the counter the customer scanned the room. Simply out of habit, Cupkiss automatically leaned very slightly to his right, correctly calculating that he would be hidden from view thanks to a large chap sitting behind him. After a long look whilst he was ordering, Cupkiss decided the new customer wasn't of interest.

Cupkiss allowed himself a despondent sigh as he took a sip of his coffee. The information he'd received from Malton had come good. The coincidences were stacking up. These two boys *were* involved in something, possibly underhand. He almost felt sorry for them. Almost.

Neither of the two apprentices sitting together in the booth against the far wall, listening to the hypnotist's assistant, noticed the very average middle-aged customer at the counter ordering a coffee. Similarly, neither of them realised a second man was watching them in the reflection of a black and white photo of the once famous Spanish City amusement park that used to occupy the land directly behind the café.

'We knew straight away you were having trouble,' Emily said to Jack, 'It was obvious as soon as you arrived on stage in Scarborough. You were three-quarters hypnotised even before Stefan assessed you… and his touch to the pressure point in your shoulder was enough to send you straight into the trauma dream. When anything like that happens, we take the subject off the stage and slowly bring them back out of the hypnosis, making sure the subject forgets all knowledge of the trauma.'

'What sort of trauma?' Cam asked.

Emily pressed her lips together as she contemplated her answer. Still wearing her stage make-up, her heavily applied lipstick wrinkled, pulling at her mouth as she started to reply.

'I don't know. Jack may not even be aware of it himself. But if he does know, he should be the one to tell you.'

Cam looked to Jack, but his friend shook his head, unable to offer anything in explanation.

'Anyway, as I said, you were in a bit of distress,' Emily continued. She turned to Cam, 'And you started to get upset. In the end, Stefan came off stage and helped me hypnotise the two of you...'

'He hypnotised both of us?' Cam stated in an urgent but soft voice.

'You were starting to disrupt the show and...'

Seeing the discomfort in both boy's faces, Emily trailed off. She scratched her neck nervously, and finding this part of her story difficult to relate, dropped her gaze away from the teenagers.

'Stefan and I put you both to sleep and left you in a quiet place at the back of the stage. Then we carefully brought you back out of the hypnosis, but not before making sure you would forget the trauma, and everything else that had happened. Stefan also spent time after the show making sure you in particular were okay, Jack. I couldn't believe my eyes when you turned up on the stage again tonight, only a week later.'

'That's because everything *isn't* okay,' Jack said in a whispered hiss.

A minute into Jack and Cam's description of their strange week and the detective work that had led to them invade her stage once more, Emily had tears in her eyes.

'You can't believe... I mean, I wouldn't do anything that could possibly hurt anyone, it's part of the stage hypnotists code... I've *never* used hypnotism like that, and I can't believe Stefan would either.'

Retrieving a paper tissue from her bag, she dabbed at both eyes, smudging her liberally applied mascara.

Cam caught Jack's eye and could tell he didn't share his view of Emily. Jack's compressed lips and a quickly flashed wide-eyed frown indicated he wasn't convinced one way or another. Cam sent his own silent message back; that he believed Emily was genuine and being truthful. Jack grimaced and took up the questioning.

'If Stefan and yourself are the good hypnotists, then tell me, have we been hypnotised by someone else?' asked Jack.

Emily sniffed, blinked her eyes dry, and blew her nose

before answering.

'After the Scarborough performance it took Stefan a good ten minutes to bring you back and check you were lucid enough to allow you to leave the theatre. That could be a sign someone left something planted there, and you in particular are very susceptible to hypnotism, Jack. If someone knew this… But we were so careful with you. With you both. We were very, very careful.'

'Careful enough to leave Cam and me hypnotised at the back of a theatre for the best part of an hour while you did a stage show,' Jack muttered angrily, 'Anyone could have come along and thrown their own commands at us. Is that what you're saying?'

Emily looked hurt.

'We have a code of conduct,' she insisted, 'And I was checking on both of you throughout the performance. If anyone did plant something into either of you, they must have known exactly what they were doing.'

'If your Scarborough gig was anything any like tonight a dozen people, perhaps more, could have wandered past us standing alone in the wings. There were a surprising number of people knocking around backstage,' Cam noted.

The conversation fell flat for a moment. Jack scratched his chin, his thoughtful gaze never leaving Emily.

'And you've now got rid of all of the, umm… stuff planted in my mind?' Jack checked.

'I watched Emily bring you back tonight,' offered Cam, 'She kept repeating that you were cleansed. Is that what you were doing?'

Emily nodded, 'I was trying to push that trauma back and make sure your mind was clear of any suggestions.'

'Be honest, Emily,' Jack pleaded, 'Could someone have got to us whilst the show was running and during the time we were left hypnotised at the back of the theatre in Scarborough?'

Emily studied the empty cups and plates on the table

for a long moment, her features scrunching up together as she considered her answer. Jack did his best to suppress the urge to bark, 'Well?' at her.

'I suppose it's possible,' she eventually replied with a despondent shrug.

Cam watched Jack roll his eyes in exasperation. He jumped in, addressing Emily directly.

'Tonight the wings were full of teenagers, or at least, young people like us,' Cam said, nodding at Emily, 'Could one of them put instructions, I don't know, *into us,* like don't win when you're riding a favourite, or ride your next horse up the gallop and bowl over your employer?'

This seemed to stump Emily and once more, it seemed to Jack she took an interminably long time to cogitate before answering.

'I don't know anything about racing, or horses for that matter. Stefan has a big following at the colleges and universities. He advertises for non-paid help at each of the gigs and so he gets lots of youngsters who turn up for a performance and help out – like Robert and um... the boy on the props table – and they get a reference, one or two free tickets, and we get free stage hands.'

Cam gave Emily a small smile, 'Do you know who was working that night at Scarborough. Were there any young men in their late teens or early twenties?'

'Of course. Most of them students, drama students mainly, or doing psychology degrees,' replied Emily, but she shook her head before continuing, 'They just turn up at the stage door two hours before we go on, and help to hump the gear in. A few get to hand out the props or actually help with anyone who has a bad reaction, you know, like getting them a drink or just chatting with them. I doubt Stefan records anything, but I can check.'

'That would be great. Can you remember any of the students from the night at Scarborough?'

Emily pressed her lips together for a second time,

'We've done three other gigs since then. They're all instantly forgettable after a while. I've probably dealt with a couple of dozen helpers just in the last week.'

Cam's hopeful smile vanished and he adopted a downcast frown. Jack sighed dejectedly.

'Listen, I don't want you thinking I'm protecting anyone,' said Emily, 'They're just students. That night it was just me and Stefan working on you. If someone else came in and sank some other instructions into your minds, it wasn't us. Please don't think I or Stefan would...'

'It's okay, Emily,' Cam reassured her, 'It's a man we're after, and it's not Stefan. The bloke we're after is young, perhaps in his twenties. We got a good look at him at Haydock races today.'

'I shook his hand and we think he tried to... or actually *did* hypnotise me,' Jack explained, 'I think he wanted me to lose the last race on the card.'

Emily nodded, 'It sounds like he was attempting a handshake interrupt. It's a method less honest individuals employ to induce hypnosis. A handshake is so normal, and the mind anticipates what it will feel like. When the handshake is strange, it confuses the mind, making the subject more open to suggestion. On the whole, it's frowned upon in the hypnotist community.'

'But it didn't work. Jack won the race and I chased off the lad who tried it,' Cam grinned.

Emily looked pleased for Cam, but Jack was left with the feeling she didn't quite understand the gravity of their situation. And he still hadn't mentioned Savage's missing notebook.

'Could a hypnotist make those things happen?' he asked, 'Could I be made to lose a race, and Cam to ride a horse into his boss?'

Emily reiterated what they already knew from their internet searches.

'Hypnotism is the art of suggestion. You're still in

charge of your own actions,' she reminded them, 'For example, if you're basically honest and understand the difference between right and wrong, you couldn't be hypnotised to steal something...'

'However...' Emily added with a grimace, 'There are definite signs of you being hypnotised, both of you. And a clever hypnotist might be able to be... creative in what he suggests.'

Cam leaned forward, 'How do you mean?'

Emily scrunched her face up as she considered how to explain, 'Well, I've read about cases where a hypnotist has achieved an outcome through indirect suggestion.'

She smiled knowingly. Cam and Jack stared blankly back at her. Reading their puzzled expressions, Emily swiftly added to her explanation.

'A talented hypnotist can uses someone's strongly held beliefs or motivations, and along with an indirect suggestion, profoundly alter their behaviour without them knowing. Indirect suggestion places an idea or motive into the unconscious, meaning the subject doesn't realise they have been shepherded towards a particular notion or action.'

The boys maintained their blank expressions.

Emily's shoulders dropped as she sought a clearer explanation.

'It's entirely possible you could be made to ride a horse recklessly,' she said to Cam before turning to address Jack, 'Or believe you're riding a race correctly when you're not. But... and I can't stress this enough, it's very unlikely. It would take a talented hypnotist, with the means, specific goals, and opportunity. They would also need to know exactly what drives both of you.'

She allowed this to settle on both boys for a long moment before adding, 'It's more likely that you both suffered some sort of reaction to being hypnotised in Scarborough and it coincided with an accident on the gallops and a poorly executed ride at the races.'

Emily looked into the boys faces and sat back, finally feeling she'd managed to get through to them. They both appeared to be mulling this over.

'We're still no further forward,' Cam told Jack grouchily, 'I was convinced that Haydock autograph hunter was trying to hypnotise you. And we still might lose our jobs.'

'Not just our jobs,' Jack explained to Emily, 'If we can't find Sebastian Savage's lost notebook it could end our careers in racing, especially if he decides to pursue his complaint against us with the racing authorities.'

'A lost notebook?' Emily queried, blank faced.

The boys shared a swift glance.

Damn it, thought Jack. He had hoped casually dropping Savage's name and his notebook into the conversation might catch Emily out. Perhaps it was her line of work, but there was something about the woman that was making him nervous. But having studied Emily, her face and her body language as well as her answers for the last forty minutes, Jack couldn't come up with any reason for his reaction. So why was he being nattered by a sense of incompleteness? Was he somehow missing something about her? It wasn't as if she was clearly hiding something... was she? However, from her responses so far, she clearly knew nothing about Savage, or his notebook. A thought struck him. It was something he'd forgotten to quiz Emily about...

'I heard Stefan using certain words as prompts that made his hypnotised group react in a certain way on stage.'

Emily nodded, 'They're hypnotic triggers.'

Jack slowly repeated the phrase, studying Emily carefully. She showed no outward signs of stress.

'And could a hypnotic trigger be used over the phone?'

Cam was frowning, not sure where Jack was going with this line of inquiry.

Emily compressed her lips and her eyes widened as she gazed into space, considering her reply.

'Yes, I don't see why not,' she said thoughtfully,

returning to meet Jack's eyes.

'Do you, um… *reuse* certain trigger words?'

'Of course. It's a stage act, Stefan uses the same trigger words every night.'

'Does he use the word 'Magpie'?' asked Jack.

Once again, Emily's gaze wandered for a few seconds.

'No,' she said with a shake of her head, 'I don't think so. Why do you ask, Jack?'

He looked over at Cam, who was leaning forward, also interested in his answer.

'It's nothing,' he replied, casually waving the question away with the back of his hand, 'Just something I needed to check.'

Somewhat deflated, Jack concluded Emily was being truthful and was indeed, honest. Apart from knowing they'd attended a stage hypnotists show on that Saturday night, and he had reacted badly to being hypnotised, they were no further forward. That sense of incompleteness was nothing to do with Emily. It was probably a reflection on his own inability to find answers.

Twenty-Two

As they left the café, Cam pulled his jacket collar up and removed his phone from his trouser pocket. It was chilly and the spitting rain was leaving small blobs on the screen as he checked the time. It was a few minutes past eleven. No wonder Jack had been yawning for the last ten minutes inside the Silver Grid Café, he'd started work at five in the morning and had been on the go ever since. Cam gave his friend a gentle clap on his shoulder.

'I can drive back to Malton. You look wiped out.'

'I'll be fine,' Jack replied, manufacturing a tired smile, 'This combination of fresh sea air and drizzle is doing me the world of good. Besides, there's something very wrong with

Corbyn's steering. That pull to the left got even worse on the way over here. I don't want you getting caught out with it.'

Initially, they began the short walk back to the Playhouse car park in silence, passing the white dome of the Empress Ballroom, and a number of sea-front amusement arcades with their shutters firmly closed. Emily had gone off in the opposite direction after apologising once again for not solving their issues and promising to ask Stefan about the young student helpers he employed that night in Scarborough, as well as asking for help from his followers on social media.

Cam noticed Jack was walking with his hands dug into his jacket pockets, his head down, concentrating on a non-existent point of interest always three paving slabs ahead of him.

'What you thinking about?' asked Cam.

Jack slowed to a full stop. They'd left the seafront and were standing on the pavement opposite the now dimly lit Playhouse. The road that led to the coastal drive ran right past the entrance to the theatre. A couple of cars slowed as they drove past, their young drivers and even younger passengers with their windows lowered, elbows poking out, gave them an assessing glare and disappointed, accelerated away to continue around the one-way system. Jack smiled to himself. That had been the highlight of his life three to four years ago, cruising around Sheffield at night, sometimes in a car he knew to be stolen, looking for trouble. He waited for the crackle and popping of their exhausts to die down.

'What am I thinking about?' Jack asked rhetorically, 'Well, pretty much everything. Even though we now know for sure that we were hypnotised last weekend, we're only fractionally closer to working out who the autograph hunter is and why he wanted me to lose races, and for you to mow Savage down and steal his notebook.'

Cam didn't reply, sensing there was more to come. Sure enough, as Jack crossed the road and they entered the theatre car park, heading for Corbyn, he spoke again.

'To be honest, I don't feel completely free of the effects of their hypnosis either. I... Oh, crap.'

There were only a smattering of cars left in the car park, and Jack had purposefully found a space lit by a lamppost. Despite this, the inside of the car remained dark. Even from twenty yards away it was clear the driver's door to the Renault was ajar, the lock and it's barrel hanging from a newly created round hole in the door's steel panel.

Jack immediately grabbed Cam's arm and putting his finger to his lips, directed him into the shadows against the side of the theatre. For the next thirty seconds, Jack simply watched Corbyn. When he was satisfied, they moved closer. At around ten yards away, Jack lay on the ground, checking underneath the Renault. Still at a distance, he walked around Corbyn, examining every tyre, sill, panel, and grill.

Cursing under his breath, Jack looked over at Cam and with a series of hand gestures, told him to stay put, several yards away from the car. Cam watched as Jack approached with care, and in one swift movement, flung open one of the rear doors and stepped back.

'Good evening, Mr Goodman,' said a man's voice from inside the car.

Cam's knees momentarily went wobbly. It was the last thing he'd expected, and was pretty sure he'd jumped back in fright. Yet Jack hardly reacted at all. He simply stood there, hands on his hips, staring in at the thin figure sitting bolt upright in one of the rear seats.

'I wonder whether we might have a nice, quiet chat?' said the man, remaining partially hidden from view.

His voice was far deeper than his size suggested, and it had a wispy, almost too British quality to its delivery. Only after he'd finished speaking did he turn his head to regard Jack.

'My name is Tarquin. Oh, and by the way, this *wasn't* my work,' he said, inclining his head towards the broken door, 'Far too messy. I found it this way. I wish to speak with you and your friend. I decided to take a seat out of the rain while I waited.'

Cam drew closer and altering his angle of approach, was able to define Tarquin's profile. A prominent nose was set between hooded eyes and a heavily furrowed forehead that stretched all the way back to a sparse covering of sandy coloured hair beyond his ears. It gave Cam the impression he had to be in his fifties. A Londoner perhaps? Mixed with the hint of another unidentifiable accent. The charcoal raincoat with collar turned up, dark dress trousers, and highly polished brown brogues made Cam wonder whether Tarquin had a hat to complete the 1950's middle-class gent look.

Without fuss or demand, Jack said, 'Get out of my car... Tarquin.'

Tarquin obediently swung his legs out of the footwell, got to his feet, and leaning back into the car, retrieved a felt trilby with a pale orange band. Placing it onto his head, he softly closed the car door. In the shadow of the theatre wall, Cam fought back a smile, suddenly reminded of those black and white BBC Two films he and his father used to sit and watch on Saturday afternoons.

'Where's the notebook?' Tarquin asked plainly.

Jack's tongue made an audible click of derision and he shook his head, cursing under his breath.

'Savage,' Jack said grimly, 'He still thinks we've got his precious notebook, does he?'

'My client is indeed keen to locate said item,' Tarquin replied, casting his gaze away from Jack and over to Cam, 'Do either of you have it with you?'

Tarquin's half-lidded eyes felt like they were boring into Cam and he found himself shaking his head and mouthing the word, 'No', before he knew what he was doing.

'So where is it, boys? I'm growing tired of searching and all I have left is direct action.'

'I don't have it!' Cam shouted, 'Jack doesn't have it!

We've never had it, and we want nothing to do with it. It would solve all our problems if we did have it, because I'd be handing it over to you right now. But we don't, so we can't.'

The corner of Jack's mouth twitched with suppressed mirth, impressed at Cam's outburst. He turned his twitch into a gesture of 'I told you so' by cocking his head slightly at Tarquin.

'Who was sitting with you in the café?'

Cam looked on with his mouth open, aghast at the thought they'd been followed and watched. Jack didn't move a muscle.

'Just a friend we met at tonight's show,' Jack replied pointing at the Playhouse, and before Cam could offer his response, Jack had added, 'I'm a real fan of stage hypnotism.'

The southerner gave a less-than-impressed sigh and adjusting his Trilby, started to walk away. He stopped after half a dozen paces and changed direction, heading for Cam.

'If the notebook turns up, call this number,' he said, holding out a small card he produced from his pocket.

Cam left his hands by his side. All that talk of hypnotic interrupt handshakes had him wary.

Tarquin locked eyes with him and flicked the card at the boys chest. The card fluttered to the ground, but Tarquin's gaze remained constant until Cam bent down and scooped the card up from the carpark tarmac. Turning on his heel, Tarquin set off again.

'If I discover you've lied to me,' he said over his shoulder, 'You'll never ride a horse again. Neither of you.'

'Why would we lie?' sputtered Cam, throwing his arms in the air.

Tarquin pulled both his lapels up against his neck, tucked his hands deep in his pockets, and walked away in the direction of the seafront without looking back.

***

What an interesting encounter, Cupkiss thought to himself as the boys car pulled away from the theatre car park, its steering rack creaking. It had been worth tailing them.

And this... *Tarquin* who had disappeared from sight around the corner of the theatre. Tarquin... he queried, allowing the name to filter through his mind. It was probably made up. He hadn't recognised him. But Tarquin had known about the loss of the notebook. That was noteworthy. And those boys were young and clueless. But Tarquin? It occurred to Cupkiss that he could do with shedding some light onto this newcomer. Specifically, who he was working for.

Waiting another five minutes for good measure, he emerged from the shadows. He'd been lurking in one of the small recesses in the Playhouse building, close enough to hear their conversation, far enough away to never be spotted. He considered his options for a long moment, then stepped out into the light of a street lamp and peered after Tarquin. With no sign of him, Cupkiss decided to call it a night. The rain was getting heavier, and a nasty little breeze was whipping up. He coughed, dug his hands deep into his coat pockets, set his jaw against the rain, and hurried away.

Twenty-Three

The Northumbrian towns and villages on the coast road from Whitley Bay to Newcastle whizzed past un-regarded by Jack and Cam. It was after midnight and the drizzle had strengthened, making driving a frustrating exercise for Jack, especially when his mind was consumed by what they'd learned from Emily and their conversation with the grimly threatening, yet enigmatic Tarquin.

Jack squinted through an endless torrent of spray being sent up by the car in front. Between his wiper blades scraping annoyingly across his windscreen he noticed with a sinking feeling that a block of grey cloud was hanging above them, removing any chance of a break in the rain, or allowing a few shafts of moonlight to lift his spirits. The dismal weather was indeed a perfect reflection of the mood inside the car.

Emily's information had at least confirmed that his poor rides, and Cam's accident may have been the result of hypnotism. Yet neither he nor Cam had been pleased with this outcome, and where to go from here was weighing heavily on their teenage minds.

'A handshake interrupt. That's what Emily called it wasn't it?' Cam asked from the passenger seat, his face lit by his glowing mobile phone.

Jack kept his eyes on the road and murmured a confirmation.

'According to this website on the art of hypnosis, the handshake interrupt is *an immediate way of shocking or confusing your subject's mind and placing it into a state of increased suggestibility.*'

Cam read on silently then lowered his mobile and thoughtfully contemplated the greasy windscreen and the blaze of lights sending lines of white, red, and yellow sliding across the glass.

'Imagine if all you have to do is shake their hand to hypnotise someone,' he wondered out loud, 'As jockeys, we must shake hundreds of hands every day at the races…'

A playful grin tugged at his lips, 'We could get all the owners doing a conga in the parade ring… or make sure the trainer only jocks you up for the ride on every horse in their yard… You could do *anything*…'

Jack snorted a laugh and shook his head, 'No, you couldn't. You heard Emily, all a hypnotist can do is place a suggestion in your mind. They can't force you to do something against your will.'

'Hold on! Didn't you throw a race?' Cam retorted, 'Wasn't that against your will?'

Jack made to answer, and whilst his mouth opened, he couldn't find any words. Emily had explained he was highly suggestable. Who knew? However, the knowledge that someone might be able to control his mind was worrying. As the journey continued, Jack allowed that thought to percolate.

Emily had promised all remnants of any previous hypnotism had already had been 'cleansed' during their time in the wings at tonight's performance… But how could he or Cam be sure this was the case? The whole idea of someone messing with his head made him feel violated.

'What was it Emily said about you?' Cam remarked into the silence inside the car, 'You're highly susceptible to hypnotism?'

Jack's mood darkened further, 'She said I'm highly susceptible to hypnotic suggestion…' he modified, 'And don't get too cocky, for all we know, someone managed to suggest to you that you should mow down Savage.'

'Mmm… I can't say scaring Savage was against *my will*,' Cam mused, 'I was in a really foul mood with him that morning. Convincing me to ram into him was probably a piece of hypnotic cake.'

'There was no pretend about it. You knocked him unconscious.'

Jack took his eyes off the road for a second and aimed a raised eyebrow at his friend, 'As you can't remember the incident, and no one else was there, we'll never know.'

He paused before adding, 'Actually, everything we heard tonight from Emily could be an elaborate pack of lies… In fact, we could still be hypnotised!'

This landed heavily on Cam. To his mind, Emily had been truthful. She had seemed so… genuine. A feeling of vulnerability swept over him and leaning back into his seat, he unconsciously hugged himself. He consoled himself with the one thing he was sure Emily had been right about when it came to himself and Jack: their minds and motivations were very different. Perhaps that's what had drawn them together and made them firm friends?

Jack returned to staring through the car windscreen.

Gripping the steering wheel firmly with both hands, he tried to ignore the dazzling lights, and concentrated on the slick road, whilst cursing the persistent rain. The headlights of the oncoming cars seemed somewhat brighter tonight and as he approached the entrance to the Tyne Tunnel the combination of streetlights reflecting off the greasy road, and headlights half-blinding him, reactivated his headache from earlier in the evening.

Who was he kidding? Jack asked himself. His headache had nothing to do with street lights and everything to do with being hypnotised, probably by some university student for a stupid prank.

As they entered the Tyne Tunnel, his grip on the steering wheel hardened. Travelling downhill, under the River Tyne, the tunnel ceiling lights began to rush by.

Jack didn't like the idea of someone he didn't know poking around in his mind, uncovering traumas he'd all but forgotten about… his mind had been burglarised. Violated.

Jack blinked hard, his attention being hauled back into the present as he battled with the Renault. Corbyn was pulling relentlessly to the left and the poor visibility afforded by the tunnel lighting wasn't helping. Try as he might, the lights in the tunnel were somehow sending long, reflective streaks down his windscreen, distracting him as they merged and crossed each other. It worsened each time any car got to within twenty yards of him. It was as if their brake lights were aiming a beam right into his retinas. It didn't help that the car following him had headlights that were blinding him when he used his rear view mirror. Not to worry, the tunnel was now on an upward gradient and the steady forty miles per hour speed limit he was adhering to meant there was little chance of an accident. They would be back onto the A19 proper within a matter of seconds and he'd pull over at the first opportunity and get himself together; it had been a long…

Both teenagers jolted forward and the car squirrelled over the double yellow lines in the centre of the dual carriageway and Corbyn swerved into the right-hand lane.

'What the hell?' shouted Cam, bracing himself with hands against the roof and passenger door. Meanwhile, Jack wrestled the Renault back into the left-hand lane to the noise of a blaring horn, care of a fellow driver he'd just cut off.

'It's the car behind,' gasped Jack, his blinking now rapid, adding the blurriness of tears to his visual problems, 'He just rammed us!'

As if to immediately confirm Jack's assertion, Corbyn shunted forwards once more to the sound of a high revving engine noise and a crunch of plastic and metal. This time the steering wheel jolted to the left in Jack's hands, the car bumping up the small kerb and swinging dangerously close to the vertical concrete of the tunnel wall.

Cam shied away from the passenger door, letting out an involuntary whine of concern as the unforgiving grey concrete came within inches of his window. The edge of the wing mirror momentarily scraped against the concrete wall before it snapped backwards with a crack.

'What the hell are you trying to…?'

The smell of burning brake pads and rubber quickly filled the cabin as Jack slammed his foot on the brake and brought the car to a halt half-way across the left-hand lane and the tunnel wall, the nose of the car pointing into the right-hand lane that was still flowing with traffic.

The growl of a six cylinder engine being revved sounded behind them.

'Brace yourself!' warned Jack, waiting for the inevitable thump from behind.

Bewildered, Cam stared over at his friend, but he did as he was told, closing his eyes for good measure.

A squeal of tyres on tarmac saw Jack doing the same. However, his eyes closed for a wholly different reason.

Twenty-Four

Jack was... in the passenger seat? His ears were ringing. Feeling small, he looked around, only just able to see over the dashboard, a white deflated sack splattered with red paint hung incongruously in front of him. Looking up, the windscreen was smashed, long, irregular cracks running to the edges of the glass. And there was blood, some of it must be his. It was pouring from his nose, his hands were streaked dark red, and suddenly there was pain...

A dull ache from various places, his elbow, knees, hips, but it was his face, his forehead and his nose... Christ, his nose felt numb... and *wrong*. But then fear took over. It wasn't finished... There was shouting, a lot of shouting. For the first time he became aware of another person in the car. The driver was clutching his arm, his black skin punctured by a jagged bone. The man... no, the boy lifted his head and gave him a pained, apologetic look.

'Run,' he wheezed, 'Run, kid.'

He could see them coming. Masks or hoods covering their faces, two, no, three of them, massing at the driver's door. Something struck the driver's window and more glass tinkled around the cabin. The door was wrenched open and a pair of strong, unforgiving hands tore... Jacko, his name was Jacko... Jackson, Iman Jackson... outside and onto the tarmac, screaming in pain, and for mercy.

Fear took over, his small, weak hands scrabbled at the passenger door, a click and a kick and miraculously, Jack was out. Iman's screams soon became distant as he ran, short, rapid strides, across the road, past shuttered shops, into a side-street...

'Jack?'

Then into an alleyway, moonlight filling the passageway... cobbles hurting his feet, the sound of steps behind him... a siren and blue lights strafing the end of the alleyway for a heart-stopping second before passing by, allowing darkness and moonlight to return...

'Jack!'

The darkness faded and light, hard artificial light burned Jack's eyes as he fought to open them.

'Thank, God for that!'

It was Cam, bent over him. He was in Corbyn, in the driver's seat, his driver's door open, Cam fiddling with his seat belt. It popped open.

'Get into the passenger seat,' Cam demanded, 'You're in no fit shape to drive. Go on, scootch over, man.'

A car horn sounded angrily behind them, echoing down the tunnel as Jack scrambled over Corbyn's gear lever and landed awkwardly in the passenger seat.

'I'm still in the tunnel,' he marvelled, pulling on his seatbelt as ordered by Cam, becoming aware he wasn't in great pain, only a throbbing from his forehead. However, he was drenched in sweat, feeling sticky, and becoming cold.

Cam got Corbyn going and after an awkward five-point turn, they left the tunnel lights behind. Jack had never been so glad to encounter squally rain and a sky filled with grey clouds. He fiddled with the buttons on the door, eventually lowering the window enough to allow cool night air to circulate, immediately making him feel better. At the first opportunity, Cam pulled off the dual carriageway and into a layby, came to a stop, turned Corbyn's engine off and turned to face Jack.

'How you doing? Feeling better?

'Sure, I've a bit of a headache, otherwise...'

'So what the hell happened to you back there?'

Jack scratched his nose, feeling the bend in it that had never straightened out properly.

'I don't know. Is Corbyn alright? Didn't we... get rammed?'

Cam shook his head vehemently, 'No, we did not! You went a bit white and ghostly, I asked if you were feeling okay and you started veering all over the road, almost smashed me into the tunnel wall, and then slammed all on and ended up blocking both of the southbound lanes. And then...'

Cam squinted at his friend, carefully studying the contours of his face. Jack waved a discouraging hand at him but Cam pushed it aside and carried on with his inspection, especially into Jack's eyes.

'...And then, you just went fsst!' Cam said with a snap of his fingers, 'Out like a light. Scared the living daylights out of me!'

'How long was I out for?'

Cam screwed his mouth to one side, cogitating.

'No more than five or ten seconds. You sort of shook a bit and then you were back out of it, but looking like a zombie. I should be taking you to a hospital...'

'I'm fine,' protested Jack, rubbing his eyes with the heel of his hands, 'I'm just tired. I was winning a Group Two ten hours ago and riding work for my boss eight hours before that!'

Cam shook his head and curled his lips into a pout.

'Blame it on a long day if you want, but I reckon you're still hypnotised. I think Emily didn't get you sorted. As soon as you drove into that tunnel, you started going funny.'

Jack didn't reply at first. Then he politely asked Cam to drive him the rest of the way back home to Malton. They travelled in silence, Cam wrestling with Corbyn and his continual desire to drift into the left-hand-side kerb, and Jack, wrestling with the memory of an event he'd tried to bury in the back of his mind for the last four and a half years.

As Corbyn virtually turned himself off the A19 on the outskirts of Thirsk, Jack remained in a quandary. He felt ready to reveal his past to Cam, but was worried sharing would somehow damage their friendship. He'd had a strong friendship before, and knew its sudden and tragic end had scarred him, and not just physically.

At that moment, Cam straightened Corbyn up and looked over at Jack, grinning like a cheshire cat.

'You going to tell me, then?' Cam asked, comically flexing both his eyebrows.

Jack returned him a blank look.

'You've been squirming around in that seat for the last hour, like your backside is on fire. Something is bugging the heck out of you. Whatever it is, just tell me. It can't be that bad… can it?'

Jack managed a weak smile, and reluctantly opened up. Within seconds, he felt better as his story tumbled out of him. He told Cam how, at the age of thirteen, the car he'd been travelling in had been rammed from behind, the result of a criminal turf war. How he witnessed the fatal stabbing of his seventeen-year-old best friend called Jackson, who'd fancied himself as a drug dealer in Sheffield. He described how he'd run from the scene scared to death, sleeping rough and dodging the other gang members and the police for several days. Eventually he'd been picked up by the police after he'd botched a burglary, spending ten months in borstal and subsequently another fourteen working under supervision at a local riding stables. Cam offered nothing, except the odd nod of his head, until his friend had run out of words.

'You relived all of that in those few seconds in the Tyne Tunnel?'

Jack grimaced, 'It started with the lights. The ones in the tunnel. It was like I was in some sort of trance.'

'Emily did say you were…'

Jack groaned, 'Yeah, I know, I know…'

Once off the A19 the minor road wound its way to Malton and Corbyn managed to turn off left into the town without Cam having to turn the steering wheel. He made a mental note to force Jack to get Corbyn fixed, but decided it could wait until they'd both had a good night's sleep. However, there was something else, far more important, that couldn't wait to be fixed.

'You're still hypnotised,' Cam stated firmly, 'You need to see a doctor, a psychologist, or somebody who can tell us you're not going to go all zombie on me again when someone flashes light in your eyes.'

Jack shook his head, 'I can't risk going to hospital. If the BHA doctor finds out he'll stand me down, and I've got four rides booked for next week and I'm riding work at three different yards on Monday.'

It was half-past-one in the morning and the town was deserted. But despite there only being a couple of taxis prowling the streets, Cam had to stop at the traffic lights in the centre of town and wait for over a minute.

'I need a driver,' Jack announced as they turned right and headed for Norton, 'Do you want the job?'

Before Cam could answer, Jack went on, 'You're not working at the moment, and I've clearly got… issues with keeping Corbyn in a straight line. And I can introduce you to plenty of trainers. I'm sure one of them will give you some riding work, or maybe even a shot at race riding, if we can sort Savage.'

Jack completed his pitch as Cam eased the car into the Racing House drive and switched off the engine. Jack didn't move, anticipating a reaction to his suggestion. Instead, Cam frowned and peering through the windscreen, swearing under his breath.

'What is it? …Cam? What's the matter?'

'See the Range Rover I've parked behind?' Cam said with a sigh.

Jack sat up in the passenger seat and followed Cam's gaze though the rain splattered window to where a dark green lump of a car crouched under one of the mature trees. The registration plate read, 'CAM 392'.

'Bloody Savage must have called her,' Cam groaned, 'My mother's here.'

Twenty-Five

Sebastian Savage woke at five fifty-eight, two minutes before his alarm was due to sound at six o'clock. There was no need for him to be up and about at this time on a Sunday, he had barn managers to check the horses and do the morning feed. No, the reason Sebastian Savage rose at six o'clock was to allow time for his personal grooming and wellbeing regime. Swinging his legs out from between silk sheets, he tapped his alarm once more and Classic FM burst forth.

After showering, exfoliating, and showering again, he deep cleansed, and moisturised. He shaved and plucked. Blessed with a full head of hair despite being in his forty-third year, his attention was then concentrated in his trifold mirror: styled, quaffed, and products introduced to ensure bounce and stability. His final act before leaving his bedroom was to add a pinch of hair thickening powder to the top of his scalp.

Savage appraised his thinning crown and scowled, adjusting a mirror to allow another area specific application. Recently, a pinch of the product had become a sprinkle, and he was afraid it would soon become a full blown dowsing. Holding back time was… time consuming, but well worth it.

At seven-fifteen he entered his walk-in wardrobe and made his choice of outfit for the morning. He swore under his breath as he caught sight of his slight paunch in one of the two back-lit mirrors, and spent a few seconds sucking it in. More expletives left his lips as he battled with the unsightly sling on his broken arm, castigating the dumb, rich, pretty-boy apprentice responsible.

Seven forty-five arrived and Savage was in his kitchen-diner, eating a slice of toast with freshly brewed coffee made with his privately sourced Robusta Beans – Arabica was so middle-classes these days – when his mobile rang, and the name 'MM' flashed up on the screen. He stabbed a finger at the call.

'Did you get it?'

There was a pause, and Savage heard his own, delayed words being repeated to him. It was a poor line. He waited a moment and then barked his question once more.

'Good morning, Savage,' intoned the caller darkly after a short pause.

'Well?' Savage pressed.

'I hope I haven't caught you at an inopportune moment, Savage?' the caller inquired innocently.

This time, Savage picked up on the thinly veiled threat in the man's voice. He held the phone away from his ear and took a breath. It wouldn't be worth upsetting this person.

'My apologies. A very good morning to you. You've caught me between bites of my toast at the breakfast table. Please accept my apologies if I was somewhat abrupt. And how are you?'

'I'm sitting in the driver's seat of my car. The same seat I spent the entire night in, on your behalf, Savage.

'Oh? Really?'

'Yes. Really.'

Savage frowned. What on earth was he supposed to say to that? Did a correct response even exist?

'So... Erm... You slept well?'

There was a pause during which Savage heard something he imagined was the ruffling of an overcoat.

'Does the business name Headingley Hypnotherapy mean anything to you, or the name Emily Harris?'

'I... Mmm... A hypnotist... could be an old... um... flame.'

In truth, he couldn't remember. But that business name... in Headingly. Now he thought... it did ring a bell. Yes... Headingly. He'd had to get his solicitor involved with someone from Headingly in Leeds, hadn't he? A less than straightforward woman... he had a feeling she had something to do with one of his Grey Horse Hustles.

Savage produced a little sly smile. The Grey Horse Hustle was the name he gave to his favourite method of maximising profit from his... less knowledgeable female owners. But that name, Harris, rang no bell. He was the first to admit his memory wasn't too good, even so, he couldn't visualise a face.

'She may be involved in the disappearance of your notebook,' suggested the caller.

'What about Camberley and Goodman?'

'I've spoken with them. They met with this Harris woman last night. I don't believe they have your notebook, although the two of them may well be trying to locate it on your behalf. I assume you're responsible for that?'

'Possibly,' Savage replied, not wishing to reveal the exact nature of the pressure he'd exerted on the two young jockeys.

'They're... rather energetic young men. Camberley is as green as grass, the other one less so. If they're not in possession of your notebook, you may have unwittingly sent them on a hunt for it... The same hunt I'm currently engaged in. Would that be correct, Savage?'

Savage's shoulders dropped. He'd been sure it was them... and he had given them that ultimatum...

'I'll take your silence as an answer in the affirmative,' said the voice, 'I'm not entirely sure that was a sensible course of action.'

'Yes, well, I...'

Savage felt a flicker of indignation light up inside him. His caller was probably right, but it didn't give him the right to point out his paymaster's shortcomings. Noisily clearing his throat, he took on an authoritative tone which he judged to be just the right side of condescending, 'At the time, *I was sure* Camberley had stolen it.'

Pausing a moment to - hopefully - lend some gravitas to his statement, he continued, 'I remember him. As I came to, he was there, Camberley that is, leaning over me, his hands moving across my chest... and fingers touching my neck. No one else was around.'

'No one was around *when you woke up*,' the caller stated levelly, 'When I spoke with the other three work riders, they said it could have been anything between three to five minutes before they caught the loose horse and then cantered back down the gallop to find Camberley with you. That's a window of opportunity of about three minutes for parties unknown to steal your notebook.'

'So Camberley must have seen them! You just need to shake it out of…'

'He may have bowled you over on purpose, Mr Savage,' the caller said, drowning out the rest of Savage's instructions, 'But I doubt Camberley knew of the notebook's existence, and certainly not its significance. Neither of the work riders I spoke with had any knowledge of you using a notebook.'

Savage was dumbstruck. It was true, he only ever made written entries, or consulted it when alone, usually in his rooms in the mansion. He rarely got it out around the yard, it was far too valuable. So who would know about it?

'I assume you take your jacket off inside your residence?' the caller inquired, prompting Savage to wonder if the man was reading his mind, 'And your lady friends are the only people to enter your private rooms who potentially get access or sight of your notebook?'

'Yes?'

'And given Camberley had led us to one of those ladies…'

Savage felt a grin grace his face, 'Ah! I see where you're going with this.'

'I'm waiting for her to leave this small, back street basement-cum-business and I'll attempt a recovery of your notebook.'

The mention of a back street basement had Savage wondering. If this Emily was the woman he'd conjured up in his head, hadn't she owned a swish retail outlet on the main street in Headingley? He cast the thought aside. The retrieval of his notebook was the important thing, and his caller sounded like he was signing off.

'… and I cannot guarantee when that will be. Rest assured, I will report again. Goodbye, Savage.'

'Yes, good…'

But the line was already dead.

Savage spent a minute trawling his mind for any further information about a woman called Harris from Leeds. He had a vague recollection of someone with a Leeds address getting flustered about a horses death certificate. His solicitor had dealt with it. But he could be mistaken. His memory really was poor – which was why he kept everything written down in his notebook. In Savage's estimation, the handwritten word was far more secure than anything kept digitally.

Sucking in a deep breath through his nose, Savage checked the time and crossed over to one of the large arch-shaped windows that overlooked his business. He stared down onto his quad, two barns, and other scattered stables, and his staff and horses, scurrying around ant-like between buildings.

He'd give work a miss today. There was something to be said for being hospitalised and carrying his arm around in a sling… even though it felt absolutely fine already. Besides, that horse, Kaleidoscope was nicely bedded in now and had already shown it was special. The way things were going, the yard would have its first runner at Royal Ascot for over six years.

What, with it looking like his lost notebook would be back in his hands before too long, that dangerous, pretty-boy Camberley off the yard, and Laura Fenwick, his wealthy, and not forgetting, good-looking new owner to concentrate his attentions on, things were finally looking up.

Savage made a call to Miguel, one of his barn managers, giving him instructions and telling him not to expect him on the yard today. After barking a few commands he hung up abruptly and removing his sling, sauntered into his kitchen to make himself another coffee and flick through one of his favourite gentlemen's clothing catalogues.

Twenty-Six

'Good morning, mother. So nice to see you on a Sunday,' Cam mumbled as Mrs Camberley entered the kitchen and took a seat at the island-cum-breakfast bar. She gave her son a sour look and didn't answer.

'So, did you sleep well?' Cam added grumpily from his stool.

He'd spent the night on Jack's floor in a sleeping bag, after the two of them had discovered Mrs Camberley snoring loudly in Cam's bed in the small hours of the morning.

Jack was interested to take a closer look at the woman, now she wasn't rolled up in a duvet and making a noise equivalent to a mis-firing engine. This would be Jack's first exposure to a member of the Camberley family. Cam had passed on several stories of their mutual dislike, and he'd been expecting a harder faced, prim and proper stickler, but on first impressions Mrs Camberley portrayed a much softer image.

They weren't alone in the kitchen-cum-lounge. Sunday mornings were the one time the whole house tended not to start work early. Charlie, in her tantalizingly short bathrobe, was seated beside Mrs Camberley, Olivia was sitting opposite. A fully dressed Grace was curled up on the sofa in front of the communal television, watching the football highlights from the day before and Ben was in one of the armchairs, checking his social media feeds.

'Good morning, Cameron,' Mrs Camberley stated testily in a thick Scots accent, 'Out drinking... and driving last night were we?'

Jack was struck dumb by the fifty-year-old's opening statement. The veracious, sarcastic nature of her comment starkly contrasted with Mrs Camberley's soft features that rested into a smile. He half expected Cam to bite back, but instead he appeared to ignore the comment and sliding down off his stool, pulled open a kitchen unit. He grabbed at a cereal box, located a spoon, and a bowl from the shelves, and added a carton of milk from his designated shelf in the fridge.

'Really, mother?' Cam queried as he crossed back and forth to the breakfast bar, 'You want to do this here, now, in front of my friends?'

Rooted to the spot, Jack was unable to take his eyes off the perfectly poised, elegant Scotswoman with wild raven hair. She revolved on her stool as she followed her son around the kitchen, firing a battery of inflammatory comments regarding Cam's attire, looks, inability to look her in the eye, and in particular, the poor state of his room upstairs.

Cam's answers, if he answered at all, were a weary, monosyllabic, yes or no. Finally, he laid out his bowl and spoon on the island and chose a high-stool opposite his mother.

'I hear you're drinking excessively, unable to do the weight to ride in races, and being argumentative with your employer, whom you also tried to kill… Were you drunk at the time?'

'No,' Cam replied, dipping a spoon into his cornflakes.

Mrs Camberley watched a large spoonful of toasted corn disappear into her son's mouth.

'What is most upsetting is that Mr Savage also reported to me that you've stolen something from him.'

'More upsetting than attempted murder, mother?' Cam fired back.

'Did you steal from him, Cameron?'

'Why, no,' replied Cam through a mouthful of semi-masticated cereal, 'He's a liar.'

'It was this friend of yours. The Borstal boy! He's responsible isn't he? He put you up to these insane acts, didn't he, Cameron?' Mrs Camberley posited whilst jabbing a pointed finger across the kitchen at Jack.

Cam froze for a moment, swallowed, and then dropped his spoon into his bowl with a clank. Slowly raising his head, he stared with the intensity of the righteous into his mother's belligerent gaze. The room held its breath.

Jack had never seen Cam so incensed – it was all in his eyes. Silent and stiff, his friend's disgust hung so heavily in the air, no one dared breathe. Jack hard swallowed, sensing he had to act quickly.

'Hey! Whoa there!' Jack remonstrated, holding his hands up. Olivia sipped at her mug of coffee at the corner of the island, making herself look small, but Charlie was already at Jack's side, arms crossed, ready to wade into the argument as and when required.

'Yes, I know all about you, Goodman,' Mrs Camberley continued, waving a desultory hand in Jack's direction, 'Cameron's boss, Mr Savage, has made it *very* clear what he thinks of your influence on my boy!'

'I bet he has,' Cam said in a soft, condescending tone, 'Tell me, mother, what did the fabulous Mr Savage have to say?'

Mrs Camberley girded herself, keen to deliver her reply in a similarly sober tone.

'He said I should take you home, Cameron. Away from bad influences. Away from all of… this,' said Mrs Camberley with an all-encompassing gesture to the room.

'How very convenient for you,' Cam said sourly, picking up his spoon once more, 'And by any chance did Savage advise you to tether me to the Camberley estate?'

Mrs Camberley took a moment to brush a thumb and index finger thoughtfully through a lock of hair that had fallen across her forehead. Giving out a little sigh, she folded the fingers of both hands together and leaned her elbows on the table, relaxing into a new, but no less confrontational position.

'No, Cameron. You know it's what *I* would like you to do,' she said, lifting her thumbs up like little flags as she finished her sentence.

'However...' she added with a grimace, 'There is the question of the item you stole from him. A notebook, I believe? If you give him his property back he has assured me that he will drop all charges against you. Although he told me you'll never find another job in racing after this incident.'

Cam provided his mother with an amused snort, 'You've had a wasted journey, mother. I'm not coming back to Scotland with you. My home is here. And for the record, I didn't steal anything from Savage. By the way, thanks for not even questioning whether I'm innocent.'

Cam glanced over at Jack for a moment, 'As for never getting another job in racing, I've already found one.'

'Is that so? What about your weight? Mr Savage told me you've let yourself go and you're too heavy for flat racing. You may as well give up, Cameron. Come home with me.'

Jack closed his eyes and shook his head, waiting for the guaranteed eruption. At five feet, nine inches, Cam was tall for a flat jockey. There were a small number of beanpole professional riders out there, but Cam was quite broad in the shoulder. Jack was aware his friend's weight was a major issue for him. Despite strict dieting, Cam struggled to keep at the eight stones, four pounds target weight. Making full use of his apprentices seven pounds allowance was almost impossible on lowly weighted horses.

At times, Jack had become worried Cam had overdone it, his skin becoming sallow and drawn in order to prove he was capable of making the weight in non-apprentice races. The withdrawal of sauna facilities at racecourses hadn't helped. But raising the issue with Cam only led to him initially biting back, and subsequently, withdrawing into himself. Jack had learned to steer clear of the subject, keeping shtum whenever the topic arose.

Cam's response to his mother, or rather, eruption, was swift, direct and largely, successful. Not without dexterous skill, Cam skimmed his bowl of half-finished cornflakes across the tabletop at his mother.

Unable to unfold her hands quickly enough, the bowl shot over the lip of the table, flipped, and the contents landed neatly into Mrs Camberley's lap. Cam remained stony-faced as his mother staggered to her feet and started to brush the milk and soggy flakes of corn off her crotch and onto the floor, whilst issuing a torrent of inflammatory language at Cam, sprinkled with expletives. Her son remained sitting stoically on his stool as solid as a statue, his mother's accusations and demands seemingly blunted by his indifference.

Grace started to giggle, but retreated to the sofa when Mrs Camberley straightened and aimed an intimidating glare at her.

'I think it's best if you leave, Mrs Camberley.'

It was Charlie. She handed her a tea towel and waited.

'You're coming with me, Cameron,' Mrs Camberley said, snatching the proffered towel. She balled it up and tossing it onto the table after a few inefficient wipes, 'Go get your things.'

'No way,' Cam hissed.

'Yeah, jog on,' Jack added.

'How dare you speak to me like that, you...'

'There are a number of us becoming very uncomfortable with you being here,' Charlie interjected before another round of tit-for-tat name-calling could develop, 'And I must warn you that the house has a security system with a panic button that links directly to the local police station.'

This news initially had a positive effect on Mrs Camberley. Scanning the young faces around the room, and particularly Charlie's, she realised any further argument would be non-productive. Rolling her shoulders, she turned to leave, but halted, lifted her arm to point an accusing finger at Cam, and delivered her parting shot.

'Why waste your time here, Cameron? You're better than this. You should be at home with your sister and me. It's your duty as a Camberley. Your destiny is to run the estate.'

Cam crossed his arms, 'I disagree. I control my destiny, not you.'

Mrs Camberley locked eyes with her son and the kitchen fell silent. A withholding of breath among the main protagonists signalled an important impasse had been reached.

Mrs Camberley drew in a long breath. She'd seen that look in her boy's eye in the past. It was the same one his father used to give her when he'd been alive. Receiving the phone call from that Savage man had been bad enough, both embarrassing and demeaning. With Cameron not accepting her calls, she'd been forced to come in person to Malton. It had been a four hour drive to get here, and then she'd had to stay overnight because her son wasn't anywhere to be found. It had been bad enough having to sleep in that pokey, terribly messy room of his, but washing the family's dirty linen in front of these youngsters was unacceptable! This whole situation was unacceptable. Frustrated and feeling belittled and beaten, Mrs Camberley resorted to uttering the words she knew would sting her son the most.

Maintaining her gaze, Mrs Camberley wetted her lips and in a tone she judged would depict her feeling of betrayal and deep disappointment, she told her son, 'Your father will be turning in his grave.'

Twenty-Seven

Jack was puzzled. Whenever the subject of the Camberley family had arisen, Cam had always spoken as if his father was very much alive…

It only took a few seconds of reflection for Jack to replay a select few of those moments in his head, before he came to realise how blind he'd been. There had been a variety of clues he should have picked up on. However, this wasn't the time to reflect on his failure to read his best friend. Right now he had to ensure Cam didn't end up killing his mother. He'd never seen him quite so angry.

While Charlie helped bundle a fearful, yet still resolute Mrs Camberley out of the house, Jack kept Cam ensconced in the kitchen through a combination of speaking soothing common sense, and delivering a number of threats. Once Mrs Camberley's Range Rover had departed it took a further ten minutes before Cam calmed down, by which time Ben was hovering, set on discovering more about Cam's home life.

Ben had busy-body tendencies. An annoying sort, he spent most of his time in the house sucking up to the girls and finding reasons to make barbed comments about the remaining residents. Ben was particularly outspoken when it came to Jack, never missing an opportunity to produce an outpouring of scathing words about his fellow apprentice. Jack had no idea why.

Jack swiftly suggested Cam and he went up to his room. As they headed for the stairs, Jack's phone burbled and he checked a message, blinking in surprise. This, at least, should cheer Cam up.

The door to Cam's bedroom was only partially fixed, hanging on one hinge and the lock still missing, thanks to Savage's boot. So Jack was careful to handle the battered door with kid gloves as he hurried Cam through. As soon as the light was flicked on, both boys were of the same mind: someone had ransacked the room.

'What the hell! Can you believe my mother?' gasped Cam as he took in the sight of all his clothes and personal belongings strewn across the floor, 'It looks like a bomb's hit the place.'

'I'm not sure you can blame this on your mother,' Jack said, carefully picking his way across the room, tiptoeing between clothes, books, drawers, and other assorted detritus. He reached Cam's bedside table and righted a photo of Cam with his family that had been knocked over. He'd seen it before, but now homed in on the similarities between an eleven-year-old Cam and his father, the two of them smiling. They were on a beach somewhere hot. He was a similar build to his son, and Cam had definitely benefitted from his father's Nordic good looks.

'Your mother said your room was a mess. It was pretty much her first comment when she met you in the kitchen this morning. It may have been like this when she got here last night. Because we could hear her snoring, all we did was poke our noses in here when it was pitch black, and we were dog tired. I doubt we'd have noticed if it was like this.'

'You think someone was in here before my mother arrived... looking for that bloody notebook?'

Jack rubbed the back on his neck, 'Yeah. About that notebook...'

'What about it?' asked Cam vaguely, his back to Jack, already busy restoring his belongings back into their correct places.

'You said it was about four inches by five, bright red leather with a raised paisley pattern on its cover?'

'Yeah, well, I only saw it once. The barn manager, Dean, told me more about it. He saw it close up and reckoned Savage kept details of all his female conquests in it...'

Cam turned to pick up his next bundle of clothes and found Jack, smiling apologetically, and dangling his phone in front of him. It showed a photo. It was a little blurred, probably taken in haste, but the image definitely showed a small, bright red notebook.

'Savage's notebook?' Cam boggled.

'From...' he checked the sender, 'Emily?'

Jack nodded.

'She's just sent it, well... forwarded it. And there's a message. Like she promised, before she left the café last night she posted a request to all of Stefan's followers on social media, asking whether anyone had seen, or picked up a missing notebook at the Scarborough gig. She says a boy replied almost immediately on her messaging app, and I should call her. That's all she's said.'

'Right! Let's get to the bottom of this,' Cam said brightly.

Jack tapped the call icon on his phone and set the call on speaker.

Emily picked up almost immediately, 'Hi Jack.'

'So this boy has the notebook?'

'Yes, it's good news isn't it?'

'Yes, of course. Do you have it then?' Cam asked.

'Oh... Hi Cam. No, this boy, well... I think he's a student, still has it. He said he's going to send it in the post to you. Give me your address and I'll pass it on to him.'

'Do you know this student?'

'No. He said he was acting on behalf of a friend who had made a big mistake and wanted to put it right.'

Jack asked, 'Did you speak with him? Or video call? What did he look and sound like?'

'Sorry, it was all by WhatsApp text messages. I did try to call him, but he'd already blocked my number and kept his own private. I guess he wanted to remain anonymous.'

'Okay, Emily. That's sound work, by the way. The social media thing was a great idea,' said Jack.

Emily paused a moment before accepting Jack's praise with a flurry of thankyou's.

'No worries, I'm just glad it's worked out okay,' she added, 'I have a good feeling he will post the notebook to you. I did ask him how he, or his friend, came across it, but he said he'd rather not say.'

'I bet he did,' Cam replied sarcastically.

Jack picked up the conversation, 'Okay, well, I'll send you the address over in a text message, and once again...'

'He did say something in his last message that was a bit strange though,' Emily interrupted, as if she'd just remembered something she had to get out.

Jack and Cam shared a hopeful look.

'He said, *I don't know what all the fuss is about. This*

notebook is full of rubbish,' related Emily, sounding as if she was reading from her phone, 'I asked him what he meant, and he replied, *'You'll see!'*

'If nothing else, it does sound like he intends to follow through and send it to us,' Cam reasoned.

Jack nodded his agreement, but soon changed the subject.'

'I suffered a few… seconds of a… umm, *dreamlike* state on the way home last night, Emily.'

'He's underplaying it,' Cam broke in, 'Jack almost crashed his car in the Tyne Tunnel. And I reckon he looked hypnotised.'

Jack rolled his eyes at Cam. He grinned back.

'Anyway, I was just wondering what you thought.'

'He shouldn't be driving, should he?' interjected Cam.

Emily didn't answer for a long moment. When she did, she started with a heavy breath.

'You were there, Cam. You know how long it took me to bring Jack out of his hypnotic state last night. The mind is a fragile instrument and some people can suffer lasting effects if they've had someone mess around and not bring them out of a trance in a controlled, properly managed way. But saying that, you said you were in the Tyne Tunnel. I suppose the regular spacing of the tunnel lights could have triggered a hypnotic state. Also, you were yawning and struck me as very tired when you left me in the café. The combination of being hypnotised earlier in the evening leaving you still quite open to suggestion, the lights in the tunnel, and sheer tiredness, may have culminated in placing you in a short hypnotic episode.'

'Episode?' queried Jack in a worried voice, 'You mean I had a fit?'

Emily was quick to reassure him.

'No. It's very unlikely indeed that you had an epileptic fit, Jack. You probably just zoned out for a few seconds. A good night's sleep is all you need. Resting your mind should see you back to normal.'

Cam smiled wryly, 'No worries there then, Jack! I'm sure you'll sleep like a baby knowing we're in danger of losing our careers. Oh, yes, being persecuted by both my mother and Savage will help make you sleepy. And I'm sure the threats by some scary joker called Tarquin won't have you tossing and turning!'

'Your mother? And Tarquin?' Emily repeated with a questioning inflection.

Jack jumped in, 'Oh, don't pay any attention to him. Cam and his mother are always at it, and the other chap is just someone trying to convince me to become my agent. We bumped into him recently and he won't take no for an answer. Don't worry about either of them, I'm certainly not.'

As he was speaking, Jack mimed cutting his throat to Cam, his eyes wide in warning. Cam responded with a grumpy shrug and mimed zipping his mouth.

Profusely thanking Emily once again, Jack finished the call, promising to send her a new message with their full postal address. As soon as he hung up, Jack was tapping it out on his mobile. Cam watched him for a short time before he spoke.

'You came up with that stuff about Tarquin pretty quickly, Jack. Why lie to her?'

'It comes naturally. You seem to forget I was a professional liar until I met you,' he said, sending the message on its way.

'That doesn't answer my question.'

Jack stowed his phone and went to Cam's bedroom door, 'I didn't want her worrying about a scary bloke in a raincoat pitching up at her next performance. She's never mentioned a husband, partner, or any family so I'm guessing she lives alone.'

'Right. Yes… that makes sense,' Cam agreed.

Gently cracking the bedroom door open, Jack added, 'Oh, and can you keep quiet about my little blip in the car last night. I don't want the BHA doctors or Cupkiss getting wind of it. They might not take Emily's explanation as gospel, and they'll use any excuse to stand jockeys down at the moment. I've got a ride tomorrow at Southwell and plenty later in the week.'

'Errmm…'

'Cam? I never like it when you make that sort of noise. What have you done?'

'I may have mentioned to everyone at breakfast me driving you back home last night because you had a funny turn…'

'Everyone?'

Cam nodded, 'Before you came downstairs. I got fed up of waiting for you to finish your shower. It was just to warn everyone that my mother had stayed over. I didn't want the girls wondering who she was, or getting upset, and we got talking…'

'Was Ben there?'

Cam crumbled inside, whilst outwardly displaying a look of desperate apology.

Jack leaned his back against the bedroom wall and visibly wilted.

Twenty-Eight

Tarquin checked out of the Leeds Metropole hotel, and reunited with his car, he was back in Headingly fifteen minutes later. Parking up, he settled down for another potentially long wait. He'd waited all of Sunday for the woman to leave her house-cum-business premises, but she'd stubbornly remained inside all day. Defeated, he'd decided to return the following day.

It was now eight-thirty. Locking his car, he walked the same circuit of the backstreet he'd covered a dozen times before the previous day. His tour provided him with the opportunity to pass the front of the three-storey terraced house twice and secure surreptitious glances into two of the ground floor room windows and one in the basement. The second basement room window was blocked out – he assumed this was the treatment room. On his first pass, he hadn't time to be sure, but on the second the street had been clear of pedestrians and he was able to pause and make a proper check. It was dark, quiet, and Tarquin smiled to himself when he noticed the lock on the basement door was a basic lever.

The car he'd tailed to the house was still parked where the woman had left it. That meant she was either still sleeping, or she'd gone out on foot.

Tarquin decided to take his chance. Walking carefully down the stone steps he reached the front door. Its glass pane provided a view straight into what appeared to be a small waiting room in the basement. Beside a hanging notice that said, 'Sorry, we're CLOSED', a handwritten sign sellotaped to the glass announced, 'Please ring bell and wait to be admitted.'

Tarquin rang the bell and waited, keeping an eye out for any returning local residents. Twenty seconds later he bent down and began toying with the lock.

'Hey! You! Get away from my door!' Emily screamed.

Tarquin scrabbled on the mat outside and when he straightened he was holding his phone.

'I dropped my phone. My apologies if I scared you in any way,' he said confidently and calmly, but loud enough to be heard through the closed door, 'I simply wished to ask a question.'

Ignoring the fact the woman was wearing a dressing gown that barely met in the middle, Tarquin kept his gaze unwaveringly at eye level. He wished to place Emily at her ease, but she was also aware of her potential wardrobe malfunction, tightly holding the garment together with both hands.

'We're shut,' Emily snapped, 'And we won't be re-opening any time soon. I'd like you to leave.'

She turned and headed for a half-open door he'd missed on his initial reconnoitre. A set of stairs, presumably up to the first floor, were just visible.

'I'm working for a client who is keen to recover a small, red notebook with a raised paisley pattern,' he called after her.

Emily paused with her back to the man. She didn't like the idea of a strange, unknown, raincoated man calling at her door at all hours and considered what level of answer might get rid of him, and keep him away.

'It's been posted to Cam and Jack in Malton,' she called over her shoulder, 'It'll be there tomorrow.'

***

Jack's Monday morning had started well, turned bad, and then gone downhill from there.

After riding four lots of work at Paddy Doherty's stables, Jack had made a late-morning trip over to Freddie Jones' yard on the other side of Malton and taken Rosy Glow onto his grass gallop to complete a piece of fast work. The colt was in scintillating form, and Jack had known they'd done something special as they pulled up. Stopwatch in hand, Freddie had beamed at the two of them once they'd stepped off the gallop. Rosy Glow had recorded a couple of back-to-back ten and a half second furlongs – easily equating to group quality sprint times. The colt was so well and full of himself, the only worry Jack shared with the trainer was that Rosy Glow might be *too* fresh by the time they reached the third week in June for the straight six furlongs at Royal Ascot.

With the main event of the morning over, Jack was alone on the gallops astride a handicapper, another of Freddie's horses, when he received a call from John Cupkiss. It soon became clear that Savage had made good on his threat to bring his riding career crashing about his ears. Cupkiss coolly informed him that he was in possession of an audio recording that, if proven legitimate, could involve a lengthy riding ban for bringing the sport into disrepute, and if so, would most likely require the BHA to forward the evidence to the police.

'I'm standing you down for three days, Mr Goodman' Cupkiss had told him in an officious tone, 'To allow me time to investigate the allegations.'

'What allegations, exactly?'

'That without provocation, you physically assaulted Mr Sebastian Savage at your Racing House accommodation in Malton.'

Jack considered whether to respond with a detailed denial there and then, but decided not to bother. Cupkiss would follow due process. As long as the notebook turned up in the post as promised, both he and Cam would hand it back to Savage and put this whole sorry episode behind them before the end of the week. All the bad blood with Savage, the hypnotic autograph hunter, Tarquin, and Cam's issue with his mother would then, hopefully, fade away.

'Your agent has been informed, Mr Goodman. It means you cannot take the ride at Southwell today, or expect to ride until the weekend at the earliest,' continued Cupkiss, 'Expect me at Racing House later this week to take your statement. To be clear, you should not attend any licensed premises until this matter is resolved one way or the other.'

With his mind in a whirl, Jack didn't answer immediately and so Cupkiss seized the initiative.

'If you want my advice, son… swallow your pride and get Savage to change his mind. If you were able to somehow convince Mr Savage to withdraw his accusation, we could nip this matter in the bud before I submit my findings to the relevant authorities.'

'And how would I go about that, Mr Cupkiss?'

Jack was sure he'd heard Cupkiss give an amused snort.

It sounded like he'd asked the question Cupkiss had been anticipating.

'Good move, Mr Goodman,' he replied, his tone warming, 'Speak to Savage. Don't allow the situation to escalate. Sort Savage out with whatever he wants before this complaint goes any further.'

Twenty-Nine

Jack got back to the Racing House in a frustrated, but determined mood. It was just past one o'clock on Monday afternoon and he'd refrained from calling or messaging Cam, deciding to update him face-to-face about Savage's complaint and being stood down by Cupkiss. At this time in the afternoon the house would usually be quiet, with only a couple of the residents around, most probably watching TV, catching up on some sleep, or playing video games in their rooms. It was a something of a shock to hear the mother of all rows seeping out of the house even before he'd opened the front door.

Most of the anger was being delivered with undiluted vitriol by a pair of females. Quietly dropping his riding kit in the hall, Jack made his way into the lounge and found Grace and Charlie nose-to-nose, shouting blue murder at each other, and between them, Cam, trying desperately to prise the two of them apart. Olivia and Ben were also there, looking on from the sidelines in the kitchen area. Olivia looked stricken, hugging herself and wincing with every new accusation that was flung back and forth. Meanwhile Ben was smirking gleefully at Cam's failure to bring the argument under control.

'I overheard her, that's how I know. It was her, I'm sure of it!' Grace insisted in a shout, poking a stiff, accusatory index finger into Charlie's shoulder.

Charlie, with arms crossed, her eyes narrowed, stood her ground, 'Poke me one more time and I'll bite that finger of yours clean off.'

'I heard you talking to Savage in your room,' Grace said in a base tone, 'You must have been planning when to raid Cam's room!'

'Really? Funny how that's the excuse you're using, because you opened the door to Savage the day he smashed Cam's door down,' Charlie retorted, 'There was no knock, or I would have heard it. From my room I can hear everyone who comes up to the house. And saying you just happened to be around won't wash, you were hanging around, waiting for him. I could hear you, the floorboards in the hall were squeaking.'

Grace pushed her bottom lip out as she decided how to respond.

'I opened the front door! I happened to be there. What's the big deal? You're the one who scuttled off to York when you heard Cam was being questioned at the police station. Why would you do that? Savage sent you to get his notebook back, didn't he?'

'I went to the police station because Cam's a friend!' Charlie shot straight back, 'And I thought he'd appreciate the company. A police station isn't a nice place to be alone in!'

Grace paused a moment and a sly smile creased her lips.

'Had experience of police stations then?' Grace goaded, pushing Cam aside, 'So it *was* you that turned over Cam's room, you little sneak thief...'

A triumphant Grace turned her head to face a tongue-tied Cam and announced, '...I told you it was her earring!' Which was when Charlie took the opportunity to land a powerful slap to Grace's cheek.

Olivia let out an involuntary shriek, and her eyes bulged, radiating a combination of shock and embarrassment.

To her credit, Grace took the slap well, simply rotating her jaw and ignoring the powerful urge to put her hand to her face. Stiffening for a moment, she slowly turned her head back to glower at her foe as her cheek, already pulsing with pain, turned a hand-shaped red. Taller and rangier than Charlie, Grace took a quick step forward and threw a straight, right-handed punch, landing it squarely into Charlie's mouth.

Jack had been making quiet progress across the lounge towards the two girls. He now dived between them, making sure to bundle Grace far-enough away to ensure she couldn't follow up with another punch or kick. Cam took Charlie in the opposite direction.

'Oh, please!' Grace harrumphed as Jack sat her down on the end of the sofa and stood over her, 'Anyone can see she's trying anything to shift the blame elsewhere!'

In a low, almost menacing growl, Jack said, 'Take a breath, both of you!

It had the required effect. All six people in the room looked over, or up at Jack, and joined in a silent hiatus.

'Now, can someone please tell me how these two have come to blows over an earring?' Jack asked once the tension in the lounge had eased.

'I found an earring in my room when I was clearing up the mess left by my intruder on Saturday night,' Cam explained, 'I brought it downstairs, and asked if anyone recognised it. Grace and Charlie each reckoned the other one owned it and before I knew it, all hell broke loose!'

'I could have guessed this argument was all Cam's fault. What a surprise!' Ben said sarcastically.

'Shut up, Ben,' Jack and Charlie said, virtually in sync.

Olivia came forward with a tissue and started dabbing at Charlie's busted lip, shaking her head at the amount of blood she was mopping up.

'Thanks, but I'm okay,' Charlie said, not unkindly as she waved Olivia away.

Cam watched on, reminded that as a breed, stable lasses were made of stern stuff. They could expect regular kicks, falls, bumps, bashes and bruises from being around horses and stables for up to ten hours a day. To most of them, a busted lip was nothing to get too excited or worried about.

'Where's this earring then?' Jack asked, looking around at the group, one by one.

Cam went to the kitchen island and picked up something small, silver, and moon-shaped, carefully placing it in Jack's hand. He took a quick look then turned to Charlie.

'It's okay, Charlie. Go get yourself cleaned up.'

He cast his gaze over to Grace on the sofa, 'You want to do this here, or in your room?'

***

Twenty minutes later, Jack and Cam left a tearful Grace sitting on her bed, being tended to by a shocked Olivia. Clicking her door shut, they wearily warned a loitering Ben to stop hanging around in search of gossip and climbed the stairs once he'd scuttled off into the lounge.

'Let's go up to your room, otherwise Ben will hear everything we say through my busted door,' suggested Cam.

At the top of the house and with Jack's door firmly closed, Cam fell onto his friend's bed face down and gave out a frustrated 'Aaargh!' into the bedclothes.

'If we needed any confirmation that there are people out there willing to go to any length to get this blasted notebook back, then we've got it now,' Jack sighed, leaning up against the wall.

He'd just learned that Grace had not only searched through Cam's room, but had also worked her way through his. Looking around his room now he was struck by how bare it was compared to Cam's. According to Grace, it hadn't taken much searching and she'd left everything in its proper place, coming out empty-handed.

Cam rolled over onto his back and lay like a dead weight, arms out, feet dangling over the end of the bed, staring up at the ceiling.

'Why didn't she just tell us?' he suggested with a tired

sadness.

Jack allowed a contemplative silence to develop before saying quietly, 'Don't be too harsh. It wasn't her fault.'

After explaining to Grace that he'd recognised her earring from their chat in the early hours a few days earlier, she'd argued that Charlie or Ben must have planted it in Cam's room. Jack had gone on to point out that she'd let slip that she knew the would-be thief was trying to locate a notebook.

'There's no way you could know that, unless you did the searching,' he'd told her, 'Savage didn't mention what he thought Cam had stolen when he was here the other day. In fact, he's been quite guarded about what he's lost... So who asked you to search Cam's room for a notebook?'

'And your room,' she'd replied, tears beginning to flow, 'My key opens every door in the place if you jiggle it a bit. So will yours if you try it. I searched your room first and was careful, then Cam's, but his mum turned up and I had to rush, so stuff ended up all over the floor and I had no time to clean up. I must have lost my earring as I rushed to get out.'

A long apology had followed, along with a plea not to report her to either the charity that ran the Racing House, or the police.

'That depends,' Cam had pointed out, 'Tell us who put you up to this.'

'It started with a phone call,' Grace had told them, 'Three calls, the first last Tuesday. It was always from a withheld number and the caller was the same man each time.'

'He said I was to try and find a red notebook that had been stolen by one of you,' Grace had added between sniffles, 'I had to search your rooms when you were out racing on Saturday afternoon, but Ben was hanging around the house all day so I couldn't start until he went out at eight o'clock in the evening.'

'And what did this chap pay you?'

'What? Nothing!' Grace had replied indignantly,

becoming more confident, 'He threatened to hurt my kid sister if I didn't do it. He knew where she lived. Knew the house, the road. Even knew which school she went to in Bootle and what class she was in! I haven't slept for days, which is why you caught me in the kitchen at three in the morning. For the last few days I've been constantly calling my mum to make sure she and my sister are okay!'

Cam had asked whether the man had called back. Grace had confirmed he'd rung on Sunday morning. It was a short conversation. Learning she'd come up empty-handed he'd sworn a lot and rung off. That was the last she'd heard from him.

'Do you believe her?' Cam asked.

'Yeah, I can't see why not,' Jack replied, 'You saw how she reacted when we told her the notebook would be back where it belonged in the next couple of days... talk about relieved!'

Cam had rolled over and was sitting upright on the edge of the bed.

'Do we agree it was Savage on the phone to Grace, threatening her sister?

'She seemed to think so, although the voice she described wasn't anything like his.'

'Mmm... She called it a deep voice that always sounded angry,' mused Cam, 'That sounds like Savage.'

'It could be anyone,' Jack sighed, 'But I was thinking of that bloke who called himself Tarquin.'

'Good God, yes!' Cam exclaimed, 'He did know about the notebook. He had a fairly deep voice and I bet he's working for Savage.'

'He wasn't angry when we met him the other night,' Jack noted, 'Tarquin was incredibly calm.'

The boys shared a glum frown.

'The sooner we get that notebook back to Savage the better for everyone,' Cam said, 'I can't believe how belligerent he's been about it. Whatever he's written in it must be important.'

Jack smiled wryly, 'You got any ideas what it might be?'

Cam rolled his tongue around a cheek, crinkling his eyes in thought, 'Poems. Really bad poems he's embarrassed about. Or a book... maybe he's written his autobiography? Blimey, can you imagine how boring that would be... Or...

'A record of his bets?' Jack offered, 'Or maybe it's just all the notes he makes about his horses, plans for runs, that sort of thing. After all, he was on the gallops with it in his pocket when he lost it.'

Cam shook his head and grinned, starting to enjoy the game, 'Miguel, one of the barn managers at the yard reckons it's a record of his female conquests!'

'Or male conquests!' Jack said with wide amused eyes.

The two boys barked out a laugh each.

Cam waved his finger from the bed, 'No way! I've heard him talking to female owners. It's sickening the way he fawns over them. I reckon that notebook will be full of nasty stuff he's written about everyone in racing, owners, staff, jockeys, trainers, and breeders, and he doesn't want it ruining his reputation. He strikes me as that sort.'

'I guess we'll see when the notebook arrives,' Jack said thoughtfully, 'I've just got a text from Emily. The autograph hunter has been in touch. He's said the notebook will be delivered to us in tomorrow's post.'

'Aren't you racing tomorrow?'

Jack's face fell. In all the excitement he hadn't told Cam about his riding license being suspended.

'No, I'm not riding work, or going racing at all this week, thanks to Savage,' he replied, and went to explain why.

Once he'd answered Cam's final question about the call with Cupkiss, Jack pushed himself off the wall and said he was going to speak with Charlie and tell her about Grace. Cam beat him to the bedroom door and insisted he should be the one to report in and make sure she was okay.

'You going to ask her out?' Jack grinned, determined to not become depressed if the answer was yes.

'Let's both go,' Cam said, pleased to see Jack in relatively good heart, given the dreadful news he'd just shared, 'We can console each other when she turns both of us down.'

Thirty

The post was delivered to the Racing House at around eleven in the morning. Anything thrust through the front door with its large, old-fashioned letterbox, complete with brass shutter, would usually lie on the hallway floor until after one-o'clock, when the first resident got home after morning stables.

Jack and Cam were ensuring that wouldn't be the case today. They were on lookout. As soon as their postwoman pushed the mail through, they would be ready to catch every item, specifically any package that could contain a small, red notebook.

They'd assumed the house would be theirs alone this morning, given they were both unable to work, however it transpired that Ben also had the day off. Cam had tried to befriend the yard man when he and Jack first arrived at the Racing House, but the twenty-three year old had made himself difficult to like. Despite their best efforts, Ben still treated the two of them, especially Jack, as interlopers. A slightly creepy way of being around the girls, combined with his tendency to attempt to know everyone's business, didn't help his cause. However, most annoying was Ben's habit of popping up when you least needed him and then hanging around on the periphery of private conversations. Incapable of taking a hint, he was often the last person left in the lounge on an evening, slowly driving each resident back to their bedrooms, rather than remain in his company.

By ten o'clock on Tuesday morning, Ben was well on the way to winding Jack up. Laid on the sofa, Ben had been peppering both Jack and Cam with questions about the girls' argument the day before, and then moved on to divining why they were both at home on a workday. Amazingly, the news of Jack's suspension hadn't reached Ben's ears yet.

Jack and Cam had been camped out in the kitchen area since nine o'clock, nervously checking the driveway through the nets at the front window every few minutes for any sign of Margaret, their usual postwoman. Easily of pensionable age, Margaret spent as much time chatting to the townsfolk as she did delivering their mail, making her and her red trolley a regular sight on the streets of Norton and Malton.

'You both seem obsessed with the driveway this morning. Expecting anyone?' asked Ben.

He'd already made the same query in a number of different ways. Jack snapped, tired of his nasal voice and having to skip around the truth.

'Listen, Ben. It would really help us if you just beggared off back to your room for an hour, okay?'

'Mmm... must be an important visitor then,' Ben replied, with a self-satisfied smirk, 'No, it's fine, thank you. I'll stick around and find out who it is.'

As Jack bristled at the kitchen window, Cam decided to try a different tack.

'Actually, we're waiting for Margaret, the post...' he strung this last word out, searching for the correct way to finish, finally plumping for, '...person.'

Ben sat up on the sofa, his interest piqued. Unable to comprehend why Cam would want to share this information, especially with such a gossip, Jack began to object, but Cam immediately closed him down.

'Yes, we're expecting a delivery,' Cam continued, 'But it needs to be signed for. I was wondering... given you're sticking around, could you stay here and sign for us? I guess it could be anything up to another hour... or two? Jack and I were thinking of going for a game of snooker.'

Cam waited with an expectant expression as the interest drained from Ben's eyes. There was no way he'd want to do them a favour.

Ben yawned, 'Sorry, Cam. I'm going out myself... was just on my way to get ready.'

Once Ben had climbed the first flight of stairs on his way to his room at the top of the house, Jack clamped a hand onto Cam's shoulder.

'... And the Oscar for best performance of a manufactured exit goes to...'

'Never mind that,' Cam grinned, 'Keep a lookout for Margaret.'

***

Postwoman Margaret Steele was in the process of pushing her Royal Mail trolley around the corner of St Peter's Street when she ran into the man standing squarely in the middle of the footpath.

'My apologies,' said Tarquin with a broad smile, stepping aside, 'I didn't see you coming.'

Margaret eyed the raincoated man keenly and for a moment, wondered how he'd been able to miss a huge trolley carrying what had often been described by passing townsfolk as a 'red coffin'.

'That's alright, my love,' replied Margaret amiably, noting how well turned-out the man was for his age in his expensive raincoat and brogues, 'This trolley has a mind of its own sometimes!'

He backed up to the nearby hedge and she pushed on past, however the man fell into stride with her as she set off up Langton Road.

'Actually, it's fortuitous I've bumped into you. I'm looking to visit my nephew, and I'm struggling to find his house. Perhaps you could point me in the right direction? His name is Cameron Camberley?'

'Cameron? Oh, aye, I know Cam. Very nice boy. Only moved here... ooh, September year before last. He's at number twenty-three. This side, just up there,' she said, pointing.

Tarquin's gaze followed her finger, but only for a moment. He knew exactly where the Racing House was. He'd already walked past it twice this morning, and also cased the alley at the back of the apprentice's accommodation.

Margaret came to a stop, engaged the trolley's brake. Checking her handheld device, she unlocked the shiny red box on her trolley.

Remaining by Margaret's side, Tarquin quickly studied the contents of the box. He tried not to show his disappointment. It was almost full, with too many packages and packets to choose from. There'd be no swift locate, grab and leave.

Margaret's fingers riffled through until she located a small bundle of letters held together with an elastic band. She did a cursory double-check of the address and closed the box with a definite click. Tarquin held onto a disgruntled sigh in his throat, not letting go of it until Margaret, in her bright Royal Mail red jacket, blue shorts, and walking boots was pushing the bundle though the letterbox of number fifteen. He greeted her return with another broad smile.

'I tell you what, if you have anything for Cameron, or for his friend, Jack Goodman. I can take them for you. They're jockeys you know!'

Whilst Margaret liked to chat, she'd held onto her position as a postwoman for thirty years for two reasons. She always finished her round, even if it took a bite out of her own free time, and she rarely got a delivery wrong. She'd learned the hard way that no one could be trusted to deliver a letter or a parcel as accurately as herself.

'That's kind of you, my love. But if it's all the same to you, I'll do the deliveries.'

'That's a shame,' said Tarquin, allowing his face to register disappointment, 'Just thought I could help, and it would be nice to turn up on his doorstep with something for him.'

Recognising that the man had begun to try just a smidgeon too hard, Margaret gave Tarquin a sharp look.

'More than my job's worth, my darlin',' she told him, 'But say hello to Cameron for me.'

She moved away up the road. Tarquin watched the postwoman lock her trolley, open the next garden gate and walk purposefully up another pathway to another front door. He'd have to bide his time. He crossed the main road and walked a little way up a side-street, stopping at a point where he was hidden from the main road but could monitor the postwoman's progress to the Racing House.

***

Savage checked his watch. Ten forty-eight. He'd been sitting in his parked car for over an hour now, glued to his mirrors. And when she finally appeared in his rear-view mirror at the bottom of the road, pushing that bright red box on wheels that looked like a coffin, his heart boomed. If his information was correct, he was about to be re-united with his notebook.

Leaving his car, Savage hurried up the road on foot.

Up in his second-floor bedroom, Ben was at his window. He often sat at, or rather, *in* his window. The windowsill was nice and deep, wide enough for him to perch on the painted wooden board with his back to the wall, legs out straight, and peer down, beyond the parking area, trees and bushes at the front of Racing House and see what was happening on the main road.

He hadn't gone out. There was no need. He could sit up here and watch the world go by, happy in the knowledge that Cam and Jack... especially the bent-nosed Jack, would have to wait for Margaret to arrive. That would ensure they missed their chance to go out for their wretched game of snooker to which he'd not been invited.

Even better, he imagined, would be a situation where Margaret was really late. Or better still, she didn't have the package they were expecting. That would be worth witnessing!

Ben's expectations were shattered a moment later with Margaret's arrival on Langton Road. He watched a man in a raincoat stand in front of her and hold a conversation with the postwoman as she got on with her deliveries. Ben slowly ground his teeth, it looked like Cam and Jack would get their parcel and their date with the green baize. He wouldn't have minded a game himself… but it wasn't the same, playing on your own.

He checked Margaret again. She was at number seventeen, and the chap in the raincoat had disappeared up a side street.

When he spotted Sebastian Savage striding purposefully along the footpath on the opposite side of the road, Ben's hopes were raised. He looked purposeful… and angry! And he seemed to be heading for the postwoman.

Ben kept his eye on Savage, mulling over the scene developing below him. What was it Cam had said they were waiting to receive? And then an idea, a wonderfully devious idea, struck him.

***

When Ben bounced down the stairs and came into the lounge calling their names, Cam did his best not to sigh. Jack had no such reservations, displaying his contempt with a hearty sigh and a disparaging expression. Ben ignored both of them. He would have the last laugh.

'Jack, Cam!'

'What is it, Ben?' Cam answered dourly.

'Savage! Savage!' he shrieked, a little too theatrically, realising he should tone it down.

He took a breath and added, 'Is the delivery you're waiting for something to do with you, Savage, and all this upset between Charlie and Grace?'

Jack shrugged back. They couldn't claim it wasn't, as Ben had been in the same room when that had all kicked off. Savage's name had definitely been mentioned, and for all he knew, the notebook too. So a shrug was the natural response.

'So?' asked Cam, making a circular motion with his finger to hurry Ben along.

'He's outside now. Savage. He's outside with Margaret!'

The teenagers glanced at each other for a fraction of a second and bolted for the front door. Ben went to the lounge window and watched with glee as Cam and Jack reached the footpath and, upon spying the postwoman, disappeared up Langton Road at a flat run.

***

There was always a joker. Every round, every day, she'd come across some jobsworth, usually men, who would complain about something that wasn't her fault, make an unfunny comment about her age, face, shorts, or her trolley, or the very worst, try to educate her by being patronising. In Margaret's experience, that sort of conversation often started with, 'If I was you…'

As the handsome man with anger in his eyes approached, Margaret got that sinking feeling. The jokers were coming at her thick and fast today.

'If I were you…' Savage announced with a plastic smile.

Margaret stood her ground, albeit with the trolley between her and the man she now recognised as being the local racehorse trainer, Sebastian Savage.

'… I wouldn't deliver the package you have for the Racing House. It will be addressed to either a Cameron

Camberley or Jack Goodman. It contains a stolen item that belongs to me. If you open it, you'll see my name inside the cover.'

'Really?' Margaret said with a low whistle, buying herself time to consider his words and place her right hand into her jacket pocket, 'That sounds complicated.'

'No, it isn't,' Savage declared in a patronising voice, 'It's perfectly straightforward. You need to open your…'

Savage appraised the trolley for a moment.

'…your *little red coffin*, find the package, and return it to its rightful owner. And that's me.'

Margaret produced a smile, 'I'm sorry Mr Savage. It is Mr Savage isn't it?'

'Umm.. yes, that's correct, it is.'

'Good. Well, here's what will happen. I'm going to deliver that package to the person it's addressed to. I can't open any piece of post, and I can't give an addressed piece of post to any Tom, Dick, or Harry who rocks up in front of me in the street. So, if you'll let me get on?'

Savage started to protest, and ignoring him, Margaret started to push her trolley along the footpath.

She only made it a few yards before Savage was at her side, wagging his finger at her and restating his demands. She reached number nineteen and gave up. Margaret took her hand out of her jacket pocket and held up a small, black device.

'This is a personal alarm, Mr Savage,' Margaret stated sternly, 'If I press this button… Oh! Looks like I won't need to…'

Savage realised he was no longer holding her attention. He swung around to follow her gaze up the footpath to where two figures were racing towards them. The postwoman gave him a sweet smile and set off with her trolley once again.

'Guv'nor!' Cam said breathlessly a moment later as he and Jack drew to a shambling halt in front of Savage. Jack noticed the trainer was no longer sporting his sling.

Meanwhile, wishing to see an end to this bunch of jokers, Margaret took her chance, picked up some speed and missing number nineteen and twenty-one, shot her trolley into the driveway of number twenty-three, the Racing House.

'Get out of my way, Camberley!' Savage demanded loudly, pushing past Cam, only to be intercepted by Jack who with arms outstretched and never losing eye contact with him, blocked the trainer's way, despite being twenty inches smaller. Cam dodged back to help reinforce their line of defence.

Beyond the two boys, and through a gap in the bushes, Savage could see the pesky postal worker had entered the Racing House drive and was rummaging around in her open trolley box. Trying to reason with these two numbskulls would take too much time. He had to intercept the old woman to retrieve his notebook. Throwing caution to the wind, he threw a few punches, only one of which connected with the Camberley boy, and kicked out at the other enough to break free. Savage rushed into the driveway of number twenty-three, shouting for his parcel not to be...

'Delivered!' Margaret said with relish as she turned back from the front door to the Racing House, 'The postal service always finds a way!'

Savage lifted his right arm, his palm flat, ready to step forward and swipe at the postwoman. But before he could unleash his anger, a pair of hands were dragging his arm back.

'Don't you dare!' Jack hissed into the trainer's ear.

'Perhaps you should leave. Quietly,' Margaret advised, pointing behind Savage to where a small group of local residents were standing at the entrance to the driveway, gawping at him. Charlie was with them, holding onto her bicycle having just arrived home from morning stables. Ignoring them, Savage went to the door and trying the handle, unsurprisingly, found it locked. He squinted inside the vestibule where Savage's hopes were frustrated once again.

His nose touching the glass, he watched as the pile of about six items, two of which bore a resemblance to his enveloped notebook, were scooped up by a boy in his twenties and taken inside the house.

With the trainer distracted, Margaret winked at Cam and walked confidently down the drive to her trolley, smiling at the five people waiting for her. One of their number gave a little cheer and a clap as she assured them she was fine, and doubled back to number nineteen to continue her round.

Savage turned away from the house and shot a hand out to grab a fistful of Jack's jumper, 'It's my... *property* in there! You know it's mine!' Savage protested in a low, threatening voice, aware he was still being watched by a couple of the neighbours.

Jack was far too quick for him. Dodging his grasping hand, he looked Savage dead in the eye and stood his ground.

'You'll get your property back when we know you've retracted the lies you've told about us. Drop all the charges against Cam and myself. Once that's done, you'll get your damned notebook.'

It was almost comical to watch Savage assess the situation – the witnesses at the top of the drive, the locked door, and now Charlie turning up - in order to make his decision to leave. The group of onlookers had grown to seven or eight people, one of them with his phone out, pointed at the Racing House's front door, presumably videoing the confrontation. Savage strode over to Charlie and said something to her before stalking off down the drive and past the nosey neighbours.

'All over now!' Cam called out to the bystanders, 'Hope you enjoyed the show!'

A couple of the neighbours continued to discuss the Racing House, casting scornful glances down the drive, but the rest soon broke off once the possibility of witnessing a fist fight had vanished.

Cam produced his key and let Jack and Charlie back

into the house.

'The packages are gone,' Jack noted as he stepped into the house, 'Ben must have picked them up.'

The post was usually deposited on the kitchen island, but neither Ben, nor the pile of mail Margaret had pushed through the letterbox were anywhere to be found in the communal area. Cam shouted Ben's name up the stairs and started up them when there was no reply.

'I'll try his room,' Cam called out to Jack and Charlie, 'Make sure he's not in the washroom or the backyard.'

On the ground floor at the back of the house a small area housed a washing machine, dryer, ironing board and a large sink in what the landlord rather grandly called the utility room. Everyone in the house called it the washroom. Working in racing meant plenty of washing, often on a daily basis. The washing machine was of industrial quality and rarely silent.

Charlie and Jack went down the hall, calling Ben's name. They pushed the washroom door open to the sound of Cam's thumping footsteps going up the two flights of stairs to Ben's room above them. The thumping ceased abruptly once Charlie screamed Ben's name, then started again as Cam came helter-skelter back down a flight and a half of stairs.

At the door to the washroom he discovered Charlie on her knees in the centre of the linoleum floor, with a comforting arm wrapped around Ben's shoulders. He was lying amongst a number of discarded letters and advertising flyers, holding his head between his knees, mumbling something about wishing the room would stop spinning.

Thirty-One

Once he'd lifted Ben off the floor, and ascertained he was conscious, semi-lucid, was suffering from nothing more serious than a mild concussion and a lump on the side of his head the size of a songbird's egg, Jack had given him a few supportive words then shot through the open back door.

Dashing through the small backyard with eight-foot-high brick walls on all sides, he burst into the back alley and began combing the cobbled street behind the house. It was frustratingly empty, save for the multitude of black bins, some of which he lifted the lids, just in case. One of them spilled fetid vegetables onto him. Finally, he ran up and down its length, but there were no signs of a lurking intruder or another backyard door having been forced. The grounds of Norton Primary School were only yards beyond the next line of houses, offering numerous escape paths and hiding places.

Returning empty handed to the Racing House backyard, he noticed for the first time the busted lock on the yard door and the smashed pane of glass in the back door. Ben and Charlie were gone and Cam was busy picking up the half dozen letters strewn across the floor.

'Any sign of him?' asked Cam.

Jack shook his head, 'No. He'll be long gone by now. How's Ben?'

'He'll live. Making the most of Charlie's attention if you ask me,' he said with a touch of jealousy, 'She's taken him into the lounge.'

Jack stooped down. It was another letter. Only a corner was showing, sticking out from under the dryer. It was addressed to Charlie. There was no sign of the two packages Margaret had been so determined to post through their letterbox. He made a mental note to thank her. The way she'd stood up to Savage had been impressive.

'Looks like he got what he came for,' noted Cam sadly, 'There's no notebook.'

'What does Ben say?'

'He reckons he was watching us on the street and when the post landed, collected it all up and was on his way to the lounge when he thought he heard something in the washroom. He went in to investigate, and got bopped by someone standing behind the door.'

'Brilliant, so he didn't see them?'

'No, by the time he'd recovered enough to look up, the thief was away on his toes.'

Jack frowned, then sniffed. 'You smell that?'

Cam sniffed.

Cam screwed his face up, 'Have you been sifting through the bins? You smell… binny.'

'You're so descriptive,' Jack said, rolling of his eyes, 'Not me, the air in here! Can you smell cigarettes?'

Cam sniffed again, 'Nope. I can smell rotten cabbage.'

'There's definitely a tang of cigarettes,' Jack insisted, 'Tarquin was smoking that night in Whitley Bay…'

Cam moved away from Jack and tried again. He shook his head.

'Nope. Still can't smell it.'

'Never mind,' said Jack dismissively, 'Come on, let's see whether we can get anything more out of Ben.'

'Just go easy on him,' said Cam as they entered the hallway, 'He's pretty shaken up, and you know how you tend to rile him.'

Jack had set about defending his handling of Ben, but was cut short. A beep from Cam's mobile saw him dive for his pocket, his concentration immediately on the small screen, rather than anything Jack had to say.

Ben and Charlie were sitting on the sofa together. To be fair to Cam, Ben did look paler than normal, and the bump on his head had swollen out to almost comic proportions. He was sipping on a glass of water while Charlie held a damp cloth to his forehead.

It turned out that apart from a banging headache, and making the most of Charlie's continued attention, Ben had regained his faculties. He hadn't seen his attacker's face, but could confirm that he'd seen the man scoop up the two small packages delivered by Margaret and made off the way he'd entered. The first had been addressed to Cam, the second to

Jack.

'Ah! That would have been my riding gloves,' Cam announced, 'I've just received a text message saying they've been delivered.'

'The other one must have been…'

He paused, not sure he should say anything in front of Ben.

'I know Savage has lost a notebook,' said Ben, 'The least you could do is credit me with a bit of intelligence.'

'It must have been the notebook,' Jack said with a weak smile.

'Oh, riding gloves. That reminds me,' said Charlie, moving a little way down the sofa from Ben so she could grab her backpack that held her riding gear.

'A young lad gave me this while you two were fighting with Savage in the street. He said to give it to you personally,' she said, dipping into the back pack.

She handed Cam a small, rectangular jiffy bag. He turned it over in his hands. It felt like a notebook.

'Open it,' said Jack, anticipating the question he felt sure Cam was about to ask.

Cam pulled on the tear ribbon, turned the package over and gave the jiffy bag a gentle shake. A silent moment later, a small, bright red rectangular notebook with a raised paisley pattern, its cover tipped with tin corners, dropped into Cam's lap.

Ben broke the silence with a rare example of his previously hidden dry sense of humour.

'After going to all that bother, I do hope the gloves are the right size for the chap who clonked me.'

Charlie laughed and Cam smiled. Jack looked on, slightly bewildered. Perhaps Ben was better for knowing?

'Is it okay if I call Meera Akbar, the policewomen dealing with myself and Savage?' Cam asked Ben, 'We should tell her we've had an intruder.'

'I don't know,' Ben said after a pause for thought, 'Send

me her number. I'll think about it.'

Jack and Cam understood. No one wanted to be stood down from riding out because of an innocent little bang on the head.

Two miles away, a car pulled off into a layby on the A64. A minute later the car door opened and a pair of brand new riding gloves were tossed onto the verge. They were followed a second later by a small, rectangular catalogue for the upcoming Horses In Training sale at Doncaster. The car door slammed shut and the car sped away.

Thirty-Two

For a Wednesday morning, there were plenty of cars on the A64, but thankfully, most of them were queuing on the east-bound side of the road, heading for a day out at the coast.

'Looks like Whitby's going to be busy,' Cam noted with a nod at the turn-off for the seaside town.

Jack murmured a nondescript reply from Corbyn's passenger seat and once again, tried to pull their conversation back on topic; Cam's mother's visit and the revelation that his father had died four years previously. Cam seemed to have swept the whole incident aside and was side-stepping Jack's attempts to discuss it any further.

'Your father, Cam,' he repeated for the third time since leaving the Racing House, 'Can we talk about him?'

'I'd rather not.'

'You gave me the impression he was alive.'

Cam gripped the steering wheel a little harder.

'Yes, it's just… easier.'

'Right. I get that.'

Jack allowed another mile to slip by in silence.

'So, you'd have been, what, fourteen when he died?'

Cam gave out a sigh that ended with a glance Jack's way and a frustrated growling noise.

'You're not going to let it lie, are you?'

Jack responded with a silly, childish smile that, combined with his bent nose, successfully dissolved Cam's resistance.

'Yes, he died when I was fourteen. He had a fall when he was riding out one morning. His horse spooked, he landed awkwardly and hit his head. My mother and my older sister managed to speak to him before he went, but I was at boarding school…'

He swallowed, 'I didn't get back in time. I never got to say goodbye.'

Jack's smile had evaporated. Allowing the rumble of the car to fill the pause, he evaluated his potential responses. Eventually he said, 'You know you look a lot like him.'

Cam didn't respond.

'I can't remember my father's face,' Jack added without much emotion, 'When I try to imagine him, it's just a blank. He was always the one taking the photos, so he was hardly ever in them. I've just got snapshots of him in my mind from school holidays. I don't know if I'm like him or not.'

Corbyn ate up another few miles, with Cam constantly tugging on the steering wheel to keep him straight. The small corrections had become an unconscious activity, with his mind elsewhere. However, when a little jolt from a pothole made the steering wheel jump alarmingly in his hands, his concentration, and his patience, broke.

Without thinking, he blurted, 'Why on earth did you buy this blasted death trap, Jack?'

As soon as he'd said it, he knew it wasn't fair. He didn't even own a car, and was forever borrowing it or cadging lifts. Still, it was marginally better to be discussing the car than his relationship with his dead father.

'It was all I could afford at the time and Corbyn had ten months of MOT to run, so it meant he could get me through the flat season.'

'Remind me, why did you call the car Corbyn?'

Jack shrugged, 'It's what the guy I bought him off called him. He said it was because he always went to the left.'

Cam barked out a laugh.

'What's so funny?'

Cam never got the opportunity to explain.

'Shh!' Jack said, indicating he was receiving a call on his mobile. Cam zipped his mouth shut and Jack accepted the call without recognising the number.

The moment Jack finished the call the two friends whooped and hollered for the first few seconds, speaking excitedly for the next ten minutes, all thoughts of family, hypnosis, hooded men, Tarquin, and even Sebastian Savage banished to the back of their minds. The caller had been Freddie Jones, trainer of Rosy Glow.

'I've got the ride in the Commonwealth Cup at Royal Ascot!' marvelled Jack for the umpteenth time. Both the teenagers sported wide grins on their faces.

'The owners agreed I deserved the leg up after Haydock…' Jack said, replaying the conversation out loud again, '… and Freddie wants me to ride out for him twice a week on the run up to the race!'

He blew out three breaths through rounded lips, creating a small hooting sound, 'In three weeks' time I'm riding Rosy Glow in a Group One race at the most important meeting in the flat racing calendar!'

This settled on the two of them for a long moment, before Cam spoiled it.

'As long as Savage's complaint about your violent behaviour gets rescinded by the BHA. Otherwise you'll still be suspended.'

***

The outside of Lucille's house had a different feel about it in the sunshine of a mid-week morning. Jack hadn't noticed the broad-leafed ivy growing up the façade on their first visit.

Its newly arrived crop of green leaves bestowed a feeling of renewal onto the house. All the windows had their curtains drawn back and the noon-day sun was making the long glass panels shine.

This time they'd called ahead with their request to visit, and perhaps because of this, Lucille immediately felt more like the woman they'd met on the train to Scarborough.

'Come on in, boys!' she hollered from the already open front door in her louder than needed voice as soon as Corbyn came to a crunching and squealing halt on her driveway.

'I can't wait to show you the library!' she gushed as soon as they were in the hallway.

Lucille led them down the hall, Cam following, but Jack paused for a moment to have a second, more detailed inspection of the photos that travelled all the way up the stairs. Perhaps it was the argument with Cam's mother, or the conversation in the car, these photographs took on a deeper meaning this time around.

The phone call ahead had been a good idea, as not only was Lucille totally relaxed, but she'd also readied herself to entertain them in her own, inimitable way. She'd asked about their trip up to Whitley Bay and Cam had provided her with the highlights, leaving out their confrontation with Tarquin.

'And this, is our library!' she announced proudly as Jack caught up. Cam was already a few yards inside, standing still, his head tilted upward, staring open mouthed at the fourteen foot tall bookcase that almost reached the ceiling, its dark, ornately carved wooden shelves wrapping around the best part of all four walls. The library had no windows. Books covered every possible inch of wall space. A ladder made of thin steel was hooked onto a rail at the top of the bookcase, and, doing a quick calculation, Cam reckoned there had to be several thousand books on the shelves.

The only area not dedicated to books was a small, neatly tiled fireplace installed with a modern, wood-burning stove. It protruded from the centre of an external wall, around which a semi-circular coffee table and two deep-seated armchairs were placed, each of the chairs equipped with its own reading lamp. A dark green velvet sofa and a large leather-topped desk placed at opposite ends of the room completed the furnishings. It seemed everything within these four walls was dedicated to the study of the written word. Cam loved it, taking time to enjoy the smell of the aging tomes. He picked up the aromas of book glue, leather, woodsmoke, and furniture polish.

Jack, on the other hand, was simply bewildered. He could count the number of books he'd read on one hand.

'And over here is the section on puzzles, codes, cyphers, and conundrums,' Lucille told them, gesturing to several shelves, 'I think that's where we might find some of the answers we're after. But first, where's this little red book?'

Jack dug Savage's notebook out of his jeans pocket and held it out to Lucille.

'You understand that this isn't ours,' he checked, 'We've... *acquired* it from someone who stole it from its original owner.'

'Yes, yes, dear,' Lucille snapped, patently more interested in the contents of the notebook than hearing its origin story once again, 'Cam explained everything on the phone, as well as Mr Savage's attempts to blackmail both of you and the rather convoluted way it came into your hands.'

'That young autograph hunter of yours was extremely naughty to use their hypnotism skills like that,' she said, tutting a few times, 'And this Savage chap sounds quite the rogue trainer!'

Jack caught Cam's eye and raised an eyebrow, wondering just how much he'd shared about the two of them.

'What could I do?' Cam said with a coy smile, 'Lucille's a good listener.'

'There's nothing like a bit of intrigue to whet the appetite, that's what my Monty used to say!' Lucille said as she accepted the notebook, laying it on her palm like a sacred text and running her fingers over the raised design in its leather binding.

'Monty was your husband, the one in the photos up the the stairs?' asked Jack.

Lucille's finger suddenly stopped tracing the pattern on the notebook's cover.

'Ah, you've caught me out,' she said, lowering her head to view Jack over the tip of her spectacles, 'I was going to reveal all to you today, but you've already worked it out, you clever boy.'

'Worked what out?' asked Cam.

Clasping the notebook to her bosom, Lucille explained the safeguards she adopted with unexpected house callers.

'As a lady of age, in a large house she doesn't want to leave because of the happy memories it holds, it does rather leave me open to unwanted callers and the possibility of burglars or charlatans believing I may be a soft touch,' she explained, 'There's been a number of thefts on this avenue of late.'

'Which is why you answered the door the other night pretending to be holding a phone conversation,' commented Jack.

'Mmm... you worked that out too. That's rather disappointing. I thought I was being quite covert,' replied Lucille, somewhat crestfallen.

'Oh, it's clever enough,' Jack assured her, 'Anyone intent on pushing their way into the house is less likely to do so if you're currently holding a conversation with someone. All you'd have to do is tell the caller you're in trouble. But... your phone lit up the home screen as you put it to your ear.'

Disappointed in herself, Lucille lifted her eyes to the ceiling and slowly shook her head.

'I could see your call wasn't connected to anyone,' continued Jack, 'Mind you, calling out to your husband in the back of the house was impressive. Cam was completely fooled, weren't you?'

Cam blinked, looking perplexed, but did manage to mumble, 'But I... saw the photos?'

'Lucille's husband, Monty, was never here,' Jack explained to Cam. He turned to Lucille, 'All the photos up the stairs are of younger versions of yourself and your husband. I'm guessing he's no longer around?'

Lucille didn't answer immediately. Instead, she held Jack's gaze, providing him with the faintest of smiles.

'I'm impressed, my dear young jockey,' she eventually replied, her smile broadening, 'You've uncovered my second little white lie... Perhaps you've underestimated your own competence and should be doing this code cracking yourself!'

Jack shook his head and wondered whether to reveal that his early teenage years spent breaking and entering had taught him to look out for such signs. On reflection, he decided not to take the chance of spooking her. Besides, he liked Lucille. Being around this rather eccentric lady was entertaining, and surprisingly educational.

He answered, 'Thanks for the compliment, Lucille, but I wouldn't know where to start with this code stuff. We really need your help.'

'So you live here alone?' Cam asked, still a little lost.

Lucille produced a sad smile and told him her husband, Montgomery Beaufort, had died in his late forties, some eleven years ago. She also assured the boys she wasn't delusional, just careful of people she didn't know.

'Someone who thinks there's a man in the house always treats me differently. It's laughable really, as Monty was as soft as a poorly tossed pancake! I'm far more likely to punch someone on the nose than he ever was!'

'Oh, right. I see,' Cam said uncertainly in return, still somewhat puzzled, but feeling he was getting there.

'So, to work, my pretty young boys!' Lucille announced loudly.

The contents of the notebook had initially proved to be somewhat disappointing. But after deeper thought, it had become beguiling, especially to Jack, who had pored over the notebook all day Tuesday and into the night, even passing it around the house to see what other people made of it. He'd also asked Ben, now fully recovered, to take a look and offer his thoughts. Jack had admitted to himself a grudging admiration for the way Ben had taken the attack. He hadn't blamed, or got angry at anyone. If anything, he'd contributed plenty of ideas to the subsequent discussions about the notebook, although the ongoing attention he'd received from Charlie had certainly aided his transformation. Cam had suggested that Ben should thank his attacker – for finally knocking some sense into him – and Ben had laughed along with the rest of his housemates.

Apart from the inside cover, that had 'Savage' printed in inked block capitals, nothing else in the notebook made any sense. The notebook ran to a hundred pages. The first eighty pages were filled with utter gibberish, the remaining twenty were blank. Each of the small, faintly lined pages consisted of up to twenty lines of seemingly random letters and numbers. Spaces and punctuation marks were inserted at irregular intervals and everything was hand written. There was a mixture of pencil, ballpoint, and most of the early pages were written in ink.

It was Ben who had suggested that all the random letters and numbers were probably a code. Jack had cogitated on this and had found his mind full of Lucille, specifically all the puzzle books, crosswords, and other mind-bending books that had been scattered around her armchair when they'd called on her.

'That day we visited her, she'd completed The Times crossword,' he'd told Cam, 'And on her side-table, there was a thick book called 'Cryptic Conundrums'. If we're to discover what's in this notebook, I reckon she's our best bet.'

Cam had considered this, then voiced his belief that they should take the notebook straight to Savage.

'Aren't you interested in what the notebook contains?'

Jack had countered, aghast at the suggestion that they simply hand it over.

Cam had given his answer some thought.

'I want to get back to riding. I was happy to stop Savage grabbing the notebook earlier, as I thought we'd be able to read it... but it could take us months to work out what it means. Think of it this way - someone has broken into your car, blackmailed Grace, searched our rooms, and bonked Ben on the head. People are getting hurt because of a silly red five-by-four inch notebook!'

'Yeah, but the fact it's in code means the information must be valuable,' Jack had argued.

'Valuable to Savage, maybe. But even if we can get the information decrypted, what will we do with it?'

It had been Jack's turn to pause for thought. Cam was right, he had to consider the consequences of holding onto the notebook long enough to understand why it was so important to Savage.

Somehow, Tarquin must have found out the notebook was being delivered by post and stolen around the back of the house when they were being harangued by Savage out the front. Had Savage's public display been just that, a flamboyant diversion? Tarquin worked for Savage, that much was clear. It also meant he had no aversion to using violence in order to recover his precious notebook.

'Ok, Cam. I agree that we have to hand over the notebook. It'll allow us to get back to riding,' Jack had conceded, 'But we need some insurance. You saw Savage today, I don't trust him. He could take the notebook back and never bother to clear our names.'

The final, clinching argument had come, of all people, from Ben. He'd pointed out that if his attacker was working for Savage, he would believe the notebook had never been delivered. Either their information was duff, or the post was late, the latter explanation the most probable. This meant Savage and his cosh-wielding side-kick would leave the

Racing House and its inhabitants, alone for a day or two, to allow the notebook to arrive.

'This offers you a window of opportunity,' Ben had pointed out, 'You have one to two days to find out what's in that notebook.'

'Besides, you can hand it over to Savage in a couple of days' time, whether you've decoded it or not. And of course, you could make a copy of the notebook's contents and continue trying to make sense of it even though Savage has the original.'

Jack had decided there and then. Ben and he had got off on the wrong foot. With Cam bought in, the only question left had been whether Lucille was the right person to be taking on the job of deciphering Savage's notebook (if indeed it was a code, and not, as Charlie had suggested, just a way of messing with everyone's head).

But within minutes of entering Lucille's library, neither Jack nor Cam were in any doubt they'd made the right decision.

Lucille was positively excited by what she found in the first few pages of the notebook. Sitting down at the desk in the library she immediately got to work, turning a page at a time, front to back, all eighty pages that contained data, poring over each page for a few seconds at a time before moving on.

Every now and again she'd nod and mumble a few words over and over to herself, like 'Caesar', 'Substitution', 'Playfair'... and make a few notes on her pad with a pencil and rubber, the rubber getting just as much use as the pencil. Without anything to do but wait, Cam decided to browse the multitude of books on codes, puzzles, ciphers, and crosswords Lucille had drawn his attention to. Meanwhile, Jack took to one of the armchairs. He wasn't a great reader, and certainly no mathematician. He closed his eyes and started dozing.

'There's tea in the pot,' Lucille called out without looking up, five minutes into her investigations, 'On the coffee table at the back of the room. It should be brewed by now.

Help yourselves! You'll find biscuits in the stripey green biscuit barrel. Left-hand kitchen cupboard at the back of the house.'

She got to her feet, crossed the library and picked out a trio of books, then returned to her desk and began cross-referencing certain pages with the notebook.

Cam and Jack were into their second helping of bourbons when Lucille called out in her loud, brisk tone to which they were quickly becoming accustomed.

'It's a transpositional cipher!'

The boys looked blankly at each other, their cheeks bulging with biscuit.

'Is that good or bad?' asked Jack after a munch and swift couple of swallows.

'A bit of both, my dear boy,' Lucille admitted, waving them over to stand behind her at the desk.

'Take this first page as an example,' she said, 'Even though there are numbers and letters, it does look like there are jumbled-up English words in there. That points towards a transpositional cipher. It means the letters or numbers are correct, but have been transposed into different places in each line or paragraph.'

She looked over her shoulder at the boys, 'If it was a simple couple of words, you could sit and try and work it out like an anagram, but that isn't the case here. It looks like Mr Savage has coded each paragraph, although when you compare certain pages, the paragraphs show similarities, so each of the pages in this notebook could hold a very similar set of information. Look… I've found one here that was quite short.'

She flicked to a page of the notebook about half-way through and pointed to the top two lines.

'I think this is someone called Lynn or maybe Lesley, and I think there's a phone number in there too,' said Lucille.

Jack cast his eye over the lines of code again. As far as he was concerned, it was simply a jumble of letters and numbers.

'How do you know there's a phone number somewhere in that lot?' Cam queried.

'I'm assuming the address only has a single digit, and the postcode has three, which leaves eleven numbers in the code, and there is a zero and a seven mixed in,' Lucille replied, her words excitedly rapid.

This was greeted with silence. Jack scratched at the bend in his nose and Cam sucked on his teeth. Before either of them could question her logic, Lucille was speaking again.

'And whilst knowing it's a transpositional code helps, I can only guess at what the rest means until you find me the key.'

'The key?'

'The *Key*,' repeated Lucille grandly, 'It will be a five or six letter word, like a password, and will unlock the code and present the text in the correct order. Here, look.'

Lucille picked up her iPad and it lit up a page from the internet.

'This website allows you to enter the encoded text, introduce a key, and it will decipher the transpositional code for you at the click of a button.'

She played around with the various input boxes and buttons for a few minutes, showing the boys how to encode and then decode a sentence of text and numbers.

Lucille got up from the desk, 'So, over to you guys!'

'How do you mean, over to us?' asked Cam, still puzzling over her comment about telephone numbers and postcodes.

'We need to find the key. It's probable that one key will unlock everything in the notebook. Hopefully, it will be an easy one. We should make a list, and mark our guesses off one-by-one when they don't work. Here, like this.'

Lucille took her iPad back from Jack and typed in the first paragraph of code from Savage's last entry.

'ANOOEKOTHNKDHNOWUHUFNACENOEOANLIT

OIHLENCHUWRSRASOLGMWODOHNEEROFKDDLIPRD
ALHSDESRFEYLEFTHTDESICEPAERTTLOPRICECLCMAB
AITVFIDINOL'

'Bloody hell,' Jack muttered, watching Lucille carefully type in five letters at a time, 'It's going to take some time to type in the whole notebook, there's seventy-odd pages of this coded rubbish.'

'Don't fret! We only need one paragraph to test all the potential keys,' said Lucille, giving him a kind smile, 'So, give me a possible key, my dear. A word with either five of six letters is most likely. Something that will have meaning to this Savage chap.'

'How about 'Sebastian Savage?' Cam suggested.

'Mmm… We can try, but it's almost certainly too long. His surname might work though… Savage.'

Cam nodded.

Lucille started typing into a box holding a small image of a key beside it, then clicked on a 'decode' button.

'No. I'm afraid that's not it,' she reported almost immediately, pointing to the results box on the same page, 'It's still encoded. So, we make a note of the key we've tried, so we don't waste time trying it again.'

'Can we try, Marsh?' asked Jack, 'Marsh Landing is the name of the stables.'

'You've got a phone haven't you, my dear boy? Do it yourself… be the detective!' Lucille trilled, 'The website is free. Carefully type in that first paragraph of code and start trying different keys.'

Both the teenagers retreated to their armchairs with a copy of the paragraph and began tapping on their phone screens. Every now again, one of them would shout out a five or six letter word for Lucille to add to the ever-expanding list of unsuccessful keywords. After forty minutes of abject failure, their well of possible keys had run dry and the enormity of their endeavour began to sink in.

'Perhaps we need to do a little research,' Lucille

suggested, 'I assume Mr Savage has a website for his business?'

'Yeah, I guess so, but he won't have the key published on there, will he?' asked Jack dejectedly.

Whilst he'd owned a mobile phone since the age of eleven, Jack was the first to admit that he wasn't technologically savvy. Watching short videos, sending basic emails and scrolling through social media messages were about his limit.

'No, absolutely not,' agreed Lucille, 'What we're looking for is information about the man himself. Does he have a wife, or children, or a pet with a five or six letter name? What about his mother and father? Does he play golf, like a certain type of music, or collect stamps, coins, or figurines… People tend to choose passwords that mean things to them, especially for code keys. For example, if we find out he likes nineteenth century art, we should try all the artists from that era with five or six letter names, like Degas, or Turner. Do you think there are any racehorses that have a special meaning to him?'

They spent the next hour scouring the Marsh Landing Stables website, plus Savage's Facebook and X pages, and even went through all the horses' names he'd trained in the last five years, plus every racing news report mentioning him, thanks to the Racing Post, looking for any small insight into the trainer's life. With Lucille's help they managed to track Savage from being a teenager, then to university, back to Marsh Landing to be an assistant trainer, and finally, him taking over the yard when his father died in the nineties.

By the time the ornate carriage clock at the centre of the mantelpiece over the fire had struck one o'clock, Cam and Jack were mentally worn out. In contrast, Lucille was still positively firing on all cylinders, apparently enjoying the challenge.

'My husband and I always enjoyed a puzzle. If I'm honest, we probably spent a little too much time on them. But it's important to keep your brain fit with regular exercise. I imagine you boys regularly go for a run, or a swim, to keep your body fit. I give my brain a workout each day, and it shows. You can concentrate longer and I like to think it keeps me sharp,' she revealed when the boys commented on the fact she wasn't tiring of the search.

'What did your husband do for a living?' Jack asked innocently.

'He worked for himself, we both did,' Lucille replied wistfully, before excusing herself and leaving the room.

'You boys must be famished!' she announced a minute later, reappearing with a tray stacked high with sandwiches, mini pork pies, and sausage rolls.

'Back with the tea in a minute!'

Thanking her profusely and offering to help, Cam followed Lucille through to the sprawling kitchen that looked out onto a large, mature garden with hedges on all three sides. He helped carry the tea, crockery, and an iced lemon drizzle cake back to the small table in front of the fire in the library.

'Your husband worked for himself…' Jack mentioned as he dug into the mountain of small, triangular sandwiches, choosing cheese and pickle, ham and mustard, and an egg mayonnaise, 'I don't suppose you worked together?'

'Hmm. You may be a digital caveman, but you've a sharp little mind when it comes to working people out!' Lucille answered with a grin, 'I suppose those photos on the staircase wall are a bit of a giveaway aren't they?'

Jack's smile said it all, 'The one of him and you accepting an award from the local Harrogate MP was the clincher. What was it for?'

'There were a few,' she said after a thoughtful pause, 'I think the one you were looking at was an award for technical innovation. We wrote computer programs, you see. Mainly to secure… well, to stop people hacking important computer systems. Our clients tended to be big internet companies or public concerns like the civil service, or the police. But it wasn't the same after Monty died. So I took early retirement.'

Cam shared a nervous look with Jack, took a swig of his milky tea and cleared his throat.

'Lucille, you do realise this notebook was stolen, don't you? At the very least, it was picked up and kept by someone before we got hold of it. All we know about that someone is that he goes by the online name of BobLege and is a fan of hoodies and hypnosis.'

'I am aware,' Lucille confirmed.

'And what we're doing with the notebook at the moment could be construed as an invasion of privacy,' added Lucille, 'I don't know whether that's illegal, but I imagine we're treading a fine line. Tell me, do you intend to give Mr Savage his notebook back?'

'Yes. We have to. It's the only way either of us will be able to continue our apprenticeships,' Cam confirmed.

'And you can assure me you didn't knowingly aim to injure Mr Savage on that horse? And how about you, Jack? You said Mr Savage attacked you in your house. Is that what happened?'

She asked this whilst eyeing both boys keenly.

'Did you check up on us?'

Lucille was forced to smile, 'I still have a few contacts.'

Jack grimaced, 'Then you'll know that Cam is whiter than white, and I'm the opposite.'

Lucille's gaze fell onto Jack and her eyes crinkled around the edges, 'White for the last two years, though.'

Jack's glowering faded into a sad smile, 'Until all this kicked off!'

'I wouldn't have let you in the house if I had any worries about either of you,' Lucille said, turning her attention back to the notebook, 'Besides, I've not had this much fun for years, my darling boys!'

Thirty-Three

The afternoon dragged on without any breakthrough. While Cam became disillusioned with the lack of progress, he was amazed by Jack and Lucille's dogged persistence. It was like a game to them; who could find that elusive keyword first? He'd worried the two of them were arguing too much at first. Raised voices had accompanied the discussion of whether Savage's ex-girlfriends names, places he'd been on holiday, or his past winning horses names held the keyword that would release the notebook's secrets. However Cam soon realised the arguments waged, and harsh comments being flung across the library were actually the two of them simply enjoying the cut and thrust of debate.

Bored with typing lists of girls, boys, horses, and place names that might be of relevance to Savage into the online decoder, Cam had been glad for the chance to leave the library in the early evening to toast some teacakes, spread strawberry jam on a few scones, and make another pot of tea.

It happened when he was standing at the kitchen counter, in front of a set of three windows that looked out onto Lucille's veranda and neat back garden. The spring sun was low in the sky, but still powerful enough to cast its warmth onto Cam's face as he worked. Smearing butter onto the last hot teacake, he felt the beating warmth of the sun vanish for a moment as a rounded shadow flitted across his face and then the bread board. Looking up, whatever had passed between himself and the sunshine must have already moved on, as the heat had returned to his skin.

The hairs on the back of his neck stood on end as Cam imagined what could have generated such a complete block to a sun that was burning in such splendid isolation between the roofs of two distant houses in a cloudless sky? He moved to the back door, turned the key in the lock, pulled the door half open and stuck his head out.

Birdsong, car noise, a distant plane... and footsteps.

Hurried, retreating footsteps? Cam stepped outside. A quick scout around determined there was no-one in the garden. A five foot beech hedge divided Lucille's property left and right, and a taller, green privet hedge sealed the bottom, he'd have heard if someone had tried to scale, or push through any of them. He paused like a statue for a moment, listening, then took three quick steps to his right. He peeked around the corner of the house, trying not to breathe too heavily even though his heart was pounding in his chest.

Along the side of Lucille's house a paved passageway led to a bolted gate and over the fence… a next door neighbour, a businessman by the look of him, was placing a bag of rubbish into his black bin. The neighbour made the ten yard walk back to his backdoor, the heels of his shiny black office shoes clacking on the paving slabs, the noise reverberating between the walls of the two houses.

Smiling inwardly at his ability to allow his imagination to run away with him, Cam breathed easily. As the neighbour's door clicked shut he was left wondering how much the episodes with Tarquin, Ben, and the ransacking of his room were still playing on his mind.

When Lucille's back door slammed shut a moment later, Cam screwed his neck around, and once the key turned in the lock and a dark figure moved away from the glass pane the duck egg on Ben's head once again came vividly to life in Cam's mind.

Seizing the door handle he found it was now locked. Wrenching at it, he started shouting out to Jack and Lucille. Moving across to the kitchen window Cam realised his mistake. What a first class idiot he had been! The kitchen was an extension, but instead of running right to the end of the house as he'd assumed, there was a small paved area set back in the far left-hand corner, accessed from another room. Whoever had entered the house must have been hiding in that alcove and slipped into the kitchen when his back was turned.

Dodging right, the last kitchen window gave Cam a

view to the hallway door, but he was too late. It was already being closed from the other side. Whoever it was, would only be yards away from the door to the library, where Lucille and Jack were working. The house was too big, its walls too thick. If his shouts hadn't alerted them already, would anything else warn them? Still shouting out he nevertheless began battering on the window panes with his flat hands, trying to register as much noise by slapping them. It was useless, hardly making more of a small thump, and he gave up within seconds.

Think! Think!

He ran his hands over his trouser pockets: no phone, damn it, he'd left it in the library. Break a window? What with? Besides, they were thick, and triple glazed by the look of them. The front? Yes, the front of the house…

It only took seconds to run around the side of the house, but far longer to negotiate the tall, bolted, and padlocked side gate. Cam scaled the neighbours fence and using it as a boost, threw himself at the gate, eventually clambered over this significant deterrent to burglars at the third attempt. He found his clothes smeared with some sort of grease as he lowered himself to the ground on the other side. Every moment of delay filled Cam's mind with thoughts of what might be happening to Lucille and Jack. What sort of cosh, or implement did Tarquin use to fell Ben? Jack might be able to defend himself, but Lucille…

Cam decided it wasn't worth giving these questions headspace. Given his present predicament, he was concerned the answers might be too distracting. Instead, he concentrated on a new query: Why on earth had he listened to Jack and put Lucille in danger?

Even that question became moot when he ran around the corner of the house and discovered the front door standing wide open. Why would it be open?

For a fleeting moment, Cam considered curtailing his hasty approach. But the urge to warn his friends was too great. He leapt over the threshold, hurried down the empty hallway, yanked on the doorknob, and burst into the library.

Jack and Lucille looked up in surprise at their sweating, panting, greased-up, and very much relieved colleague.

'You've forgotten to bring the tea,' Jack observed.

'Someone... in the house...' puffed Cam between gasps.

Thirty-Four

In total, they lost an hour and a half of keyword search time. Instead, they searched Lucille's house from top to bottom, inside and out, sticking together for fear of Tarquin stepping calmly out of the shadows and coshing them one by one.

Cam's frenetic explanation following his shambolic entrance back into the library had included several references to the incident at the Racing House the day before, so Jack had found it necessary to bring Lucille up to date, and apologise for not mentioning what happened to Ben, and also their run-in with Tarquin in Whitley Bay.

She seemed completely unfazed by this news and if anything, more determined to complete their grown-up version of hide-and-seek properly, leaving no stone, cupboard or curtain unturned. This meant a sortie into the dusty loft for Cam, he being the one already covered head to foot in goo. The goo in question turned out to be anti-climb grease, meant to dissuade potential burglars.

'After Monty died I was feeling a little vulnerable, so I had a security company come in and strengthen all the locks and add extra safety features to the house,' Lucille explained as they combed the fourth bedroom, 'It's just as well you didn't fall into the man-trap I've had installed around the other side of the house!'

Cam didn't question her statement, uncertain whether Lucille was joking or not. Her grin told him she was... probably.

It was twilight outside and dark inside by the time everyone was back in the library, their search completed to Lucille's exacting standards.

'Our snooper knew escape through the hedges into a neighbouring garden was likely to get them heard, or spotted, so they nipped inside the kitchen when your back was turned,' explained Jack, as he held a toasting fork to the open stove, carefully ensuring his half a teacake browned evenly, 'They must have run through the hall, opened the front door and high-tailed it down the drive to freedom, which explains why the front door was left open.'

'Or an attempt at a clever double-bluff.'

Both boys looked to Lucille who had just taken a large bite out of a teacake. They patiently waited for her chewing to cease.

'It's a large house. By leaving the front door open we assumed they'd scarpered. If all three of us had gone outside to search, the hidden burglar could lock the door behind us and search the house at their leisure. Or they might have waited until we started to search the house, leaving the library empty, and swiped the notebook while we were all upstairs.'

The boys stared at Lucille in horror.

'You're mind works on a completely different level to mine,' Cam noted.

Standing, Jack scanned Lucille's desk. The notebook wasn't there.

'Don't worry yourself, my darling boy!' she smiled, bending down and lifting the hem of the skirt that almost touched the floor. She revealed a pair of sensible flat shoes and a pair of bright green woolly socks that presumably reached her knees – thankfully, you couldn't be sure. The notebook was easy to spot: a small rectangular shape inside the right-legged sock, half-way up Lucille's shin.

'Excuse me,' she said with a wink, 'Avert your eyes, darling boys.'

'There you go,' she said a moment later, holding the

notebook out to Jack, 'Your turn to look after it.'

'You did that…'

'Before we left the library, yes,' Lucille confirmed, 'Can't be too careful, you know.'

'On the subject of not being too careful…' said Cam, seeing his opportunity to broach a tender subject, 'Jack and I have had a bit of a chinwag, and we were wondering whether you'd be okay with us staying the night.'

Lucille eyed Cam keenly over her spectacles.

'It's not for us, you understand,' he added quickly, 'We do have a home to go to. It's just… we thought it might be sensible for you to have some company, given we don't want to bother the local constabulary with what's gone on today.'

'Tarquin is probably responsible for today's scare,' explained Jack, 'We reckon he works for Savage and we know for certain he's after the notebook because he told us he was. One of our roommates, a lad called Ben, saw a man answering Tarquin's description talking with the postwoman a few minutes before he got coshed. We think Tarquin was trying to intercept the notebook.'

Lucille leaned back in her armchair and quietly clapped her hands together as she cogitated.

'Surely the moment you leave, this Tarquin person will follow you, and leave me alone? Oh, and by the way Jack, I'd toast yourself another teacake, yours is a little well done.'

Returning his attention to his toasting, Jack groaned when he found nothing more than a lump of charcoal attached to the end of the long brass fork.

'We thought that too,' Cam replied, 'But now that someone has been in this house, Jack and I both agree that we don't want to leave you alone in the house. Tarquin must know why we've come here.'

'Ah!' responded Lucille thoughtfully, 'That does, annoyingly, make perfect sense. So, one way or another, he may target me, believing I'm able to reveal the notebook's secrets.'

'We'd be much happier if at least one of us stays here,' said Jack, noticing a grin slowly creasing Lucille's lips, 'Although we completely understand if you want us to leave…'

Jack stopped talking when Lucille's grin had become so broad her entire face was a sea of creases.

'I'm flattered, and I absolutely adore you both!' Lucille gushed, 'Stay, please stay. It's been far too long since I had any proper company. And with two young bucks staying overnight, it will do my reputation in the street no end of good! My neighbours can be so conservative.'

'We'll do our best to be as visible as possible, Lucille,' Jack promised.

'But before I forget,' she replied, snapping her fingers at Jack, 'Give me the notebook back. I need to take photographic copies of each page before you take it back to Savage tomorrow.'

Jack and Cam traded an uncertain glance.

'Give him it back?'

'Yes, of course, my darling boy. How else are we to work out the keyword?'

Three minutes later, as Lucille was snapping the final few pages of Savage's notebook under the brightness of her desk lamp, the doorbell rang out. It was a proper bell, loud and insistent, making Cam flinch from its shrill demand for attention.

Jack looked to Lucille expectantly.

'I'm not expecting anyone,' she shrugged, 'I rarely expect any callers these days, especially this late in the evening.'

'Give Cam the notebook for safekeeping. I'll come to the door with you, just in case,' said Jack.

'Gosh this is exciting! It looks like a woman,' Lucille reported in a whisper, cocking her head to one side as she approached her front door.

'Hello?' Lucille ventured though the four inch crack

allowed by the chain on her door.

'Good evening,' the woman said with a smile that stretched her bright red lips wide, 'My name is Laura Fenwick. I.. er, want to speak with you about the… umm…notebook?'

Laura allowed this information to land and settle for a moment. The few inches of face hung back from the gap, as if unsure.

She continued, 'Erm… I know this might sound strange, and I could completely understand if you…'

She faltered, noticing Lucille's face was now pressed into the gap between the door and the frame. The older woman's eyes were popping and her eyebrows climbed up her forehead as she looked her caller up and down.

'Umm, this is a terribly awkward situation,' Laura muttered, trying to regain her thread, 'But I wondered whether I might have a word with you and your… jockeys?'

Thirty-Five

'How difficult can it be!' screamed Savage into his phone.

Crossing his lounge to a window, he scanned the quad, fearful his voice may have carried down to the yard. However, it was late evening and quiet. One lass, a yard girl, was trundling a barrow piled high with muck to the container behind the barns. She kept her head down and satisfied he hadn't been heard, Savage moved back from the window.

The line had remained silent but Savage soon heard what he imagined to be an exasperated breath being exhaled.

'Those wet-behind-the-ears apprentices have got my notebook. The information you got from that woman in Leeds… what was her name again?'

'Harris. Emily Harris.'

Savage allowed the name to revolve around his mind

for a few seconds. It meant nothing to him. He'd always been pretty good with names, faces, and... bodies, female ones that is. It was the small details, like their private life, and the nature of his deals with them that he could never recall clearly. It was one of the reasons he'd diligently kept his notebook updated. Holding the bridge of his nose for a moment, he fell back onto a sofa, giving up trying to place her. He was too agitated, too wound up after this morning's debacle with that wretched postwoman to give it any meaningful thought.

'I still can't place her. But it looks like she told you the truth. They had it delivered to them... So where were you?'

'I'm not your lapdog, Savage.'

Savage snorted derisively, 'Well, you're certainly no Golden Retriever. I thought you had it covered if I couldn't intercept the package?'

'The notebook wasn't delivered in the post.'

Savage considered this new information a moment, but swiftly found his anger bubbling up once more.

'It's in that house,' he seethed, 'The notebook has been seen in that house this morning! It arrived today. It must have been posted!'

'It wasn't. I intercepted their mail. If the apprentices have it, it must have already been there, or delivered by hand.'

Savage squeezed his eyes shut and shook his head.

'How it got there hardly matters now. We *know* they have it, so go and get it! You don't seem to be grasping the importance of locating that notebook... for *both* of us.'

A long sigh reverberated down the line.

'If you'd destroyed it as I suggested, you wouldn't be in this mess.'

'And you know why I couldn't do that,' Savage replied tartly.

Another silence developed, eventually broken by Savage.

'Where are they now?'

'Harrogate.'

'What the hell are they doing there?'

'They're visiting an old lady.'

'What? Family?'

'Nope, she's a loud, school teacher sort. Fancy house, lives on her own. Impressive security though, I almost had to deck another youngster.'

Savage was on his feet again, pacing the lounge, sweat breaking out under his arms, 'Another?'

'Listen to me, Savage,' replied the man, his voice suddenly brusque and impatient, 'How I sort out this screw-up is my business. Have you even considered how many copies of that notebook might be out there by now? Hell, if they wanted to, they could have the entire thing posted to their damned Facebook pages…'

Savage halted mid-perambulation around his lounge and leaned against a bare piece of white wall. No, he hadn't considered that possibility. And the thought of his notebook being digitised and… He swallowed hard. It was dry and painful.

'Solving *that* little problem will take drastic measures. You're either up for that, or we sit back and allow these snotty-nosed youngsters to decide how they're going to make us dance.'

Savage's knees wobbled. He slid down the wall until he was sitting on the floor, knees tucked into his chest, his phone still held to his ear.

'They still have to decode it,' he replied finally, a thin ribbon of hope running through his words.

'You want to take that chance?' the man said drily.

Savage's mind raced. He fired a short burst of questions at his caller, and received one word answers.

Finally, he asked, 'How will you do it?'

'The only option left to us is…'

'I don't want to know,' Savage said, cutting across the man, 'Just get it done.'

Thirty-Six

'I'll save you the time in googling me,' said Laura, 'I'm Laura Fenwick, and I live in York with my husband, Andrew…'

'…Fenwick, the MP for York Central!' Lucille exclaimed in fascination.

Lucille was at one end of the sofa, closest to the library fire, their visitor was sitting at the other end, quiet, compact and attractive. Cam was back in his favoured armchair, although unable to get comfortable, the arrival of this beautiful stranger into their midst was making him nervy. Meanwhile, Jack remained standing. He faced Laura with his arms crossed, unable to take his eyes off the woman since they'd been introduced. He found himself unconsciously tilting his head and studying her face intently. There was something about her he couldn't quite fathom. Deep in the recesses of his mind a memory was scratching at him, trying to become whole, attempting to surface.

Laura was far from imposing. She was sitting, knees and feet held neatly together, hands on her lap, a brand new pair of black training shoes melding into black jeans and a less than flattering thick cotton sweater that covered her lean frame up to a neck that was swathed in a dark blue cravat. And yet, her outfit seemed incongruous with her perfectly made-up face, shiny blonde hair cut into a perfect bob, and her salmon pink painted fingernails.

Jack guessed she was in her late-thirties, but he could be convinced to go ten years either way. She had the sort of plain, wrinkle-free face that retained enough vitality to make her age difficult to interpret. However, one thing was certain: she didn't look right in that outfit. She was uncomfortable, pushing at the baggy material under her arms, regularly shifting her backside on the sofa cushion. She gave the impression she was wearing someone else's clothes and just the thought of it was making her uneasy.

'The reason I'm here is rather embarrassing...' Laura went on, 'Blast it, I had this speech all worked out, and now I don't know where to start! I'm such a scatter-brain...'

She did indeed come across as being somewhat lightweight. Her voice had a girlish quality that didn't quite chime with her age, and her soft blue eyes held a slightly vacant, nice-but-dim quality.

Lucille lent over and placed a hand on the woman's arm, 'We're ready to listen, my dear. Relax your shoulders. Take a breath. In through your nose, out your mouth. Then tell us in one sentence, if you can, why you're here.'

Cam regarded their host, suddenly even more impressed. Lucille was generally loud, and terribly outspoken, to the point of embarrassment. He'd concluded she was certainly entertaining, but perhaps only in carefully measured doses. However, this version of Lucille could charm birds from the trees.

Doing as she was told, Laura breathed. Then she spoke, and once she got going, the words tumbled from her in a steady rhythm. She started by relating the events that led to her transferring her racehorse to the Sebastian Savage stables. How a drink at the racecourse Owners and Trainers bar at Beverley early in the season had become a conversation, then a visit to Savage's stables, and finally the rooms in his wing of Marsh Mansion. And when faced with no alternative, she described how she had acquiesced to Savage's demands.

'I was so ashamed. I've always been flattered by the attention of handsome men, but never, ever, gone that far. I can't for the life of me work out why I did,' Laura admitted with head bowed, unable to meet anyone's eye, 'I was so confused, upset, and angry afterwards! Angry at Savage, but probably more at myself for being so stupid. The next morning I was on the verge of telling Andrew, but Sebastian called me before I could pluck up enough courage.'

She stared at her clasped hands on her lap, shuddered, and took a stuttering breath that lifted her shoulders.

'Savage realised I was married to a politician,' she said, her voice laden with doom, 'And said he had… photos and video of me… and he'd make sure they would ruin Andrew's political career, my reputation, and my marriage. I had no choice. I had to keep quiet, immediately transfer my horse to his yard, and pay his extortionate training fees.'

Laura sighed. It was a large, heartfelt sigh that had no defined finish. She seemed to cave in, dropping her head once more, shrinking into herself.

'I followed you here tonight on a whim. Then I saw that man come out of the house and hurry off down the street. I got worried and couldn't… help myself. Em' will be beside herself if she knows I've spoken to you. That dratted notebook! I don't suppose you've decoded it?'

'Em?' queried Cam.

'Emily,' she replied bitterly into the hands on her lap she was now wringing, 'My partner in…'

'Crime?' suggested Jack.

'My partner in… all of this,' Laura stated earnestly, not picking up on the sarcasm in Jack's voice, 'You've met her… at the Whitley Bay Playhouse?'

Cam said, 'We did, but what's Emily got to do with you?'

'I've been desperate to find a way out of this mess. I started to monitor all the stable socials, following everything the lads and lasses were posting. Savage isn't well liked… I found that out within minutes!'

'I discovered Emily on one of the social media websites. I'd been doing lots of searches on Savage and I came across a couple of her really old posts. Although she never said it outright online, I was convinced she'd had a similar experience to me. I got in touch, and I was proved right - Savage defrauded her out of tens of thousands of pounds. I met her about two months ago and for the last few weeks we've been trading thoughts, ideas… ways to extract me from this nightmare, and perhaps get some compensation for

Emily.'

Cam shared a disappointed look with Jack. He'd been so sure Emily had been telling the truth that night at the theatre in Whitley Bay. It now appeared Jack's suspicions about the woman had been spot on. He was becoming something of a whizz when it came to identifying people with villainous intentions. He'd never trusted Savage, hadn't been too sure about Grace, and was now proven right about Emily.

'Is Emily with you? Is she outside?'

Laura shook her head at Cam, 'She's working with that hypnotist of hers in Darlington tonight. She knows I've come here alone to watch the house in order to…'

Laura's voice trailed away to nothing and her shoulders sagged.

'It's okay, my dear,' Lucille assured her, 'May as well get it all out in the open.'

'I wasn't supposed to get too close,' she whined, 'I wasn't supposed to knock on your door, and I certainly wasn't meant to be in here, unburdening myself like this… but Emily… I've realised Emily is willing to go much further than I am… I'm just *so tired* of the lies!'

'Emily doesn't know you're speaking with us?'

Laura shook her bowed head again and it was Lucille's turn to mouth the boys a silent, 'Wow!'

Laura continued, 'Emily and I set out to find something on Savage, something damning enough to ruin him.'

'What's good for the goose…' said Lucille knowingly to a trio of blank faces.

'…is good for the gander,' she added with a frown, 'Don't tell me you haven't heard of that idiom before?'

She began chuntering something about the state of education in the country. Meanwhile, Jack gestured to Laura for her to continue.

'We were after evidence. Anything that proved his wrong doing. It had to be indisputable. Or we had to capture him in the process of duping another woman… but, it was impossible. We couldn't find anything... he's squeaky clean. It's like he's got conning women down to a fine art!'

'After a month of trying, we both realised we didn't know enough of what was happening in the Savage yard. I could visit my horse of course, but the one visit I made, Savage was very careful to never leave my side. We needed someone actually *inside* the yard to help us.'

Laura met Cam's gaze, 'And then you turned up on the same train as Emily. She couldn't believe her luck! What's more, you told her you'd argued with your boss – with Savage. She decided you had the right... profile and she had to make the most of it.'

She turned her attention to Lucille, 'Emily isn't much of a conversationalist, but you got on with these two so well...'

'I do have that effect on some people,' remarked Lucille, loudly and happily.

'When Emily convinced you all to take the free tickets to her show, she was winging it, hoping to benefit from the opportunity that had fallen into her lap. She didn't have a plan, it just developed as she got to know more about the two of you. Emily said she couldn't put you fully under on the train, so instead, she used a suggestion technique, especially on Jack, as he was easier, sitting right beside her. She suggested you both attend the Stefan Kreihn's show, and that you offer yourself up for being hypnotised.'

Laura's expression became troubled.

'Once you'd got up on stage Emily immediately took the two of you into the darkest area of the wings. That's... when it happened. She spent the rest of the evening performing deep hypnosis on both of you.'

Laura glanced nervously at Cam, 'Emily made sure you'd fall off your horse on the gallops.'

'She *did* hypnotise me! What, so I'd charge into Savage on the gallops?' Cam gasped.

'No, no!' Laura cried, 'It wasn't like that. Emily meant for you to gently drop off your horse twenty yards beyond

Savage.'

'Gently drop off?' Cam replied in an exasperated tone, 'I was doing a three-quarter pace gallop! What did you think... that I'd bounce and spring up like a jack-in-the-box?'

Laura's eyes became teary. Sniffing, she soldiered on.

'It wasn't about you. It was the notebook. Savage's notebook. We had to find out what was in his notebook.'

'I'd seen for myself how much he coveted that notebook of his. On the day he took me back to his rooms in Malton, as soon as we got indoors I saw him take that red book out of a zipped pocket of his jacket. It was like he couldn't relax until he knew it was safely locked away. Emily reckons he has a safe and that notebook always goes in there when he's in his rooms. When he's outside, it's always in that same, zipped jacket pocket.'

'I can see why you might think the notebook held details of his nefarious activities,' Lucille noted, 'Digital media is so easily hacked these days.'

Jack and Cam turned their heads to stare incredulously at Lucille. She smiled wanly and waved a wrist at them, 'I'm no one-trick pony!' she gently scolded, her attention returning to Laura.

'We'd watched Savage every day for weeks on the gallops. As long as it was nice weather, Savage did the same thing every day,' said Laura, warming somewhat to her subject.

'He'd park his car behind the hedge, walk over the grass to his little raised piece of ground and after ten or fifteen minutes he'd get hot and remove that lined jacket of his and hang it over the post at the far edge of the plinth, only a yard or two away from him.'

Cam imagined all those rides up the Malton All-Weather gallop. He could see Savage in his mind's eye, standing on his plinth, either clutching binoculars or scrolling through something on his phone. And behind him, nine times out of ten during the summer months, he'd have that jacket of his, slung over a fence post he'd had planted at the back of his plinth.

'We thought Savage would see you drop off the horse, and if you laid there for a few moments, he would go over to make sure you were okay. Savage would be distracted and I would nip out from the hedge and grab the notebook from his jacket. Emily said you'd be okay, being young and fit.'

'But it went wrong when he dropped his phone and got too close to the gallop,' said Lucille, 'Cam fell into Savage and knocked him out. Cam stayed on the deck for a few seconds, as he'd probably been hypnotised to do, but then found Savage injured and unconscious. Meanwhile you'd used those seconds to steal the notebook from Savage's jacket.'

A demure Laura nodded her agreement.

'I did. I sneaked over to Savage and took the notebook from his jacket pocket. I know what you're getting at, and I'm not proud of what we did. But…'

'Not proud…?' interrupted an indignant Jack, unable to keep silent any longer, 'Why on earth was I hypnotised to lose races? What possible reason did you and Emily have for doing that?'

Laura's cheeks reddened, and her lips tightened into a thin crease as she considered her reply.

'Oh, bother! You know about that…' she said sheepishly.

'Emily didn't tell me what she'd done. At least, not until after the first race you lost. I didn't realise how desperate things were for her… financially. Savage left her with absolutely nothing. Look, as soon as I found out she'd hypnotised you, and she was betting on one of those exchange-thingy websites, I put it right.'

Jack tilted his head one way, then the other. It was infuriating, he still couldn't place Laura's face. As soon as he edged closer to the answer, the memory would immediately fade. It was unbearable.

Laura had noticed the frustration building in Jack.

'Just a moment,' she said, taking another tissue from the box Lucille had placed on the coffee table in front of her. She began dabbing at her lips, then her eyes. Cam realised she was removing her make-up. Finally, she reached behind her head and flipped over a hood and cinched it tight, removing all sight of her hair.

'Recognise me?' she asked Jack with a tight, uncertain smile.

'The autograph hunter,' he said under his breath, then repeated it, only louder, 'You were in the waiting room too, at the police station…'

It felt like a dam had burst and a wave of memories were flooding into Jack's mind.

'And at Haydock…' he said in a whisper, all these instances, the boyish good looks, the sharp, perfectly sculpted nose, the grin… suddenly they all blurred together for a moment. Jack slammed his eyes shut and tried to clear his mind.

'I read a stable lass's post about you being taken to Fulford Police Station,' Laura said to Cam, 'You were never supposed to get hurt, and I was horrified when I learned that you might be charged by the police, so I went along to make sure you'd be okay. Emily was dead set against it, but if the police hadn't released you, I was going to hand myself in and explain everything. But in the end, you and your friends were able to leave.'

'According to DC Akbar, I'm still under investigation,' Cam said huffily.

Jack, still with his arms crossed, pitched in angrily, 'What about me? Emily lied. She reckoned some hypnosis junkie must have got to me?'

'I lent her some cash, but a few days later Emily was suddenly flush. She said she'd won some money and I became suspicious. In the end, Emily admitted she'd had winning bets on two of your rides to lose. I told her she had to stop immediately. It wasn't fair – we'd caused you both enough trouble. She was actually pretty good about that, especially after I offered to give her some money. But she wouldn't put it right herself, she was frightened of being recognised. So she taught me how to shake your hand and put you into a trance long enough to remove her hypnotic instructions that were stopping you winning on favourites. It was easier for me because you'd already been primed by Emily. Also, Emily said you were incredibly suggestive…'

She glanced back at Cam, 'I'd just managed to get it done, remove the instructions to lose on favourites, that is, when you saw me and chased me out of Haydock Racecourse. I was so relieved when the name Jack Goodman popped up in first place on the results for the last race…'

Laura slowly undid the tie on her hood and peeled it back over her head, shaking her bob back out.

'I was convinced you were a boy,' said Cam, now able to place Laura's boyish face.

'That's down to Emily again, I'm afraid,' Laura admitted, 'She did something when she hypnotised you in the wings of the stage at Scarborough. She implanted the notion that you couldn't recognise a boy in a hoodie. It was meant to stop you seeing me going through Savage's jacket on the gallops, but there were other times...'

'Like when?'

'I passed you on the street outside your house when I brought the notebook to you. You were racing to meet the post woman at the time, and you looked straight through me.'

'It was you who gave the notebook to Charlie?'

Laura nodded, 'Neither Emily nor I could do anything with it, and I told her we had to give it back, otherwise Savage was never going to leave you alone. I didn't want to see you lose your careers because of that nasty man and his rotten notebook. I decided at the last minute not to post it, just in case it got lost in the mail system, but when I got to your house in Norton it was like your street was full of madmen. You two were rushing around, that wonderful postwoman was being accosted by everyone, and then Savage turned up! There was no way I could deliver the notebook myself, so I gave it to your friend. She was so nice at the police station, I felt certain she would pass it on.'

Jack was still on his feet, but his hand was massaging the back of his neck, trying to put the events of the last week into some sort of order.

'You've said Savage blackmailed you to send Kaleidoscope to his stables, but how is Emily involved?'

'I'm not proud of what I did. I still can't quite believe it. And I'd understand if you have no sympathy for me...'

'Your story I believe, but I want to know about Emily,' Jack insisted, his irritation growing, 'She lied to our faces. She may be lying to you, and *still* lying to us. Perhaps you are too.'

Laura blinked, and a tear dropped onto her hoodie, creating a dark smudge in the cotton.

'All I know is that Savage swindled her out of lot of money,' she sniffed, dabbing another tissue at her eyes.

'That's not good enough,' Jack challenged, 'Committing adultery was your choice, and you're paying for it. In Emily's case, most owners lose money when they buy racehorses. If she couldn't afford it, she shouldn't have got involved! It sounds like we're mixed up in some stupid vendetta you two have against Savage...'

Jack lowered his voice, despite his surging anger, 'Hypnotising me to lose races and Cam to fall off a horse... So you can steal, and bet on fixed races. These are criminal offences. And yet you've passed on Savage's notebook for us to return, as if we're the ones who stole it!'

Jack took a breath, 'I suppose you'll want to know whether we've decoded it?'

Laura didn't answer.

'Tell me, why should we do anything to help you?'

A steady stream of tears were now flowing down Laura's cheeks. Jack wasn't swayed, he glared down at the woman, daring her to reply.

'Steady on, Jack,' Cam said, holding up a hand to his friend, 'To be fair, most trainers wouldn't blackmail their owners and employ dodgy men to threaten and clout their stable staff.'

Laura took the tissue proffered by Lucille. She blew her nose and took a few seconds to centre herself, 'I know. It all sounds terrible. I don't blame you. I'd run a mile from myself and Emily if I was in your shoes. I was just hoping his notebook… might help us to prove the real criminal is Sebastian Savage.'

Laura raised her chin and looked hopefully over at Lucille, 'Have you solved the code in the notebook?'

'No.' Lucille stated firmly, 'I'm afraid not, my dear.'

Laura's disappointed frown was so deep it sent a wave of wrinkles up her forehead that immediately aged her by a decade.

'I was hoping you'd have it solved before you gave it back to Savage. It may have brought this whole sorry episode to an end.'

'You don't think it will end if the boys give the notebook back to Savage?' asked Lucille.

'No… at least, I don't think so. Emily sounded a little… unhinged the last time I spoke with her,' said Laura, tears once again forming in the corner of her eyes.

'That's why I insisted on giving the notebook back to you. I thought it would remove you two from any blame and further danger.'

She issued a ragged sigh that squeezed another tear from her eye, 'I'm afraid Emily might be planning something even worse for Sebastian Savage, and it might involve the two of you.'

Thirty-Seven

'Emily's lack of empathy always worried me,' said

Laura, fluttering her eyelashes.

Lucille had suggested Laura took a moment to collect herself. She'd returned from the bathroom with newly applied make-up, freshly brushed hair, and looking altogether less emotional. Jack couldn't believe the transformation.

'With Emily betting on you to lose races, and the lies she told you in Whitley Bay. I was afraid she'll stop at nothing to bring Savage down,' continued Laura, 'She has this warped expectation that hypnosis will solve all her problems, that's why I never handed the notebook over to her.'

'She's never seen the notebook?'

'Oh, she'd seen it, but I always kept hold of it. I may be a bit of an air-head, but I didn't trust her with keeping it safe. She became increasingly angry about that, especially when I insisted we hand it back to you. I haven't seen her for a week and we haven't spoken since this morning, just before I dropped the notebook off. She should be working at a show in Darlington tonight, but to be honest, I can't be sure she isn't sitting outside in her car right now.'

Laura continued to explain herself for the next half an hour, going over events in more detail and trying to answer the many questions Cam, and, in particular, Jack threw at her. Uppermost in both their minds was whether they were still under Emily's hypnotic influence. It became apparent that Laura was troubled with the same worries and was unable to guarantee anything when it came to Emily's influence over them. Apart from repeating the jerked handshake and the few words in Jack's ear at Haydock she'd been taught by Emily, Laura had next to no knowledge of hypnosis.

By the time she'd finished speaking, Jack had taken a seat, Cam was on the edge of his, and Lucille, having been silent for over thirty minutes, was now sitting beside Laura on the sofa, holding the younger woman's hand.

'When I saw that man coming out of your house, and the door left open, I knew I had to check you were all alright, even more so after I spotted Cam scrambling over the side-gate. What with Emily, Savage, this strange man, and the police... I was really worried he'd done something horrible,' Laura explained, looking fretful once more.

'You do still have the notebook, don't you?' she asked.

Lucille produced the red notebook from an inside pocket.

Laura brightened, managing a small smile and immediately her younger self returned.

'I thought he'd stolen it,' she said with a relieved sigh, 'And I'm so glad you're all fit and well. I had this awful image of you all being...'

Laura sniffed and blinked twice, doing her best to not ruin her newly applied make-up with more tears.

'He was skulking in the back garden and ran through the house to get away,' said Cam.

Laura frowned, 'Through the house?'

'Time for a hot beverage and a slice of Battenberg,' Lucille announced loudly, slapping her knee for good measure, 'Nothing like marzipan to get you feeling better. Just the name... *mar-zi-pan!*... does it for me, my sweet girl!'

She got to her feet, steadied herself against the back of the sofa, and with a roll of her eyes she signalled for Jack to join her in the kitchen.

'Look after this poor woman, will you, my dear boy?' she half-asked, half-instructed Cam who accepted the command without question and immediately went over to join Laura on the sofa.

'What do you think to all of that then?' Lucille asked as soon as she and Jack were ensconced in the kitchen, the kettle making enough noise to be sure to muffle their voices.

'It's a hell of a story... but believable.'

'Do you trust her?' asked Lucille.

'Not completely.'

Lucille contemplated his reply as she placed three tea bags in the pot and cobbled together the rest of the elements onto a serving tray.

'I've had an idea,' Lucille said with a sly look, 'It's a little bit tricksey, but I think it could get both your apprenticeships back on course, sort out this Emily Harris, and possibly catch Mr Savage with his fingers in the cookie jar.'

'Go on,' urged Jack.

By the time Lucille had finished speaking, the kettle's contents had cooled enough to warrant another quick boil while Jack mulled over her suggestion.

As the kettle clicked off for the second time, an excited Lucille asked, 'I know it means cracking that notebook's code, but what do you think, Jack?'

He looked her straight in the eye.

'I think it's a brilliant idea and we should absolutely do it... if the notebook does contain what you think.'

Lucille grinned, the light from the spotlights in the ceiling dancing in her eyes, 'I absolutely adore you!' she announced in her standard broadcast volume voice, 'You are so fearless!'

Taken aback, and unable to meet her gaze at first, Jack soon found himself swamped with dopamine. It was as if he'd just ridden a winner, the only other time he experienced this sort of inner euphoria. It felt like a soft, comforting, welcoming pillow for his soul, and in returning Lucille's grin, he soon found the muscles in his cheeks beginning to ache. And when Lucille started to giggle with excitement, he couldn't help but join her.

After calming each other down, they returned to the library and found Cam chatting amiably to Laura about her racehorse and why she'd given the colt that racing name.

'I was looking through a child's kaleidoscope in an antique shop the first time I met Andrew,' she explained, 'He blocked out the light from the window, and when I dropped the kaleidoscope from my eye, he was standing there. It was love at first sight.'

They ate Battenburg, Jack told Cam to stop groaning

with satisfaction after every bite of the cake, and eventually the conversation slowly went full circle and back to the code within the notebook.

'I should leave,' announced Laura, 'I'll be worse than useless at helping with that notebook.'

She thanked them all, especially Lucille, and left her contact details, promising to be in touch over the course of the next few days.

'So how do we crack his code?' Jack asked once the front door had closed behind Laura.

Once again, it was Lucille who jumped in.

'Come with me. Come on, both of you!' Lucille said encouragingly, back on her feet again. Just for a moment, she seemed to go slightly off-balance. Jack took her by the arm.

'Got up too quickly, my dear,' she explained, gently removing his hand, 'Just keen to get on!'

She led them out of the library, down the hall, then up the stairs to the first floor landing where she turned and walked to the end of the corridor, stopping in front of a door sporting a serious looking padlock. Apart from the odd little creak of the floorboards as they were standing waiting, Jack could hear a low hum coming from inside what he'd assumed had to be a bedroom. Lucille took out a small bunch of keys and slotted one into the lock and twisted.

'You did check this room for our intruder earlier?' asked Cam.

'No. We never checked it,' she replied, 'There was no need. He'd never get through this door!'

Jack and Cam traded a shrug.

'I told you my husband and I worked together. Well, this is what we did for twenty-five years,' Lucille said as she removed the key and grasped an uncommonly solid looking door handle, 'I met Monty at university. We were on the same course. And in 1997 we were the original internet geeks! And the work we did there turned into a nice little business.'

She pushed the door open and stepped inside. The

door, whilst wooden on the outside, was in fact attached to a secondary, thick steel door. A wall of uncommonly cool air wafted out as they entered a large, square room. It was shrouded in darkness, although the hum of electronic equipment and the odd flashing light and line of small green pulsing LED's were the big giveaway.

'Computers?' asked Jack.

Lucille flicked a switch on the wall and several small pinpoints of light sparkled from the ceiling, yet they were so dim they only served to provide shadowy outlines of the room's contents. Jack and Cam narrowed their eyes, squinting at what turned out to be two racks of blinking metal boxes and a half-full water cooler placed beside a small table upon which one of Lucille's ubiquitous serving trays was sitting. Another trio of hidden beams of light were directed at the other end of the room and a desk that filled the far end of the room. It was tiered, with several keyboards tucked under the primary desktop. And behind the desk, Jack could just make out a metal framework and a set of blacked out windows. He counted six flat monitors of differing sizes on the frame that, one by one, were busy sparking into life. In front of this altar to the digital world sat two black office chairs that were works of art in their own right.

'Monty and I were employed to hack into huge corporate or government computer networks,' Lucille explained in a soft voice as she crossed over to the two chairs, waving Jack and Cam over.

Running her fingertips over the ergonomically designed head support on the left-hand chair, she added, 'We'd advise those companies how to make their systems more secure.'

'Wow!' Cam cooed, 'There must be enough computing power in this one room to run a small country!'

Lucille smiled, 'You might think so, but actually, it's knowledge of networks, systems, and most importantly, the entity, corporation, or even the person you're attempting to hack into that counts most. If you have the right knowledge, you can break into any system with just an average laptop and a decent internet connection.'

'Blimey, Lucille, remind me never to troll you on social media!' Cam said with a chortle.

'Never used them. Never will,' Lucille replied, 'And I'd advise you to do the same. Spawn of the devil, most of it. But you're right, back in the day, we did have quite a bit of processing power here. We used this setup to mine Bitcoins...'

Lucille grasped the top of the chair, massaging the edges of the backrest with both hands, and seemed to be elsewhere for a moment.

'Are you okay, Lucille?' Jack asked as the silence lengthened.

His query appeared to disconnect her from whatever thoughts had been troubling her and she swung around, 'Yes, my dear boy. All good, now where was I?'

Before anyone could answer, she answered her own question.

'Ah, yes! Knowledge. The *right* knowledge. Knowledge that will allow the algorithms I write to do their work more effectively. That's what I need to crack this replacement cipher.'

'So how do you get this knowledge?' Jack asked.

Lucille produced a broad smile.

'You two, and only you two can get it for me.'

The two boys smiled back uncertainly and privately shared a puzzled glance as Lucille headed back to the thin rectangle of light that represented the half-open door.

'Come on, I'll explain downstairs,' she said airily, 'It should hopefully put your riding careers back on track as well.'

'I'm all for that!' Cam agreed, as he and Jack followed her onto the landing.

'And looking at the time, I think its gin and tonic o'clock!' Lucille added as she locked the door to her server room behind them.

Thirty-Eight

Cam hadn't felt this content for months, but to balance this out, he was also experiencing intense guilt. After a wonderful night's sleep, in a bed so comfortable he'd slept on through his phone's alarm, Lucille had cooked them both a full English breakfast: sausage, bacon, mushrooms, tomatoes, fried egg, black pudding, and a fried slice of bread. It had been glorious, all washed down with one of the best cups of coffee he'd ever tasted.

'I reckon I've put on five pounds thanks to that breakfast,' he complained to Jack as Corbyn trundled through the Malton traffic, heading to the Marsh Landing stables.

'Good job you can claim seven pounds then,' Jack replied, concentrating on the road ahead.

'Ha, ha, haaa!' Cam replied sarcastically from the passenger seat, 'What can I say, I'm five-foot-ten-inches tall and I like my food! I only have to look at a pack of butter…'

'We're here,' Jack interrupted with some relief.

They pulled off the main road and passed a large sign directing them into the Sebastian Savage Marsh Landing Stables. He'd heard Cam's speech about his weight control, or lack of it, many times before and wasn't in the mood for another rendition just at the moment.

The yard looked exactly the same as when Cam had left it a week earlier. He didn't know why, but he'd expected it to have altered. A week away from riding seemed much longer than just seven days.

'Now remember what Lucille told us. I'll keep my eyes and ears open,' said Jack, 'And you'll do all the talking, right?'

Cam grunted his agreement. They'd checked with Charlie that Savage was on the yard, then called ahead, but only ten minutes ago. Savage knew they were coming, but with any luck, he wouldn't have time to get Tarquin over to beat them to a pulp.

Both barn managers, Miguel and Dean, intercepted

them before they reached the quad. Dean held onto a smirk, whilst Miguel looked uncomfortably wary.

'Hiya, Cam. How's tricks?' Dean inquired without a smile, looking him up and down, 'Working in the sewers now, are we?'

Despite Lucille's valiant efforts overnight, the anti-climb grease had refused to completely relinquish its grip on his clothes, and Jack hadn't wanted to return to the Racing House just in case Tarquin was waiting for them. Without a change of clothes he was sporting black patches all over his sweater and jeans. They looked slick and sticky, but were in fact, rock hard.

'Anything's better than working for Savage,' Cam replied sweetly.

'Where is he?' Jack asked, sensing the chilly reception might be because Savage was close by. He was proved right when the man himself emerged from the darkness of a stable fifteen yards away. Beside him, Jack could feel Cam bristling with resentment as the suave trainer, who looked like he'd just walked off a country clothing photo shoot, approached.

Jack shot Cam a swift, 'You got this,' glance.

'I'll deal with this, Dean, Miguel,' Savage ordered, dismissing the two of them with a flick of his fingers.

'Okay, where is it?' Savage demanded as soon as his employees were out of earshot.

'Not here,' Cam insisted, 'We'll discuss this in your… umm.. rooms.'

'Right here is good enough for you two. Hand it over. It's my property.'

Both boys shook their heads.

'In private. In your rooms in the mansion,' Cam repeated, 'We're not discussing terms out here.'

'Terms!' spat Savage defiantly, 'I'll give you some terms to deal with…'

Cam held up a flat palm, 'Fine, we'll deal with this now… Jack, have you got that cryptologists telephone number?'

Jack took out his phone and began tapping at the screen.

'It may take weeks, or months... But we'll get there in the end. I imagine artificial intelligence will help somehow. And then we'll see why you're so desperate for this little red book to be returned to you.'

Cam's hand went to the inside pocket of his jacket and studying Savage, he fingered the red notebook, toying with it. Savage watched him intently. Presently, Cam pinched the leather between finger and thumb and tugged, sliding the notebook up so that an inch of the paisley indented pattern could be seen poking out invitingly. Savage's face went ashen and his pupils became as large as pennies. He licked his lips. It was as if the mere presence of his notebook was enough to make the trainer salivate.

Jack stiffened. In that moment, Savage resembled a hungry animal. Dangerous, brutal, and ready to pounce. Instead of recoiling, Jack calmly looked on, appraising the wild flash of insanity in the trainer's eyes.

As quickly as the animal within Savage appeared, it vanished from his expression without a trace, replaced with the trainer's smarmy resting face. Had that desire remained any longer, Jack wouldn't have been surprised if Savage had produced a gun from under his sports jacket and calmly shot them both dead. He wondered whether Cam had seen that momentary flash of danger? Glancing at him, Jack thought not. Cam was exuding calmness and determination. Jack attempted to do the same.

Unbidden, a woman's voice entered his mind. It took a few words, but he soon pinned her Yorkshire accent down. It was Emily. She was reminding him. He rode every race without fear. He lived his life without fear. Emily was telling him a traumatic event in his past had removed his fear... and he must use this gift to reach his goal, a new goal...

Exactly when had Emily told him this? Jack asked

himself. He didn't know. Swiftly pushing this query aside, he concentrated on Savage. There were more pressing questions right in front of him, in the here and now.

Jack examined Savage once more. Having experienced a split-second of this man's undiluted, pure evil shouldn't he be filled with dread? He'd imagined the trainer shooting Cam and himself dead, hadn't he? Instead, Savage's flash of potential darkness only made Jack more determined to discover this man's secrets.

Had they underestimated Savage? Did this small, but thick book of devilishly complex codes hold information that was far more sinister than coaxing women to cheat on their husbands and then blackmailing them?

'Alright. Alright!' Savage growled though gritted teeth, 'We'll go into my rooms. Follow me.'

He'd backed down a tad too easily, Jack decided as he and Cam tracked Savage between the barns and over the quad to his private residence. No matter. This was what they wanted.

Savage took them to the back of the mansion, to what Cam decided was the tradesman's entrance, rather than the grandly pillared entrance on the other side of the mansion. Through a communal hall and up a set of stairs, they entered Savage's rooms via a tall, heavy, oak door and were hit with the smell of wax and stargazer lilies. Passing what Jack assumed were a couple of bedrooms, they walked down a short corridor with a wooden floor laid in a whalebone pattern and entered a large room that seemed to serve no purpose, other than for Savage to hang up his coat, change into a pair of moccasin slippers and admire a vase of flowers on a small, shiny wooden table. Cam explained afterwards that it was a reception room. Jack thought it was a huge waste of a room.

At the end of the hallway Savage led them into a large square lounge and watched the boys sink down into an 'L' shaped leather sofa, the largest of the three sofas in the room.

The trainer remained standing, which irked Jack as he realised it was a conscious effort by Savage to dominate them.

The lounge had a minimalist feel, white painted walls, with glass replacing wood wherever possible. The coffee table was a section of sawn tree trunks fitted with an oval glass pane. Two bookcases also boasted shelves made of glass, although they were mostly bare. Compared to other trainers' homes Jack had visited, there was a surprising lack of racing memorabilia. The shelves held a few small sculptures of the naked human form, specifically the female variety, and there were large framed paintings on each wall that Jack presumed had to be originals, again, mostly avant-garde stuff mixed in with nudes. He really likes his nudes, noted Jack.

A large sheepskin rug lay in front of a fancy flame-effect fire, whilst all the furniture pointed towards the focal point; a huge wall-mounted flat-screen television.

There was hardly any reading matter on show. A magazine rack held a trio of racing publications, but they didn't appear to be well-thumbed. A small shelf, glass again, boasted a few hardbacks and unable to read the titles, Jack made a mental note to tour that way whenever the chance arose.

Beyond the lounge lay the kitchen, a set of glass and steel double doors providing a window into a sparkling array of cream units with black marble tops interspersed with various appliances. Shiny steel saucepans and other implements such as ladles, spoons, knives, and strainers were hanging on the walls or sticking to magnetised strips.

'Not satisfied with trying to kill me on the gallops, I presume you're here to blackmail me with my own notebook?'

Savage's arm was back in a sling, merely a band of a spongey substance that did a figure of eight from his wrist up around his neck. There was no full arm sling, no plaster cast.

Not as serious as he'd made out to the police then, thought Cam. They'd been under the impression it had been a full break, but from his experience of several broken bones, Savage was carrying nothing more than a minor fracture.

'I'm sure you're recording this meeting. So for the purposes of your hidden video cameras, I can confirm that neither myself, Cameron Camberley, or my colleague, Jack Goodman, stole anything, or purposely set out to attack you, Mr Savage. Those are false accusations.'

Savage, standing behind one of the leather sofas, stared fixedly at Cam whilst gripping its backrest, his fingernails making indentations into the soft animal hide.

'Once bitten, Mr Savage... We won't be making the mistake again of allowing you to edit our words so you can lie about us,' Cam stated in a steady, low timbre, 'And by the way, we haven't received a copy of that recording of yours. You know, the damning evidence against Jack... I wonder why that is?'

Jack was impressed. Cam's voice boomed around the room. He was sounding like someone three-times his age and twice his height. The two hours practice in Lucille's library last night had been worth it, as had recalling and analysing every recent encounter they'd had with Savage. Lucille had methodically quizzed them on every detail.

Savage remained rigid, his perfectly sculpted features giving nothing away.

'Just so we are completely clear, we are recording this meeting, with a video link open to a third-party who will have no hesitation in contacting the local police if contact is lost, we are attacked, or we are intimidated in any way,' Cam added, tapping the breast pocket of his shirt to indicate where his phone's camera was poking out. This last claim was false. Whilst the phone was recording, Cam doubted the quality of either the video or sound quality would be good enough, and his internet connection was too weak to do a live broadcast.

Savage eyed the small lens silently recording him, resisting the urge to immediately jump up and tear it from the boy's chest. A moment later he was wondering whether he was telegraphing his thoughts to the apprentices.

'If you have any ideas of taking the notebook by force, or perhaps you have Mr Tarquin waiting in the wings, ready with his cosh, think again,' stated Cam, smiling.

Jack caught a quiver of a reaction from Savage, a muscle in his cheek pulsing, and he wondered whether Tarquin actually *was* in the next room, ready to pounce. If he was, it held no fear for him. He pushed the thought away. He had to remain concentrated on the task Lucille had set them.

'Now for the detail, Mr Savage,' continued Cam, leaning forward and placing his elbows on his knees and steepling his fingers, 'We want our riding careers to be resurrected with a blemish-free record. This means halting the progress of your complaint against myself with DC Meera Akbar so she may close the case regarding the accident on the gallops.'

Cam paused, waiting for a response. Savage remained stony-faced and silent.

He continued, 'You must also contact Mr Cupkiss at the BHA and Meera Akbar at York Police Station to retract your statements and the false evidence you've submitted accusing Jack of attacking you with no cause.'

Cam took a breath, and with Savage again failing to respond, he soldiered on.

'Finally, you will immediately release me from my apprenticeship. You will make these two phone calls now. With us in the room. When our demands have been met, we will hand over the notebook.'

Both boys sat back and waited for a response. Aware there were beads of sweat forming on his forehead, Cam tried to ignore the urge to mop them up with the back of his hand, instead, studying Savage's face for a reaction. When it came, it wasn't the response either of them had anticipated.

Thirty-Nine

DC Meera Akbar removed her phone from her ear and ended the call. She shook her head, thoroughly confused. She took a long moment to consider what Sebastian Savage had just told... no, what he'd demanded of her. If anything, the conversation had served to make her suspicious.

Transferring her attention to her PC monitor, she brought up the relevant search box and typed in 'Cameron Camberley'. As expected, the boy had an unblemished record. There was only one incident in that file, the interview she'd been duty-bound to conduct with him a few days ago.

Meera checked, and as expected, the last update to the file regarding the accident on the Malton gallops had been by herself, several days ago. She'd closed the incident file, marking it for no further action.

Despite the initial protests of Mr Savage, there were no suspicious circumstances, nothing officially reported stolen, and the incident had been categorised as an accident. She'd spoken with Savage two days ago to inform him of that decision, although Meera noted she hadn't got around to informing Cameron Camberley. She added it to her 'to do' list. In her opinion, Camberley was an honest lad who through inexperience in the saddle, had incurred the wrath of a less-than-wholesome employer as a consequence of a simple riding error.

Her next query saw her bring up the record for Jack Goodman. This made far more interesting reading. However, despite what Savage had said on the phone, she couldn't locate any recent report of a complaint against the boy. And Savage hadn't lodged a contact with any other police force in the last week, not since his accident... in fact, despite some meaty charges for burglary as a minor, Goodman had kept a clean sheet for over two years, which was odd, given Savage's assertion that he'd lodged a complaint of physical assault and attempted blackmail against the nineteen-year-old several days earlier.

It wasn't his non-existent complaint that had Meera Akbar wondering about Savage, or that he'd seen fit to contact her to drop an imaginary complaint. It was the sound of someone's voice in the background reminding Savage of which accusations he should rescind.

Meera was suddenly reminded of Savage's conversation she'd overheard in the hospital. She ticked herself off for not following that up. As a double-check, she searched for Sebastian Savage and waited patiently for the computer system to display his file, should one exist.

***

Jack groaned. If anything, Corbyn's preference for pulling left towards every nearside kerb was getting worse. Driving him was becoming something of a battle of wills. He eased down the single-track road from Marsh Landing Stables and at the junction with Beverley Road, Corbyn managed to turn left without having to touch the wheel.

'Well, that went easier than I expected,' Cam stated happily as Jack gunned the engine and the Renault sputtered its way into Norton.

'After that initial welcome I was half-expecting him to batter us with a cosh and steal the notebook,' added Cam, 'But he did everything we asked… it was like he was rushing to tie up the loose ends.'

Both hands on the wheel, Jack was frowning at the road ahead, creases of concentration etched into his brow. Recognising that Jack was preoccupied with keeping Corbyn straight, Cam continued the one-sided conversation.

'That phone call he had with DC Akbar was a bit stilted, didn't you think? And having to give him our phones to prove we didn't have copies of his notebook was a bit odd.'

Still Jack offered no reply.

Cam soldiered on, 'Once he saw his precious notebook

and we told him we'd not got anywhere near decoding it, he was all business…'

Cam left this hanging, but Jack remained mute.

'Still, he wasn't to know Lucille had taken photos of every page on her own phone last night,' Cam added as they negotiated a couple of speed humps on the edge of the village.

'And Savage was keen as mustard to release me as his apprentice. I was surprised how quickly he agreed to that. To have the papers in the next room, already signed…'

Cam offered a couple of seconds of opportunity for Jack to comment before continuing, 'Makes you think, doesn't it?'

The car pulled out of the next junction and Corbyn trundled out onto Langton Road. Cam twisted in the passenger seat and squinted at Jack.

'And Cupkiss sounded really hacked off when he was told to cancel his investigation, and restore your riding license, wasn't he?'

Jack, staring ahead had begun chewing on his lower lip.

'Are you listening to me?'

There was no response. Jack maintained his furrowed brow, rolling his lip between his teeth, and didn't lift his gaze from the oncoming road, his hands constantly edging the steering wheel to the right as he corrected Corbyn's tracking.

'Jack? Seriously, Jack, you're not hypnotised again are you? Jack!'

'It was… far too easy,' Jack croaked in reply, speaking in a slow, deliberate tone. He cleared his throat.

'Savage didn't care. We could have asked for anything. It didn't matter to him. Only the notebook mattered. Once he knew we had it, he was willing to agree to pretty much anything to get it back.'

'What do you suppose he meant by, 'The notebook contains my recipe for success?' Cam continued, 'I had to ask him what was in that notebook, if you don't ask, you don't get! But what a half-assed answer!'

'His recipe for success…' Cam snorted, 'Like Savage

knows anything about success… he's a hopeless horseman.'

Jack's frown deepened and he failed to respond.

'Yes, Cam. I'm fine, Cam. Thanks for asking, Cam!' his passenger stated sarcastically.

'That phone call to that DC… It was like…' said Jack, as if in a trance.

'You mean Meera?'

'…she sounded surprised when Savage mentioned the false accusation against me.'

Without thinking, Jack indicated right and with a squeal from Corbyn's steering rack, pulled into the Racing House drive, parking in his usual spot under the sycamore tree.

Cam huffily exited the car, whilst Jack remained behind the wheel, fervently trying to understand. He should be happy… elated even! According to Cupkiss, he could start riding again immediately. He should be calling his agent, booking in rides… confirming with Freddie Jones that he would be riding Rosy Glow in the Commonwealth Cup in only ten days' time. Yet his thoughts were being drawn back to that meeting with Savage. It had taken barely twenty minutes for the trainer to fold. He'd given in to every single one of their demands in order for them to hand that notebook over, including making the phone calls in their presence. As far as Jack was concerned, the entire meeting with Savage had felt… staged. Maybe because he'd been sent there to watch intently, listen, observe Savage's body language… Had he read more into their meeting? Or had it all been a set-up? Had he witnessed utter capitulation from Savage, only for it to prove to be an elaborate plot with a sting in the tail?

'He was too quick to accept our terms,' Jack stated out loud, unknowingly speaking to his empty car, 'How did Savage know we hadn't made any extra copies?'

Jack realised a moment later that Cam wasn't there, and he was speaking to himself. Opening his car door and stepping out, he called out the same question again. But Cam was already standing stock still a few yards from the front door, his phone held to his ear. He was beckoning him across.

'It's Laura,' Cam told him as he drew closer, 'Emily has been in touch with her.'

Jack tensed. The serious edge to Cam's voice cleared his mind of all thoughts concerning the meeting with Savage...

'There's been a fire. Emily's house in Leeds was gutted this morning... She almost died. She's frightened, and has left Yorkshire and won't tell Laura where she's gone... and Laura's the same. She wants nothing else to do with us or Savage.'

***

Lucille smacked her lips, placed her cup of tea onto her desk and edging her chair closer, peered at one of her fifty inch monitors. It was good to be working again, she'd missed that spark of enthusiasm that used to greet her every time she woke in the morning and contemplated which computer system she was going to penetrate today... Being a widowed retiree didn't supply the same buzz.

She was also reminded of how she and Monty used to work together, side by side. A quick glance at his empty seat bubbled up enough emotion for her to pause and remind herself not to get swamped with the pain of grief. What had that counsellor told her? Reminders of loss can be positive, but don't dwell on them too long. Perhaps it was time to move Monty's chair out... But not today, there was work to be done.

The photographed pages of the notebook's code had already been converted through an image-to-text converter, and now all seventy-two pages were in one long text file. Having knocked up a quick bit of code to allow her to automatically introduce large tranches of possible keywords to the online decoder, she was busy ironing out the bugs. The program would automate the process of checking keywords, and as the latest test results scrolled down the monitor, Lucille experienced a rush of endorphins and an inner warmth. Initially, the program would be running against a dataset of girls names.

With any luck, the boys would be ringing soon to report back after their meeting with Savage, and hopefully point her in a more specific direction, rather than having to set her program to work its way through random datasets of commonly used passwords and keywords.

As she set her program running once more, this time picking up a dataset of flowers, Monty entered her thoughts once more. Despite being an adept programmer, he'd adopted the role of salesman, the liaison with clients, the negotiator. It hadn't been her strong point, dealing with people. Ever since her childhood, Lucille had been aware of a disconnect, a puzzling moment when an invisible switch was flicked in the eyes of the people around her, and they would drift away. But not Monty. That switch had never flicked for him.

The program finished running, with the results… unfavourable. Lucille screwed her mouth to one side and after making another small edit, set the program running again, this time on a database of East Yorkshire town and village names she'd digitally scraped from Google Maps.

She watched as the program tried Atwick, Aughton, Bridlington, and then Beverley. Despite the length of some of the place names, it was worth trying all of them for the tiny extra effort it took. Her phone rang and she seized it upon seeing Jack's name displayed.

'Lucille?'

'I'm here, darling boy! How did…'

'It went fine, Lucille. But please listen, it's important. Emily's place in Leeds was burnt down this morning…'

'Oh, dear! That's terrible, you know, I…'

'Lucille!' Jack hollered, 'Please! Shut up and listen!'

Lucille, taken aback, blinked and realised the switch had just been flicked. She collected herself and concentrated on listening.

'Savage has got his notebook. The fire could be a coincidence, but I think he's making sure there aren't any copies of the notebook. Savage and Tarquin will know myself and Cam, Emily and yourself have had access to his notebook. Laura's probably safe. She only contacted Emily by phone recently. But we have to assume Savage knows about the rest of us.'

Jack's voice was becoming laboured. He sounded like he was on the move. Lucille could hear other voices and heavy footfalls.

He continued, 'Cam and I are checking our rooms at the Racing House now, but it… oh, crap!'

'Jack?' Lucille cried, repeating his name two more times in increasing volume before she received an answer.

'Cam's room has been trashed again. I'm on my way up the stairs to mine. One minute.'

Jack swore under his breath. There was the sound of a door creaking and more expletives peppered his language as he confirmed his own room was also in a shambolic state.

'They've taken the iPads, and even an old bashed-up phone I hadn't thrown away,' Jack reported, but a moment later the disappointment in his voice was gone.

'You've got to protect your house and yourself, Lucille,' he told her, 'Do you understand? I'm certain Savage and Tarquin will know about you. I reckon it was Tarquin that was snooping around your house yesterday – he must have followed us from Malton. Lock the doors and bolt everything. I'm coming over. Cam will stay here, just in case they try to set fire to the Racing House.'

'Understood,' Lucille confirmed, insisting he give her a potted version of his meeting with Savage.

'Okay…' Lucille replied once Jack completed his one minute round-up of the meeting at Marsh Landing Stables.

'Listen carefully, Jack,' Lucille said slowly, sounding flat all of a sudden, 'You said Savage *handled your phone* for more than a minute…'

Jack thought the emphasis on certain words was a little odd, but his mind was still full of other things, primarily Emily, the fire over in Leeds and the implications for Laura and Lucille's wellbeing.

Lucille left a meaningful gap before continuing, 'Savage *will* know everything... do you understand, Jack?'

He said he did.

Lucille bit her lip, convinced he really didn't understand. He'd missed the meaning behind her words. If she could get him to finish the call quickly, it could be turned to their advantage. The best thing to do would be to end the call. Before she could do so, Jack spoke again.

'I'm worried they will know about Laura. We need to warn her. At least she hasn't got a copy of the notebook...'

'Jack!' Lucille said, poking desperately at her phone screen. But he was still speaking.

'Only you have the last remaining copy...'

Lucille sighed.

'Lucille?' Jack queried, falling silent.

'The phones, Jack. The phones. Savage needed to know who had access to the notebook...'

Lucille's words finally sank in, and Jack cried out in anguish.

'He's tapped our phones,' Jack said in a small voice, 'He wasn't checking them for photos of his notebook, he was installing... And I've just...'

A stream of shouted swear words were married to the sound of rapid movement. It sounded like Jack was jumping down a set of stairs two or more steps at a time.

'Call me back on one of your friends' phones,' Lucille advised, and ended the call.

She immediately started to type on her keyboard, but as she looked up, realised it was too late. An error message was displayed on her monitor. The latest run of her program had crashed. Her internet connection was down.

A shiver of fear ran through her as Lucille considered

her options. Like Jack said, securing the house was paramount. She jumped up from her seat and went to the office door, pulled it open, dashed out onto the landing...and her world became a miasma of shooting sparks, pain, all wound up in the smell of stale sweat and leather as a pair of hands shook her violently from behind.

Forty

'How many times must I remind you?' an exasperated Meera Akbar said, rounding on Jack, 'There is no evidence to support your accusations against Mr Savage! You're actually lucky I'm not charging the two of you with harassment!'

'Have you seen what he did to Lucille?' Jack admonished, pointing through the open door to a small hospital room containing four patients, 'He beat up a defenceless woman!'

'What's happened to your... friend, is despicable. But Savage was not there! I have twenty witnesses, including yourselves, that make it impossible for him to have been in Harrogate on Thursday morning.'

She held up a hand to fend off Jack's response, 'And before you start again, I and a number of my colleagues have done an exhaustive search of known criminals, and all her neighbours on the street where Mrs Lucille Beaufort lives. We've found no-one called 'Tarquin'. No one has seen, spoken with, or has any knowledge of a man in a raincoat, least of all Mrs Laura Fenwick.'

Meera watched Jack's reaction with interest. Up until now, their ten minute conversation had been a batting match back and forth. At this news, he faltered and dropped his gaze to the hard enamel floor, and rendered speechless, adopted a contemplative expression.

Making the most of Jack's entrenchment, Meera continued, 'Mrs Fenwick has no knowledge of Lucille, nor you, beyond knowing you're an apprentice jockey. Furthermore, she gives Mr Savage a glowing reference as a trainer and friend.'

'He thinks he's won,' Jack muttered.

The detective groaned and started to back away, a sure sign she was done with the conversation.

'I would strongly advise against pursuing this matter with Mr Savage. You and your friend, Mr Camberley, were lucky he didn't press charges when you threatened him at his stables.'

Jack lifted his head and met her stern gaze. He'd known going over to Marsh Landing Stables would be a mistake, but he'd needed to let Savage know he wasn't about to roll over. He was going to be a thorn in that man's side for as long as it took.

'It was Savage,' Jack said firmly, 'It may not have been *his* fists that broke Lucille's nose and left her with two black eyes and bruises all over her body, but make no mistake, he ordered it. He almost killed a defenceless woman, and as far as anyone knows he did kill Emily Harris.'

Meera blew out an exasperated sigh.

'The fire investigators are still going through what remains of the premises in Leeds. It looks like it was started by a spark from a faulty wall socket. So far, there are no signs of a fatality. Neither have we found anyone with the name Emily Harris linked to that address. The owner was a Pearl Harris who died seven months ago. The place has been empty ever since.'

'All very convenient for Savage,' Jack said pointedly, 'What about Emily's job with Stefan Kreihn?'

'That is a lady called Emily *Green*. I've spoken with her. She knows nothing about any of this. However, she did say you have been pursuing her with a wild accusation about being hypnotised!'

They held each other's gaze for a few seconds, Jack determined, Meera shifting between disappointment and concern.

'Stay away from Emily Green and Sebastian Savage, Jack. Let this obsession go,' she said as she turned her back on him, 'If you don't, the consequences could be disastrous for your riding career.'

Jack watched the detective travel down the hospital corridor for a few seconds, but was forced to look away when a blinking ceiling strip light sent an arrow of pain through his eyes and into the back of his head.

Lucille welcomed him back to her bedside with a smile he felt he didn't deserve.

'Have you been haranguing that poor policewoman?' she asked in her usual piercing voice. A large woman in the next bed grumbled to herself and made a meal of turning over, pointing her back, and her fat posterior, at the two of them.

'And I'll keep on doing it, if that's what it takes to see Savage...'

'The doctor says he has to see me later. I expect I'm leaving today,' Lucille cut in, speaking in an untypically small voice. She leaned over and gently tapped Jack's arm, 'Keep that anger of yours under control until you need it, my dear boy. Rattling your cage when there's no-one around is a waste of time.'

Jack smiled back, trying desperately not to allow his residual anger to show in his face. It had been three days since Lucille had been assaulted in her upstairs office, and only now were the two black eyes starting to fade. A large wad of cotton padding secured with plastic tape straddled her nose. It had required some minor surgery to straighten. By God, thought Jack, Savage would pay for that too.

'That's great news, Lucille. Tell you what, I'll come back here after racing and take you home in the car. I could stay the night if you'll have me... Does that sound okay?'

'Ah! Adore you! My wonderful boy. Yes, that would be much better than me taking up the precious time of an ambulance crew, and to be honest, it would be rather nice to have a bit of company. Mind you, Lord knows what state the house is in!'

'Cam and I did a bit of a clean-up,' he admitted.

Lucille's intruder had scoured the house for every possible electronic device that could hold data, making a mess of several rooms. Lucille's computing room had been the worst hit, as he'd set about the servers, ripping out the hard drives and stealing every USB stick, back-up drive, and handheld device with a screen he could lay his hands on.

'How's Cameron?' she inquired.

'On the gallops this morning. I introduced him to Freddie Jones, the chap who trains Rosy Glow and he's been riding out work for him the last few days.'

'Ah! That's good. You need to keep busy at your age,' Lucille responded sagely, 'And where are you off to this afternoon, you busy young boy?'

'My agent managed to get me a couple of rides at Catterick. I'm heading off there straight from here.'

Jack pulled out his phone, 'Actually, sorry about this Lucille, I need to get going. My first ride is in the two-ten.'

Lucille's hand shot out, pinching the cotton in his shirt between finger and thumb, tugging him closer. He bobbed down until he was only inches away from her face.

'We're still on…' she said in a conspiratorial whisper.

Jack frowned, 'Yes, of course. I'll pick you up this afternoon. I should get back here for about half-four.'

Lucille rolled her eyes, 'No, silly! Look!'

She turned over, casting a glance over her shoulder to make sure the other three patients, or their visitors, couldn't see what she was doing. Undoing the top button of her nightshirt, she dug in a hand and produced her necklace, the gaudy one with a large green stone at its centre, hanging on a thick silver chain.

'It's in here,' she said.

Jack squinted at the jewellery, uncertain how to

respond.

Becoming frustrated by his lack of understanding, Lucille grasped the necklace in both hands and to Jack's astonishment, proceeded to break it in half.

'It's in here!' Lucille said in a low growl.

Jack peered at the break in the green stone, which in fact, was hinged and had split in two down a barely visible seam. Just about poking out was a tiny, rectangular steel socket.'

'It's intelligent jewellery. Among other things, it's a memory stick masquerading as a pendant,' said Lucille proudly, 'Monty had it specially made for me. It's so clever!'

Jack found himself smiling back at Lucille, amused by her childlike excitement.

'My Bitcoins are in here too. It goes everywhere with me,' she whispered proudly, clipping the green stone back together and tucking the pendant back inside her nightdress, 'And so does a digital copy of Savage's notebook!'

'You're kidding me!' said Jack, gawking at her.

'Soooo, you adorable young rascal,' crowed Lucille, 'What did you learn when you visited Savage's rooms?'

Forty-One

Walking a six-year-old handicapper around at the bottom of the Wold gallop, Jack waited his turn. He was about to take the gelding up the long, sweeping ten furlong track that hugged its southern-most edge when his phone rang inside his jacket. Ignoring its insistent demand to be picked up, he allowed the call to be redirected to his answerphone. He was under strict instructions from his Guv'nor to ensure the gelding, with the stable name of Croc, was given an even-paced, but not testing, swinging gallop up the hill, and that needed concentration. It had to take precedence over a phone call.

The gallop was bathed in early summer sunshine and quiet with it being late morning. The late slot suited Jack as he enjoyed the isolation. There was a sense of freedom about being alone on the gallops, just him and the horse, rather than part of a large group.

Jack's license holder, Paddy Doherty, had the gelding entered for a valuable mile race on Saturday at Haydock's evening meeting. Croc had earned his stable name as a two-year-old, sinking his teeth into stable staff's shoulders and arms and refusing to let go - his idea of fun, but the cause of several bite-sized bruises. All was forgiven by the end of his first season as Croc had won three times and was rated in the late eighties, becoming one of the best horses in the Guv'nor's pint-sized yard. Jack hadn't been confirmed for the ride at the weekend, but he was hopeful.

Pulling his goggles down, Jack waited until his mobile had ceased chirping and vibrating, gave the strapping gelding a squeeze and, keen to get going, Croc gave a little excited buck and was soon into a good stride.

There really wasn't anything more enjoyable. Alone with a powerful, mature racehorse on a perfectly sunny day for a ride, travelling easily on a hillside that, once at its summit, provided grand views over the Vale of York. Despite the glorious sunshine and enjoying his work, Jack's mood was uncommonly dark, and for once it wasn't down to Sebastian Savage.

It was Wednesday, and Royal Ascot was already into its second of five straight days racing. At ten o'clock this morning the final declarations for the Commonwealth Cup had been made. There were eighteen in the race, and whilst he'd been relieved to see his name confirmed as Rosy Glow's jockey, Jack had been less than pleased when the draw had been announced, with the colt being drawn in the stall one berth, right on the inside of the field. To compound his misery, the current going was good, good to firm in places. The Commonwealth Cup, due to run on Friday, was only two days away and Rosy Glow desperately needed persistent rain to fall at Ascot.

Whatever happened, Rosy Glow would take his chance – his syndicate had already shelled out close to eight thousand pounds in entry fees to be in the line-up - but his chances of running well would be vastly increased should the word 'Soft' appear anywhere in the official description of the ground. The weather forecast for Ascot was for isolated showers over the next few days, otherwise, lots more sunshine.

Though difficult, Jack shook away all thoughts of Rosy Glow, Ascot's draw bias, and the lack of rain. Instead, he concentrated on bringing Croc up to a three-quarter pace gallop.

Life had slowed in the last ten days, returning to what Jack considered normal - almost. He was back race riding three or four days a week for a variety of trainers, and although his form hadn't been sparkling, he'd managed a couple of placed efforts on unfancied runners. Lucille had been back home for almost a week now, seemingly no worse for being attacked by the mysterious Mr Tarquin. And although Lucille provided an update every day, she'd only made one small breakthrough in cracking Savage's code.

Meanwhile, Cam was enjoying his new role. Thanks to Jack's introductions, he was splitting his time between Paddy Doherty's and the Freddie Jones' yard, taking on anything they cared to throw at him, whether it be on top of a horse, in a horsebox, or in front of a computer. Paddy in particular had recognised the potential of Cam's warm personality and had no hesitation in sending him off to represent the yard in an Owner facing role at the races. Being in his late sixties, and more of a horseman than an entertainer, Paddy preferred spending his time on the yard these days. The availability of a well-spoken, good-looking chap to do the travelling and replace him at the races had put a smile on the face of the Guv'nor. A similarly pleasing smile was back on Cam's face.

And all of this was fine. Just fine. Apart from that itch.

The itch that was nagging relentlessly at Jack every waking hour. He couldn't seem to let go of it. It was unfinished business, a wrong that hadn't been righted, and if he was being honest with himself, an almost pathological need to bring Savage down.

He and Cam had come across Savage several times since handing his notebook back and following Lucille's run-in with Tarquin. It was hardly surprising, Malton was a small town and Savage inevitably had runners at the same race meetings he and Cam attended. Virtually every morning the odious man could be found, standing on his personalised plinth halfway up the Wold All-Weather gallop, and Jack regularly passed him at the races, the two of them studiously avoiding eye contact as they went about their daily life.

Jack had tried several times to contact Laura and Emily, but they never picked up, and his voice and text messages remained unanswered. With Cam happily concentrated on his newfound role in racing, it seemed to Jack that Lucille was the only one who shared his enthusiasm for toppling Savage and his web of misogynistic deceit.

At the top turn of the gallop, Jack angled the gelding against the rail and allowed his pace to slowly drop as they approached the gate at the top of Langton Road. His ride snorted playfully, and pulling a little, let Jack know he was capable of far more. Nevertheless, Jack eased him to a trot and they walked the last few yards off the top of the gallop.

It was approaching noon as Jack brought Croc to a stand. He was alone, and with the sun beating down, he turned to take in the view down the hill, immediately filled with the feeling that everything from the grass to the birds twittering behind him in the hedgerow was busy bursting forth, growing, living. And still, he felt that itch…

He slipped off Croc, intending to open the gate, when his phone began vibrating again. Keeping a firm hold on the gelding's reins, he dug the phone out of his inside pocket. It was Lucille. Not only that, she had called three, no, four times whilst he'd been making his way up the hill.

'Lucille?' he answered, his tone filled with hope.

'I've made a breakthrough,' she told him in an excited shout,' I've found the keyword…'

Jack held his breath, aware his heart was pounding in his ears. He could hear the clicking of keys on a keyboard, '…to about a third of the notebook.'

'What? How…? Why only a third?'

'It was your info… when Savage said something about the notebook holding the recipe for success? I searched a set of keywords that incorporated recipes, then kitchen appliances, forks, spoons, you name it… then I hit ingredients, and that was it… the middle section of the notebook was decoded with the word SPICE.'

'What's it say? Can we bring him down with the information?'

'That's a big fat no, my precious boy,' Lucille replied, 'But you could make a terrific meal.'

Jack was left puzzled, and somewhat winded. She still hadn't explained why she could only decode a third of the notebook. And what did she mean by…

His mount snorted impatiently and stamped a foot. Croc was wanting to go home and enjoy a few hours out in the paddocks.

'Pages twenty-two through to forty-six are recipes,' Lucille confirmed, 'They start with an olive-oil ice-cream sandwich with halva and pistachio, the next is twice-baked Roquefort soufflé with poached quince…'

'What the…?'

'I agree! You should see the instructions. What a faff!' exclaimed Lucille, 'It looks like Mr Savage fancies himself as a bit of a gourmet.'

Jack's mind whirred. What did this mean? Were they *his* recipes? Surely Savage wouldn't be desperate to recover the first few pages of a pretentious cookbook?

Or had he and Cam made a monumental mistake? Had

they been fooled by Laura and Emily into thinking Savage was a monster when in fact he was… an arrogant chef?

'Just a couple of seconds,' Jack told Lucille, 'I have to sort a gate out.'

He stuffed the phone into his jacket pocket and led Croc through the gate, tied it back up, then leapt athletically up onto the gelding's back. He and Croc began the ten-minute downhill walk alongside Langton Road back to Paddy Doherty's yard.

Jack's mind was swimming with new possibilities. Savage certainly wasn't a particularly likeable individual, and had been adept at almost ruining both his and Cam's careers in racing, but had he really blackmailed both Emily and Laura? Or were they simply seeking revenge for being seduced, then discarded. When you stripped away the stories and hearsay, only one thing was proven – with Laura's help, Emily had hypnotised Cam to harm and help her steal from Savage, and what's more, she'd hypnotised himself to lose two races for her own profit.

The gelding plodded on and although Lucille had begun speaking once again, Jack wasn't listening. His thoughts were elsewhere. He was re-evaluating the last two weeks and wondering whether Emily or Laura had good reason to be working *with* the cosh-wielding Tarquin. But *who was* Tarquin?

'Jack? Jack…? JACK!'

Realising his name was being bellowed from his pocket, he retrieved his phone and raised it to his ear. By gum, Lucille could project her voice… he imagined she would have made a hell of a head teacher.

'I'm here, Lucille,' he said quickly, not wishing to have her scream his name out at close range, 'I'm sorry, I'm just a bit… confused by what you've found. Could I run a few things by you?'

Detailing his thoughts took longer than expected. By the time he'd shared everything with Lucille, he was almost back at the Doherty yard. She had been mostly quiet throughout, only offering timely mmm's and aah's.

'It is disconcerting, the way Laura and Emily have disowned us since the fire in Leeds and my brush with an intruder,' Lucille agreed, 'But I'm not convinced Laura had anything other than good intentions. She didn't strike me as someone who was capable of contriving a complex fraud.'

Lucille continued, 'On another subject, given we still have two further blocks of code to untangle, I've been examining the original photos I took of the notebook.'

'You saved them too?'

Lucille barked a sharp laugh, 'Never discard data, my dear boy! You never know when it may come in useful. Anyway, I took a long look at the way some of the code has been written, and I'm fairly sure the first third of the notebook was created by a different hand to the rest.'

'So a different person?'

'I thought that, but I also investigated the strange indentations on the notebook's cover. Christian Arles originally manufactured that style of notebook from 1974 until 1989. It could be that the first third of the code is from a young man, and the second third by the same man, only older. Or, we could be looking at a notebook that has been used by two or three different people, or generations, each using the same codebase, but different keywords.'

'I'm back at the yard. I'll have to go,' Jack apologised again.

'Talk later,' Lucille agreed, and rang off.

Walking the gelding past the makeshift car park, he noticed Corbyn was the only vehicle remaining, the other two members of the stable staff having already left. Paddy himself emerged from a stable with his feed bucket in hand, and looked expectantly up at his apprentice as he slipped off Croc's back.

The silver-haired trainer was adept at readying his horses for one or two valuable races each season, whilst playing the handicapping game between times. Happily training no more than twenty horses with his hands-on approach, Paddy possessed a dry sense of humour, smiled easily, and was generous, sharing his time and expertise with horses and staff alike.

Jack gave his license holder a breakdown of how Croc had gone, and set about washing the horse down, drying him off, and led him to the walker to warm down for twenty minutes.

On his way back to check the gelding's stable, Jack was still turning Lucille's findings over in his mind when he heard a moan come from a nearby stable. He found the Guv'nor bent over in the back of the box, sifting through a pile of straw with his bare hands. An unraced two-year-old filly had been closely tethered to an iron ring embedded into the wall and was staring over at the trainer's backside.

'Everything okay, Guv'nor?'

'The little beggar has stepped on her shoe and prised it off again,' Paddy complained, 'Feet like dinner plates this one. If I can find it, it should go back on easily enough.'

Jack joined his boss on the floor of the stable, the two of them searching in silence, the thought of Savage still uppermost in his mind. It took another minute or two, but presently Jack spotted the glint of steel beneath a pile of bedding and withdrew the horseshoe. It was almost complete, with most of the blacksmith's nails still attached.

He was about to leave when a thought occurred to him.

'Paddy, did you know Sebastian Savage's father?'

'Aye, of course. He was a bit older than me. Knew him enough to say hello to, but not much more,' Paddy replied, his attention directed at picking the straw and dirt from the filly's recovered shoe.

'Was he, y'know… honest?'

This brought a smile to Paddy's face, 'It was a different game back in the seventies. No television cameras at every racecourse, or regular drugs testing.'

'Does that mean no?'

'All I'll say is, like father, like son. I've heard about your run-in with Sebastian, by the way,' Paddy said, glancing up to gauge his apprentice's reaction.

Jack acknowledged him, but didn't offer a reply.

'Sebastian's father, David Savage, was as ambitious and just as unwilling to put in the hard work it takes to be successful,' Paddy added, 'Too happy to take shortcuts, I reckon. David did get one Group horse. Bred it himself. But like a lot of his better horses, he got greedy and over-raced it.'

'Can you remember the name of it?' asked Jack.

'Oh, aye, Lost Post. Grand little filly, she was.'

Jack thanked him, then left Paddy to the re-application of the filly's horseshoe. After checking and cleaning up Croc's stable, he called Lucille back.

'What you were saying about different generations…' he began, 'Can you check the pedigree of a racehorse called Lost Post? She was a filly in the seventies. And try using all the names of the stallions and mares on that first third of the notebook. You'll get them from the Racing Post website. It's a longshot, but you never know.'

Ten minutes later, Jack was leading Croc back to his stable when Lucille called back.

Breathless with excitement, she immediately launched into a step-by-step rendition of what she'd accomplished since they'd last spoken.

'… so after that I had a look to see if Lost Post had any foals, and sure enough, she'd had two. It was her first offspring backwards!'

'What? Sorry, Lucille, run that by me again.'

'Lost Post's first foal was a colt named, 'Postcode'.'

'Okay, I've got that…'

'That didn't work as the keyword, but I always try things backwards, it's a regular thing with passwords and keywords… and bingo, or ognib!'

Becoming slightly frustrated, Jack tried not to raise his

voice.

'Bingo?' he intoned as a question.

'The keyword was EDOCTSOP. That's postcode backwards. I suppose your post would go missing if the postcode was spelled backwards!' Lucille said with a snort of laughter.

'Does it work for the last third of the notebook?'

'Afraid not, beautiful boy... But you really need to read those first twenty pages.'

'More recipes?'

Lucille paused a moment, 'Mmm... you could say that, although from what I've read so far, it's more like a series of cocktails.'

Jack did sigh this time. A deep and disappointed sigh. It was a recipe book. Nothing more. What the hell did Savage think was so important about recipes?

'Cocktails,' Jack repeated sourly.

'Particularly, milkshakes,' Lucille announced, 'Although I wouldn't want to try any of them. Whoever wrote this was using some pretty weird ingredients... and none of them appear to include milk...'

Jack froze, a bright, shiny vista of understanding making him suddenly feel lightheaded.

'Still, I've not got through all twenty-odd pages yet, and I have a feeling there's more to this notebook than convoluted and complex recipes,' Lucille asserted, 'There's a lot of text in the last few pages of that first third that reads like a diary.'

'I adore you, Lucille,' Jack breathed, 'I'll be with you in an hour.'

'Adore you!' she trilled back.

Forty-Two

The giant Union Jack flags flanking each side of the Ascot Grandstand entrance tried their best to billow and flutter in the light breeze, but the torrential rainfall had made the fabric heavy. They hung vertically, darkened and listless, as raindrops splashed, ran down in rivulets, and steadily streamed off the base of the flags and onto the concrete walkway below.

Jack and Cam, leaning against the rails on the parade ring terraces, took a moment to admire the sunken oval of pristine turf, its two trees, and the horse walk around its perimeter. To their delight, the rain was pinging the grass and bouncing off the artificial surface of the walkway. The rain had come overnight and continued into Friday morning, the current lighter precipitation being the last hurrah of a thunderstorm that Ascot hadn't expected to catch.

'Impressive,' Cam said, allowing his gaze to rise up and rest in admiration on the colossal grandstand, 'I've never been here before.'

'Neither have I, and I'm about to ride in a Group One race with half a million pounds in prizemoney,' Jack replied soberly.

Cam clapped his friend on the shoulder, 'We had better get on and walk the track then, there's only two and a half hours to the first race.'

***

Sebastian Savage pulled into a parking bay beside a brand new Rolls Royce Phantom and smiled to himself, a surge of pride and accomplishment delivering him a natural high. This was where he belonged. In the vanguard. At the pinnacle of achievement in his chosen discipline. Contesting Group One races worth millions of pounds.

It was early, yet the car park was already three-quarters full. Owners making the most of their free lunch, he thought to himself. Another car drew in and parked beside him. He took his time, waiting until it had disgorged its passengers before following his practiced system of ensuring he would enter the racecourse in immaculate condition. Eyes, nose, teeth and ears first. Cravat, collar, shoulder blades next. He left the drivers seat and brushed his trousers, combed his hair, unhooked his suit jacket from its hanger in the back seat, and wiped a small smudge from his shoes before donning his top hat.

The hat had been his father's. It was over half a century old and yet the silk still shone like it was brand new. His father had fielded runners at Royal Ascot twice, but only in the handicaps. The thought that *his* runner was racing in a Group One contest forced his lips to curl into a smile. Finally, he placed a carnation in his buttonhole, checked his overall look one more time, locked his car and turned towards the Ascot Grandstand.

'Oh!' he gasped, on finding Laura Fenwick standing right in front of him, 'Laura! It's…um, lovely to see you.'

It certainly was, he thought. His owner looked absolutely stunning.

'Erm.. is Andrew…?'

'My husband couldn't make it today,' she said with a prim but pretty smile that advertised her white teeth.

He smiled back, 'Ah, that's such a shame.'

'Isn't it,' she stated coyly, 'So I'm an owner in need of a… companion for the day. I happened to see your car, and wondered…'

Savage raised one eyebrow, 'Even though I rather twisted your arm in order to train your horse?'

'That day at Beverley was… an experience I wouldn't mind repeating,' she replied, making sure the tip of her tongue lingered suggestively on her upper lip as he considered her suggestion.

Savage stepped closer and locking eyes with her, he held out an arm, 'I'd be delighted to escort you…'

Laura grasped his hand, tugged it violently towards her, and started to speak into Savage's ear in a low, soothing voice. Confused, he tried to pull away, but soon felt a light touch on his shoulder... and all his concerns fell away.

***

'Isn't this exciting? The last time I got dressed up like this was for a charity ball. That must have been... oh, almost twelve years ago!' announced Lucille, adjusting her fascinator.

Charlie growled Lucille's name under her breath and gave her companion a hard, expectant stare.

'Too loud, my dear?' Lucille ventured.

She smiled hopefully at the young woman's cringing response and added, 'Oh, my! Again?' in a whisper.

'We're supposed to be moving silently around the crowd, trying to locate certain people,' said Charlie irritably, 'If Jack wanted you to act like a foghorn in order to draw people to us, I'm sure he'd have said so.'

The two women had just entered the Queen Anne enclosure and had paused beside a small tree to get their bearings. They'd waited in Jack's car for the rain to stop, and as they moved over to the top of the parade ring gantry and took in the view, the clouds cleared and the sun broke through, bathing Charlie's bare shoulders and arms in a welcome wave of warmth.

Lucille wore a long, flowing floral print dress and Charlie, over a foot shorter, a sleeveless black cocktail dress with a deep v-neckline and a pair of stiletto shoes she was still breaking in.

'I'm sorry, Lucille,' Charlie said, touching the older woman's hand, 'I guess I'm nervous. I didn't mean to snap at you.'

Lucille shook her head, felt a little dizzy, and took a moment before she replied.

'Nonsense, child. I'm well aware I have a tendency to broadcast, rather than speak discreetly. You were right to point out my blathering.'

She drew closer and nudged Charlie playfully with her

hip, 'I'm sure that's why Jack has put us together. I need a strong hand to keep me on the straight and narrow. My Monty used to say that I was like a tame wolf who hadn't learned not to howl, but nevertheless extremely useful when someone needed savaging!'

Charlie threw an arm around the taller woman and gave her a squeeze.

'Thanks, Lucille. And I'll bear your savaging skills in mind. They could be very useful later this afternoon.'

Lucille grinned, 'Let's hope so!'

Jack had introduced Charlie to Lucille only two days earlier. Knocking on Charlie's door late on Tuesday evening, he'd explained what they'd uncovered. It hadn't taken too much convincing to get her to meet Lucille. She'd spent Wednesday afternoon over in Harrogate and soon realised that what they had planned for Friday at Royal Ascot was far too much fun for her to miss. Besides, Lucille was enjoyably whacky, Savage deserved to be exposed, and… she was developing a soft spot for Jack.

'I guess we should start mingling,' suggested Charlie, 'But let's stick together. We might get lucky and run into…'

'Excuse me, I saw your fascinators… are you Lucille… and Charlie?'

A busty, blonde-haired woman in her mid-forties was standing alone behind them. Her wide-brimmed baby blue hat went perfectly with a strappy, low-cut silk dress that was just about keeping her fulsome bosom contained. She smiled hopefully and shot her hand out in greeting when Lucille confirmed her suspicions.

'I'm Tabitha,' she said nervously, 'I think I spoke with you on the phone?'

'That was me,' Charlie grinned, stepping forward to introduce herself, 'Great to meet you, Tabitha.'

'Fabulous outfit, my dear,' Lucille said generously and loudly enough for a few people in the locale to turn their heads and stare.

Charlie didn't comment. There was little point. Lucille was a law unto herself. It was, at least, the right sort of comment and it deserved to be shouted.

Tabitha pursed her lips and self-consciously brushed a stray strand of hair away from her eyes, 'Thanks so much. It took me ages to choose the right look. I wanted to show him he hasn't taken my confidence away, as well as my money.'

'You aced it, my dear girl,' Lucille told her confidently, and to Charlie's relief, in a lower register, 'His jaw will undoubtedly drop to the floor. You're gorgeous, my dear.'

Tabitha bounced on her heels with pleasure.

'So, when will you be needing me?'

***

Laura watched Savage as he emerged from the dark corridor that led into the airy weighing room reception. A slight inclination of his head to acknowledge another northern-based trainer was his only notable interaction before he pushed his way through the glass doors and out onto the parade ring steps. She didn't call to him straight away, far better for him to catch a glimpse of her, waiting alone for him.

Savage smoothed his hair, replaced his top hat and scanned the crowd. On his second pass, he spotted Laura. She was waiting patiently under a gazebo, holding onto two glasses of champagne, and looking gorgeous. He made his way over, holding onto a confident smirk all the way.

'It's done,' he told her in a whisper, taking her hand and planting a dry kiss on her cheek, 'There's no way that snivelling stable boy will spoil our enjoyment of Kaleidoscope's run in the Commonwealth Cup.'

She passed him his half-finished glass of champagne.

'I'm so glad,' she breathed, 'I couldn't face being embarrassed in front of so many important and influential people.'

Savage puffed out his chest, 'Don't worry about that,

Mrs Fenwick. The only embarrassment caused today will be to those owners and trainers who have been put in their place once Kaleidoscope wins by half a dozen lengths.'

Laura took another sip of her champagne and giggled appreciatively.

***

Cam ducked down under the rails in front of the grandstand and waited for Jack to join him on the walkway that led under the impressive grandstand. Jack was staring down the home straight, his eyes set on the green and white starting stalls in the hazy distance. They were standing at the six-furlong start for the first race of the day, The Albany. And only thirty-five minutes later, at five-past-three, the eighteen runners in the Commonwealth Cup would charge down the home straight over the same distance.

'The Albany will be an interesting race,' Cam said to Jack from the rails.

Jack turned to him, 'You're a mind reader. With the ground going soft, it could throw the draw bias out of shape. Maybe being drawn low could turn out to be a positive?'

Cam shrugged, 'We know you've got the ground you wanted for Rosy Glow. We'll find out after the Albany whether you've managed to get the plum draw.'

They both took another long look up the straight, its undulations clearly visible from ground level. Now the rain had cleared and the course was being warmed, a fine mist was being sucked up out of its low points. The sprints went downhill until the horses met the round course after which the ground gradually rose to the finish. The addition of several undulations meant you needed a well-balanced horse. Rosy Glow had never run on anything but a dead flat track.

'I'd better get going,' Cam said after consulting his watch, 'I promised Charlie I'd meet up with her.'

A little way up the walkway, Cam wished Jack good

luck. Jack did the same, adding, 'Your role is just as big as mine today.'

Cam was about to leave when Jack asked him the question. They'd danced around the subject for the last week, and he'd thought Jack might have forgotten, or simply discounted it. But his form in the saddle hadn't been great in the seven races he'd ridden since that evening in Whitley Bay.

Cam shook his head, 'Naa! There's no way you're still hypnotised to lose races.'

'You know me better than anyone. We spend a ton of time together,' pressed Jack, 'Have I seemed... *normal* to you in the last week?'

Cam considered giving a flippant reply, but the look in Jack's eyes was dead serious.

'Yes, absolutely normal,' he replied stoutly, 'Emily said she'd cleared your mind of all her suggestions. Laura told us the same. Apart from that weird dream of yours brought on by the lights in the Tyne Tunnel, you've not had any other episodes have you?'

Jack shook his head, 'No, but my rides... I've ridden two favourites into the places this week. You don't think Emily is still...'

'Absolutely not,' Cam interrupted, clapping a hand onto his friend's shoulder, 'You rode those favourites perfectly. They simply weren't good enough to win. Those losses were nothing to do with any of Emily's mind games.'

A silence developed and they studied each other from close quarters. Without warning, a smile crept across Cam's face.

'What?' inquired Jack.

'You're worried that if Rosy Glow is made favourite, your suggestive subconscious will make you throw the race. And at the moment your mount is contesting favouritism with Kaleidoscope, and they keep flip-flopping at odds of about four to one, yes?'

Jack frowned, replying with an uncertain sounding,

'Okaaay?'

Cam took out his phone, tapped it a few times and brought up a bookmaker's website.

'There!' he declared jubilantly, 'Look at the betting.'

Jack took the phone and swept the screen for the odds for the Commonwealth Cup. Kaleidoscope was at the top of the list, trading at 7/2, and Rosy Glow was currently 4/1.

'What are you on about?' Jack complained.

'Remember this screen. This market. This list of odds!' Cam insisted, wagging his index finger at the small screen. 'You're riding the *second* favourite. If you don't look at any more betting between now and the off, there's no way your subconscious is going to know any different. If Emily's voodoo mind control is still in that head of yours, it won't kick in during the race because...'

Cam waited, wide eyed and expectant.

'Because as far as I'm concerned, I'm on the second favourite...' Jack trotted out.

'Regardless of the actual betting market at the off,' Cam concluded triumphantly.

Jack took a moment to consider the merit of Cam's argument.

'Thanks for trying, Cam. But I'm not sure...'

'Forget Emily's hypnosis,' interrupted Cam, staring earnestly at his friend, 'A hypnotist can't make you act upon something you know in your heart to be wrong. She's told us so.'

Jack tried to force a smile, but soon gave up. He wasn't in the mood. Appreciative of Cam's attempt to bolster his confidence, the fact remained; Emily had found a way to make him lose that race at Wolverhampton. With the most important ride of his career only hours away, he needed to know for certain. He needed reassurance that what happened out on the Ascot racecourse this afternoon was all his own doing, and not some malevolent suggestion embedded in the recesses of his brain.

Cam grabbed Jack by the arms, 'You're the most driven, fearless person I've ever met. Go and win your race.'

'Thanks, Cam,' replied Jack sheepishly, 'And you go and sort out those ladies!'

They shared a tight smile, and parted, both feeling bonded by a shared sense of purpose.

As soon as Cam had melted into the crowd, Jack took out his mobile phone. Bringing up the contact's details, he paused, staring at the name, 'Emily'.

It was answered within two rings.

'Haven't you worked it out yet, Jack?' Emily said, not unkindly, a minute into their call, 'I've told you before, the suggestion to lose races was removed by Laura at Haydock...'

The relief was sweet. Jack felt cleansed, but he waited, sensing there was something else Emily wanted to share.

'I thought Laura might have told you,' she went on, 'I got her to replace it. With another suggestion. It's the reason we're all here at Ascot.'

She spoke in a light, positive manner that Jack took as a good sign, but she wasn't making much sense.

'I'm... confused, Emily. What do you mean?'

'Laura came up with it. You were the perfect subject, incredibly suggestive, driven, and with no fear because of your... umm, *life experiences*.'

'Stop talking in riddles, Emily,' growled Jack into his phone, a feeling of unease growing within him, 'What did you do to me?'

The line fell silent and for a moment he wondered whether she'd rung off, upset or offended. A moment later she was back, this time speaking in a serious, slightly apologetic tone.

'At Haydock, after removing the suggestion not to win if you were riding a favourite, Laura planted the suggestion that you should concentrate all your efforts on decoding Savage's notebook and finding a way to bring him to justice... and if this afternoon goes to plan, you'll have succeeded!'

***

Up to now, John Cupkiss had been enjoying his Royal Ascot experience. As a senior employee of the BHA, experiencing top class racing in sumptuous surroundings at someone else's cost was a significant perk. He did love his racing. He loved the horses, the people... and the intrigue, even though it was his job to root it out. So being called away from the BHA's box at the top of the Ascot grandstand halfway through his complimentary seafood lunch hadn't placed him in a positive mood. Once that text message had arrived on his phone, he knew he had to be elsewhere, managing things.

Sitting in the small room allocated for BHA use in the bowels of the weighing room, Cupkiss had a decision to make. Information had been passed to him, and as the most senior Integrity Officer at the racecourse, it was in his gift whether to act upon it or not.

He lit a cigarette, enjoying the nicotine hit of the first few inhales, but soon transferred his thoughts to his immediate problem: a certain young apprentice. This name had crossed his desk a number of times in the last few weeks. It was why he'd made that trek up to Whitley Bay. It seemed the lad was intent on destroying himself.

Cupkiss leaned a hand onto his forehead, closed his eyes and considered how to deal with the apprentice. If this latest information proved to be correct, the lad could kiss goodbye to any sort of career in racing.

Forty-Three

Jack watched the twenty-runner Albany Stakes on the television monitor at the far end of the huge weighing room dressing area. A high-class six-furlong race for two-year-old fillies with only limited racing experience, the Albany kicked off a cracking Friday card worth millions to the owners, and tens of thousands to winning jockeys and trainers.

Following a ragged break from the stalls, the field divided into three groups. All the pace was up the middle of the track until the fourth furlong, where the nearside group took over and three runners from double-figure draws took over, shot clear, and fought out a well-contested finish with a two lengths gap back to the pack. Jack corrected himself, you couldn't really describe the other runners as finishing in a pack, as the field was randomly scattered right across the track.

As the replay played, Jack concentrated on the far-side group. Six of the juveniles had gone to the far rail and run their own private race. The television coverage moved onto an interview with the winning jockey. Grabbing the TV's remote control, Jack rewound the live pictures and watched the last furlong through twice again. The dressing room was buzzing, and several other jockeys joined him in trying to analyse the potential track and draw bias.

Less than ten minutes later, Jack was among the eighteen jockeys who spilled out into the airy weighing room foyer. Some of the riders spoke, a few joked. But most, like Jack, remained silent and concentrated. Following the first half dozen through the glass double-doors, Jack felt the sun touch his cheeks and then the soft turf of the parade ring under his booted feet.

Jack scanned the oval. Few parade rings in Britain are built as amphitheatres, and Ascot is singularly impressive because the racing public are not only stacked high, but almost complete a full circle around the equine and human players about to compete for glory. Jack's stride shortened as he took in the majesty of the place, with its waves of expectation crashing around this crucible that represented the pinnacle of British racing excellence. Drinking the atmosphere in, Jack felt like a gladiator entering the Colosseum for his first top-flight fight.

Freddie Jones left David Haywood and his syndicate to meet Jack on his way to the impatient eight men and two women. The syndicate were standing, looking on, nervously waiting for him to arrive. Bending over and craning his neck, Freddie slowed their approach, managing to get a few private words across before they reached the syndicate.

'Nervous?' Freddie asked.

Jack considered his answer, opting to shake his head and give a determined smile. He wasn't nervous, but perhaps he should be?'

'This bunch are bouncing with enthusiasm and expectation,' Freddie warned, 'Let me do the talking, if you want. Leslie is proving a bit of a handful again.'

'I'm fine, Freddie,' Jack assured him levelly, 'Seriously, I rarely get nervous. I can speak with Leslie. He's the professor isn't he?'

Freddie looked the eighteen-year-old up and down for a long moment.

'Blow me, Jack,' he admitted with a shake of his head, 'You're the cool one!'

The syndicate were indeed up a height. Jack hardly had a chance to get more than a few words in between their excited banter. In and amongst the talk of whether the ground had actually gone too soft, the possible poor draw, and the importance of a clean break, the subject of betting came up, and the news that despite being on the wrong side of the track, Rosy Glow had been heavily backed. Jack zoned out for that conversation, instead engaging Freddie in a discussion about the possibility of taking his chances up the far rail.

'There was a longshot in the Albany that finished fifth,' Jack pointed out, 'The filly went to the far rail and stuck there. Rosy Glow liked being out on his own last time, and that strip of ground could have enough cut for him.'

'There's always talk about that far rail when the rain comes,' Freddie agreed, 'Some trainers reckon its better ground when its wet, due to the turf getting compacted during the longer distance races. Either way, I don't think we have a choice. You may as well make use of your stall one draw, cross over there after the kick and give it a good go.'

At the sound of the 'Jockeys. Will you please mount,' instruction over the public address system, Jack tipped his cap to the syndicate members and he and Freddie walked to the edge of the parade ring.

As they waited for Rosy Glow to make his way around the walkway, led up by his stable lass, a voice Jack recognised drifted past him.

'…of course these immature apprentice jockeys tend to find this sort of day all too much…'

A smirking, morning suited Savage was standing six yards away with his arm around a stunning woman. Beside him, a less-than-impressed pro-jockey flashed Jack an apologetic glance and resumed his inspection of the parade ring turf. It took a second or two for Jack to recognise Laura Fenwick, and he immediately felt sorry for her. She looked like a rare orchid that was in the process of being overrun by a rogue weed.

'Ignore him,' Freddie advised, 'Don't let Savage get under your skin.'

Jack acknowledged Freddie's advice, but didn't furnish him, or Savage, with a reply. If everything went to plan, Savage's smirk would be wiped from his face soon enough. Since Lucille had cracked that set of recipes and the second, then third sets of code, apart from riding work each morning, Jack had spent every other moment over at Lucille's house. Charlie's help had been invaluable, as Cam had been too busy with his new employers. As he'd hoped, Charlie and Lucille had hit it off immediately, sharing a similarly jaunty sense of humour and forthright view of the world.

An image of Charlie working together with Lucille in her library sauntered through Jack's mind. One side of the girl's perfectly symmetrical face lit by a desk lamp, the other cheek remaining in shadow. She'd looked up at him, smiled, and... called his name? Jack snapped out of his daydream... someone was shouting his name. It was coming from the crowd around the parade ring.

There they were. Charlie and Lucille. Waving at him from halfway up the terraces. He had to smile, both of them wore identical, incredibly intricate hats he'd been informed were called fascinators. And sticking out of both hats were two ludicrously long pheasant feathers. The feathers bounced around as the ladies heads bobbed or turned, making the two of them stand out. Exactly as intended.

Once they'd caught his attention, the two women started pointing to a lady standing with them and then provided him with thumbs up and radiant smiles. Before he could respond, Rosy Glow and her stable lass were upon him and Freddie was offering to lift him into the saddle. As soon as his toes poked into his stirrups, all thoughts of anything other than the race left his mind.

The colt was on his toes a little, but no more than any of the others, and more importantly, Jack could sense the restrained power beneath him. Holding his head higher than normal, Rosy Glow swaggered around the bottom end of the parade ring giving Jack the impression the colt was enjoying the attention. The colt seemed to know today was special.

Rosy Glow snorted in anticipation as they dipped into the shade of the underpass beneath the grandstand, the colt having spotted the green expanse of the racecourse further down the chute. As he and Rosy Glow stepped into the sunshine once again, Jack caught a glimpse of another recognisable face, staring up at him from amongst the throng of racegoers against the rails to his right. An unsmiling Emily regarded him, arms crossed. The two of them locked eyes for a fraction of a second and she gave him a half-smile. Then she turned away and was immediately lost among the sea of people.

As the stable lass led Rosy Glow onto the racetrack, Jack wondered whether that's all it took. One look... Would one look be enough to hypnotise him? Would that one look be enough to influence the outcome of the most important race of his career? He took one last look around at where Emily had been standing in the crowd. She'd gone, but he recalled her attempt at a smile… and rather than disturb him, he was soothed.

The stable lass released Rosy Glow, the colt gave an excited little buck and went unexpectedly sideways a few steps. Unbalanced, Jack went out the side door.

Forty-Four

As the last of the runners disappeared into the darkness beneath the grandstand, Cam checked the contents of his inside pocket one more time. Instead of moving with the crowd to fight for a position in the stands, he stayed on the third step of the terrace, sizing up the parade ring rails. He followed them around to one of only two breaks in the oval, where two members of Ascot's race day staff maintained a hawk-like vigil. Only owners with access badges for that specific race could gain entry to the parade ring. It was vigorously policed, after all, the King and Queen were known to venture into the parade ring a couple of times each day.

Cam nervously fingered the breast pocket of his morning suit once more. He'd nipped back to Corbyn and changed after walking the course with Jack. He hadn't needed to hire his morning suit and top hat. Thanks to his years at his extremely traditional private boarding school, he already owned several morning suits and top hats. Making the round trip yesterday, up to his mother's estate in Camberley in Scotland had allowed him to be reunited with one of his standard, black morning suits and a grey top hat, but there had been another reason for his visit. He'd wanted to speak with his mother.

The estate hadn't changed much, even though he'd

been away for almost two years. However, he'd detected a change in his mother as soon as he walked through the scullery door and into the huge kitchen at the back of the house – the only room in the entire hall that was always warm. His mother had been sitting at one end of the massive oak table with his sister, the two of them quietly consuming one of the housekeeper's heated-up shepherd's pies.

Unexpectedly, Cam had been met with an air of acceptance, and possibly, resignation from his mother and sister. It was a shock, given the conciliatory nature of the speech he'd rehearsed at length during his journey up to Scotland and had been ready to deliver. That combination of factors had resulted in both Cam and the remaining members of his immediate family parting on favourable terms, the best they'd been since he'd left his school and the estate behind.

He was jolted back to the present by a third man joining the two gatekeepers at the entrance to the parade ring. Cam recognised him, and immediately moved to place himself behind a tall couple who, like him, were staying to watch the Commonwealth Cup on the huge television screen behind the grandstand, rather than be jostling with tens of thousands of racegoers.

Forty-Five

The crowd surrounding the parade ring chute produced a collective, 'Ohh!' as Jack tumbled onto the turf.

A one-handed grip on Rosy Glow's rein saved him from embarrassment. He'd landed awkwardly, but his body protector took the sting out of his fall. As Jack got to his feet the colt backed away and snorted its disapproval, but presently stood rigid. Signalling to everyone around him that he was absolutely fine, Jack received a leg up from his stable lass and Rosy Glow trotted away as good as gold, as if nothing had happened.

It was still a relief to reach the starting stalls and be told by the stalls handler checking over his tack that everything was in good order. There was a definite air of tension at the start. The usual banter and commonplace ribbing and chat of a small mid-week meeting was missing. Instead, a higher state of professionalism existed. Led into his stall one berth early, Jack took his weight off the colt for a minute, standing on the side-struts of the stall, keeping careful watch over the interminably long loading process.

It felt like four, maybe five minutes had passed, yet looking around, there were still three, perhaps four horses left to load. A number of the horses to Jack's left had shown signs of restlessness, and when one of them reared, Rosy Glow bobbed his head up and down a few times and produced a frustrated whinny. Jack returned to his saddle at once and the colt settled after he'd run his gloved hand down the three-year-old's neck a few times and made soothing noises.

After the starter shouted, 'Two to go,' another full minute ticked by before six stalls handlers managed to inch the last runner forward and clamp the stalls gate shut behind its recalcitrant backside. By this time, Rosy Glow had been a prisoner inside his stall for almost six minutes.

From the parade ring terrace, Cam watched the big screen, his attention split between the stall furthest from the camera and keeping an eye on the Ascot parade ring gate staff. Forty yards away, and directly opposite, DC Meera Akbar leaned against the topmost rail of the terrace. Looking over the parade ring, she kept a watchful eye on Cameron Camberley.

On the Queen Anne lawn, close to the furlong pole, Charlie stood on tiptoes, with Lucille beside her. They were both peering to their right, at the small white and green blob in the distance that represented the starting stalls. Lucille was jigging from one foot to the other in anticipation of the start.

For the third time in as many minutes, Laura deftly removed Savage's roving hand from her left buttock. It was cramped in the Owners and Trainers area in the grandstand and for Laura, waiting for the race to start had become a constant battle against Savage's covert advances.

'Not here...' she whispered smoothly into his ear, 'You'll have to wait. But imagine my appreciation if we win!'

Savage's face creased into a salacious grin.

On the concourse, Emily had no interest in the race. She was scanning the grandstand, her plain face turned upwards. She soon pinpointed the people she was seeking. They were standing thirty yards away. And she caught them in time to watch a giggling Laura lean into Savage. When he turned and gave his owner a lecherous grin, Emily silently snarled.

In the foyer of the weighing room, Cupkiss had one eye on the television screen on the wall, and the other on his mobile phone. Tapping the call button, he phoned the same number a fifth time, and grimaced when it went to answer. Cursing, he gave up.

As the starting stalls opened and sixteen colts, two fillies, and their hopeful pilots rushed forward, Tarquin took a long draw on his cigarette, straightened his hat, pulled up the collar of his raincoat and breathing blue smoke out through his mouth and nose, left the balcony of the private box. The race commentary rang through the almost empty corridors of the grandstand as he waited for the lift to answer his call and by the time he'd exited on the ground floor the horse leading the Commonwealth Cup entered the second furlong. As the commentators voice built the drama by creeping up in volume, Tarquin was striding towards the parade ring.

Jack cried out in frustration. Rosy Glow had been standing idle for too long. When the stalls opened the colt jumped awkwardly, as if stiff, bumping his shoulder, then his backside against the stall walls, in the process wrenching Jack's toe from his right hand stirrup. It took two attempts and a loss of a length, maybe more, before he was back on an even keel, in full control, and angling Rosy Glow towards the far rail.

Stealing a glance to his left, Jack saw a wall of horses. Bar one straggler only just emerging from his stall, every other horse was settling into a gallop. None of them had followed him over to the inside rail. The entire field was ahead of him, already two or three lengths closer to the finishing line. Disappointment hollowed Jack out for a moment until Rosy Glow found his rhythm against the rail and stretched out. It was then that the enormity of his task hit home.

With his inner monologue screaming alternatives, Jack took control. There was no use rushing Rosy Glow forward, it would expend too much energy at the wrong time. The start hadn't been kind to them and as such, the race he'd intended to run was irretrievably lost from this position. From here he had to sit tight, and allow the colt to run his own race, in his own way. Use his speed and stamina in a different way and hope… hope the colt would co-operate, be taught on the job… and would rise to the challenge.

Jack eased back, completely motionless, perfectly balanced, allowing the thundering pack on his left to edge further ahead.

The five furlong pole was soon left behind and Jack concentrated on nothing else except the regularity of the colt's breathing, the thump of his hooves, and the maintenance of balance as Rosy Glow gobbled up the turf. But it all had to be done within himself. There could be no straining, no… racing. The thought almost brought a smile to Jack's face. Thankfully, there were seven, maybe eight horse widths to his nearest rival, the rest of the field being a colourful melee of movement, muscle, and mud clods flying in the left-hand corner of Jack's vision. It meant Rosy Glow wasn't going to be pestered or cajoled into a match too early.

The fourth furlong marker flew past his right-hand shoulder and Jack felt Rosy Glow stretch underneath him for the first time as they hit the first of the undulations. Jack responded, by not asking the colt for anything. The hand they'd been dealt meant the conservation of energy was critical. The colt relaxed again, travelling through the turf to the crest of the small hill with a loss of half a length on his rivals, but no more.

The pack started to break apart. Jack could sense it before he chanced a sideways glance. The stamina sapping ground was claiming its first victims, and as some fell away, others sought clear paths through, which brought them closer as they fanned out. The sound of whips encouraging effort started with a single pop, but soon became a crackle as more and more riders seized on its persuasive qualities. Rosy Glow maintained his even, calculated pace, running past the two marker. Jack pulled his whip through, but had no intention of using it. Not yet.

Walking the course had only strengthened his view that the second, and final climb from two out to the furlong pole was the more challenging. And so it proved. On his outside, more of the competition fell away. At the same time, people, a crowd on the outside rail, and sounds of the crowd suddenly swamped them. All of it. All of those distractions had to be ignored. Four, maybe five rivals dropped off the back of the pack. Yet that still meant there were five... no, six lengths for Jack to make up on the leaders, way, way over on the far rail. It was time to see what Rosy Glow had left, whether his solo path up the inside rail had handed him any sort of advantage, whether the waiting game had worked. Jack pushed the colt for the first time.

As it had been at Haydock, the response was instant. Jack couldn't be sure, but it sounded like Rosy Glow had given a squeal of excitement when he asked him to quicken. Did that mean he had plenty more to give? Or was he asking too much from the three-year-old this time? The colt answered by pointing his toe, dipping his head, and extending.

Jack ignored the pack now. Out to his left it seemed the field was lighter, somehow more spaced out, but in full flow, asking for his mount's maximum effort wasn't the moment to be sightseeing. Working as one unit, a marvel of momentum,

Jack and Rosy Glow reached the crest of the hill as the furlong marker loomed large. The run to the finishing post was all that was left to accomplish, and still, they hugged the rail.

The noise from the crowd seemed to be swirling around them, a cacophony of shouts and screams interspersed with the race-caller's increasing volume. Twenty-thousand people had read the script, seen what was about to happen, long before Rosy Glow and Jack Goodman were to become part of the story. A sudden and intense gasp of horror punctured the roar.

It happened within a few strides. As if conjured up out of nowhere, a challenger careened into Jack's view, crossing over and taking his ground, bumping its backside into the plastic rails and bending them inward. Jack stopped riding, for fear of running into the back of the errant competitor.

This former trail blazer was under severe pressure and couldn't be relied upon to stay straight. In another heartbeat horse and jockey had edged out from the rails again, leaving an opening, a thin channel between horse and rail.

There was a split second decision to be made; stop riding, take a pull and lose momentum, and all chance of finishing in a place, or grab the gap on the rail, barely wide enough, and somehow squeeze through. Almost on top of the horse and its jockey in dark silks, Jack paused a fraction, to bring Rosy Glow's head away from the competitor's heels, then thrust his willing partner's head into the space between the rail and the colt's backside.

Rosy Glow bounced off the plastic rail and they were through, leaving the faltering challenger to weaken away in their wake.

Jack pushed, and now, as the half furlong marker slid past, chanced a glance to his left. To his astonishment, there was only one horse, two, maybe three lengths in advance of them, way over on the grandstand rail, its jockey flailing his whip, the colt's stride shortening. The rest of the field had disappeared, presumably blown away, emptied of stamina by the combination of the ground and the testing nature of Ascot's six-furlongs.

Giving Rosy Glow a flick of his whip, Jack crouched lower in his saddle and continued to thrust the colt's head forward, firmly but careful to maintain balance. He could feel the horse straining, trying to stretch. Punishing him with another strike, risking unbalancing him as he forged forward would be detrimental… wouldn't it?

The image of Emily's half smile suddenly leapt into his mind. She wasn't interested in winning a race, even a Group One. She sought revenge over Savage… and he had enabled her…

Jack didn't chance another look across at his rival. Neither did he give Rosy Glow another crack. Jack pushed with all his might, and with his willing partner's nose diving low, the last three strides of Jack's Commonwealth Cup were completed in perfect harmony and to a tumult of shouting and screaming from the grandstand. Rosy Glow swept past Ascot's white finishing post wall, scraping the paint off the rails.

Forty-Six

A photo finish, and yet, there was no announcement. The public address system was uncharacteristically quiet.

The parade ring terraces were full and ringing with cheers as Rosy Glow appeared from out of the gloom of the grandstand tunnel. Jack wasn't sure whether they were for his mount or not, but nonetheless, he accepted them via several deferential touches of his cap.

Freddie Jones' stable lass, close to his right-hand boot, was on her toes, literally bouncing with expectation.

'It has to be a close one for the photograph to take this long!' she said, smiling up at him, 'That was some race. What a clever boy, Ronnie!'

Jack automatically smiled back, suddenly becoming aware that the lass was speaking directly to Rosy Glow, and not to himself. Ronnie, eh? Of course! Ronnie was the colt's stable name... Yep, it suited the colt. He'd always thought Rosy Glow was a shade too feminine for such a powerful individual.

The public address system rumbled into life, and the racecourse chatter fell to a precipitous murmur. In one of the most memorable anticlimactic moments of Jack's life, the announcer did a callout for the representative of a trainer with a runner in the fourth race to attend the weighing room, which drew a bemused gasp from the crowd.

Members of Rosy Glow's syndicate were soon swamping the stable lass and calling congratulations up to Jack in the saddle, asking whether he thought he'd got there on the line. Jack could only smile, shrug, and keep reiterating that he hadn't looked over to the other side of the track for the last three strides.

Looking up, Jack saw Freddie Jones waving from in amongst the melee, loitering outside the entrance to the horseshoe-shaped winner's enclosure. He had a smiling David Haywood by his side. And only a few yards away, Jack spotted Sebastian Savage. Laura was at his shoulder and the two of them were staring fixedly up at him.

For a terrible moment, Jack's mind snapped out of race mode and into another orbit completely. His challenger on the far side of the racecourse... had it been Kaleidoscope? He'd been certain they'd been light blue colours, not the purple and black silks of Laura Fenwick. As Rosy Glow stepped to his left to avoid a photographer, Savage's gaze remained focused... Jack realised it was on the horse *behind* him. Craning his neck, Jack finally understood. Kaleidoscope and his jockey were following him across the parade ring. It was the same pairing that had caused him to stop riding for a stride or two in the final furlong as they wandered across the track and bounced off the rails. Laura and Savage were standing close to the third placing board, and Kaleidoscope slotted straight into his placed position.

Still no news on the photograph.

Scanning the crowd Jack soon picked out Cam, exactly where they'd planned him to be situated. Another search over at the Owners and Trainers entrance to the parade ring found Charlie. He gave her a thumbs up as he kicked his toes out of his stirrups. She beamed back. Right beside her was Lucille. He was amazed to hear her voice over the hub-bub. She was telling the woman beside her, 'I know him! I know that jockey! Isn't he adorable!'

Still the public address system remained silent.

All too quickly, he was slipping off Rosy Glow's back, the colt being surrounded by owners, reporters, television cameras, and other well-wishers. A second horse and jockey did the same beside them, an outsider named Mike's Eighty, his jockey in pale blue silks with a white star. Both horses and their connections remained outside the winner's enclosure.

Jack recognised the jockey immediately and went to shake his hand. It was Leo, another young apprentice, and like him, a graduate from the Doncaster Riding College, albeit a year older.

'Best of luck, Leo,' Jack called over to him. The apprentice replied with a similar sentiment, his swarthy Asian face lighting up with his trademark white-toothed smile. The ring was emptying of unplaced horses, and most of the owners and trainers had vacated the space. Three horses and their entourages remained, members of the press circling the principles.

The public address system sparked into life with three graduated tones that echoed around the racecourse. For a second time, the crowd dropped silent.

'There is a Stewards Enquiry. Please retain all…'

The crowd emitted another frustrated gasp and several people around Jack, now collecting his tack together, gave out derisive howls of frustration. However, immediately after the enquiry announcement, the electronic bongs were played again and the same voice said the words the racecourse was waiting for.

'Here is the result of the photograph for first place...'

Over at the other end of the parade ring, a man measuring five-feet-ten-inches sprang up and vaulted over the parade ring rails, landing with grace on the springy surface of the horses' walkway. He remained crouched, as if waiting for a starting gun to signal him to spring into action. Several shouts went up in the crowd, alerting the parade ring staff to his illegal entry, and as one, three fluorescent bibbed men rushed from their positions at the entrances to the parade ring.

The thin, powerfully made man maintained his crouch, and with the alertness of a hare, pivoted to ensure he had a clear view of the approaching men. He removed his top hat, that had miraculously remained on his head, and grinned. All three of the men headed purposefully his way were over fifty, and two carried what could be best described as several pounds overweight.

Once the leader had closed to within ten yards, the crouching man slowly stood and reaching into his morning coat, he withdrew a small red notebook and held it aloft as if he were a referee issuing a red card to a undisciplined footballer.

Cam's grin widened as the three men slowed and spread out. They were immediately joined by another, quite different man. This late addition to the bouncer crew strode up to spearhead their approach.

Resplendent in top hat and tails, Cupkiss glared at Cam, then at the red notebook he was waving above his head.

'Hand it over, Cameron,' Cupkiss hissed quietly, aware as many as a hundred racegoers crammed into the nearby terraces were enjoying this impromptu stand-off.

In a louder voice he stated, 'Please, Sir. I need you to surrender yourself and leave the parade ring.'

The public address system drowned out the BHA man's

last few words as the announcer completed the result of the Commonwealth Cup.

Forty-Seven

'Here is the result of the photograph for first place. First, number thirteen, Mike's Eighty. Second, number nine, Rosy Glow. The third horse was number two, Kaleidoscope. The distances were, a nose and six lengths… and the placings of the winner and second placed horses will not be affected by the stewards enquiry…'

Cam shrugged, the grin falling from his face as he cast his gaze to the other end of the parade ring where Rosy Glow, Jack, Freddie Jones, and the colt's connections had started to move onto the area of turf under the second placing board.

Seizing his opportunity, Cupkiss lunged forward and grabbed at Cam's left arm, deftly twisting it up his back, satisfied with the grunt of pain it brought forth from his prisoner. As the stewards converged, bolstered by another two new arrivals from the other side of the parade ring, Cupkiss stepped back to allow his crew to restrain the miscreant.

'Hello, Cupkiss,' said Cam drily, readily submitting to his rough handling.

'Better check him for weapons,' Cupkiss suggested, 'We have no idea why he's jumped in here.'

'Seriously? No idea, Cupcake?' Cam volunteered, flinching as behind his back a zip tie nipped at his wrists.

Cupkiss ignored the apprentice.

'Empty his pockets,' Cupkiss ordered the nearest steward, acknowledging another two members of the BHA's Integrity department.

'It's okay,' Cupkiss assured them once they'd stepped back from Cam, 'I'll take it from here.'

Car keys, a thin wallet and the small, red notebook

were dutifully handed over to Cupkiss. As he was pushed in the direction of the weighing room, the BHA man leaned in on Cam.

'Your riding career is finished, boy. It doesn't matter how much money and land your family own, you're fin…' Cupkiss began, but a kerfuffle at the other end of the parade ring cut him short. A woman was shouting.

A grin blossomed over Cam's face and he raised an amused eyebrow at the BHA man.

Another shout, this time from a man, was soon drowned out by several female voices.

'You're a fraud!'

The loud, and clear accusation cut through the parade ring's atmosphere, forcing Cupkiss, all five of the security men around him, plus most of the crowd who up to now had been entertained by the parade ring rails jumper, to turn their heads and gawk at the tight ring of well-dressed, and extremely angry women, and the handsome middle-aged man at its centre. A cameraman who had been focused on a microphone touting TV reporter's interview of the connections and trainer of the winning horse, was now pointing his camera in a wholly different direction.

'I wonder how that little lot managed to get into the parade ring?' Cam asked innocently.

The word, 'Blackmailer!' uttered by several females at once, travelled around the ring. Losing interest in Cam, the parade ring crowd went quiet, their attention inexorably drawn to the trainer of the third racehorse home in the Commonwealth Cup. Even the connections of the first and second horses home were now staring over at the ring of women who appeared to be connections of Kaleidoscope.

Cupkiss swung around and studied Cam anew for a second. Taking the newly confiscated red notebook out of his pocket, Cupkiss swiftly flicked through the pages.

Cupkiss rolled his eyes and swore under his breath. This spawned incredulous looks from the stewards surrounding Cam and a satisfied smile from their prisoner.

'Take him,' Cupkiss growled at the nearest two stewards, throwing his hand out in the direction of the weighing room, then he hurried off after his two colleagues from the Integrity Department, who were already stalking over to the other end of the parade ring.

Tack in hand, Jack passed the BHA men on his way to the weighing room. His initial disappointment at finishing second, and being beaten such a close margin, had soon dissolved as Freddie Jones, David Hayton, and the rest of the syndicate, delighted with their second placing, heaped praise onto him and his handling of Rosy Glow. In particular, his fearless passage up the far rail to avoid running into the back of the wayward Kaleidoscope had come in for specific shakes of his hand and claps on the back. Passing through the open weighing room doors, he headed straight to the Clerk of the Scales and weighed-in. Giving Cam a surreptitious wink, he disappeared into the back of the building. Now the race was over, he had other important matters to attend to.

Sebastian Savage didn't notice Kaleidoscope being led away, or his jockey leaving to weigh-in. He was too busy being boggled by eight women, only a couple of which he recognised. He was unable to escape from them, or get a word in edgeways.

Uncomfortably embarrassed to witness his runner weaken away so badly, Savage had been tearing into the rider with a venom he usually saved for his private debasements back at the yard. To make it worse, Kaleidoscope had been the favourite in the betting. His choice of jockey had, in his opinion, judged the pace of the race all wrong, and it didn't help that Jack Goodman had been the one to slice past Kaleidoscope with such ease. He'd been so agitated, Savage hadn't noticed an array of females, all wearing Owners' badges with Kaleidoscope's name written on them, surround him. That was confusing enough, but when they began speaking in voices purposefully loud enough to carry into the crowd, he'd tried to leave, but a small, sour-faced woman had said something to him and puzzlingly, he'd found himself rooted to the spot, allowing this circle of ladies to continue to bawl accusations at him.

Laura had seemed to be satisfied with third place, straight after the race, but she was no longer by his side. She had inexplicably pulled away and joined the circle of women. Indeed, she had been among the first of the women to deliver an accusation of blackmail once the other seven witches had arrived. Bemused, Savage tried again to step away, but he couldn't. It was as if his feet were magnetised to the turf and the ring of evil women seemed to be taking it in turns to scream abuse at him.

'He blackmailed me as well…' said a new, different voice.

A blonde woman at nine-o-clock, wagged a finger at Savage and added breathily, '…. I lost seventy-thousand pounds.'

'That's rubbish. What evidence have you got for any of these allegations!' Savage responded angrily, trying again to move forward, but finding his legs were still refusing to co-operate.

Next to her, a woman with long black hair and striking brown eyes agreed, 'It was fifty-seven-thousand from me! Stolen!'

'I don't even know who you are!' screamed an incredulous Savage, although a second inspection of the lady brought faint recognition. In truth, he now recognised about half the faces in the circle.

Emily held up a flat palm. Speaking in a loud, shrill voice she asked for silence from her fellow accusers. Savage recognised this woman immediately. She'd popped out of the woodwork and had been difficult to silence. It had reminded him of a couple of golden rules… don't get over-confident, and do your homework on your mark's family and friends.

'I've had an exclusion order served against you,' he

asserted, then to the growing number of stewards surrounding the group, 'This woman… ermm… Sandra, um, Emma…'

Emily allowed him to flounder for a few more seconds before loudly stating, 'For a serial fraudster, you have a terrible memory. My name is Emily Green, you extorted money from my mother, Pearl Harris, for a grey racehorse you never had any intention of paying for, or training.'

Savage drew himself up to his full height and pointed a finger at Emily, 'This woman, shouldn't be within three miles of me. I have an exclusion order against her, agreed by a court of law!'

'Well, then, you'd better come and get me,' taunted Emily with a devilish grin.

Savage willed his legs to obey, but they steadfastly refused to co-operate.

'Sebastian Savage,' Emily shouted, spitting his name out, 'You fraudulently took a hundred-and-sixty thousand pounds from my mother. As a result, she lost her business,'

Savage shook his head, 'Absolutely not!'

Emily continued, her voice louder and more emotionally charged, 'She was shattered. Depressed. With nowhere to turn. And that's when she committed suicide.'

There was a mass intake of breath from those racegoers listening at the far end of the parade ring.

'You made that happen, Savage! You killed her!' Emily exploded.

Savage started to scan the faces beyond the circle of women, seeking a friendly face, anyone who might come to his aid.

'And what's more, Mr Sebastian Savage,' said Lucille, loud enough for the *entire* ring to hear, 'You've defrauded twenty-three women in the last twenty years, using the promise of good-looking grey racehorses from Ireland. According to you, every one of those grey horses died whilst in transit to your stables. And if a woman complained, or became problematic about losing her money, you had the perfect insurance policy.'

Lucille became even louder, 'None of these women actually *wanted* to sleep with you! You used Rohypnol, took compromising photographs of these women, and if the need arose, produced your snaps in order to blackmail and silence your victims.'

Clearly stung by this latest accusation, Savage was stuck for words. Glaring at Lucille, a growing realisation of what her statement meant filtered through him. Not a single soul knew how he staged his photo sessions with the women he brought back to his rooms. His mouth went dry... this woman had decoded and read his notebook.

Once again, he lifted his eyes beyond the mouthy woman he didn't recognise, and sought out the one person he could rely on to extract him from his torrid situation. But this area of the parade ring had become swamped with stewards, officials, and... Savage gulped. There were reporters, and a television camera was pointed at him.

He couldn't find him. The one man sure to be on his side wasn't there.

Lucille had paused to allow the stricken man to glance guiltily and desperately around. Now she struck her final blow, her eyes reducing to thin slits, her voice hard and brimming with contempt.

'You're not some loveable rogue, or handsome lothario,' she told the immoveable Savage, 'You're a cold-hearted, calculating con-man.'

'Okay. That's enough,' interjected a male voice.

Cupkiss shoulder barged his way between two of the women, breaking the circle's seal. Aware of the television camera, he held up a hand to the woman with the loud voice and cleared his throat. He spoke with as much authority and gravitas as he could muster.

'That's quite enough ladies, and also from you, Mr Savage. Some serious allegations have been made by yourselves... and they have been refuted by Mr Savage. This spectacle is disrupting the ceremony for the winning connections of the last race. Let's take this somewhere private. Please follow me.'

There was a general admission from the circle of women that their fun was over, however, one of their number didn't agree. Emily darted towards Savage, placed a hand on his shoulder and said the words, 'Dancing Queen!' into his ear.

Savage stared at the small woman as she backed away from him, and despite the warm afternoon, and the beads of sweat swelling on his forehead, he shivered. Suddenly able to move, the grass beneath his feet dissolved and became a stage. He was a dancer... and not just any dancer. The crowd became his audience, and he was a great performer!

'Go on!' Emily shouted savagely, 'Show the crowd what you've got!'

Cupkiss stared at the women, confused. He set off to handle Emily himself, but a sudden movement and a shriek of 'Oh, yes!' from Savage stopped him in his tracks. Cupkiss swung around and realised he had a much bigger problem.

Beating both his fists on his chest like a male gorilla, Sebastian Savage leapt to his right, pirouetted, and reaching down, pulled off a shiny black shoe and extravagantly tossed it aside. He cavorted around the parade ring, carefully avoiding capture by Cupkiss and the race day stewarding staff, skilfully leaping and spinning between them. He swung his jacket around his head a few times, then tossed into the crowd. The jacket was closely followed by the second shoe, his cravat, his waistcoat, and a sock.

Lucille groaned. She'd seen this performance before, but not with Savage as it's star. It was a routine Stefan Kreihn had delighted his audience with that night in Scarborough. This hadn't been part of the plan she and Jack had meticulously created once all three codes had been solved and they'd read the horrifying contents of Savage's notebook in its entirety.

Cupkiss bore down on Emily.

'What the merry hell have you done to him?'

'Isn't it obvious?' she replied, as Savage dodged a steward, removed his top hat and swung it over his head by its rim.

The parade ring crowd, initially bemused by the public roasting of the trainer by a bunch of female owners, were now faced with the spectacle of the forty-two-year-old performing a striptease. Savage raced around the horseless parade ring dodging stewards and tossing garments aside with abandon. His actions managed to produce an equal reaction of both amusement and disgust. Some of the ringside watchers were cheering Savage on and laughing as he performed a series of hip thrusts and tossed his top hat into the crowd like a frisbee, whilst others booed.

'Stop this now!' demanded Cupkiss angrily as Savage, now barefoot, managed to sidestep a rushing steward and complete an off-balance star-jump in front of the presentation stage that was set ready with several trophies.

'No need,' Emily noted with a satisfied smirk, as one of Cupkiss's Integrity Department colleagues rugby tackled Savage, bringing him down before he could expose any serious flesh. Cupkiss went over and manhandled Savage, hauling him back up to his feet and grabbed him around his waist to keep him still. The confused trainer looked tired, but happy, and was mumbling the lyrics to 'Waterloo'.

Emily ambled across and said something to Savage and he immediately lost the big grin that had graced his face during his cavorting. Instead, his confusion was quickly followed by a flush of embarrassment, which soon turned to white-hot rage as realisation dawned. Cupkiss helped Savage cross the parade ring and enter the weighing room, courtesy of bending his arm up his back and a hand firmly holding onto the trainer's shoulder. Following at a walk, Lucille, Emily, Charlie, and the rest of the women were escorted by a number of wary race day staff.

Forty-Eight

Still a shade confused, Savage came to a shambling stop in the weighing room foyer. He rubbed at his shoulder, then at his face. The nine women, chattering and complaining in equal measure, came in close behind, filling the space and effectively blocking the flow of foot traffic in and out of the weighing room. To add to the confusion, a dozen jockeys, some still wearing silks from the Commonwealth Cup, squeezed into the foyer from the changing rooms, keen to discover what all the fuss was about.

The women were the subject of a stern reprimand from the Clerk of the Scales for impeding several jockeys trying to make their way out for the Coronation Stakes. Taking a hold on the situation, Cupkiss quickly assessed each woman and divided them into two groups.

'Take their contact details, then let this lot go,' Cupkiss told the racecourse security staff, indicating the women with Owners' badges for Kaleidoscope.

'I want the rest of them into a meeting room,' Cupkiss ordered, 'I'll deal with *them* personally.'

'And take laughing boy over there, too,' he added angrily, indicating Cam seated against the far wall. A steward was standing, arms crossed, directly in front of Cam. Bobbing his head around the steward, Cam shared a thumbs-up with Charlie and Lucille, and waved goodbye and shouted his thanks to the Kaleidoscope ladies.

With Cam and his steward following in rear, Savage, Laura, Emily, Charlie and Lucille were escorted by two young Integrity Department officers down a dark corridor. They were directed into a medium-sized meeting room dominated by a tightly fitting rectangular table surrounded by a dozen hard plastic chairs. The room boasted cheap partition walls, one of which was fitted with a large window onto the corridor. Once locked, an Integrity Officer could be seen, standing guard outside the door.

Savage took a seat at the head of the table. Cam directed his team to the other end, leaving Savage isolated.

'So how did it go?' Cam asked his co-conspirators.

Charlie rolled her eyes, 'As planned, until Emily hypnotised Savage and made him do a striptease.'

Savage, sitting alone at one end of the table, was looking unusually dishevelled. His usually slick hair was scruffy, sticking out in clumps. Collar unbuttoned, and shirt tail untucked, he leaned both his elbows on the table and held his bowed head in both hands. Lucille couldn't decide whether the trainer was about to explode with anger, or start crying.

'You're kidding!' Cam exclaimed excitedly, inviting further discussion.

'I didn't think we'd done enough to ensure he would be detained,' Emily said innocently.

'Yeah, right!' Charlie scoffed, 'You could have ruined everything if he'd been carted off and simply ejected from the racecourse. How would that have helped your cause?'

Emily considered this with pursed lips.

'No,' she announced defiantly, 'It was worth the risk,'

A small voice stated, 'Embarrassing me will be your only victory today.'

All five of them eyed Savage, some with interest, others with undiluted disgust.

Savage sniffed and straightened, leaving both hands palm down on the table, his fingers wide, as if composing himself prior to playing a church organ. He slowly flexed his fingers, examining them intently as he spoke, rather than meeting the stares of any of his accusers at the opposite end of the table.

'So you cracked the code in my notebook,' he said with a shrug, maintaining a quiet, measured tone.

'Speak up, I can't hear you,' Lucille said loudly.

Savage smiled down at his hands, 'Nice try, whoever you are. I know there's an Integrity Officer just outside the door. I won't be broadcasting to the authorities. My words are for your ears only.'

Lucille grimaced internally at the failure of her ruse, outwardly remaining stoney-faced.

'What you've all forgotten is that you no longer have the notebook. It doesn't matter what accusations you level at me, it's simply my word against yours. Anyone can compile a list of people I may, or may not have dealt with. Just remember, any complaint against me in the past has either been immediately dismissed by the BHA, or ignored by the police. The Crown Prosecution Service won't have enough evidence to bring any charges and I will, of course, deny all knowledge of any wrongdoing.'

His smile broadened, 'That may not be the case when it comes to you… Emily, is it? I congratulate you on your little piece of stage hypnotism. From my attire I assume I made a fool of myself… However, it will ensure I have a strong case against you. I doubt you'll ever be able to hypnotise anyone ever again. Rest assured, I will be asking Mr Cupkiss to involve the police in this episode… I believe the denigration of a man's reputation is frowned upon by the judiciary.'

Charlie glared expectantly at Laura and Emily.

Laura cracked first.

'We thought it was only fair, given what we'd been through.'

Charlie rounded on Savage, 'What about your use of Rohypnol on these women? It's all in your notebook! We have the proof!'

Savage looked up for the first time, his eyes burning with repressed anger, 'Is it?' he asked in a low hiss, spittle flying from his mouth, 'Is it, really?'

Dipping into the inside pocket of his morning suit jacket, Savage produced a red notebook.

'You mean *this* notebook?'

The room fell deadly silent as Savage's words sunk in.

'You've re-written it, haven't you,' Lucille said, watching as he waggled the notebook between finger and thumb, a triumphant grin on his face.

Buying an old, blank notebook on the internet to replace his original would be easy enough, thought Lucille. Burn the old evidence filled version, and replace it with a benign version. Who wouldn't believe it wasn't the original? After all, thought Lucille, they'd done virtually the same thing to ensure Cam's distraction tactics in the parade ring were believable.

Identifying and then tracking down five women from Savage's notebook in order to convince them to help expose the trainer inside the parade ring had been Jack's idea. But he'd needed Laura and Emily to play an integral part in the deception. Both ladies had been difficult to contact, but had come back on board once they'd been sent the details of what the notebook contained. Laura especially had jumped at the chance to become involved, once she'd learned that beyond little doubt, it had been Rohypnol that had rendered her helpless, rather than excessive alcohol, or Savage's dubious charms.

'Righty ho!' Lucille stated loudly, 'Enough of your self-satisfied bleating, Mr Savage. I hate to burst your bubble...'

'Actually, that's wrong, she said, correcting herself, 'I'm *delighted* to burst your bubble... Tell me, did you ever manage to decode your father's notes?'

The grin on Savage's face slumped into a contemptuous slit-eyed look of disbelief.

'No, I didn't think so,' Lucille said matter-of-factly, 'Thing is, Mr Savage, we did. We managed to decode your father's portion of the notebook.'

Lucille looked over at Cam and smiled. He'd been desperate to be the one to tell Savage what they'd found in the first half of the notebook. But he'd insisted it had been

Lucille's excellent work that decoded the notebook, so she got to make the reveal.

'We know you haven't been able to decode your father's part of the notebook,' Lucille announced loudly, 'Because if you had, there's no way we'd all be sitting around this table. In fact, I doubt you'd be a racehorse trainer.'

She smiled at Savage. He returned a scowl.

'It strikes me that you would have been better served as a chef, assuming you didn't *spice* up every dish with Rohypnol.'

That reference disarmed Savage somewhat. He lost some of his rigidity, slumping even lower in his seat.

'Remind me, how did your father die?'

Savage uttered a torrent of expletives under his breath. He'd tried for twenty, maybe thirty years to decode his father's part of the notebook, without getting anywhere. This… loud woman couldn't have done it in what…? A few days? His father had died suddenly, without warning… and left him in such a mess. He'd only been eighteen, no mother, then no father. God, it felt so long ago.

'It was a heart attack, wasn't it? That's what the racing papers reported at the time,' Lucille continued, 'At that time in the mid-eighties I doubt the police or the local coroner were too thorough with a desperately sad, but straightforward death…'

'Shut up about my father,' Savage demanded, a feeling of vulnerability swamping him.

'We believe he was murdered.'

Lucille met Savage's gaze and could see the hurt that lived within him. A hurt she had just resurrected.

'I'm so sorry, Mr Savage but we did decode your father's notes, or rather, what developed into an encoded diary…'

Unclipping her clutch bag, Lucille removed a thick wad of folded paper and asked Charlie and then Cam to pass it down the table.

As he leaned forward to pass the papers on, Cam noticed a water cooler, complete with little paper cups, set up against the back corner of the room. Suddenly thirsty, he rose, and squeezing past both empty and occupied chairs, poured himself a drink.

Savage was silent, his concentration held by the papers he'd been handed. He riffled through the pages, only reading a line or the odd paragraph before continuing. Everyone in the meeting room waited. Lucille began to speak. Her voice was soft, almost regretful.

'It's all there, Mr Savage. Everything… It was within the pages of your notebook all along… Your father was being blackmailed.'

Savage looked up and fixed Lucille with a disbelieving stare.

'Allow me to provide a snapshot of what the first part, your father's portion of your notebook, contains,' Lucille said, holding Savage's stare.

'Your father was using milkshakes on his horses in the seventies. He was using anabolic steroids to enhance their performance. The first few pages of the notebook are his record of how he sourced and then administered the drug to his horses. I have to admit, he kept incredibly detailed records… rather like yourself.'

'However, someone discovered what your father was doing and began to blackmail him. But as is often the case, the blackmailer forced your father into even more serious actions. He began to lose races to order, in the process, defrauding his owners. Once he went down that road, he couldn't escape his blackmailer's clutches.'

Lucille paused for a moment, suddenly aware she might be sounding like an Agatha Christie denouement. She shrugged the thought off. Why not? She was enjoying herself!

Lucille continued, 'The last few pages of your father's section are a detailed account of how he tried to extract himself from this tangled web of deceit. Reading between the lines he realised his business, and indeed his life, was spiralling out of control. In short Mr Savage, thanks to his blackmailer, your father became a broken man. He went to his blackmailer with an ultimatum; he would expose his own wrongdoing, and that of his blackmailer, unless the deception ceased.'

Lucille paused, her head felt like it was swaying slightly. In the distance, the sound of a race commentary filtered into the room. She swallowed hard and continued.

'His last entry was on the morning of the day he died, two weeks after your eighteenth birthday. You may wish to acquaint yourself with the passage I've highlighted for you?'

Savage riffled through the pages. Passing over his father's notes detailing his use of milkshakes and anabolic steroids, he found the last five pages were a set of diary entries. The final entry, as Lucille had indicated in yellow highlighter pen, was dated fifteen days after his eighteenth birthday... the same day his father died. He scanned the first few lines on the last page, but read the final paragraph three times.

As Savage silently read his father's words, Cam got up from his seat and drew himself another cupful of water from the cooler, whispering something into Lucille's ear on his way back to his seat.

'Sebastian, my son, I trust you will read these words. This notebook is my confession. I'm not proud of the things I have done. Yes, I have benefitted, but I bear a deep, unrelenting guilt. I am writing this for you, so my mistakes will not become yours. You're decent. Untainted. Try to remain that way. UX is attending yard this afternoon. Will inform him I am done. No more fraud, lies and deception. UX will try to turn me, force me, but I shall not be turned. Be under no illusion - UX is evil. He may react badly to my news. He may threaten to hurt me. If this happens, believe nothing he says. However, my mind is set, I cannot continue to be involved in his evil.'

Lucille waited until Savage's tear-filled eyes rose from the decoded page.

'I could never work out the keyword,' he said in a hoarse whisper.

'The first foal from his favourite mare, reversed,' Lucille revealed.

One side of Savage's mouth rose into a fleeting wry smile. He fractionally shook his head.

The third race of the day was well under way, with the Coronation Cup commentary echoing down the corridor outside, yet inside the meeting room everyone's attention was concentrated on Savage's reaction.

Cam got up from his seat again and filled his cup with water at the cooler, spending much longer at the plastic bottle than he had the two previous times.

'The type of fraudulent activities your father committed are strikingly similar to yours,' Lucille said, 'And Cameron, Jack, and Charlie believe you couldn't have been such a successful embezzler using your 'Grey Horse Hustle' as you refer to it, without the aid of an accomplice. That help would have to come from a certain type of person, someone holding a powerful role within racing. In your father's time, this person would have been working in the field. However, to ensure your criminal activities weren't noticed, and that any complaints, or evidence of blackmail would be quietly filed away and forgotten, this person would need to be operating in the upper echelons of the racing industry.'

Lucille paused, hoping Savage might confirm this assumption, or even offer a name. Unfortunately, he seemed preoccupied with his own thoughts, scratching his shoulder and looking off into space.

'Your father called his blackmailer and co-conspirator UX. In your notebook, you refer to your accomplice as MM...'

Lucille waited. Savage blinked, but remained mute.

'Who is MM, Sebastian?'

Savage slowly shook his head. He was hunched over the table, exhibiting the same distant, vacant expression. Lucille caught Cam's eye and they shared a shrug. They couldn't be certain Savage was even listening.

'Let me hypnotise him,' said Emily, growing impatient, 'I'll get it out of him.'

Laura, still managing to look gorgeous, incongruously so given the shabby surroundings, voiced her support for the hypnotist.

Lucille, Cam, and Charlie said nothing in reply, but the glares they sent back to the women spoke volumes. Both women, remembering the instructions they'd received the night before in the conference call, retreated.

Lucille asked the question again. Again, Savage appeared not to register her query about this 'MM' character.

There was a long pause during which the commentary for the Coronation Stakes reverberated noisily down the hallway. The race caller's voice increased markedly in volume as he described the runners entering the last two furlongs and the roar of the crowd echoed his excitement.

Lucille glanced through the glass wall to where the Integrity Officer was still standing outside the door. Cupkiss and the other Integrity Officers were bound to be coming back soon. They were probably watching this blessed race. She didn't have long to get through to Savage.

'UX, UX… UX!' Lucille chuntered, 'Have you worked it out yet, Mr Savage?'

'UX?'

Savage began mumbling the query repeatedly, more to himself than his audience around the table.

'We think the U indicates a cup,' Lucille responded, 'And the X is a kiss… would you agree, Sebastian?'

Forty-Nine

Jack changed into his street clothes as quickly as he could and grabbing his mobile phone, ran out of the back of the weighing room and onto a concrete concourse, a designated area from which he was allowed to make calls on his personal phone. As soon as the device switched on it started vibrating and beeping with incoming messages. They would have to wait. With Cam and the women being held with Savage, all of them awaiting their ticking off, or perhaps something worse, he had his part of the plan to uphold.

It had all come together over the two days following Lucille's cracking of the key for the older part of the notebook. He'd soon come to realise it was one thing to uncover blackmail and fraud, but quite another to expose it.

Being the honest person he was, Cam had wanted to hand everything over to DC Akbar for her to investigate and eventually bring Savage down. Jack hadn't agreed and supported by Lucille, they'd convinced Cam there wasn't enough evidence from the photographed pages of the notebook. Besides, there was definitely more to the notebook than just Savage's wrongdoing. It was clear he had an accomplice, and if his understanding of the notebook was correct, something far more serious lurked in those pages.

The public address system rumbled into life with the commentator, his echoing voice bouncing around the back of the grandstand, announced the loading process had just started and the Coronation Stakes would soon be underway.

Contacting the people Savage had conned had been tough. Almost entirely made up of women, some of the names and numbers had been over a decade old. Even if they managed to contact the individual, convincing them to come to Royal Ascot in order to take part in a shaming exercise that would hopefully result in Savage breaking down and admitting his guilt was a tough sell. However, Cam had been up to the challenge!

It took conversations with only the first three ladies for Cam to realise some of Savage's victims hadn't understood they had been defrauded. They'd assumed Savage was honest and the death of their young horse, associated costs, and loss of the purchase price had all been legitimate. Only in a very small number of cases had there been a need for Savage to drug someone and take compromising photos. Many of the ladies had quickly written the loss off, often quoting the same thing - that it was just, 'One of those things.'

Over the past twenty years Savage had recorded eighteen ladies in his notebook with whom he had engaged in what his notebook referred to as, 'The Grey Horse Hustle'. Most of the ladies were similar in three respects; they were of a certain age, more often than not, recently divorced or separated, and finally, they'd never owned a racehorse before. The other qualifying factor was that they were extremely rich.

Laura Fenwick's case was quite different. Savage had taken a step into a far murkier level of criminal activity. It was the first time he'd targeted a racehorse to actually *train*, rather than stealing the cost of a non-existent horse from his victims.

Emily was another who didn't fit the profile of a normal Savage victim, until Lucille had realised her name didn't appear in his notebook at all. Being under thirty, and enduring a frugal, hard-working lifestyle, it wasn't until Lucille had found 'Pearl Harris' among Savage's list of victims that the penny had dropped. Emily was Pearl's daughter. She had married to become Emily Green, but was now divorced. Emily had been the one who, seven months ago, had discovered her mother's body after she committed suicide.

The torching of Emily's mother's house had shaken Laura and Emily into a nervous silence. Both had received death threats following the fire in Leeds, with a warning phone call to stay clear of Savage, and the apprentice jockeys.

Eventually, after two days and many, many phone calls, they had responded to Cam's messages. It had been during a late night Zoom call to try and convince them to help, that

Emily had finally opened up and explained her true involvement with Savage.

Widowed abroad at forty-three when a heart attack took her husband, Pearl Harris and her then seventeen-year-old daughter, Emily, had returned to her home town of Leeds after spending many years touring the world on cruise ships, performing as a stage hypnotist. Pearl sank the insurance money into a hypnotherapy practice in Headingly and for the next ten years she and her daughter had made a good living helping her clients overcome bad habits such as smoking, drinking, and over-eating. Phobias were also a mainstay of the hypnotherapy business and this was how Pearl had met Sebastian Savage. At the time, she'd been based on Headingley Lane, a swish address in the Leeds suburb, her shop front being on the main throughfare.

'I'm sure the business was what attracted him, rather than my mother, but neither she nor I saw that at the time. As far as I was concerned, Sebastian was a breath of fresh air for my mum,' Emily had told Jack via Zoom.

She went on to recount her mother's first encounter with Savage, 'It had been almost twelve years since dad had died. Mum always rebuffed any advances from men up until then. But Sebastian arrived in her waiting room, good-looking, smooth-talking, and a racehorse trainer. My mother had always loved horses. Once she'd sorted Savage's issues concerning fish, he asked her to dinner.'

Jack had goggled at her. Listening in the background, Lucille and Cam had laughed heartily.

'He detested fish,' Emily had said with a shrug, 'Believe me, I've had to deal with worse… much worse. Savage couldn't bear to be in the same room as a fish, dead or alive. It was the eyes… Anyway, he had problems eating at restaurants that served them from a tank, or whole.'

Emily went on to detail how, over the course of the next few weeks, her mother and Savage had got to know each other, culminating in a visit to his Malton yard and his wing of Marsh Hall.

'It was autumn when Savage suggested my mum should buy a racehorse, and he would train it to race the following summer. I told mum it was a bit of an extravagance, as thanks to vaping and these new weight loss injections, the hypnotherapy business was going through a tough period. Savage had explained my mum could limit her cost by owning a small share of ten percent but still get all the benefits of ownership. He showed her photos and video of this fantastic young, unraced grey colt he'd been to see in Ireland and said he was going to buy it before it went to the sales in October.'

Emily had continued, 'It was going to cost my mum sixteen-thousand pounds for her share, plus the transport from Ireland over to Malton. Savage claimed he had another one or two like-minded people who would make up a very small, select syndicate of his close friends.'

'She admitted to being a little dazzled by him. He was good-looking, younger than her, and we imagined, financially secure. And the thought of my mum having fun going racing with Sebastian and meeting other people over the summer at the races, did appeal,' Emily stated sadly, 'I should have asked more questions, or checked with the breeder he was buying the horse from, but I didn't know any better, neither I nor mum had bought a racehorse before, and we both trusted Sebastian implicitly. Mum paid sixteen-thousand pounds into his business account and expected to see the colt at the yard a few days later.'

There was an inevitability about Emily's story. Jack had heard plenty of bad luck stories about the purchase of horses, especially juveniles, but when the downturn in Emily's story came, its evil twist was a shock even to him.

'Sebastian called my mum the day before the colt was supposed to arrive. He said he'd gone to pay the full amount, one-hundred-and-sixty-thousand pounds, but the remaining one-hundred-and-forty-four-thousand he was due to collect from an owner based in Corfu hadn't arrived, something to do with the Greek banking system. It wouldn't arrive until after the weekend. But the horse was due to go to the sales, and the breeder wouldn't hold it unless he got paid in full... could she possibly cover the remaining hundred-and-forty-four-thousand-pounds and he'd pay her back when his friend's money arrived in two days' time?'

Emily had sighed heavily, 'To cut a long story short, my mum agreed. She took the money from the business account and her savings. It took all our reserves and wiped the accounts clean. But she was sure it would only be for that weekend.'

Jack had shaken his head at this news, 'Let me guess. The friend never paid?'

'Oh, no, Savage was cleverer than that,' Emily had responded, 'Mum got a call from him on the Monday to say the money had been sent and he was awaiting its arrival in his account. Also, the grey horse was already on its way to the ferry and everything was going smoothly. The deal with the Irish breeder had gone through and the yearling would be at Marsh Landing Stables the next day. My mum was so excited and had made arrangements to go and see it the next day.'

Emily had paused for effect.

'Then Savage called back only an hour later to say the colt had died. It was a heart attack, just like my dad, enroute to the catch the ferry. All the grief came back for my mum, it was awful. But unlike my dad, the colt hadn't been insured. And it wasn't until a day later mum realised she still hadn't been paid back for the extra money she'd loaned Savage for the purchase. Sebastian fobbed her off at first, saying it would arrive forthwith, but it didn't. Eventually he admitted his 'best friend' in Corfu had recalled his payment once he'd learned the horse had died, so Sebastian didn't have the money to pay my mum back. He was apologetic, but said there was nothing he could do... he'd paid the breeder and didn't have the money himself, and this chap in Corfu wasn't taking his calls anymore. My mum's one-hundred-and-sixty-thousand-pounds was lost.'

After taking a gulp of her drink, Emily had taken up the story once again, 'Mum told me about her bad luck, and I did some checking. It took several months, and a trip to Ireland to determine that Savage was lying. He'd groomed my mother and taken her life savings from her. There was no 'friend' in Corfu, just a man's name that couldn't be traced, and there was no horse worth a hundred and sixty thousand pounds. There was a grey horse, but it hadn't gone anywhere near a ferry port. It had a badly turned-out foot and was placed on a horsebox and taken straight to an Irish abattoir and euthanised, with no reason for its premature death being recorded. I tried to get out of the breeder how much Savage had paid for the horse, but he refused to answer and blocked me after that.'

'Mum's business immediately came under pressure and we couldn't pay the rent. We had to leave the prime position on Headingley Lane and run everything from a little rented place in a backstreet. It killed the flow of clients. Eventually Savage stopped taking our calls and even though we complained to the police, the British Horseracing Association, and the Irish Breeder's Association, nothing came of any of it.'

'Savage is a thief. He's a fraudster, preying on… vulnerable women of a certain age by… flattering them.'

'Or drugging them,' Jack had added.

'And the authorities are toothless, they can't do anything,' Emily had added, 'Savage took my mum for every penny and then took…'

Emily had suddenly gone quiet and looked uncomfortable in her seat.

'I had to get a job with Stefan Kriehn to keep things going,' she admitted, 'Mum got depressed and then, ten months ago I came home and found her… '

Jack winced as Emily finished her story. Incensed at the injustice and deep in the abyss of grief caused by her mother's suicide, she had hounded Savage, resulting in him being granted an exclusion order against her for unnecessary harassment.

'Which is why…' Emily had looked to Cam first, then Jack, 'When you two sat down on that train, a little bit drunk, and in such good spirits after your wins at the races, and announced one of you worked for Sebastian Savage, I stupidly thought you would be a means by which I could exact my revenge.'

Emily's story had shocked everyone, but also galvanised them. By Thursday afternoon Cam's excellent verbal skills on the phone and on Zoom had rounded up four ladies willing to make Savage squirm, each of them with similar stories, thankfully without the suicidal conclusion.

The grandstand suddenly erupted with noise as the public address system announced there were only two horses left to load for the Coronation Stakes.

With Emily's story still fresh in his mind, Jack called Meera Akbar's number. They spoke for thirty seconds after which Jack hurried back into the weighing room, down two corridors and out into the parade ring. Entering the Queen Anne enclosure he leapt up the half-empty parade ring steps and scanned the terraces. He spotted an Asian woman waving at him just as the Coronation Stakes was about to start. He waved back and started to move along the terraces towards Meera.

A roar of approval swelled forth from the Coronation Stakes crowd as the stalls flew open and the race got underway. As the line of fillies settled down Jack noticed a much taller man had fallen into step just behind the policewoman. Tall, with a grimly grey face, he was wearing a raincoat and a deep-brimmed fedora hat, despite the fine weather.

Fifty

John Cupkiss paced the small, private room designated as the Integrity Department's temporary office for the day. A headset clamped to his head, he was listening to the conversation in the meeting room, thanks to the listening device he'd secreted behind the water cooler. His mind was racing, and it didn't help that the whole racecourse was alive with the sounds of a cracking finish in the Coronation Stakes.

The makeshift office was thick with smoke, thanks to a lack of any air conditioning and his illicit chain-smoking of three cigarettes in the last fifteen minutes. He'd needed them, to help him concentrate. Bringing his pacing to a halt, Cupkiss wiped a hand over his head, slicking back his thinning hair, plastering it to his scalp with a mixture of pressure and sweat. Savage was compromised, and thanks to that infernal notebook of his, those apprentices, and that strange, older woman, it wouldn't be too long before he was implicated.

Cupkiss swore, repeating the same word over and over as he listened to Savage's voice. The trainer's earlier belligerent denials had dissolved, his tone had become that of a broken man making a confession. Cupkiss swore again. It was time for him to move.

Briefly checking the contents of his briefcase, he tossed his headset in and locked it. Cupkiss dabbed his cigarette out against the rim of the waste-paper basket and checked his pockets to make sure he had his phone. The right-hand pocket of his morning suit jangled. He drew out a set of car keys… Of course, they'd come from Cameron Camberley's pocket!

***

'I need to visit the ladies!' insisted Lucille loudly, 'This is what happens when you offer unlimited water during meetings.'

The young Integrity Officer who had opened the door

to her insistent raps looked her up and down a second time. Tall and wiry, his morning suit hung off him. She wondered whether he'd lost a lot of weight, or he'd borrowed the outfit.

'You're to stay in the meeting room until Mr Cupkiss is ready to interview you,' he repeated in a tired monotone.

'Listen, chum,' Lucille said, poking her index finger into his flat chest, enough to make him take a step back, 'I'm going to the ladies. Try and stop me.'

She pushed past him and without looking back, beetled off down the corridor. Cam had been right; she *was* the most likely to be allowed to wander around the weighing room building on her own!

'Second door on the left after the right turn. If you get to the foyer, you've gone too far!' the Integrity Officer called after her, keen to recoup some of his lost self-esteem.

It was Cam who had found the listening device, taped to the back of the water-cooler bottle, clearly visible once the water level had dropped. The question was, who was listening? Lucille thought she knew the answer.

Almost every room along both sides of this corridor was the same: an office or meeting room with ceiling tiles, three flimsy walls and a floor to ceiling glass front that included a glass door. Lucille ambled down the empty corridor, looking left and right into each of the small offices. She turned right at the end of the corridor and stopped dead. Like the one she'd just left, this corridor was also empty, however the glass in the first office on her left had dark, tinted glass and there was the whiff of cigarettes. She backtracked a few steps, considered her options, and decided bare-faced cheek was best.

Rounding the corner, Lucille pumped the door handle and walked straight into the room whilst loudly proclaiming, 'Aha!'

The room was empty, although a pall of escaping smoke immediately made her eyes water and her throat feel itchy. The tobacco odour was unexpectedly heavy. She started backing out, noticing a crumpled packet of cigarettes in the bin, along with a number of crushed butts and plenty of ash.

Lucille clucked her disapproval at the plastic wastepaper basket. If this was supposed to be a smoking room, they really hadn't catered for their target audience.

The sound of approaching footsteps from the foyer made Lucille falter. Should she go back in, or brazen it out? The idea of re-entering the pre-breathed smoke emporium made Lucille shiver. Instead, she closed the door and standing rigid in the corridor, waited to see who came around the corner.

John Cupkiss barrelled into view at the top of the corridor and flew straight into the first available office. He was in such a rush, he didn't bother to look down the corridor towards Lucille, more concerned with peering over his shoulder at where he'd come from. Lucille held her breath and dodged into the smoky recesses of the tinted office. A few seconds later three dark figures passed by. She waited, still holding her breath, then edged the door open a crack.

Without warning, the handle was wrenched from her grip and the door flung wide open. The smell of burnt tobacco and the stench of stale nicotine was so overpowering it made Lucille want to dry heave. She fought it back.

'Hello there! We meet again,' said the man brightly.

He immediately filled the doorway and grabbed hold of Lucille's shoulders, ready to shake them, or move his hands to the woman's scrawny neck. But he saw she was calm. Surprisingly so. He pushed her back into the office and went to place a hand over her mouth and lean in, fearful she was about to scream, or at least call for help. Instead, she flapped a hand close to her mouth and twisted her mouth out of shape.

'Seriously, Mr Cupkiss. You should do something about your bad breath. It's very unbecoming. I think I've got some mints in my handbag, if you'll give me a minute...'

John Cupkiss stared in wonder at the woman for a moment before catching himself and closing the office door behind him.

'Remember me?' he said quietly, 'I was your uninvited guest in Harrogate.'

'Oh, yes, I remember you. About those mints…'

'Screw the mints!' he snapped, holding up a car key, 'Come on, Mrs Beaufort, you're going to show me where this car is parked.'

Fifty-One

Lucille was impressed with the alacrity with which Cupkiss managed to travel through shady corridors, out the back of the weighing room, into an area meant for horses and stable staff now empty of both, through another nameless building and out though a fire door onto Ascot High Street. She could hear the crowds returning to the parade ring after the latest race, the cheer as the victor entered the winner's enclosure, the announcements. Cupkiss certainly knew his way around Ascot racecourse. She didn't complain, speak, or try to slow him down – he wasn't that quick anyway - but he was surprisingly clean-winded given the severity of his smoking habit.

'You do realise you honk of cigarettes, don't you, dear?' she observed as he led her tightly by the arm across Ascot High Street, his palm becoming sweatier and slicker with every step. Cupkiss grunted something unintelligible in return.

Jack's car was buried in the centre of the Owners and Trainers car park, but Lucille led Cupkiss straight to it without incident.

'Huh? He hasn't fixed the driver's door yet,' Cupkiss noted with a shake of his head upon finding the lock hanging out of its housing, 'That was over a week ago. These youngsters have no pride.'

'You were in Whitley Bay?'

Cupkiss grimaced, 'I was the one who broke into it, trying to find that bloody notebook.'

He did a complete circuit of the ancient Renault, still holding tightly onto Lucille.

'Mind you, who's going to steal this old pile of junk?'

Lucille was purposely prickly, 'It looks like you are.'

'I came by train,' he said absently, pulling open the driver's door and bundling Lucille in.'

'Oh, right, I'm driving then,' she said as Cupkiss hurried around, jumped in beside her and pulled on the passenger seat belt.

'Where to, Guv'nor?' Lucille said in a ropey cockney accent as he handed her the key fob.

'Drop the clever comments,' he warned, 'We've a long drive ahead of us. Get going, we're heading north.'

***

Sebastian Savage was disappointed. Surely he should be feeling much better than this? He'd always imagined confessing to his crimes would allow the guilt to lift from him, lighten his load, so to speak. But since the Akbar policewoman, Goodman, and the older man in the raincoat who'd introduced himself as Tarquin had arrived, he'd been struggling. His chest had started to ache, and by the time the shooting pains started down his arms, Savage had reached the conclusion that confessing sucked.

Olivier Tarquin was speaking, but Savage wasn't listening that closely. Once he'd learned the rather dull, nondescript man in the raincoat was a private investigator hired by the BHA, he'd guessed they were onto Cupkiss.

Serves him right, Savage told himself as he rubbed at a sharp, insistent pain just under his ribs. Cupkiss had gone too far. Yes, holding onto his father's notebook for so long had, in retrospect, been a bad move, but burning a house to the ground and attacking people in their own homes?

He glanced up at Tarquin. The man spoke with a French accent, and Savage was finding it increasingly difficult to concentrate sufficiently on what the hell the man was saying. Savage gave a little groan as the pain in his chest stabbed a little deeper. He really didn't feel too well.

Charlie was the first to notice. Savage's skin had changed to a sickly shade of bluey-grey, he was rubbing the top of his arms and the bubbles of perspiration on his forehead appeared to be coalescing into flowing lines of sweat.

'I think he's having a heart attack,' she cried, silencing Tarquin. She jumped to her feet and crossed the meeting room to cradle Savage before he fell off his seat, 'Someone call 999 and get a defibrillator in here. Now!'

Jack traded a look with Meera Akbar. She nodded her understanding of the situation and was dashing down the corridor a moment later, on her way to the foyer in search of medical aid.

Jack pulled out his phone and switched it on. Now wasn't the time to be heeding the jockey communications ban within the weighing room complex. Instead of calling the emergency services, Jack jabbed a finger at the contact details for the Clerk of the Course at Ascot and was relieved when he picked up within three rings. A succinct description of the situation soon had Jack listening to the Clerk barking commands into his walkie-talkie.

There are at least two ambulance crews on the racecourse at any time during a race meeting. It's a health and safety requirement. No race can be run without that minimum level of medical coverage. Jack knew this, and hopefully, one of the ambulance crews would arrive soon.

With nothing else to do but allow Charlie room to get busy with her CPR skills, and with Tarquin remaining at her side, Jack, Emily, Cam, Meera, and Laura left the meeting room to stand somewhat aimlessly in the corridor with the Integrity Officer. The young man looked to be in shock, his officious stoicism having drained away as soon as Savage had fallen off his seat clutching his chest.

Emily and Laura were also quiet. They may hate the man now lying on the floor, Jack thought, but they clearly weren't keen on him dying. He took another glance into the meeting room and grimaced. Savage didn't appear to be moving at all now, lying flat on his back, his eyes open, staring at the ceiling tiles. Tarquin had joined Charlie, kneeling over the trainer, talking to her as she continued to pump away at Savage's chest.

'What's this Tarquin like then?' Cam asked, coming up to stand over Jack's shoulder and watch the man, now with his coat off, take over the rhythmic chest depressions from the spent Charlie.

'Olivier Tarquin,' Jack said quietly, 'He's an investigator, seconded from France Galop and working for the BHA. Meera Akbar informed the racing authorities she was attending Ascot and might make an arrest today, given what we told her about Savage. They asked her to involve him. The BHA hierarchy employed him a couple of months ago to investigate the Integrity Department.'

Cam scrunched his face up, 'Any particular reason for investigating the Integrity Department?'

'Tarquin said there were, a few anomalies, whatever that means. He's been following us around too. As well as being in Whitley Bay the night Emily lied to us in the café, he had been staking out Lucille's and Pearl Harris's place in Leeds. He also knew about Savage's notebook and tried to intercept its delivery.'

'What about him bashing Ben with a cosh?'

Jack shook his head, 'Wasn't him.'

Their conversation was cut off by Meera Akbar arriving back to the room at a run, accompanied by a uniformed first aider carrying a chunky plastic suitcase that turned out to be the defibrillator. It was used a number of times before the medic checked Savage over for the third time, admitted defeat, and shook his head. It had only been a matter of minutes between Savage going pale, to his death being confirmed.

A flustered Charlie stumbled out of the meeting room, red in the face, forehead glistening from her exertions. She met Jack's eyes. Without a word, she fell into his open arms and hugged him tight for a long moment. He could feel her taught body trembling as she held her thin frame against him, and for some reason, he thought of Lucille.

'Where's Lucille? Jack asked.

'She went off to find Cupkiss. She reckoned he was listening into our conversation in the meeting room,' Cam reported, 'I found a bug... oh, damn it! She's been gone far too long.'

'Perhaps she found him,' Jack wondered out loud as he scrambled for his mobile phone.

***

The Owners and Trainers car park was full to bursting, but luckily for Lucille, almost all of the cars were parked and their owners were still inside the racecourse awaiting the fourth race on the afternoon card. She hadn't driven a car for twenty years, Monty had always done the driving. In fact, she couldn't remember if she still owned a valid licence - she certainly didn't own a car. Nevertheless, she had driven a stick shift before, so she engaged reverse, pulled out of the parking space, stuck Corbyn in first gear and slowly guided Jack's car down a long avenue of parked cars before managing to find one of the main exit routes out of the car park.

Lucille was chattering away, while Cupkiss was fiddling with a small, thin box he'd produced from inside his briefcase. At first, Lucille thought it could be a fancy pencil case. He snapped it open. She stopped mid-sentence and looked over at what Cupkiss was doing. It soon became clear the contents weren't writing implements. Two stunted, preloaded hypodermic needles lay alongside each other, each pressed into a perfectly sized slot. A third slot was empty. They were the spring loaded type, allowing you to automatically push the contents of the reservoir into the bloodstream without the need for a plunger, even through clothing. Cupkiss fumbled in his suit pocket, removed a used hypodermic, and placed it into the vacant slot.

Glancing back at where Corbyn was heading, Lucille dragged the car back into line and away from the parked cars she'd unknowingly been aiming for. Cam had complained all the way down from Harrogate that the pulling to the left was gradually getting worse and she could now see what he meant. Maintaining Corbyn's forward motion in a straight line was impossible, but with constant minor adjustments, you could settle for a vague meander.

'Let me guess,' Lucille ventured, nodding at the open case on Cupkiss's lap, 'Savage?'

Cupkiss snapped the case shut, hoping it would make her jump, but she seemed unflappable. He regarded his driver for a few seconds before relaxing into his seat.

'I knew his father, Terry Savage,' he told her as they approached the main road, 'A good horseman. He used to set horses up for big punts back in the late seventies and eighties when anabolic steroids were all the rage. Insisted the drugs only allowed the horse to produce it's best possible performance, rather than making them any better. The racing authorities didn't see it that way when they finally did something about it.'

'Is that when it started?' asked Lucille, pausing to allow oncoming traffic to pass before turning left onto Ascot Road, 'The blackmail?'

Cupkiss ignored her question, instead asking one of his own.

'What's wrong with you?'

He didn't ask this with any exasperation, this was a straight forward inquiry.

Lucille looked over at her passenger. Cupkiss was staring at her with what she read as genuine anticipation.

'I mean, there's obviously something wrong with you,' he continued, 'You've a kitchen cupboard full of drugs, there were dozens of letters from the NHS stuffed into one of your sideboards, and when I gave you a shake, upstairs, beside that bedroom full of technical kit, you immediately fell unconscious. I got a bit of a shock, I can tell you!'

'Answer my question and I'll answer yours,' Lucille replied.

Cupkiss gave her a humourless grin, but to her surprise, played along.

'Yes, the blackmail of Sebastian started when his father, Terry, died. But I prefer to call it extortion,' he said, pleased to see his driving companion twitch her nose distastefully in response to his admission, 'Terry Savage was a valuable source of income for me. Back in the nineties, racing was doing well, prizemoney was relatively high. Unfortunately, my field officer's salary at the BHA wasn't. I'd found Terry's milkshake drugs stash on one of my unannounced drop-ins and in return for not reporting his illicit use of performance enhancing drugs on his horses, I took a regular fee from him.'

'Why did you have to kill him?' Lucille asked.

Cupkiss produced a phlegm-ridden half-laugh, 'Oh, no! Stick to the format. Your turn to answer.'

Lucille pouted, 'Okay... Yes, I'm suffering from stage four cancer. I have a melanoma... two in fact, as a result of an inner ear cancer. The tumour is inoperable.'

'How long you got?'

'Two, maybe three months,' Lucille replied without displaying any emotion, her eyes set on the arrow-straight road ahead, 'So, did you murder Terry Savage?'

'Like father, like son,' sighed Cupkiss, 'Terry had a crisis of conscience and had to be dealt with, and Sebastian... Well, that boy showed huge promise... he took to the dark side of racing with a vengeance. I didn't really have to threaten him... he was lazier than his father, and didn't share his penchant for guilt, or his ability as a trainer. It was a sweet arrangement. I had contacts with a bent breeding operation over in Ireland, and we'd...'

'Yes, I know how you managed to dupe unsuspecting first-time female owners,' Lucille broke in, 'I assume it was you who sourced victims and fended off any of the more energetic complaints you received from them?'

'Of course,' Cupkiss agreed, 'My promotion to Deputy, then Head of Integrity provided all sorts of opportunities to bury negative feedback. Besides, the system I'd created was infallible, all Savage had to do was work his manly magic on the gullible women I sourced for him. It worked perfectly for almost twenty years.'

'I assume you've murdered him too? Lucille asked presumptively.

'Why do you say that?'

'I think either Savage got greedy, or you decided to take a bigger piece of the cake running your Grey Horse Hustle on any old owner who came along, like Emily Green's mother, Pearl Harris. But I'm guessing Savage picked her. She wasn't like the others, she was far too down market. Your victims could always afford to lose a hundred to two-hundred-thousand-pounds and not kick up a stink. I also think Savage started to run his own little fraudulent side-hustles.'

Lucille slowed the car a little, trying to recall Jack's exact words when he'd explained about Kaleidoscope.

'Like Laura Fenwick... that was all about Savage getting himself a Group quality racehorse to train and little else. I don't see you getting your usual cut out of that deal. And his increasing use of Rohypnol must have worried you? Yep, Savage was becoming a loose cannon, and you couldn't allow that.'

Cupkiss threw his half-finished cigarette out of the passenger-side window and sighed deeply, 'I should have cut him loose years ago. Sebastian became arrogant and worse than that, sloppy. He got out of his depth. Tried to run the grey horse hustle on his own and paid the price. That Pearl Harris was a bad choice of mark. I couldn't believe it when he came to me for help. Faking her suicide was easy enough, but then that blessed daughter of hers pitched up and started stirring things up even more.'

Cupkiss grimaced, 'And then he lost his bloody notebook. Who the hell records all their black deeds in a notebook? It implicated me, so... I had to step in again.'

Lucille was pleased the traffic had backed up. Shocked at learning that Cupkiss was also responsible for Emily's mother's death, she took a moment to stare fixedly at the road and compose herself. And he'd mentioned it in passing, as if murder was a normal, everyday activity for the man! Concentrate, she told herself. Make Monty proud.

'I noticed you've used one of your spring-loaded syringes today. You put Savage into that meeting room with us so you could listen to how he performed, just to be sure you'd done the right thing.'

'And what was the right thing?'

'I'm disappointed I allowed it to happen,' Lucille admitted sadly, 'You'd already decided Savage had to be silenced after the debacle with that notebook of his. He's had you running all over Yorkshire to track the notebook down. He must have been desperate for your help. Who could have imagined that a criminal would keep a detailed log of all his past wrongdoing? And that performance in the parade ring today was the final straw. You knew he was going to drag you down with him.'

Lucille drew to a stop at a zebra crossing to allow a woman in a motorised scooter to zip across the road.

'I found it strange that you took personal responsibility to walk Savage across the parade ring and into the weighing room,' Lucille said, casting a quick glance at the case on Cupkiss's knees, 'As far as I'm aware, you're not the chummy sort. You slapped him on the shoulder and he jumped with fright. I think that's when you administered the drug.'

Traffic was light, even so, Lucille didn't take Corbyn above twenty miles an hour. She glanced over at Cupkiss again, wondering whether she shouldn't have been so direct. He was drumming the fingers of his right hand on the hypodermic case and gazing thoughtfully up the road, although Lucille doubted his mind was concerned with where they were travelling. If she were to describe his demeanour at the moment, it would have to be… content. What the hell, she'd always been direct. It was why Monty had loved her. Why break the habit of a lifetime?

'I'm guessing it's Pentobarbitol or a derivative? You'd have access to it, being around horses all the time. I believe at the correct dose it can cause a heart attack in humans and it leaves the system quickly… So am I right, did you kill Mr Savage?'

Cupkiss's contentment morphed into mild irritation as he wrenched his attention back onto Lucille.

'You like your little puzzles, don't you?' said Cupkiss a touch sharply, 'Your house was full of quiz books and crosswords. You must like a good brainteaser. So work this one out: how do you think I'll be dealing with you?'

Lucille smiled wanly as she checked her rearview mirror, 'Oh, I expect you'll want to kill me, just like Savage and his father. After all, I'm the one with a fully decoded version of Savage's notebook. Without Savage and his notebook I doubt you could be convicted, unless the original turned up, or there was a paper trail of Savage's payments to you…'

'Do you really think I would risk any link back to myself? Cupkiss replied scornfully, 'That money was laundered so many times between Savage and myself, even a forensic accountant couldn't track it down, and as for the original notebook…'

Lucille recognised the small red notebook immediately. A grinning Cupkiss dipped into the breast pocket of his shirt and displayed its tin reinforced corners, then tucked it away again, patting it through the white cloth.

'I liberated it from his discarded jacket when he started that little strip of his,' he said airily, 'You've got that silly hypnotist to thank for that.'

Lucille frowned, she and Jack had worried about Emily. They'd needed to distract Cupkiss and the ringside staff long enough to allow the ladies to enter the parade ring unseen, in order to confront Savage. They'd also required him to stay put whilst they hit him with their accusations. Despite their reservations, Emily's hypnotism had proved invaluable. And Laura's acting skills had been exemplary, tricking the somewhat foolish and arrogant Savage into thinking she was genuinely attracted to him.

Bringing Emily and Laura back on board had initially been tough, but easier with the new evidence the notebook had provided, but Emily was overly emotional when it came to Savage. It was understandable, the man had ruined her mother's life. Savage's inability to move when they'd surrounded him had been a nice touch, but the strip… Emily really was eaten up with hate, thought Lucille, she'd needed that, to laugh at him, belittle Savage in front of his peers.

'Congratulations, you seem to have all the angles covered Mr Cupkiss. You've every copy of the notebook, all the primary witnesses to your deeds are dead, and you'll only have me to finish off.'

Cupkiss shocked Lucille by laughing. It was a sustained, whole-hearted belly laugh that had him dabbing the corner of his eyes. Lucille kept the car trundling along at a steady, slow pace, only a little concerned her passenger was displaying all the hallmarks of a madman.

'You're a real hoot!' Cupkiss exclaimed only seconds later, suddenly recovering from his laughing fit.

'I've had a good ride,' he said in a more subdued tone, 'It's time for me to enjoy the fruits of my…'

He ruminated for a few seconds.

'Evil, self-serving criminality?' Lucille offered, taking one hand off the steering wheel to emphasise her suggestion. The other hand firmly maintained the car's current direction, the constant tugging to the left a reminder of Corbyn's preferred angle of travel.

Cupkiss laughed again. This was a deep-throated laugh, the sort that can only be generated by those long-term smokers who have ingested enough tar to shrink their throat and lungs. The laugh became a cough, which insanely prompted Cupkiss to produce a packet of cigarettes from his hip pocket.

Lucille looked at the packet, then Cupkiss's grey face... and the last piece of the jigsaw fell into place.

'Marlboro Man,' she muttered to herself. Try as they might, she and Jack couldn't see how MM in Savage's notebook related to Cupkiss, but there it was, in plain sight. Cupkiss chain smoked Marlboro branded cigarettes.

Rather than be pleased as Cupkiss lit up, Lucille was kicking herself. That odour... it was reviving a memory. Marlboro toasted their tobacco, and that was the strange tang that had been left in her computing room... she could have worked this all out days ago!

It had been Jack's recollection of the line of books on Savage's only bookshelf that had finally allowed her to crack the notebook's third and final keyword. Among the eclectic titles, Jack had recalled a dog-eared copy of the Penguin Book Of Classical Myths. Savage had used 'Peitho' as his keyword, a goddess of seduction and persuasion. It was horribly suitable as the goddess was often depicted fleeing from the scene of a rape...

Cupkiss's coughing abated as he lit his cigarette.

'You were saying... you've had a good ride?' prompted Lucille, wrinkling her nose against the blue smoke Cupkiss was blowing into the cabin.

'America, then the Caribbean Islands,' Cupkiss answered shortly, 'I'm retiring. With a boat load of cash. I'm finished with horseracing.'

Lucille nodded sagely, checked her mirrors and decided Cupkiss would need to run one more race.

The roundabout to which she'd been slowly calculating her approach was now only a hundred and fifty yards away. She'd noticed its significance this morning as they'd come upon the huge Ascot grandstand in the distance. At the roundabout's centre, stood a large marble plinth on which the statue of a single horse was standing, a memorial to the war horses lost in the first world war. She'd also noticed the large number of trees, both on the roundabout and beyond.

Lucille stole a quick glance his way. Cupkiss was busy sucking on his cigarette. Now that there weren't any cars ahead, Lucille pressed down on Corbyn's accelerator. Their speed crept up to forty, fifty, then sixty miles an hour.

Her gradual build-up of speed did the trick. Cupkiss didn't notice how fast they were travelling until it was too late… way too late. Relieved there wasn't another car in sight, Lucille veered hard right and hit the roundabout junction with Corbyn doing his top speed of seventy miles per hour.

Suddenly aware something was wrong, Cupkiss thrust both hands onto the dashboard, insisting she slow down. His cigarette was stuck, wobbling on his bottom lip, as the statue of the war horse flashed past. Lucille noticed with pleasure that the marble facia beneath the statue was facing the afternoon sun and the memorial veritably shone down Ascot High Street. This marked the moment Lucille allowed Corbyn to do the rest.

Taking her hands from the wheel, foot still hard down on the accelerator, Corbyn lurched to the left.

Lucille crossed her arms and turned to Cupkiss, a smile on her face and said in a loud voice, 'Enjoy your retirement, Mr Cupkiss!'

Fifty-Two

Jack pulled into Lucille's driveway. No one spoke as the car crept up to the house, wheels crunching as inch by inch, it came to rest opposite the front door.

Neither Cam in the passenger seat, nor Charlie in the back made a move. Instead they both stared out of their windows and up at the huge house. Jack leaned on the car's steering wheel and did the same, trying not to become emotional again. There had already been enough of that today, and Lucille's short message to the congregation had been perfectly clear, they should be shedding tears of joy, not sadness.

Presently, Charlie sniffed and said, 'It's really... yours?'

'That's... what the solicitor said,' Jack replied.

He leaned back in his seat and rootled around in the driver's door, producing a set of shiny steel keys, holding them up by the fob to allow them to sparkle in the July sunshine.

Cam held out a flat palm, 'Come on, give them to me. My family have an estate for crying out loud, I know how to welcome home the head of a wealthy household.'

Jack shook his head, but dropped the keys into Cam's hand anyway.

'One minute,' said Cam, 'Come on Charlie.'

Following a lot of bowing and use of the word, 'Sir', a giggling Charlie and Cam reverently prostrated themselves even lower as Jack stepped into his newly acquired residence. He couldn't bring himself to admit he felt numb... and unworthy.

Lucille's funeral had been a short, minimally attended affair at Harrogate crematorium that morning. She and Monty hadn't had children, and with both sets of parents long gone, there was hardly any family present. Emily and Laura made the effort to attend, as did Meera Akbar. Lucille's next door neighbour had introduced herself beforehand, but the other three mourners kept themselves to themselves.

After a short, generic service that barely referenced Lucille, a middle-aged man and woman had come up and asked straight out why Jack, Cam, and their friends were there. Affronted by their rudeness, Jack had repeated the question back at them, only louder. Clarissa Bone introduced herself as Monty's sister, freshly come up from Wales with her husband to say goodbye to her dearest brother's wife. The woman had bleated on and on about how close they'd been and how she'd never heard of Lucille being involved with, 'Anything as dreadful as horse racing.'

Tiring of the woman and uncertain what to do next, Jack, Cam, and Charlie had made excuses and been about to make their way back to their car when the third of the unknown attendees, a short, stout chap with a strong Yorkshire accent caught up with them and had asked for, 'Mr Goodman.'

After shaking the man's hand, he announced himself as Laurence Fleet, Lucille's solicitor, which had the Wales contingent buzzing around them like angry hornets. Once Mr Fleet had made it clear that Mrs Bone wasn't going to benefit from Lucille's will, she swiftly departed, displaying the true depth of her love for her brother's wife.

To Jack's astonishment, Mr Fleet broke the news that Lucille had wanted him to inherit everything she owned. According to the solicitor, Lucille had renewed her will only a few days prior to their Ascot trip, altering it entirely in his favour.

Jack entered Lucille's house and turned left into the room she had shown them into the first time they'd visited her. Choosing a seat on her... *his* sofa. This was so weird. The only thing he'd properly owned apart from the clothes on his back, had been his car, Corbyn. To think, he was inside a house that he owned! His bank account was brimming with more money than he'd ever dreamed of... and yet... this was still Lucille's house, and it was Lucille's money in his account.

That feeling of being unworthy returned. Perhaps he'd share some of it with his friends and one or two worthy charities...

Charlie seated herself beside Jack and realising her boyfriend was a little overwhelmed, clasped his forearm in both her hands. She shuffled up close, tugging a little to force him to meet her eyes so they could share a sad, understanding smile.

Meanwhile, Cam fell into the closest armchair with a loud, contented sigh.

'Hey! What about the letter?' Cam asked immediately.

'Cam!' Charlie admonished, 'I don't know if Jack's up to it. Anyway, should I be here when you two read it?'

'It's okay with me,' Jack shrugged. Cam nodded his own agreement.

Jack blinked himself lucid, then reached into his pocket, withdrawing a thick, creamy envelope with his and Cam's names written across it in Lucille's large, spidery handwriting. Underneath, in small capitals were the words, 'To be opened by Jack Goodman and Cameron Camberley.'

'We might as well read it now I suppose,' Jack said, searching for a way into the missive.

Cam pulled himself up to the edge of his seat in anticipation.

'Out loud, Jack, 'Cam insisted, 'I reckon Lucille liked a bit of theatre.'

Jack smiled, unfolded the double-sided page, cleared his throat, said, 'I reckon you're right,' and began to read.

Dear Jack and Cameron,
You'll know by now that I've left my little bits and bobs to you, Jack. If this is news to you, collar that slack Mr Fleet, give him a shake and get him to explain! Cameron, I thought about leaving you half, but given your family appears to own a good chunk of Scotland, I think you'll agree that Jack has the greater need. But if he wants to give you some of it, I'm fine with that.

I'm pretty sure you've both worked it out, but again, just in case, I'll state it for the record. I'm in the latter stages of an unwinnable fight against cancer. One way or another I'll be gone before the year is out. That's okay. I had a lovely life with Monty, and to be honest, it's been awfully quiet since he died. To compound this, I've been a bit of a hermit since my diagnosis eight months ago.

What you won't know is that when I met you both on that train to Scarborough I wasn't expecting to go to watch a Soft Cell tribute act and a stage hypnotist. I'd taken the train to the coast for an entirely different, and somewhat morbid reason. I've always been drawn to the east coast – Scarborough, Whitby, and Robin Hood's Bay - Monty and I loved the walks along the cliffs and I had this romantic notion of ending my life there, on that Saturday evening, before the cancer made my life intolerable.

Fortunately, my dears, I met you two. You were so much fun! I laughed so much that night that the muscles in my cheeks were still aching the next day! Fancy that! A dying middle-aged woman being chaperoned by two fit young bucks! You were both so kind and genuine, it gave me pause for thought.

And there you were the next day, back on my doorstep! Not only had you saved me from myself, you proceeded to give me a tangled web of intrigue and a fiendish problem to solve! Since being a little girl reading Agatha Christie novels, I'd dreamed of being a detective and solving crimes, and you brought one right to my door... literally! You'll never know how pleased I was to see you again, and working with the two of you was simply sublime!

You'll notice that I'm writing this letter ahead of our trip down to Royal Ascot. I should be fine, but I'm told that one bad knock to my head could see me pop my clogs. I haven't told you because I'm sure two nice lads like you two wouldn't allow me to come, and there's no way I'm missing all the fun! Hopefully you'll win that big race of yours, we'll out-manoeuvre Savage, and if our reading of his father's portion of the notebook is correct, we might catch out his dastardly co-conspirator!

Cameron, I believe you will be successful in whatever you turn your hand to, as long as it involves people. You're a gregarious force of nature. Your mother will see it too, and set you free. I hope that relationship will work itself out. I imagine she loved your father just as fiercely as you did, and perhaps, she is afraid of losing you too. Only recently have I really understood the incredibly life-giving value of having friends around you.

Ah, Jack, Jack... Fearless Jack! You fascinate me. Despite having a torrid time as a youngster you've carved out a decent, successful life for yourself. What's more, you've surrounded yourself with good, trustworthy friends. I also understand from Cameron that you're, in his words, 'A bloody good jockey!'. Make use of my house and money and above all, remain fearless, Jack. Believe me, life is far too short to waste on being timid.

I can't tell you how much I've enjoyed being around the two of you. I truly believe I've finished on a high. Thank you, both of you.

Adore you, darlings! Simply adore you!'

Lucille, xx.

It was Charlie who finished reading Lucille's letter. Jack had been struggling after the first two paragraphs. She folded the letter neatly and placed it onto the coffee table.

'Did you know?' she asked quietly, 'About the cancer?'

Jack coughed and wiped his face with the back of his hand, 'I mentioned something to Cam. There were letters, quite a few empty pill packets in her kitchen bin, and she was prone to getting dizzy...'

'We thought it was her business, not ours,' Cam confided.

'I had no idea about... the other thing... her reason for going to Scarborough,' Jack added.

'No...' Cam agreed.

The room fell silent for a long moment.

'She got him though,' Cam said with feeling, 'She got Cupkiss.'

Jack smiled tightly, 'That she did.'

Epilogue

Excerpt from The Guardian's coverage of Judge Graham Francis Heard's sentencing in the case of The Crown versus John Leslie Cupkiss.

"…In handing down a sentence amounting to a prison term of fifty-eight years for the murders of Mr Sebastian Savage, Mr Terry Savage, and Mrs Pearl Harris, Judge Heard drew particular attention to the evidence provided by Detective Constable Meera Akbar of Leeds Metropolitan Police.

DC Akbar had reported that Ms Lucille Beaufort, fatally injured when the car she was driving crashed into a group of mature trees located on the roundabout at the end of Ascot High Street, was discovered with a recording device around her neck, disguised as a pendant.

Ms Beaufort was not wearing a seat-belt at the time of the accident, a major factor which contributed to her death. Her passenger, the accused Mr John Leslie Cupkiss, survived the crash with a broken leg and other minor injuries and was apprehended by police when attempting to flee from the scene. The covert recording of a conversation with Mr Cupkiss, made by Ms Beaufort inside the car just prior to the accident, provided detectives with enough evidence to secure a conviction on three counts of murder, and aided the tracking of a large sum of money linked to the case.

Judge Heard highly commended Ms Beaufort. He also thanked Ascot Racecourse, the British Horseracing Authority and the police for the parts they played in curtailing Cupkiss's criminal activities."

Enjoyed reading The Grey Horse Hustle?

I do hope you have enjoyed this story. If you have, I'd *really* appreciate it if you would leave a rating and perhaps a short review with your favourite bookseller. Your ratings and reviews help more readers find my books, which in turn means I can dedicate more time to writing.

Simply visit your bookseller and search for 'Richard Laws', or submit a review and rating through your digital reader.

You can also register for my book alert emails and news on upcoming books at **www.thesyndicatemanager.co.uk**

Many thanks,

Richard Laws
July 2025

Printed in Dunstable, United Kingdom